PASSION'S MAGIC

With his hand, Louis gently lifted the curtain of
fragrant hair from his face, then pulled the young
woman across his chest. The tantalizing feel of her
silken skin under his caressing hands inflamed him.
He captured her protesting mouth the moment she
tensed against him and lifted her head.

"Let me go," Manuela demanded, squirming to free
herself from his embrace. "You may have kept me
from breaking my neck, but that does not give you
the right to kiss me."

"I think it does," Louis said as he held her head
firmly between his hands. He leaned closer to her and
kissed her again, and this time she responded to the
warm pressure of his lips.

As his kiss deepened, she found that she wanted
nothing more than to return his ardor. Never having
been kissed before, she wondered at the searing swirls
of sensation that coursed through her. She became
completely enraptured by the molten magic of his lips
on hers, and she suspected that he might be taking
away her breath forever . . .

EXHILARATING ROMANCE
From Zebra Books

GOLDEN PARADISE (2007, $3.95)
by Constance O'Banyon

Desperate for money, the beautiful and innocent Valentina Barrett finds work as a veiled dancer, "Jordanna," at San Francisco's notorious Crystal Palace. There she falls in love with handsome, wealthy Marquis Vincente — a man she knew she could never trust as Valentina — but who Jordanna can't resist making her lover and reveling in love's GOLDEN PARADISE.

MOONLIT SPLENDOR (2008, $3.95)
by Wanda Owen

When the handsome stranger emerged from the shadows and pulled Charmaine Lamoureux into his strong embrace, she knew she should scream, but instead she sighed with pleasure at his seductive caresses. She would be wed against her will on the morrow — but tonight she would succumb to this passionate MOONLIT SPLENDOR.

TEXAS TRIUMPH (2009, $3.95)
by Victoria Thompson

Nothing is more important to the determined Rachel McKinsey than the Circle M — and if it meant marrying her foreman to scare off rustlers, she would do it. Yet the gorgeous rancher feels a secret thrill that the towering Cole Elliot is to be her man — and despite her plan that they be business partners, all she truly desires is a glorious consummation of their vows.

DESERT HEART (2010, $3.95)
by Bobbi Smith

Rancher Rand McAllister was furious when he became the guardian of a scrawny girl from Arizona's mining country. But when he finds that the pig-tailed brat is really a ripe, voluptuous beauty, his resentment turns to intense interest! Lorelei knew it would be the biggest mistake in her life to succumb to the virile cowboy — but she can't fight against giving him her body — or her wild DESERT HEART.

Available wherever paperbacks are sold, or order direct from the Publisher. Send cover price plus 50¢ per copy for mailing and handling to Zebra Books, Dept. 2227, 475 Park Avenue South, New York, N.Y. 10016. Residents of New York, New Jersey and Pennsylvania must include sales tax. DO NOT SEND CASH.

RIVER TEMPTRESS
MYRA ROWE

ZEBRA BOOKS

are published by

Kensington Publishing Corp.
475 Park Avenue South
New York, NY 10016

ZEBRA BOOKS
KENSINGTON PUBLISHING CORP.

*To Cindy and W.C., for their constant,
loving support.*

ZEBRA BOOKS

are published by

Kensington Publishing Corp.
475 Park Avenue South
New York, NY 10016

First printing: December, 1987

Printed in the United States of America

Part One

"The red rose whispers of passion
  And the white rose breathes of love;
O the red rose is a falcon,
  And the white rose is a dove."
                              —John Boyle O'Reilly

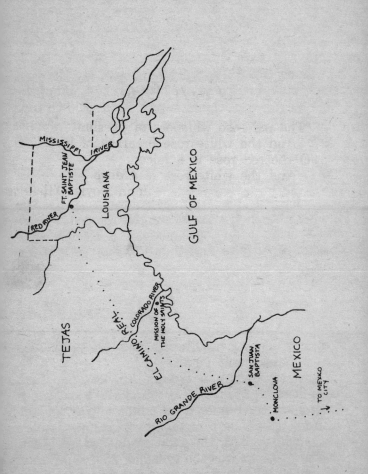

Chapter One

Far behind the solitary horseman lay the vast uncharted area known in 1714 as the Land of the Tejas. Only two leagues south of the Rio Grande River that May morning, Louis Juchereau de Saint-Denis hooded his eyes with a practiced hand.

From where he sat upon Diablo, the black stallion that had carried him all the way from French Louisiana, the handsome young Frenchman gazed upon what he sought: Mexico, Spain's little kingdom in the Americas. A light-headedness claimed him and the daring of his dangerous mission into alien territory brought a finer angle to an already proud chin.

Urging the horse farther up what seemed to be a natural levee of a small river, the lone rider glimpsed something far more captivating than the stretches of sand, cacti, and mesquite. And Louis Saint-Denis smiled.

A water sprite, a nymph, a vision of such delightful proportions as to cause the French lieutenant to wonder if he might not be hallucinating, gamboled in the river below. Louis's smile widened, for the sight gladdened his heart.

The distance was too great for the young man to determine the fineness of her facial features, but he could tell she was beautiful as she noisily splashed through the water's edge, apparently

7

chasing an elusive fish. Suddenly a burst of delicate laughter reached his ears, a sound for which he knew in an instant he had been long hungry.

Spellbound, Louis watched the morning sun dance on the mass of black hair streaming behind her, its shimmering ebony highlighting unique ivory tones in olive skin. Twin mounds of flesh topped with rosy peaks might as well not have been covered with the wet white shift, so seductively did they bounce and beckon to the weary traveler. A narrow waist connected those upper delights with winsome hips. The flimsy garment covered no lower than the dark feminine triangle, and Louis stared with quickening pulse at long legs of near perfect formation when their owner suddenly lay back against the water and floated. Even the way she brought her hands up to her face to rake back the ebony hair charmed the unseen observer.

"Be still, Diablo," Louis whispered when the horse stomped restlessly, no doubt eager to sample the water below.

Lean and lithe, the young man slipped from the saddle and tethered the stallion to a nearby willow. Close by he had glimpsed a pile of clothing and, filled now only with thoughts of the young beauty, he approached with a stealth learned well from Indians over the past eight years. Before him lay a dainty white cap and apron much like those worn by the little maids with whom his friends and he had dallied during their "learning years" in Paris. A stiff white petticoat, a dark skirt, and a matching blouse had been tumbled in a pile near small black slippers stuffed with filmy stockings and yellow

8

garters.

Sneaking another admiring look at the grace-ful swimmer, Louis sighed. How long had it been since he had glimpsed any feminine form outside an Indian's? As he pocketed a perfumed garter of yellow satin, a grin lit the craggy features of the Frenchman, sparking mischief in gray-blue eyes and subtracting some ten years from his twenty-eight.

So, he mused, the silver cross on the steeple spotted from the trail and the low buildings in the near distance glimpsed from the top of the levee meant he was, indeed, close to San Juan Batista, the northernmost post of the Spaniards. Where else in the wilderness would there be homes with servants so properly dressed? Or undressed, he corrected with wry amusement, wiping his suddenly moist forehead with one of the white monogrammed handkerchiefs he in-variably carried, even when on the trail.

Diablo stomped a foot and blew out a blubbery breath then, transforming the little pastoral scene below into one of frantic, feminine sounds and movements. Not missing the glimpse of ex-quisitely rounded buttocks as the swimmer let out a squeal and made a fast retreat beneath the water, Louis bent his tall frame low and hurried up the levee to his horse.

Startling him, a dove cooed nearby in that singular, throaty way before fluttering out of sight, a blur of gray against the greenery and the blue sky. Tender briars from wild rosebushes grabbed at his legs, their young tentacles unable to snare the leather leggings. A pleased look still playing on his wide mouth, he raced back toward the Rio Grande to meet his companions.

As he rode northward, the vision of the young woman clouded the Frenchman's mind and emotions far more than he realized. His immediate mission centered for a brief time on meeting and bedding her, not on gaining peaceful entry into a hostile Spanish *presidio* with his pack animals and trade goods. Memories of glorious, romantic nights in Paris rose enticingly, and, not finding his handkerchief, he removed his neckerchief to wipe the perspiration from his brow. The sound of the swimmer's peal of laughter still soothed some desolate space inside, one he had not known lay waiting until the moment she laughed.

All along something had told the admittedly ambitious Louis Saint-Denis that to make the seemingly impossible journey from Louisiana to Mexico would have rewards enough to make it feasible, but he had not dared hope to find such a delectable maiden as *lagniappe*. And what a perfect "little something extra": Ripe and ready for bedding, he enthused to himself, unconsciously easing up his hand to touch the small crescent-shaped scar riding his left, jutting cheekbone. Rosy and rounded, he added with an amused chuckle, falling into his habit over the past eight years of playing little word games while carrying out his varied missions in Louisiana.

Manuela Ramon surfaced and tread water, black eyes searching the bank near her clothing. She had not actually seen anyone spying, but she had experienced an uncanny feeling that someone was watching. Had she heard something other than the snort of her horse? Her mount was tethered downstream, but since she could make out its shape through the sparse bushes and willows, she decided the noise could have carried that clearly over water.

After all, she assured herself, no one would dare spy on the granddaughter of Colonel Diego Ramon, commandant of San Juan Batista. Using the powerful, unladylike breaststroke her brother, Carlos, had taught her, Manuela swam to the bank where she had discarded her borrowed clothing.

Taller than most Spanish young women of sixteen, she picked her way gingerly across the rocky bank to the group of spindly willows, spitting little oaths when a sharp edge pricked her toe. Recalling how ever since their birthday last month Carlos had been trying, without success, to curb her tendencies to talk and act like him rather than a properly reared young woman, Manuela grinned. The rules of upper-class society weren't for her. If Carlos could enjoy freedom of mood, expression, and action, why couldn't she?

Carlos, Manuela's twin, was her dearest friend and companion. Ever since their mother had died soon after their birth, they had been more or less dependent on each other for companionship and moral support. Until the past few months, their only separations had been those enforced by their having to attend different schools.

A well-to-do merchant in Mexico City, their father, Valesco Ramon, had been devastated by the death of his beautiful young wife from a mysterious fever. He never again took an active part in the supervising of his elegant household. When his son and daughter learned of his drown-

11

ing while on a business trip to Puerto Rico, they were not yet ten and felt only a fleeting sadness that Papa would no longer visit with them even briefly in their quarters during holidays.

Already the twins were attending school in the city, Manuela at the Convent of San Francisco and Carlos at the Monastery of the Capuchins. Valesco's death produced only a slight ripple in their well-ordered lives. They had each other.

Her thoughts having skipped off to such musings while she allowed the sun to dry the thin shift, Manuela now returned them to the moment and reached for the clothing removed an hour earlier. The olive forehead creased with puzzlement. Thick eyebrows knit above narrowed, widely spaced black eyes. She shook both shoes another time to see if the second garter might be lodged within. Full lips bunched up in pink annoyance before puffing out a vexed sigh. Lifting each remaining article then in exasperation, she saw the crumpled handkerchief and gasped.

By the blood of Mary, there *had* been someone watching her swim practically naked! With breathless haste and furtive glances all about, she donned the apron with trembling hands, pulling it tightly to hold up the loose skirt. She grabbed the alien handkerchief to toss it in the river but had second thoughts upon feeling its softness and tied it above her knee to serve for the missing scrap of yellow satin. Realizing that her wet mane was no place for the dainty cap, she thrust it in her pocket before hurrying to her horse.

When Manuela arrived at the *presidio*'s stables amidst a flurry of hoofbeats and powdery swirls of dust, a black-haired young woman emerged from within the shadowy interior to hiss, "Missy, you're late. Mama has already rung the warning bell for the noon meal." With unconcealed agitation, she grabbed the reins and tied them to a post, then went on in ominous tones, "You're going to get us both in bad trouble one of these days."

Dismounting and snatching off her outer clothing at almost the same time, Manuela aimed a conspiratorial grin at the distressed young woman who was also disrobing with speed.

"Conchita," she chided, "you worry too much. And how many times do I have to tell you not to call me 'Missy' when we're alone?"

From much practice, they made a perfect exchange of garments by tossing them in the air toward each other. Stepping into the starched petticoats she was permitted to wear with her morning gowns, Manuela allowed the maid to slip the full-skirted yellow gown over her head and lace up the back. She was grateful she did not have to wear the despised *panniers* until after *siesta*—not only did they hamper her movements, but also they required more time for dressing.

"There, you look almost respectable," Conchita muttered, her round face screwed up in concentration and worry. She was pretty in her darker way but knew that she served a true beauty. The only features they shared were black hair and eyes. "You're getting so tall, you're not going to be able to pass for me much longer, even at a distance." She pushed at the swinging mass of her mistress's still-damp hair with a sigh. "Your grandfather is going to scold both of us again for not having your hair dressed properly."

Shorter than Manuela and of thick body build, Conchita gazed at the slender, long-limbed young woman who had only a few minutes ago been wearing her uniform and riding one of the stock horses bareback. A compassion emanating from her four additional years and her servile position in the commandant's household filled her soft eyes and brought a concerned frown.

"Conchita, you're going to have so many wrinkles before you're twenty-one next year that no one, not even one of the Indians, will ask for your hand." Disappointed not to have brought a smile to the serious face turned toward her, Manuela looked hurriedly into the shiny piece of metal hanging near the open doorway and grimaced at the untidy image. "Stop worrying, you ninny." Affectionately she patted the maid's shoulder. "I can handle Grandfather."

"What about Don Domingo?"

"Is my uncle back home already?" she threw over her shoulder, already on her way toward the large courtyard leading to the main house, not waiting for Conchita to finish her own toilette and follow.

Manuela's heart lifted at the thought of seeing her uncle after his absence of several weeks. He had probably brought her some fashionable new gowns and pretties from Mexico City. Ever since the commandant had succumbed to her pleas four years earlier that she and Carlos be allowed to leave their schools and live fulltime at the *presidio*, she had not made the two-week journey southward to the capital.

Still unmarried, Don Domingo Ramon often played the role of surrogate father during those times when her grandfather was too involved with the activities of the post to attune himself to the needs of a young woman of sixteen. The latest in fashion itself held little appeal for her, but she adored all things beautiful, whether from the hand of an artisan or from nature.

"Manuela," called the prim voice of Doña Magdalena from the receiving room stretching across the back of the main house. "I watched you sitting in the courtyard beneath the chinaberry tree this morning plying your needle, and I was extremely pleased. You seemed so peaceful and contented. May I see your progress?" Her large eyes tried to focus on the young woman's hands, but even after she squinted against the bright sunlight streaming through the open doors and windows, she could not locate the handiwork.

"I didn't bring it with me, Aunt."

Manuela was never impolite to the younger, widowed sister of her deceased grandmother, but she was never warm either. She had accepted that all young Spanish women must reconcile themselves to having a *dueña* after reaching their first stage of womanhood. She concluded that she could have done worse than to have a blood relative serve as her chaperone and instructor in the ways of upper-class society, especially one as beautiful and kind as Doña Magdalena. And as nearsighted and hard-of-hearing, she would add when she was being painfully honest with herself.

"I'll show it to you after *siesta*," Manuela offered. "I think you'll like it." Her conscience smote her not at all for the partial lie, for Conchita really did do nicely with a needle and thread.

Upon hearing the double bell signifying that the meal was ready to be served, the *hacienda*'s only two resident ladies went into the dining room. Dutifully looking past the younger man who walked to greet Doña Magdalena, Manuela smiled with affection at the white-haired man in uniform. She rushed to put her arms around Colonel Diego Ramon and planted a kiss on his lean cheek.

"Grandfather," she cooed, peeking up at him through thick, long lashes, hoping to distract his attention from the damp hair falling down her back, "you grow more handsome each day."

With precise timing, but with the air of impulse, Manuela bestowed a second kiss upon the other cheek and squeezed his upper arms in the way she had done as a little girl when impressed by his muscles. A hint of a dimple danced in her olive cheek as even teeth flashed whitely. The slight, arresting slant of large eyes lent an exotic look to her finely sculpted face with its classic nose and high cheekbones.

"And what about your uncle?" teased the other man after seating his aunt. He turned toward the one charming his father with inherent grace.

Does she know how beautiful she is? Domingo wondered. She was apparently unaware that her looks weren't those of an ordinary pretty young woman. Did he dare tell her that during his stay in Mexico City he had seen none throughout the round of parties whose loveliness of face or body equaled hers, not even the beauteous daughter of the viceroy? Manuela seemed as easy and comfortable with herself as when she had been a skinny, leggy tomboy making every track her twin brother made.

Raising black velvet eyes to those of similar hue gazing down at her with a new, measuring look, his niece smiled coquettishly and came into his open arms.

"You're the most handsome uncle a girl could ever wish for, Uncle Domingo," she exclaimed with warmth. "And I've missed you terribly."

Although Manuela knew the words were what was expected of her by all present, even the cook, Juanita, and the uniformed maids waiting at the kitchen entrance to begin serving, she meant each one. Like his father, her uncle was tall and straight without a spare measure of fat. She accepted his brief kiss on her lips, loving the tickle of his neatly trimmed beard with its little streaks of silver contrasting with the blackness. For a moment, she laid her hands lightly alongside his olive cheeks. The vigorous, manly scent of him always made her feel so secure, so loved.

The four devoured the cold, tasty soup, the vegetables spiced with tomatoes and peppers, and the fried corn *tortillas*. They ate from imported shiny porcelain, sat upon chairs carved and fashioned by Spanish artisans. Their speech rose and fell in the same elegant cadence that could be found in the finest homes in Mexico City or Seville.

Because Diego Ramon held a lofty military position and came from Spain, as had his long-deceased wife, their children were looked upon generally as true Spaniards rather than Creoles, the somewhat derogatory term often used for the second, and always for any later, generation of Spaniards unfortunate enough to have been born in Mexico. To the citizens of New Spain, "Creole" meant "native-born to Spanish parents" and was

17

often synonymous with "second class citizen."

It was Diego's greatest wish to have his only two grandchildren accorded permanently that exalted status of "Spaniard" in the colony where class was regarded with a zeal keener than that practiced in Europe. He fretted that he would not always be around to ensure their acceptance, that their large inheritances from their father might not be sufficient to guarantee their places.

A sad but known fact was that if officials so desired, upon whatever trumped-up charge after Diego's death, his son, Domingo, could also be relegated to the lower status of Creole. Rarely did one not born in Spain advance to a rank high enough to command a *presidio;* he knew well that such was Domingo's ambition.

There had long been an unspoken agreement between Diego and Domingo that Domingo, as well as Manuela and Carlos, must marry no other than a true Spaniard in order to remain in the ruling class. An unfortunate marriage by either a Spaniard or a Creole could result in an instant relegation to the third, undesirable class of mixed blood, the *mestizos.*

Though Diego rarely thought upon the plight of the numerous *mestizos,* he accepted that they were not allowed to serve even as troop soldiers, positions reserved for Creoles. Further dividing themselves into more than a dozen sub-classes, based on the varying mixtures of Spanish, Indian, and Negro blood, *mestizos* lived the lives of laborers or servants, saddled with inevitable poverty. And at the bottom of the social ladder were the Indians. Foreigners rated no position, for, outside a few imported slaves from Africa, none were allowed.

Content to wool-gather about the enforced caste system in Mexico while the others talked, Diego recalled how he, the youngest in a family of shipbuilders, had come to Mexico as a lieutenant when he was young. Unlike most Spaniards, who came for quick fortunes from the silver mines and hastened back home to live in indolent luxury, he had never had any desire to return to Spain.

The New World had rewarded Diego handsomely through the years with a Spanish wife, sons, grandchildren, military position, and a goodly share of wealth. He saw no reason why the same prizes should not be forthcoming to his beloved Manuela and Carlos in time. Proper marriages for both could achieve his greatest wish. He would settle for no less.

A lull in the lively conversation about Domingo's visit to the capital snapped Diego back to the present, and he asked, "What is the news from Viceroy Alencastre, the revered Duke of Linares?" Guilt nudged, and he added, "How is our honorable Governor Anya? I assume you stopped over in Monclova last night on your way home, as usual."

Diego addressed his third son, the only one still living. It grieved him that Domingo, already into his thirties, seemed inclined to remain single in spite of his dubious social position. Domingo disappointed him in other ways too, though he dodged that thought for the moment. He watched the maids clear away the dishes and bring coffee.

Domingo nodded and replied with a note of asperity, "Governor Anya seemed free of pain from his gout while I was there. To hear him talk, one would think governing the sparsely populated province of Coahuila is the most taxing position in all of Mexico. He was complaining that the *rancheros* allow their livestock to roam too freely. The man is never satisfied with anything the Creoles do, when they actually contribute more to our province than any other group." An inner thought brought a pained look to his face then, and he continued in an even tighter tone, "I suspect the man never stops thinking of himself as a Spaniard due all manner of personal pleasures here in New Spain simply because he was born in the motherland." His lips clamped shut, as if unwilling to allow further news from Monclova to escape.

The aroma of freshly brewed coffee mingled pleasantly with the fragrance of yellow roses arranged in an imported cut-crystal vase centering the long table. As all four preferred to drink the thick brew black, serving took only a few minutes.

Taking a sip from his cup, then dabbing at his trim mustache with his napkin, Domingo answered his father's first question with a far more pleasant expression on his face. "The duke is well and is looking forward to my escorting Doña Magdalena, Manuela, and Carlos down for a visit in the fall. The duchess is already planning parties to introduce the young people to the city's social circles. He sends his personal best to you, Father, as well as a large packet I've already sent to your office. He seems encouraged about the latest from Seville." Waiting for the maid to place a large dish of fruit on the table and then leave, Domingo went on. "Since his mother's death, King Philip has taken a new wife, the young

Isabel from the House of Savoy. Everyone seems to think there's a good possibility of an heir."

"I wonder if a Bourbon king will ever win the Spanish heart," the older man said. "The French seem determined to stick their meddling fingers in our affairs." He was proud that in his family the girls had always been educated along with the boys and that, unlike the majority, they could take part in all kinds of social intercourse upon maturity. Grateful for his dead son's having endorsed that tradition, he turned to his granddaughter. "You see, Manuela, this absurd war over who shall sit on the throne of Spain has been going on most of your life and has cost more than it could possibly be worth to the treasury or to the people."

Domingo spoke up. "But King Philip *is* the grandson of Louis XIV, Father, and it has been difficult for the citizens to believe a Bourbon means to rule Spain on his own from Spain rather than Paris. Frankly, I doubt that he does, but maybe now that he has married. . . ." His voice trailed off as he concentrated on peeling an orange.

"What goes on over there doesn't have that much real effect on us, does it?" Manuela inquired, not truly understanding about the significance of the battles fought across the ocean after the death of the childless King Charles II in 1700 over who should rule Spain. She realized with a shock that she had been a child of two then and that treaties had been signed only the past year.

"I'm afraid it does, especially when it comes to trade," replied her uncle, looking across the table at her. "From the beginning of the Spanish con-

21

quest of Mexico nearly two hundred years ago, the Crown has insisted that all trade with the colonies should be carried on through Seville."

"Why is that?" she asked.

Manuela rested her chin in her hands while awaiting his answer, a chin decidedly strong yet feminine. The slanted, black eyes gleamed with interest and intelligence. She noticed that Doña Magdalena, though quiet as usual, was following the conversation diligently. Lately Manuela had suspected her great-aunt's air of concentration was caused by her need to compensate for her loss of hearing by reading lips.

"Because it was Castilian money and blood that built this overseas empire, my dove," her grandfather replied with strong feeling, heavy brows settling into a forbidding line above snapping black eyes. "You must never forget that fact."

"And any profit made from trade should belong to Spaniards," Manuela concluded, her look of puzzlement clearing. "Not the French, nor the English." With her fingers, she accepted the orange segment Domingo offered across the table, not daring to glance at Doña Magdalena and see her disapproval of such informality. Had her twin, Carlos, attempted such a breech ... From behind half-lowered lashes, she shot an admiring glance at her uncle for his boldness. "Not the French, nor the English."

"You are right, dear one. And, you might add, no profit for the natives of New Spain either," Domingo intoned with noticeable sharpness. "Mexican silver only for its mother country."

Domingo smiled approvingly at his bright niece until he realized her conversation was prov-

22

ing what he hated to face: She was becoming an adult—no, she was one already. He shifted his tall frame, squirming inwardly at the unpleasant news he would have to reveal soon.

Both men sipped coffee with studied casualness. Mealtimes were not occasions for them to become embroiled in differences of opinion about the enforced, subservient relationship of Mexico to the mother country.

"Unless we might suffer here from a shortage that can't be supplied by our countrymen," Domingo grated, unable to keep back his conviction any longer. His eyes shifted from the intent face of his aunt to those of his niece and father as he went on, eager to make his point. "We should never lose sight of the fact that though we are subjects of Spain—and loyal ones at that—we're also citizens of Mexico and our needs deserve homage."

"I doubt the viceroy or your other superiors would agree with that," Diego snapped, casting disapproving eyes at his son, obviously ready to defend his statement at the table if the need arose. The chiseled features of his face seemed made of granite.

"Let us leave such heavy matters until another time," said Doña Magdalena in her nasal, yet cultured, voice. A warm smile toward the stern face of her brother-in-law at the other end of the long table softened the reprimand. "It's almost *siesta* time."

Acquiescing as usual to the silver-haired woman's genteel reminders of proper etiquette, all left the dining room with promises to meet again after their *siestas*, those private times set aside each day from midday until later in the after-

23

noon when the heat of the sun had lessened.

"Tonight at dinner," announced Manuela with a pert smile and a flip of her waist-length hair before leaving the foyer for her bedroom upstairs, "we'll make it a gala family affair to celebrate Uncle's return. I wish Carlos were already back from his hunting trip—especially since no one will allow me to go along anymore."

Dried now in a straight curtain hanging down her back, Manuela's hair, so black as to suggest hidden tints of dark blue, formed a shimmering frame for the beautifully sculpted face. Openly questing for argument, the fine, slanting eyes brooded from within frames of thick, sooty lashes. The three being challenged avoided making comment in the heavy silence. Too well they knew Manuela's spirited, unorthodox views on society's demands from young women.

When it became apparent that no one wished to pick up the subtly thrown gauntlet, Manuela turned toward the staircase, ending the family gathering in her customary sweet temper. "We'll hold our own little family reunion and refuse to talk about anything serious until after we leave the table."

None could have predicted how wrong she was.

Chapter Two

San Juan Batista, a mere two leagues below the southern reaches of the Rio Grande, claimed no title as an imposing settlement according to Old World standards, but on the desert frontier of 1714, it seemed an oasis. The central, boxy buildings making up the Spanish *presidio* squatted behind massive adobe walls.

Fronting the large open area called the *plaza* were the offices and quarters of the officials and soldiers, a workshop, and several supply houses. Small dwellings for the few Indians living inside the walls were arranged in parallel lines on one side of the *plaza*. Within close proximity sat a spacious, open workshop where the Indian women and children wove baskets and fabric and made pottery for the population: the commandant and his family; the troop of thirty soldiers, some with wives and children; a dozen *mestizos* serving in the commandant's *hacienda* and in the stables; and a Lipan tribe.

Fashioned of the identical, sand-colored adobe as all other *presidio* structures, twin buildings on another side of the *plaza* served as granary and stables. It was on the back side of these long, parallel buildings that the private *hacienda* of the commandant and his family stood, encompassed by its own, more gracefully formed walls.

As at almost all *presidios* in New Spain, the

church beckoned from a short distance outside the protective walls, for it welcomed the few scattered ranchers, sheepherders, and Indians, as well as those inside the walls. Along with its soaring bell tower, topped by an imposing cross of silver visible for miles in the flat area between the Rio Grande and the foothills of the Serranias del Burro, the adobe building aspired to dignity with unusually tall proportions and arched double doors of gleaming mahogany. The red tile roof, though brighter because it had been built last, was a repeat of those humpbacking repetitiously across the tops of the numerous buildings within the *presidio*. Father Dermoza, the resident priest, enjoyed comfortable quarters inside the walls, similar to those set aside for officers and visiting officials.

Since the Crown-stated purposes of the outpost were to channel the energy and loyalty of the regional Indians toward glorifying the Spanish flag, to be as self-supporting as possible, and to prevent foreign powers from infringing upon Spanish territory, Commandant Diego Roman considered himself extremely successful. His immediate superior, Governor Gaspardo Anya of the northern province of Coahuila, as well as the viceroy of Mexico, the Duke of Linares, shared his good opinion of himself, as was evidenced by written commendations and treasured gifts of land and goods.

Colonel Diego Ramon had been in charge at San Juan Batista ever since its establishment fourteen years earlier, in 1700. The cultivated fields just outside the fort attested to the loyalty as well as to the peaceful intentions and diligence of the Indians. From the Lipan council, the tribe had chosen to join the Spaniards at the fort after being promised protection from the war-minded Tejas to the north. The well-stocked storehouses and infrequent requests for shipments of supplies from Mexico City proved that the *presidio* was self-supporting, insofar as was feasible.

For several years there had been no Indians or foreigners drifting from the territory Diego liked to think of as Texas—a term used once by someone from the viceroy's staff during a meeting of officers—rather than the Land of the Tejas. The Tejas were a fierce and hostile nation of many tribes, and in his only clash with one of their warring parties during his early years at the *presidio*, he had not ended up the decisive victor. The very name brought an unpleasant taste to his mouth. However, the Indians had attempted no retaliatory raids. Commandant Diego Ramon had rested easily for a number of years.

And so the gates of the Presidio of the North, as it was sometimes called, stood open on rusty hinges. Over the peaceful years, several Indian families had asked for and received permission to build small adobe huts outside the walls, nearer their gardens, fields, and water sources. In time they had moved out their animals to rudely constructed pens near their homes, coming inside the walls only occasionally to trade or perform the required work in the craft hall.

Soon after arriving at the desolate area of sand, cacti, and mesquite bushes, Commandant Ramon had ordered an irrigation ditch to be dug from the Santa Rosa River some fifteen leagues away. The channeled water, following an old, dry river bed with its own levees, turned the little patch of desert into a spot of beauty and prosperity.

Carefully nurtured fruit and shade trees soon reached above the dusty walls. Colorful flowering vines trailed graceful patterns across the sand-colored, boxlike buildings. A few years later, Diego Ramon commanded that a small lake be dug to be used for fishing and laundering by the Indians, the soldiers, and the ʼervants of the officers' families.

All in all, San Juan Batista was a pleasant place in which to live that May afternoon in 1714 when the Frenchman from Louisiana arrived at its opened gates on his black stallion. With him were his two companions, pack animals, two dozen Indians, and the fluttering blue flag boldly emblazoned with three golden *fleurs-de-lis*.

"S – S – Sir," stammered Sgt. Santo Guerra when Commandant Diego Ramon responded to the sharp rap on the door of his office. "An officer to see you." The sergeant looked straight ahead, his Adam's apple jumping in fits and starts. Despite his olive skin, the Creole's face seemed ashen.

"An officer?" repeated the commandant foolishly, still a bit groggy from the *siesta* taken on the couch in his office. "From where?" He gave his sergeant of the past five years a quizzical look. No one had notified him that an officer was to arrive. Visits to his outpost from the governor's force in Monclova, a half-day's journey southward, were rare but were generally heralded by a messenger.

"From French Louisiana, sir," Sergeant Guerra replied, still avoiding his superior's eyes.

Diego whipped about and stared beyond the soldier at what seemed for an instant to be a foe of inestimable strength and power—a man charged from an inner zeal alien to the character of the average, pleasure-loving Spanish soldier—until the stranger smiled. That usually ordinary rearranging of lips and facial muscles created an extraordinary transformation. A morning sun might have just risen behind the handsome, clean-shaven face and pale, sparkling eyes.

Judging the young man was not yet thirty, Diego watched him walk forward from where he waited in the *plaza*, a relaxed air of suggested nobility marking his military bearing. He stopped upon reaching conversing distance.

"Commandant Ramon, I presume?" the Frenchman asked in flawless Spanish, his use of the language as surprising as the change in his lean face at the appearance of the dazzling, disarming smile. Gray-blue eyes seemed uncommonly silver against deeply tanned skin when he doffed his three-cornered hat and offered a slight bow of deference. "Permit me to present my passport and introduce myself. At your service, sir, is Lt. Louis Juchereau de Saint-Denis, recently Commandant of Fort Saint Louis de la Mobile, presently an officer on a special religious mission at the request of the Governor of New France, Sieur Antoine de la Mothe Cadillac."

Commandant Diego Ramon possessed equal skills as a military officer and as a diplomat. Surely, he mused, the young Frenchman was as aware as he that their countries had just ended a bitter war the previous year and that relations were anything but friendly. In fact, the edict ordering that any such foreigners be thrown in prison to await trial and likely death as spies lay in his desk drawer at that very moment. A rumor had reached his ears that a trading vessel of the same Governor Cadillac had been turned away forcefully from the port of Tampico within the past six months and warned never to return. The story went that shots had been fired across her bow to emphasize the order.

Choosing diplomacy, Diego returned the man's bow with a brief nod and asked, "Will you join me in my office, Lieutenant Saint-Denis?"

At the Frenchman's approach, Diego studied him even more carefully. It shocked him to realize what he would have ordinarily noticed right away: the Frenchman's angular but pleasing face was tanned and cleanly shaven, this in a day and age when most white men cultivated some growth of hair upon the face. He wore a snowy linen shirt, its sleeves cuffed and trimmed with the same lace adorning his full cravat. A gold brocade waistcoat fell stylishly from broad shoulders over the upper portion of tight black breeches caught below the knee with silver buttons.

When the Frenchman walked with him into the building, the older man, no stranger to European fashion himself, could not help but admire the well-developed legs encased in white silk stockings and the overall perfection of a tall, manly physique and stance. He noted also that the lieutenant's polished black shoes with low, curved heels sported the stylish wide tongue and filigreed silver buckles. Although the stranger did not wear a periwig, his thick brown hair was fluffed in the curly style of one. A lovelock lay pulled forward over his shoulder, the longer piece of hair bound near the ends by a silver clasp bearing what looked like a crest.

Louis Saint-Denis met the Spaniard's blatantly appraising look with apparent candor and lack of concern, lowering himself gracefully onto the proffered chair in front of the imposing desk after they entered the office. His air was that of one cultured man accepting a courteous invitation from another. Half smiling, half at rest, the wide mouth was set in a pleasant way, though the alert eyes seemed as busy at cataloguing as the gray-haired commandant's.

The Frenchman appeared so at ease, both inwardly and outwardly, that Diego found himself relaxing, until he recalled that not all persons or things turn out to be what they seem at first glance. Calling upon years of self-discipline, the Spaniard warned himself against breathing too easily before he investigated the trespasser more thoroughly.

"I believe you mentioned having a passport?" Diego questioned authoritatively, wondering where the Frenchman had learned to speak Spanish so well.

Though Diego knew that his granddaughter, Manuela, had studied French at the convent and often read French books from his well-stocked library, he doubted that she spoke it fluently. Never having studied any language other than Latin and his own, he had always been in awe of anyone who could express himself in more than his native tongue.

"Yes, Commandant Ramon. I have here my passport, which I am most happy to present for your pleasure and perusal." Deftly Louis extracted a folder from inside his waistcoat and pushed it across the desk toward the older man. His hands then moved with light, loving strokes along the gold-tooled leather top of the handsome piece. With open admiration riding his deep voice, he said, "What a fine example of workmanship, sir. Only the Barcelonans can work so well with leather. I compliment you on your choice of desks."

A handsome gold ring flashed during the caressing movement along the desk top, and Diego made out sharply raised letters and two small emblems set in a triangle. He could imagine its creating an impressive mark in sealing wax. The Frenchman raised gray-blue eyes to his host's inquisitive black ones and smiled as though they had long been friends and fellow connoisseurs.

Up close, Diego mused, the man's teeth appeared as dazzling as his linen. Only then did he notice the little crescent-shaped scar on Louis's left cheekbone. For an unguarded moment, the older man felt inclined to ask about it, to listen to what would surely be a dramatic, exciting account of how he had received it. Instead, he pulled himself together and recalled that this was hardly a social occasion.

"Thank you," Diego replied gruffly, not understanding his temptation to relax all his guard and confess that the desk had indeed come from Barcelona and, mayhap even more impressive, had been a gift from the viceroy to show his appreciation.

The perturbed Commandant Ramon picked up the papers and read the passport, thankful that it was written in both French and Spanish: "The Sieur de St. Denis is to take twenty-four men, and as many Indians as necessary, and with them go in search of Father Francisco Hidalgo and his Mission of the Holy Saints in response to

32

his letter of January 17, 1711. While there, he is to purchase horses and cattle for the province of Louisiana."

The Spaniard glanced over the top of the vellum at the calm face of his visitor, then studied Governor Cadillac's signature and seal with deliberate concentration.

Next Diego read with care the accompanying letter from the missionary, remembering that Father Hidalgo had indeed been recalled before 1700 from the Spanish mission formed years earlier on the Colorado River in Tejas, and that since that time, the mission had been allowed to deteriorate. His conscience nagged a bit. He himself had chosen to ignore the priest's written appeals enlisting his aid over the past ten years. Why would any white man, even a priest, desire to live among the treacherous Tejas?

In the letter, over three years old if the date was accurate, Father Hidalgo indicated his concern was not whether the French or the Spanish Catholics rebuilt the Mission of the Holy Saints, so long as someone did. He stated that he was getting old and longed to return to his "children," those Tejas he had converted, and that the Spanish no longer seemed interested in those inhabiting the Land of the Tejas. From his limited sources, the missionary pointed out, he had learned that the majority of the Tejas had reverted to the worship of their pagan gods, and his heart was heavily burdened.

"Does all seem in order, sir?" asked the seemingly relaxed Frenchman from the chair. He rested his ostrich-plumed black tricorn on crossed legs, idly smoothing the feathers with two fingers. "Are you familiar with Father Hidalgo and his lost mission?"

"Yes, Lieutenant Saint-Denis." Diego toyed with his full moustache before saying, "He's presently at a mission on the western boundary of this province, Coahuila. I was unaware of his continuing efforts to reestablish the settlement in the Land of the . . . in Texas." The hated word "Tejas" would not form. Returning the papers to the folder and placing them in a drawer, he said, "Perhaps we should postpone any discussion about this matter until I've had more time to think upon it. Your passport indicates that you didn't travel alone, and yet I don't recall having seen any others with you in the *plaza.*"

"I instructed my men to wait outside the walls; for I had no wish for you to think I was a threat in any way, Commandant Ramon. One of your post guards spotted us and sent out a scouting party, but I told them I'd ride in alone. I would expect that your soldiers have by now escorted my party inside."

Louis Saint-Denis, though only twenty-eight, also recognized the value of diplomacy and had courted its art in a manner similar to that of the older man sitting before him. He kept his countenance in repose, but his mind reflected upon the amusing thought that it would have furthered his intentions not at all to reveal what had actually happened: The singular reason that the guard in the tower ever spotted him outside the walls was that Louis had whistled, yelled, and waved his hat to awaken him and gain his attention. The French lieutenant had had no desire to startle the Spanish or make them suspicious of his motives for appearing at a hostile fort. Everything was going as planned, so far.

"Of course," replied Diego, intrigued at the thought that the dapper young Frenchman must have stopped just out of view of the fort to change into his elegant clothing. No man, not even one so obviously cultured as the one before him, would venture across such a distance as that between New France and New Spain in fashionable finery. What was the lieutenant up to? "How many are in your party?"

"Only two more Frenchmen, sir. Medar Jalot, serving both as my personal valet and field surgeon for my men, and Sgt. Phillipe Penicault, my assistant and historian. Also with me are some twenty-five Indians of the Assinai tribe. The remainder of my unit stayed behind to hunt and fish along the Colorado with the Assinais after their warriors joined us in conquering a war party of Comanches. They'll be along later."

"Comanches, you say?" asked Diego, lips thinning, voice sharpening. "They are one of the most volatile Tejas tribes — as I suppose you learned." He remembered all too well just how violent they had been during his own encounters with them. Though he knew the answer, he could not resist adding with undisguised awe, "And you say you defeated them?"

What was it about the young man that fascinated him so, kept tempting him to forget that he was an enemy and likely up to no good? Diego wondered. He watched the lean face take on a look of humility.

A broad shoulder lifting in a careless shrug, Louis replied, "After our first battle, we were able to bargain with them and make peace. I've found over the past eight years that a few bolts of cloth and baubles buy a goodly measure of contentment among Indians. They're always eager to smoke the pipe and put on a show for visitors in exchange for news of other tribes and good hunting areas. But I'm sure, sir, that you're even more aware of such things than I."

Diego fought to suppress his admiration for one who had bested a group of warring Comanches without having to fight unto death. Having won that little mental battle, the Spaniard turned to more immediate matters. Within a short time, he had conferred with Sergeant Guerra and found that the newcomers were, indeed, awaiting further instructions out in the *plaza*

The soldiers of the *presidio*, no doubt fearful of what the Frenchman might be revealing to the commandant about having caught them asleep, had stationed themselves among and around the intruders in such a way as to suggest imprisonment.

Diego ordered, "Sergeant Guerra, assign quarters befitting the ranks of these newcomers. They are to be restricted to the confines of the walls until further notice."

"Aye, sir." The sergeant dared not mention that the rusted hinges prevented the closing of the gates. A discreetly exchanged look with the Frenchman told him that he no longer had to worry over having his indiscretion reported to the commandant he had served faithfully for the past five years. Saluting and breathing far more easily, Sergeant Guerra led the strangers away.

Then the commandant personally assigned to Lieutenant Saint-Denis the most luxurious guest quarters near his own office.

Noticing the quantities of large packets soon

being unloaded from the packhorses into the suite, Diego wondered at the store the young man beside him obviously placed in his personal grooming. He assumed that the numerous tarp-covered bundles contained personal clothing. Why else would they be placed in the lieutenant's living quarters? By that time, there was little doubt in his mind that Louis Saint-Denis was an enigma—with one hell of a personality.

"Will you join me again in my office?"

"My pleasure, sir." This, with another disarming smile.

If there were valid complaints to be made about life at San Juan Batista, Diego reflected as the two moved across the tree-edged *plaza*, they would center around the sameness of the days, the dearth of visitors, and the lack of news from the outside wold.

On the road to Monclova, the nearest settlement, a few Creole *rancheros* lived and eked out a living by grazing goats and cattle in the foothills and small grassy slopes. Though, as commandant and therefore a representative of the Crown, Diego kept friendly relations with the *rancheros*, neither he nor his family socialized with them, for class distinction reached throughout New Spain. The *rancheros* and their *mestizo* herders came often to services at The Church of the Blessed Virgin outside the *presidio* walls, where Diego was wont to acknowledge their presence and the baptism of their children. He even invited them to the frequent *fiestas* at the *presidio*, but never did he ask them to call at his *hacienda*, despite frequent criticism of this policy by his son, Domingo.

Before he realized what he was doing, Diego

had insisted that Louis and he use first names. Bringing out a choice bottle of wine and sharing it, he engaged him in further conversation about his recent experiences with the Comanches.

Another unplanned, uncharacteristic move followed the lively exchange when Diego said, "Though we both know I must look upon you as being under 'house arrest,' I'd consider it an honor if you would take your meals with my family and me while we await Governor Anya's orders from Monclova. I'm sure this matter will be cleared up without problems."

"You're most kind, sir, and I accept with pleasure," Louis replied graciously, without a trace of surprise showing on the handsome face.

A flashing inner thought did bring an added sparkle to the gray-blue eyes of Louis Saint-Denis: the hope that the maid spied swimming earlier that morning at a distance would be the one serving the table.

Chapter Three

"Have you seen the intruders?" Manuela asked Conchita.

From where she sat upon a bench before her dressing table, the commandant's granddaughter watched idly in the mirror while the maid turned the straight fall of black hair into an artful combination of chignon and tumbling ringlets. The curling iron hissed when she formed two wispy curls to fall in front of her mistress's ears and dangle below.

"Frenchmen!" Manuela fumed, letting out a sigh of disapproval. "As Grandfather says, they seem always to be meddling in Spanish affairs."

"Be still," warned Conchita, bottom lip held between her teeth until she had removed the hot metal from the perilous position alongside the creamy olive cheek. "I don't want to burn you, and I'm sure you don't want to be late for dinner and have Doña Magdalena give you a lecture on the ways a proper young lady should act." With affection she met the black eyes in the mirror after she returned the iron to its stand. "Yes, I've seen them. They don't look at all like anyone on the trail for months. And they don't look like spies either."

"I don't see why Grandfather had to invite

them to dinner with the family. Aren't they prisoners now?" With slight interest, she viewed Conchita's handiwork, tugging carelessly at a curl resting on a bare shoulder.

"Mama says only one officer is in the group and that he's the only one invited. The other two Frenchmen are underlings, one a valet and one a sergeant."

The maid's tone indicated that she had no problem in accepting the existence of the varied social classes, or her own place in one lower than that of Manuela. Seeing her mistress rise with nothing on except beribboned drawers and a thin chemise, she eyed the gored and boned corset lying on the bed in the adjoining room and moved toward it.

"You need not touch that torturous garment, Conchita," snapped Manuela with a rare show of temper toward the pretty maid. "I refuse to wear it."

Manuela hated the way the corset pinched her waist and came up high in front, pushing her breasts up in a painful way. When Doña Magdalena had brought it to her a few months ago, she had expressed her dislike in great detail to both her great-aunt and to her maid. The despised garment had not been brought out again until tonight. That she had to repeat her personal preferences about such matters to Conchita annoyed her more than any other negative trait the maid possessed.

"What will Doña Magdalena say?"

"Bother! With her poor eyesight she hasn't noticed before. Why would she tonight?" She looked down at high, rounded breasts and her slender body. "Why do I need to look smaller than this? Surely there's no need to impress a hated Frenchman with stylish appearances here in my own home. The man will probably be shot before sunset tomorrow . . . and justly so."

"Things aren't always as simple as you'd like."

A resigned smile on her face, Conchita fetched the *panniers* and tied the strings of the basket-like contraption around Manuela's narrow waist. The full-skirted gown to be held out gracefully from her hips tonight was of rustling yellow taffeta shot with silver threads.

Giving in to a convention too obvious to discard, Manuela touched the *panniers* on her hips with distaste before skipping back to the earlier conversation.

"Juanita learns everything being in the kitchen, doesn't she? And she's a good mama as well as a good cook. You're lucky, Conchita," she said, her voice thoughtful.

Most of the time Manuela felt much older and wiser than Conchita, even more so than her sixteen years warranted. Not that she brooded upon such matters, but she sometimes wondered how much her having lived and studied within the demanding confines of a convent until age twelve had to do with it. And how much had her always having to face inner problems without the love and guidance of a mother contributed to that feeling of being grown-up at sixteen?

Well, she knew that most young women her age were already married, or at least betrothed. It puzzled Manuela that those she had known while in school had always seemed younger and more content to accept social conventions than she. Mayhap her unorthodox ideas came about because of the close relationship with her twin

41

brother, she mused.

Manuela viewed her image in the oval mirror standing in the corner of her bedroom as Conchita, trying to conceal the absence of the corset, tightly laced up the back of the gown, forcing firm breasts upward to form a more pronounced cleavage. An edging of creamy lace around the low, squared neckline brought out the same tones lurking in her olive coloring, a gift from her unusually fair-skinned mother—or so she had been told at those times when she sighed at not being as dark as Carlos. For just a moment, she panicked at the thought that her stints in the river were causing an obvious darkening around her face and shoulders. Would Domingo or Diego question such a change and become curious?

"A little corn powder will make your skin lighter," came a consoling voice.

As on numerous occasions over the four years she had served Manuela, Conchita seemed to be reading her mind. Deftly the maid fluffed the tiers of ruffles on the sleeves reaching just above the elbow before straightening the yellow ribbons decorating the silver-embroidered stomacher, or center panel, of the bodice. She retied one of the large bows holding the overskirt to the sides, designed that way to reveal the underskirt embroidered as ornately with silver thread as the stylish stomacher. Obviously satisfied with her efforts, the efficient young woman smiled when she stepped back to admire. She then brought out slippers of silver and brocade and helped Manuela slide narrow feet into them.

"Pearls?" Conchita asked, eyes squinting in thought while they roved over the beautiful young woman. The handsome jewelry cabinet

42

with inlaid patterns of jade, pearl, and rosewood sat alongside the dressing table. She fished the key from beneath a stack of handkerchiefs in the table drawer and awaited her mistress's decision.

"What difference does it make? You choose."

Manuela gazed out the second-story window at the deepening twilight, drinking in the multiple shades of purple, mauve, and pink of the diminishing sunset and wishing she were out there somewhere over the horizon to breathe in the heady scents of summer forests. Out there lay freedom. And Carlos, her beloved twin and companion.

From the balcony encompassing the entire second floor of family bedrooms, a fluttering sound blended with a raucous squawk and captured Manuela's attention.

"Zorro?" she called. "Why are you hiding on the balcony? If you're going to try your trick of aggravating the pigeons and horses out in the stables, I'll have to put you in your cage and close the door." When no reply came, Manuela scolded with affection, "You'd better listen to me, you bad bird."

She turned back toward the mirror. A flash of green therein, plus a flapping of wings, told her that the parrot had come to rest upon its perch near the open door. Her uncle Domingo had brought Zorro to her from Mexico City four years ago, soon after Carlos and she had left their schools to live at San Juan Batista.

Convinced as always that the bird understood every word she spoke to him, she smiled to see him preening in assumed innocence. Her dislike of fastening her pet inside its cage often led to reprimands from her grandfather, for the bird

43

loved to range freely about the stables and annoy the animals, especially the pigeons in the cote upon the stable roof.

"Promise you'll stay inside tonight," Manuela coaxed in the soft, caressing voice she used when addressing the parrot. "Stay, Zorro."

Zorro mimicked in that way she had taught him, "Stay, Zorro."

As she usually did, Conchita rolled her eyes at the ridiculous exchange going on between Manuela and the brightly colored bird. The parrot seldom spoke for any but its mistress. Both young women had learned that Zorro generally did as he pleased when left outside his cage, though he always returned to his mistress's bedroom after his bedeviling forays about the *presidio* stables.

The parrot's most unforgivable mischief was that played around the pigeon cote sitting atop one end of the stable roof. For some reason, the carrier pigeons could not seem to accept Zorro as a fellow bird. They would set up all kinds of throaty calls and protests when the parrot chose to perch near the cote and go through his several recitations. Always this bit of deviltry was done at night after the commandant had gone to sleep. The last time Zorro had upset the pigeons at midnight, their plaintive cries had awakened Diego. In thunderous tones, he had threatened to wring the yellow-feathered neck if Manuela allowed such to happen one more time.

Opening the top section of the jewelry cabinet, Conchita admired the selections of jeweled combs, small purses, and fans lying upon the green velvet lining. She chose an ivory fan edged with silver-dipped lace, opening it to reveal large yellow roses highlighted with silver leaf.

Then she slid out the top drawer. At first she lifted a string of pearls but seemed to have a better idea. From the third drawer she took a gold chain with a lavaliere of small pearls and good-sized emeralds. Next came earrings with identical dangles. The matching ring she found in the smallest drawer, one designed with slitted, uplifted pockets of velvet to hold only rings.

"These were my mother's," Manuela murmured with a touch of wistfulness for never having known the young woman who had given birth to Carlos and her. "Grandfather says my father loved her very much." She slipped the ring on her finger and watched in the mirror as the necklace and earrings became part of her costume. The square neckline of the yellow gown and the warm tones of her exposed neck and upper part of her breasts formed a lovely background for the contrasting dazzle of emeralds.

After applying a light dusting of powder to the tanned areas and pouring a drop of rosehip perfume into each of Manuela's palms. Conchita said, "You look as fine as any young lady from Paris." She stood back to admire. At her mistress's slight frown, she added, "Or Seville."

When Manuela acknowledged the compliment with a doubting, uplifted eyebrow, the maid continued, more in the role of *confidante* now that the grooming was completed, "How can you be so uncaring about the way you look? Don't you know half the ladies of the world would be tempted to kill to be so beautiful? All you care about is roaming in the foothills or riding around on a horse—bareback as often as not—like a boy or some Indian girl. One of these days you're going to have to face up to being a young woman – and a wealthy one of marriageable age. When we go to Mexico City this fall –"

"That's why I like you, Conchita," interrupted Manuela with a wry pursing of generous lips. Black eyes reproached the maid for what she recognized as a fair yet unflattering picture of herself. Some things were better left unsaid. She knew only too well that she moved to a rhythm all her own and that she understood it no better than Conchita did. "You're so tactful."

"I've had a good teacher for four years." She shot a mischievous grin at the one she served, the following exchange of measuring looks more one of two friends than that of mistress and maid.

Manuela assumed a haughty air, upping the natural proud lift of her strong chin and raising her shoulders and breasts to an even higher level. With the stylish grace Doña Magdalena had taught her, she unfurled the fan and held it before her oval face, leaving in view only the wide, velvety eyes with their unique slant beneath thick black brows. She blinked and fluttered long lashes in a lazy way peculiarly her own, then asked, "Is this the way you would have Miss Manuela Sanchez y Ramon appear before the unwelcome French lieutenant?"

Both young women caught the giggles then. From his perch, Zorro joined in, his noises uncanny echoes of the feminine sounds. Holding on to the perch with scaly, strong toes, the parrot rocked his body back and forth in imitation of their swaying bodies, the yellow beak opened wide to give more volume to his own version of giggles. Only the jingle of the first, warning dinner bell broke up the trio's merriment.

As soon as Diego greeted his guest, he realized that Louis Saint-Denis had dressed with a fashionable flair for the evening with the commandant and his family. Except for the generous silver braiding that outlined wide cuffs above the lace ruffles of white shirtsleeves, his coat of blue broadcloth was plain. The well-tailored garment accentuated the manly shape of his broad shoulders and trim middle. The skirt fell from the waist with an outward flare and had a slit at each hip, at which point the material was pleated into a reversed fan shape and accented at the apex by a silver button.

Above the tight knee-breeches of matching blue fabric and beneath the unbuttoned coat, the Frenchman wore a brief waistcoat of white brocade enhanced by embroidered silver *fleurs-de-lis*. A ruffled cravat of soft linen fell over silver buttons. White silk hose defined muscular calves above shiny black shoes, shoes cut up high to surprisingly narrow ankles. Diego noticed again that the enigmatic young man wore his brown hair in the style of a wig, only this time the longer lovelock was tied with a white ribbon.

"Sir, I am greatly honored to be a guest in your home," Louis intoned with a formal bow from the waist when Diego welcomed him. Both seemed to choose to ignore the fact that he was more prisoner than guest.

"We are the ones honored," replied his host, giving a courtly nod before introducing his son, Domingo.

As was their custom, Diego and Domingo had

47

dressed formally for dinner. Both wore fashion-able black coats and pants with white shirts beruffled at the cuffs in a manner similar to the Frenchman's. Diego's waistcoat was of black satin etched with scrolled patterns in silver thread, while Domingo's was of red brocade trimmed with black braid. Their shoes had the same low heels as their guest's but were lower cut with silver buckles gracing pointed toes. Fringed white cravats filled the upper openings of their waistcoats.

Neither Spaniard wore his hair in the long style that Louis chose. Thin and white, Diego's hair was pulled back severely over his ears into a neat crimp on his neck. Domingo's slightly gray-streaked black locks were softer and fuller, but even shorter than his father's. Their moustaches and full sideburns marked other notable differences between their smooth-faced "prisoner" and them.

"It has been far too long since I've been privi-leged to dine with such a lovely lady," Louis said, his voice lowering with reverence as he bent to kiss the frail hand of Doña Magdalena when she appeared and introductions were made. Aware of her appraising, skeptical looks, he remarked, "Black silk is never as striking as when on a beautiful lady with silver hair, such as yourself. That you chose to wear a jeweled comb com-pletes my mental picture of an elegant Spanish lady." He watched with satisfaction as the smile of pleasure he strove for began pushing at her pinched lips. "Your brother-in-law is to be compli-mented on his choice of hostesses to grace his table."

Stealing a quick look at her older but still

handsome brother-in-law, Doña Magdalena lifted her silvery head to a finer angle. A becoming flush crept beneath faintly netted olive skin when she noted that Diego seemed to be sizing her up in a new way. Her snapping black eyes took on a softer look as she made small talk with the charming Frenchman.

"What could be keeping my granddaughter?" Diego asked during a brief lull, turning in the large foyer to look up the staircase. She was not usually late.

Louis jerked his head at the words, unaware that anyone else would be joining them for dinner. Neither his valet, Medar, nor he had had time enough to find out much about the in-residence Ramons. Doña Magdalena had just revealed that Carlos, the grandson, was away on a hunting trip in the mountains. No one had mentioned a fifth family member.

Just then a blur of yellow glowed in the upper hallway and Manuela descended, halting all conversation and leading Doña Magdalena to feel rewarded from the tedious hours of instruction given. The beautiful young woman seemed to float down the stairs, so effortlessly did she drop one foot down ahead of the other without once lowering the proud head.

Like a full-blown rose upon a slender stem, one stirring from a tender breeze, the yellow gown billowed and swayed from the tiny waist. The searching light from the chandelier in the foyer played a losing game in the ebony depths of her hair, managing only to bounce off the swaying curls and highlight their gleaming blackness. Not until she eased from the last step onto a small rug brightening the earth-toned tile

49

squares did Manuela smile.

Along with the others, Louis gazed in admiration at the beauty who approached without seeming to move by ordinary means. But then, he amended his dizzying thoughts, there was absolutely nothing ordinary about her in any way. The commandant's granddaughter was one of a kind. He was stunned, struck almost deaf and dumb. He had no doubt that before him stood a young Spanish lady of supreme dignity, breeding, and culture. Never had he seen such a captivating smile as she was bestowing upon her grandfather and her uncle. Her full, pink lips fascinated him, reminded him of dew-kissed rose petals seen at dawn in some forgotten garden.

With the lightning speed of a falcon falling toward its doomed prey, Louis sensed an aura of immediacy about her such as he had never before found in any young woman, a hint of mystery having to do with destiny or with some kind of unrecognized force emanating from her very pores. He acknowledged that whatever assailed his being was more than mere alluring femininity. In vain, he searched for a label. A great pounding of his pulse roared in his ears. An alien dryness settled upon his tongue. Was his reaction to the young beauty caused by his having been cheated of the company of genteel young women over the past eight years?

When it was time at last to hear her precious name and be introduced, the Frenchman reeled inwardly from the incredible beauty of the heavily lashed black eyes fixed upon him unwaveringly, eyes set at an unusual, almost exotic slant above flawless cheeks. The wayward thought that some long-ago Moor or Turk had tainted a

Spanish bloodline in a most attractive way rippled through his befogged brain.

"Charmed, Miss Ramon," Louis managed to say over his still-racing pulse when his hand took hers, aware for the first time that what had formerly been a term of courtesy was at that moment one of earth-shattering fact.

With fingers suddenly turned tender, as though they were handling the petals of a delicate flower, the French lieutenant took the arrogantly proffered hand while he leaned over to plant a proper kiss upon its softness. A faint scent of roses floated to his nostrils, triggering a memory too elusive, too removed, to identify.

Later, Louis would recall that he forgot to check to see if the young woman was pleased with him and his appearance, something he had never before failed to do. And he would moan to realize that he forgot to utter one of the glib compliments he usually found so ready on his tongue, another action he had long accepted as easygoing habit. If he had been asked to write down exactly what had happened next, or who said what, the befuddled young man would have had to leave the vellum blank.

Though Louis felt less in control than usual, felt almost like a spectator suspended above the table, dinner went well. He sat across from Manuela and enjoyed watching her as the conversation dipped and twisted around what was happening in Europe, insofar as the citizens of the New World could learn.

Despite her appearing to be very young, the elegant Miss Ramon possessed remarkable composure, Louis mused, realizing from the first blatant look in his direction that she felt some

51

kind of animosity toward him. Once they were seated, she chose not to favor him with a direct gaze. That she was remarkably intelligent and well-read shone through the casual conversations with clarity.

Louis had an urge to know what went on in that pretty head, to peer into the workings of her mind. Manuela Ramon was a young lady blessed with far more than physical beauty, he realized. If he were ever to get to know her—and the thought that he might not never entered his mind—he had to find a way to break through the icy barrier she seemed to have erected upon first laying eyes upon him.

"I'm sorry your brother is absent," Louis addressed the subject of his thoughts.

Held by ornate silver candelabra, the candles were burning low, their steady glow lending mysterious sparkle to Manuela's black eyes. The servants had removed the dessert dishes and had begun to serve coffee. Despite Louis's enchantment with the black-haired beauty across from him, the aroma of the strong brew tempted his taste buds and snatched him back to halfway sanity.

"I look forward to meeting your twin, Carlos," Louis said to her. "Doña Magdalena told me earlier that he's away on a hunting trip."

Fanning thick black lashes up in her lazy, heavy-lidded way, Manuela turned to fix a haughty stare upon the dinner guest and nodded with minimum politeness. She felt the luxuriant fall of curls move from her back to drape across a bared shoulder, all the while marking the way the Frenchman's silvery gaze followed the dance of hair, then dipped to drink in the expanse of fashionably exposed bosom. A hint of a smile hovered about her full lips at the thought of Carlos's probable reaction to the Frenchman in their midst. He was also anti-French, and not even as observant as she of the rigid social rules set up by the upper-class Spaniards and observed by Doña Magdalena and their grandfather, and sometimes by their uncle Domingo.

Granted, Manuela reflected, the stranger sitting across from her was indeed handsome, far more so than the lieutenants who came from time to time from Governor Anya's headquarters and fawned over her. She had first noticed it when he took her hand and kissed it, but there seemed an aura about him that set her senses on edge.

At Louis's touch upon her hand there at the bottom of the staircase, a kind of stirring inside Manuela's blood had prickled like a warning. Something about the way his eyes, appearing silver at times and, from the reflection of his handsome coat, startlingly blue at others, had raked over her face all evening disturbed her. It was almost as if invisible fingers feathered against her skin, took liberties she could only imagine. Never before had she seen a young man's tongue touch at the inside of his upper lip the way his was doing at that instant. The momentary sight of his tongue and the heat of his piercing gaze brought an unexplained skip to her heartbeat. In spite of her earlier resolves to ignore him, she admitted that the Frenchman was intriguing.

"Yes, Carlos goes hunting often and is a remarkable hunter," Manuela responded without a note of friendliness. Black eyes challenged the pale ones sending a new barrage of exploratory trails across her face and bared shoulders. She repressed a rising little shiver. "He can down an antelope with one shot."

Louis's heavy eyebrows rose. "Perhaps the brother likes to tell tall tales to impress his sister." The obvious loyalty to her brother charmed him to a greater degree.

"Carlos would never do that," she denied with elevated chin and disdainful stare. Suddenly aware that the others seemed intensely interested in the conversation between the Frenchman and her, she clamped her lips shut.

Manuela had been tempted to tell Louis that up until the past Christmas, when Doña Magdalena had come to serve as *dueña* and put a stop to such freedoms, she had accompanied her twin on countless hunting trips and had seen for herself what he could do—and that she was no stranger to the hunt herself. With pride she recalled that Carlos was not bad with a bow and arrow either, having learned from his Indian companions at the fort.

"Your *presidio* seems to be quite self-sufficient," Louis said, turning to Diego when he saw that Manuela had no intention of warming toward him or continuing their conversation. "You're to be commended for having carved out such a place in the upper regions of New Spain. I look forward to seeing more of it during my stay."

"We are quite comfortable at San Juan Batista," replied his host, puffing up a bit at the compliment. Only another of good breeding and experience in the New World would be able to appreciate the efforts he had made to create a

54

place of both utility and beauty. "My only regret is that my granddaughter is so cut off from the cultural events of a city." With a fond smile toward her, he went on, "This winter, Doña Magdalena and Manuela will be going to our City of Mexico for her first season in society. Here we have fairly frequent contact with our governor and his family and staff in Monclova, and occasionally we have visitors from Saltillo, a larger mining settlement on the way down the King's Road to our City of Mexico. Our lives are not entirely dull."

"That's easy to see," remarked Louis, trying, but failing miserably, to keep his gaze from returning to the beautiful but guarded face across from his.

As the evening tripped along, Louis noticed again and again that Manuela's thick, black lashes appeared almost too long and heavy for her eyelids. Each fanning sweep seemed marked by a languor suggesting a sultry sleepiness. Yet he sensed her total unawareness of using her eyelashes in a provocative manner. The movements never varied, whether she was looking at her family, or him, or inanimate objects. He could not recall ever having seen anything quite so fascinating as the varied parts of Manuela Ramon, her eyelashes included.

"Shall we move to the living room to finish our coffee?" asked Doña Magdalena, rising upon receiving a nod from Diego. She had not missed the Frenchman's reaction to Manuela all evening, or Manuela's cool rebuff of him.

The massive doors and windows of the large room across the back of the house were open to the refreshing night air. Louis found himself in a room unlike any other he had seen. Of smooth white adobe, its lofty walls suggested coolness and spaciousness. Giant support beams of the same polished dark wood as the doors stretched at spaced intervals across the high ceiling. Hanging from an obviously hand-crafted silver chain was a mammoth silver chandelier, a miniature forest of tapers filling its crystal holders and dispersing soft light all about the restful room.

Glad to see that his eye for tasteful design had not withered away from his lack of opportunity to exercise it, Louis admired the three coarse-textured, handwoven orange and beige rugs covering separate areas of the same earth-toned tile squares he had noted in the foyer and the dining room. Each area contained an upholstered couch in echoing hues and two chairs with high, straight backs. Tall pottery vases held clusters of fragrant roses and a frothy-headed desert grass he had never before seen used in an arrangement. Decorating the walls were colorful paintings of still life and of scenery that smacked of what Louis guessed must be the work of Spanish artists.

"Your *hacienda* is both charming and unique," Louis remarked to Diego and Domingo as the men excused themselves and stepped outside into the walled courtyard to smoke thin cigars. Bright moonlight revealed a circular fountain in the center, as well as a large chinaberry tree and several fruit trees the Frenchman could not identify at his distance. Flowers made their presence known through blurs of pale colors and an abundance of pervading sweet smells. "One gets the feeling of having removed himself from the cares of the world here."

56

"A man's home should always suggest that, don't you think?" asked Domingo, who had been quiet for most of the evening while he had studied the "guest prisoner."

Louis Saint-Denis possessed both uncommon cleverness and great charisma, Domingo acknowledged without reservations. And he was apparently as smitten by Manuela as every other young man who had seen her over the past year had been, though he did seem to be trying to hide it. Domingo found it incredulous that she had so little knowledge of what her beauty did to men. In almost all other ways, Manuela seemed wise beyond her years. He wondered if she should ask Doña Magdalena to speak to her frankly about what goes on between men and women. After all, she had lived such a sheltered life at the *presidio*. He shelved that troublesome thought for later and let his thoughts swing back to Louis.

Like his father, Domingo puffed on his cigar at intervals and puzzled over what had brought the enigmatic Frenchman to San Juan Batista. Also like his father, he doubted the journey had come about because of an outdated plea from a Spanish missionary. Before Louis had arrived that evening at the *hacienda*, the two had talked at length in the library. They had reached no conclusions. Conversation at dinner had shown little except that Louis was, indeed, a cultured young man with noticeable pride, a keen intellect, and a decided gift for conversation.

Inside the living room, Manuela turned to Doña Magdalena, demanding, "Why can't I go

57

outside with Grandfather as I usually do when he smokes his cigar?"

Having the hated guest for dinner was bad enough, she fumed. Now she was being denied privileges she had long taken for granted. If pressed for honest appraisal, even Manuela would have to admit that the men in her family spoiled her, and she battled against turning and sending an angry look outside.

When her great-aunt made no reply, Manuela showed she knew the answer to her own question by asking, "He won't be dining with us anymore, will he?"

Manuela had no desire to say the Frenchman's name, as if to speak it might prove as intimidating as had his presence. With a sigh of exasperation, she leaned her head against the high back of the chair.

"Don Diego told me earlier this evening that he'll ask Lieutenant Saint-Denis to take all his meals here while he's awaiting further orders from Governor Anya," the silver-haired woman replied in her precise diction.

How Manuela could fail to respond to the handsome young man's obvious overtures was beyond Doña Magdalena's understanding. She could not recall having met a more charming, handsome young man before. Not that she wished to see her grand-niece become interested in anyone but a true Spaniard, she reminded herself with a twinge of guilt. Diego and she had planned the upcoming season in the City with the hope that some properly blooded young man would seek her hand and guarantee Manuela a lifelong position in the upper class.

Still, Doña Magdalena reflected, it could do no

harm for the young innocent to have behind her a few harmless flirtations. Worldly young men might not care for one so totally lacking in the accepted, even desired, art of flirting, no matter that she was ravishingly beautiful and wealthy. She repressed a sigh. Nothing about Manuela fitted a pattern. If only she had known that before she had accepted her secretly adored brother-in-law's offer to come serve as *dueña* . . .

Upon that troublesome thought, Doña Magdalena continued, "For Diego to get to know the lieutenant has something to do with finding out more about the activities of the French in Louisiana. He says that with no Spanish missions remaining in the Land of the Tejas, he finds it difficult to learn much about the settlements in New France. For all we know, they might be intruding on land claimed by Spain."

"Poor Grandfather," came the heartfelt reply.

Manuela had already learned that ever since coming to the *presidio* at Christmas, her long-dead grandmother's youngest sister seemed as concerned over Diego's welfare as over Manuela's. At times she suspected Doña Magdalena had long passed the stage of mourning her late husband and that she looked upon Diego with an uncalled-for spark of warmth. An avowed romantic, the young woman was not at all sure that her grandfather had not begun to return those secretive looks. The idea of the two older people getting together both amused and pleased her.

Putting away such fanciful thoughts, Manuela said, "When there are no wars to fight, Grandfather has to stay busy trying to find out what all our enemies are up to. He does have a tedious job, doesn't he? And poor us. We'll be stuck with that conceited man for no telling how long before we hear from that gross, old Anya."

"Manuela," warned Doña Magdalena, "you must never again use such words about our governor. Such terms do not belong in the mouth of a proper young lady."

Manuela took the reprimand in silence, concentrating on the remaining coffee in the small cup she held. To become a "proper young lady" held no priority with her. A mysterious, restless spirit lived within, and it was that which nipped at her and led her to seek a private path. What pained her was that she was unsure herself about what it was she sought.

"I gather you don't care for our guest." Doña Magdalena sat upon the chair next to Manuela's and watched the expression on her face.

"He gives the impression of one not needing any other's approval since he so obviously has his own."

"Sometimes that can be an asset," the older woman pointed out. "You haven't been around any young man as well-traveled as Lieutenant Saint-Denis. While living in Mexico City over the years, I met many such men, and I well know that they're different. They can sometimes give off an aura of sophistication that one so young as you might not feel comfortable with."

"Perhaps." She smothered a yawn.

"He seems to approve of you, Manuela."

Manuela tossed her head and smiled knowingly. "You of all people must know that men act like that around women just to see if they can get them flustered and maybe take advantage of them."

"My, but you sound knowledgeable for one

having entered the social world of adults so recently." Her tone was far from light. Where did her grand-niece get her ideas—most of them unconventional and shocking? Only moments ago she had thought that Manuela was too much the young innocent. What she was learning would call for a long, private talk with Diego. Not that she didn't admit to looking forward to having an excuse to claim his full attention—even if the subject discussed was his restless granddaughter.

" 'Tis true I don't know much from actual experience," Manuela confessed with the candor she could use as naturally as artifice. She set down the cup, empty now. "But I have read numerous books from Grandfather's library, and I gather not all can be completely misleading about what goes on between men and women."

Manuela could have added that she had been in the forests and around the stables so often over the past four years that she also knew the facts about sex. To transfer the actions of the fierce, animal couplings she had observed to those of humans making love had seemed incongruous at first, yet she had made the transition in her mind some time ago. When her thoughts strayed to that territory, forbidden by convention from discussion with with one's *dueña*, Manuela experienced a wild torrent of heartbeats and dizzying questions. What would it be like to—

The cultured voice broke into her thoughts. "Manuela, you probably shouldn't be reading so much, especially those French books. There's no telling in which directions those stories are leading your young mind." Doña Magdalena's role as *dueña* seemed to be coming to the forefront. Her eyes snapped. So that was where Manuela was picking up her ideas. "Before I came here to act as your chaperone, I hadn't been around very young ladies for a number of years. Perhaps I'm a bit too demanding at times, but I question whether or not your reading anything French is good."

Manuela threw back her head and laughed with pure delight at the pompous assumption, unaware that from the darkness outside the Frenchman watched with fascination. While still seeming to be listening attentively to his hosts, Louis allowed his imagination to play with the question of what could be causing such a lovely laugh.

The feminine, musical notes soothed his ears and tempted his lips into a smile, and tugged at his mind for a moment to retrieve a memory. For the life of him, though, Louis could not recall Manuela's having laughed aloud all evening until just then. It seemed enough for the present to be able to gaze in secret upon the captivating profile, to glimpse the provocative curve of young breasts, the sparkle of white teeth in candlelight, and the dance of blue-black curls as the Spanish beauty gave herself up to the joyful sound.

Surprising him, an unbidden thought flagged on the horizon of the French lieutenant's mind: Not once had he remembered to be on watch for the maid he had seen swimming that morning.

Chapter Four

Back in his quarters, Lieutenant Saint-Denis's ravings about the commandant's beautiful granddaughter brought a grin to Medar Jalot's slim face. He went about the routine of helping his employer undress, then putting away the finery Louis insisted upon wearing at each available opportunity. The young man's inordinate pride in his appearance and actions seemed as much a part of him as the thick brown hair and the easy, winning smile. Medar had served him ever since a relative of Louis's had urged the valet to present himself to the young French-Canadian soon after his arrival in Paris twelve years ago.

Theirs had been a sturdy relationship. Medar, ten years older than his employer, had never had the desire to settle down and so had welcomed the chance to follow Louis to Louisiana. Incapable of living vicariously on his own, he seemed to thrive on sharing the escapades of the younger man, escapades that involved affairs of the heart in Paris and those of life and limb in the New World.

"Do Phillip and you have decent quarters? How was the food?" Louis asked. "Every dish at the *hacienda* seemed laced with hot peppers. I'm not sure if I liked it, or if I would have eaten anything just to be able to watch the lovely Miss Ramon."

Now that he wore only sleeping drawers and a short robe of blue silk, Louis lay propped up on the settee in the spacious bedroom, sipping at the brandy Medar had obligingly fetched. The neat little man nodded and continued his job of brushing and hanging up clothing. Through the open windows a breeze stirred at the day's accumulation of heat inside the adobe quarters and lent a welcome coolness to the night air. Strains of a plaintive melody from a distant guitar floated across the moonlit *plaza*.

"Are Black Eagle and his men satisfied with their arrangements?" Louis asked, not content with a mere nod.

"They seem to be. They took over a section of rooms formerly occupied by the Lipans—the tribe living here—before they moved to private huts outside the fort. Black Eagle told me they preferred to sleep on the ground, so I suspect they're not inside. As for the food from the soldiers' kitchen, it too was heavy with peppers, but a welcome change from game and fish."

Pouring himself a shot of brandy now that his chores were completed, Medar moved to the footstool near Louis and lowered his wiry body. A tidy dark moustache and goatee went well with his small face and features. "Phillip and I have adjoining rooms in a building down from yours. He's already at work on the records of our journey down."

"I'll dictate a letter to Governor Cadillac tomorrow and ask a couple of Black Eagle's couriers to take it back to the fort for dispatching to

Mobile." Louis stretched out his legs and crossed them, liking the feel of the fresh air on his bare feet and calves. To be housed in civilized surroundings again brought a keen pleasure. Edging into his consciousness was the thought that an equal pleasure awaited him at his next stay upon the ground beneath the stars. A zest for living rewarded him with appreciation for whatever the moment brought. "The governor will be pleased to learn we've been well received."

"Well received?" Medar snorted. "Do you call being told we're prisoners being 'well received'?" He brought the glass up to his mouth, rolling the sip of brandy upon his tongue before swallowing.

"We're alive and we're not behind bars," Louis pointed out with an emphatic wave of his hand. "Can you imagine how we might have treated a few armed Spanish intruders back at our own Fort Saint Jean Baptiste?" He swirled the amber liquid and absently watched its sluggish movement in the candlelight. The whitewashed walls of the comfortable but unpretentious room appeared softer and less forbidding in the gentle light. "We've much to be thankful for, Medar."

"True," came the quiet reply.

Medar watched his friend and superior close his eyes as though deep in thought and, as he had learned to do at such times, waited. It seemed strange, he reflected in the silence, that Louis had reported no positive response from the young woman whom he had so enthusiastically described. If she were to be immune to the charm and good looks of Louis Saint-Denis, she would be the first since he had known him over the past twelve years.

"Did I tell you she has the blackest eyes I've

65

ever seen?" Louis asked dreamily, his eyes still closed.

"You did."

"Never have I seen eyebrows and lashes so black without their having been painted. The only times I've seen eyelashes behave in that maddening, slow moving way were in bedrooms. But I tell you, Medar, it's as natural with her as breathing. She's a coquette and an innocent all wrapped up in one." Gray-blue eyes opened and fixed on Medar with intensity. "You won't believe how beautiful, how regal, this Manuela Ramon is. She is the epitome of a princess, true royalty."

"Of course you told her these things," Medar said, a knowing smile lighting his intelligent face and bringing merriment to dark eyes.

"No." A sigh followed the deep, bass utterance. The distant song of the guitar faded into stillness.

"Why not? You've always said that flattery is the way to any woman's heart. Long before you reached twenty-eight, you seemed to have worked out a method to win over beautiful young women. Don't tell me you're changing tactics after all the years of success?" He lifted his glass in good-humored salute.

"She's not just *any* young woman, Medar, or haven't you been listening? I could sense from the looks she gave me that I would be offending her if I made personal remarks. Manuela—isn't that a musical name?—would not like hearing reference made to her body by a stranger. She's very elegant, reserved in the way of carefully reared young women."

"What about the servings maids?" the valet asked before Louis could get carried away again.

After all, with his own good looks and way with words, Medar had always been as popular with the back-door ladies as the younger man had with their mistresses. He glanced through the window at the bright moonlight. It was nearly midnight and there seemed to be no one up and about – a perfect time for trysting, if he only had someone with whom to tryst. "Did you see many comely damsels? Did you catch a glimpse of the one you saw swimming this morning?"

"I forgot about all the maids once I saw Manuela." Louis sat up, paying no attention when the blue silk robe opened to reveal a hairy chest above loose sleeping drawers. "I don't think I'll pursue that morsel until I see how I fare with the princess." With his free hand he absently touched the little scar on his cheekbone, saying after a moment, "However, she would be nice to help while away the lonely evenings *after* I've been with the lovely Manuela. You could ask around; mayhap I would have an itch that needs a bit of scratching."

Louis's handsome face lit up in the devil-may-care way Medar remembered from the times in Paris when he had spoken of his love affairs. Both men were aware that many lovely young women had sought and captured the ambitious young Frenchman's attention back then. Also they knew that none had ever touched deep inside his heart.

Soon after a brief exchange of plans for the morrow, the lieutenant and his valet parted, each welcoming a chance to sleep on a real mattress for the first time in months.

But Louis found himself too keyed up to find the bed inviting. Sliding his feet into leather slippers, he lit a cigar and wandered about the moonlight-drenched *plaza*. With appreciation for the lush growth of the fruit trees and flowering shrubs Diego had brought to the remote *presidio* in the desert wasteland, the French lieutenant threw back his head and sniffed at the welcome fragrances riding the night breeze. He glimpsed the roof and upper section of the second floor of the commandant's *hacienda* rising above the adobe wall. Did that spot of candlelight behind a filmy curtain mark Manuela's bedroom? he wondered.

Not welcoming the warmth kindling in his loins at the unbidden thought of how the commandant's granddaughter might look in her sleeping gown with her hair unfettered, the Frenchman ambled toward the stables. He had not checked on Diablo personally since their arrival that afternoon, and sometimes the frisky stallion needed his owner's reassurances when they first arrived at a new place. A dog's bark challenged Louis for a moment from down near the craft shed, the only sound indicating that not all within the *presidio* walls slept.

The light Louis Saint-Denis had seen had, indeed, come from Manuela Ramon's second-story bedroom. She had sent Conchita away to her room in the kitchen wing right after the maid had helped her prepare for bed.

Once alone, Manuela prowled about the room, even wandering out onto the balcony looking out over the private courtyard of the *hacienda*. Her restlessness and an inchoate longing for some unformed desire seemed to have no cause, or at least none of which she was conscious.

Vaguely she wondered if she might be missing her twin. Unbound hair cascading down the back of her yellow sleeping gown, Manuela reveled in the contact of bare feet with cool, smooth tiles, wriggling her toes to capture the feel. With customary satisfaction, she leaned over the wrought-iron railing to sniff in the sweet smell of roses wafting up from the bushes below.

Somewhere on the other side of the wall, a guitar began a low, haunting serenade. The sound seemed as natural and as much a part of warm evenings at the *presidio* as did the distant calls of night birds and the close-up hum of nocturnal insects seeking the flame of the candle inside.

Her thoughts tripped back to the events of the evening. When she remembered how she had earlier wished it to be a gala family affair, she rated the night dull. The presence of the ogling Frenchman had done little to further gaiety, though the others had seemed enthralled by his wit and personality. She felt no guilt that her preformed ideas against the French dictated her unfriendly manner toward the stranger.

As an image of the handsome lieutenant began to form, Manuela swished her hair and marched back to her bedroom, yellow silk whispering sibilant protests against the tiles. No matter that he might be handsome and able to charm everyone but her, the man was an enemy. She would not waste thought upon him.

Once back inside, Manuela took her favorite book of poetry from a shelf and began reading, soon lost to all around her. It was the French poem, *Roman de la Rose*, which always soothed her when she could not sleep. The work had been one of the first she had managed to enjoy after she had mastered French, and she never failed to get carried away by the account of the Art of Love.

The Lover, whom Manuela pictured as some imposing Spanish count or *conquistador* who would come charging up to San Juan Batista some day to take her away to a Land of Perfection, allows Idleness to lead him to a garden of roses. There he meets such characters as Pleasure, Riches, and Sweet Looks. But the Lover is attracted to one particular rosebud and tries to pluck it, only to have the God of Love stop him and explain the sufferings required of lovers before they can win their Heart's Desire.

Each time she read the poem, she pictured herself as the rosebud, but no one appeared who fit the mental image of her Lover. In her mind, she had already suffered enough by having to wait to reach age sixteen and thus be looked upon as an adult ready for the delights of courtship and marriage. When her Lover came to claim her, he would spirit her far away to a place not hemmed in.

Encumbering walls and close spaces created waves of repulsion inside Manuela, had ever since her early years at the convent school in the City of Mexico. The dreamy-eyed young woman had no doubt that she would know her Lover the instant she spied him—or soon thereafter. To expect to do so was a part of the magic.

All she ever saw, Manuela fretted when she finally laid aside the volume, were officers, officers, and more officers. Or pompous government officials, more intent on feeling important than on making a young woman's dreams come true. Her discontent of tonight, she told herself, was probably the culmination of her disappointment that the latest arrival at the *presidio* – although from an enemy nation and therefore not acceptable as a candidate for Lover – was another young man there only to serve his own ends, whatever they were.

She recalled the talk that day at noon about Spain's policy regarding foreigners, and a taunting question formed: Why had a French lieutenant presented himself at a Spanish *presidio?* Surely he had known that to do so would be to invite imprisonment. Putting away the puzzle as too trifling to bother with, she returned to her earlier thoughts. Someday, she assured herself before turning to blow out the candle, her Lover would appear.

A familiar noise coming from the stables stretching across the back of the private courtyard startled Manuela, snatching her awake again. Guiltily she realized that she had not checked to see if Zorro was perched inside the sheet-draped cage in the corner. Muttering at the parrot's willful ways, she padded over to peek. Holy Cockroach! The errant rascal was gone.

Fearing that the increasing protests of the disturbed pigeons would awaken her grandfather before she could retrieve Zorro, Manuela rushed from the bedroom just as she was. Bare feet skimming down the stairway, through the darkened living room, then out onto the stone walkway through the flower garden, she gave silent thanks that moonlight brightened her way.

Some time ago she had heard the tall clock in the foyer toll midnight and knew that on a weeknight such as this, everyone was likely already asleep. What did it matter that she wore only a thin, silk sleeping gown without robe or undergarments, or that her hair streamed behind her? Quiet haste was the only way to save her spirited Zorro's neck from Diego's promised wringing.

She reached the shadowed stable and hurried inside, pausing to allow her eyes to adjust. Muted squawks and throaty notes from overhead drowned out all other sounds.

"Eblo?" Manuela called first. When no answer came, she moved on toward the end of the stable. "Zorro? Where are you?" She used the sweet, intimate voice reserved for him.

Not to have found Eblo, the old Indian in charge of the pigeons, asleep in the first stall surprised Manuela. Had he found him a lonesome squaw out in one of the small huts? she wondered with an indulgent smile.

She could reach the pigeon cote on the roof by climbing one of two ladders — one leading straight up at the end of the stables, the other leaning outside. She felt so at home in the long building that she ran across the hay-strewn floor toward the one inside. The horses stabled in that end belonged to the family and made no protest when the familiar figure flew by, the full skirt of the yellow sleeping gown rustling and billowing behind.

"Zorro? Come to me, Zorro."

Usually when the parrot heard her voice, he would stop whatever mischief he was up to and wait for her to reach him and hold out her hand. Already the pigeons seemed calmer, she noted with relief. Zorro must have stopped the inane, part-human chattering that always seemed to set them off.

Placing one bare foot carefully after the other, Manuela started up the steep ladder attached to the end wall. Her long gown threatened to trip her, and she grabbed up the skirt in one hand to free her legs for faster assent. The surfaces of the roughly planed crosspieces scrabbled at the tender soles of her feet.

"Zorro?"

From the other end of the long stable, Louis Saint-Denis thought he heard the squeak of a door being opened and then a feminine voice calling a name. When the call sounded again, he came from within the stall housing his horse, checking to make sure that the belt of his robe still held the front together. Shafts of moonlight pierced through opened vents, half the size of regular windows. As he had been inside the darkened stable for some time, rubbing down Diablo after talking to him, his eyes were already accustomed to the partial light. He was fairly certain that no one had come into the building after he had, and he had had no reason to suspect anyone was already there when he arrived, for he had called out more than once. What was going on?

Louis could make out the back of a scantily clad figure scrambling barefooted up a ladder at the opposite end. Whoever searched for this Zorro was in one hell of a hurry to reach him, he mused. A sudden hitching up of the gown rewarded him with a dim yet tantalizing view of rounded hips and long, shapely legs below a

73

swinging curtain of black hair. Intrigued, he walked down the aisle as she disappeared into the overhead loft, the hay dispelling the sound of his footsteps.

No masculine voice replied to her continued calls. Louis wondered if perhaps the young woman—there was no doubt in his mind that it was a household maid trysting with a soldier up in the loft—might not run into trouble. Although he had heard the soft cries of obviously restless pigeons somewhere nearby, he had not searched out their location. Now that he had reached the other end, he realized they must be up in the loft or upon the roof. If some wild animal had come to swipe at the birds and taunt them, it could be one that might harm an unsuspecting young woman. Owls often played such nighttime tricks, as did wildcats.

Upon the thought of wildcats perhaps wandering down from the foothills seen in the distance that afternoon, Louis paused at the bottom of the ladder. If the young woman made no outcry or did not come down soon, he could go on back to his quarters and assume that she had met her Zorro. From the sweet tone of her voice and the hasty clambering up the ladder, he would well imagine what kind of reception the lucky man must be receiving—if he were actually in the loft.

Within a short time, Louis heard the soft voice again. There was still no second one. Puzzled when the next words seemed to hold wrath, he stepped away from the ladder and peered upward.

Manuela had climbed on through the opening in the roof and had coaxed Zorro to fly to rest upon her hand. Not having brought the glove she usually wore when handling him, she flinched from the curving claws against her bare hand but began inching back down the ladder with caution. She had only one free hand to clutch her gown and hang onto the rough boards of the near-vertical ladder, the other serving both as perch for the parrot and as a balance up close to the wooden sidepieces.

Cautiously she sent each foot to feel for the next lower step before permitting it to leave the one above. Once she dropped the tail of her gown and had to lean hard against the ladder to stoop and retrieve it. Each time she tried to step with the full skirt down around her ankles, she trod upon its silkiness and almost lost her footing. Meanwhile, Zorro sat with careless arrogance upon the other hand, head twisting to watch her progress and then her face, as if he doubted she would make it. Splinters caught at her bare feet.

"By the blood of Mary, Zorro," she muttered, no longer trying for the sweet voice to charm him. "If I fall, I'll wring your neck myself."

How much farther to the bottom, she agonized. Feeling a warm wetness on the bottom of one foot, she suspected that blood was oozing from an embedded splinter. And it hurt!

"Damn you!" Manuela grated, sneaking a look at the bright-eyed parrot and grimacing from pain. By then her head had left the darkness of the loft. She could hardly wait to traverse the remaining steps and reach the much lighter stable.

"Allow me to help," came a cultured masculine voice from somewhere below and behind — one the shocked young woman knew that she had heard before, but could not identify in her moment of panic.

Manuela gasped and twisted to look down and behind, so startled at the intrusion there in the half-darkness that she missed her footing and fell. Zorro flitted from her hand back up into the shadows of the loft.

Instinctively Louis held out his arms to catch the flying hair and legs hurtling down toward him. The impact of her body upon his knocked him backward, and they ended up in a tangle there on the cushioning hay covering the earthen floor. Though completely winded, he delighted in the warm softness resting against his body and the scent of fragrant hair flung across his face.

Struggling for enough air to recapture her breath, Manuela was aware of hard, nearly naked masculinity beneath her and of well-muscled arms holding her upper torso close. Somehow in the falling, she had twisted her body forward to face her would-be rescuer. Even so, the time was too brief and terror-filled for her to identify him in the partial light.

She realized that her hips slanted off to the side of his, and her legs angled across the hay-covered earth. Her face lay buried in a mass of chest curls, her breasts crushed against the planes of the heavily breathing man who had broken her fall. Was he naked? her frantic mind asked. What was he doing here? another part of it hastened to add. Who dared to be stalking around in the commandant's wing of the stable past midnight?

She became achingly aware that her gown was bunched up around her shoulders. At the rate her heart was pounding and her lungs were fighting, she would never regain her breath. Sweet

Mary! She had worried that he might be naked, and here she was the one exposed. How could she ever look him in the face, whoever he was? Her nose burrowed deeper against the heaving chest just as her starving lungs sucked in air with a huge, unladylike sound.

When he had heard the obviously disenchanted voice muttering above him and had looked upward to see that the young woman was backing down the ladder, Louis had assumed she had not located her lover. He had been struck by the beauty of the long, tapered legs nearing him in the partial darkness. The memory of the swimmer's graceful limbs had assailed him. Had he found the maid? It had been then that he had spoken, causing her to lose her footing and fall into his opened arms.

Now, even when his breathing could not seem to settle down from her having plopped face forward, smack into his middle, Louis was lost in the thrill of holding what he was certain were those very charms he had admired in the stream. At first he feared she was hurt and tried to murmur words of consolation, failing to find wind enough to form speech. When he felt her stiffen after the air returned to her lungs with a heavy swoosh, then snuggle back against him, he discarded the worrisome fear and concentrated on recovering his own breath and ability to talk.

Obviously the maid was enjoying the enforced embrace as much as Louis—or so it would seem, he reassured himself. She had not bothered to snug down her gown, which was serving more as a neck ruffle than a covering for her body. Her upper torso lay upon his heaving chest, while her legs and hips angled off a bit to the side of his own. He noticed how her wonderful softness melded against his near-nakedness in the most delightful way. His robe might as well have been discarded, so open was it; and the band of his sleeping drawers had slipped down below his waist.

All manner of flash fires blazed within the Frenchman. Dizzying waves of excitement and anticipation tore at him, reminding him of those times when he had been in neck-and-neck horse races, almost to the finish line. The moment he felt he could speak coherently, he would ask her who she was.

Who could the young man be whose voice had startled her and made her lose her hold on the ladder? Manuela wondered for the tenth time in the few seconds since her fall. She kept her flaming face buried there on his chest, not ready to meet the inevitable. The Spanish words had come too softly for her to recognize the voice, yet she sensed she had heard it before.

Even if one of the officers or soldiers dared to be rambling about the Ramons's private section of the stable past midnight, he would not risk the commandant's further censure by approaching his only granddaughter. Was the man a traveler not wishing to disturb the sleep of those in the *presidio* and deciding to bed down his horse himself? Not likely, or else she would not have suspected she had heard him speak before.

Lightning-quick detours in thought led Manuela to consider her perilous position of the moment. Though she knew she was capable of movement, she felt paralyzed. Now that she could breathe with less effort, she needed to protest, assert her position of importance, and remove herself from the enforced entanglement of bodies and limbs. Never before had her naked breasts spilled upon a man's furred chest. Never had her body lay unclothed before anyone other than a servant tending to her needs.

Manuela sought to be objective. How could she handle the necessary rising and rearranging of her sleeping gown without rewarding the man holding her with an unrestricted view of her nakedness? She had become accustomed to the murky light inside the stable and assumed that the one holding her had as well. Like it or not, she faced some young man's scrutiny.

On an unobjective level, some inner voice asked Manuela how she could explain the tingling, feathery spurts of heat wending their way from her breasts to some deep core within. She flinched from the telling question. The close-up smell of the man invaded her nostrils, leading her to think of the haunting scents riding the night winds from the desert and those of the spicy woods at the base of the foothills . . . and exhilarating maleness as she had only imagined it. Her heart galloped anew as smooth hands slowly tracked a fiery path up her back and across her shoulders. Did she truly wish to leave the enveloping arms and confront reality? What was happening?

With one hand, Louis gently removed the wayward curtain of fragrant hair from his face, then pulled the young woman upward across his chest. He heard the welcome pile of straw beneath them whisper against her outspread feet and legs during the swift movement. She was so light that he had no problem in positioning the trembling young woman.

The problem came, he acknowledged, from the voluptuous way her full breasts nestled upon his chest, the tantalizing way her silken skin felt to his caressing hands and fingertips. A bass note purred back in his throat. Definite signs of arousal spurred him on, increasing his heartbeat and lending him courage. Though he had planned to peer into her face and talk with her before he kissed her, Louis discarded the idea. He captured the protesting mouth the moment she tensed against him and lifted her head.

Practiced lips claimed untried ones. Manuela squirmed to free her mouth, but a firm hand wandering in her hair positioned itself at the base of her skull and held her face to his. All she could see of him were closed eyes and shadowed forehead there in the dimly lighted aisle of the stable. She did not know why she shut her own eyes, only that she did. The warm pressure from the young man's lips seemed to demand a response in like manner. When his lips firmed, she found her own doing the same. When he pressed with ardor and half opened his mouth, she fought to remain unmoved but found that she wanted nothing more than to return each fascinating movement he made. She complied—again and again.

Manuela wondered at the searing swirls of sensation emanating from the meeting of their mouths as he taught her the subtleties of advancing and retreating, claiming and disclaiming. Never having been kissed before, she felt that she was both ebbing and flowing from the molten magic of his lips on hers. She suspected he might be taking away her breath forever. And she didn't even care.

All at once the kneading fingers at the back of

her head seemed less of a hold and more of a spine-tingling caress to the innocent but eager Manuela. The desire to touch him in the same way led her to slip her hands up to wander in his hair and settle along his neck. When he moaned deep in his throat and kissed her even more fervently, she sensed she was giving him pleasure akin to her own. An answering vibrato in her own throat startled her almost as much as his sending his tongue to trace the shape of her lips. The biggest surprise came when his tongue invaded her mouth in search of her own, the wondrous movement causing the flame flickering deep inside to flare into a pulsating blaze.

Exactly what her throbbing breasts had to do with all that was happening to her mouth, neck, and heretofore hibernating core of womanhood, Manuela could not fathom. She wondered if it might not have something to do with the way it felt to have the twin mounds resting naked against the furred chest—rather scratchy yet wickedly pleasant, a bit like having a spot on the back to itch in search of a soothing hand. But what could her breasts be yearning for?

As suddenly as the fiery kisses began, they ended. Louis brought up the hand from her back and joined it with the other to cradle her head and lift it up from his. For a moment, his fingers caressed high cheekbones, a delicate nose, a strong chin. No longer could he wait to speak, to look upon what he had sensed all along was a face of beauty.

"Tell me your name, lovely one," Louis whispered, letting his eyes feast on the features so close in the near darkness. His lips burned from those peppery kisses. He could feel the unclad body tense against his. Lazy-moving eyelashes fanned open enough to allow enormous jet eyes to meet his gaze, eyes with an intriguing slant beneath heavy black eyebrows. His heart thundered anew. His mouth went dry.

Manuela had been dreading the moment she would have to meet the eyes of the one whose kiss had initiated her into the devastating, thrilling ways of lovers. The tender brush of his fingers across her face canceled her earlier plan to haul off and clobber him for forcing himself upon her. When he spoke, she could no longer hide behind lowered lashes and sort out her prerogatives. She knew that voice now, recognized the face directly beneath her own. A hastily applied harness of cold stone tried to slow her wild pulses and failed.

"You're . . . ?" Her voice sank in a well of despair. Holy Cockroach! The Frenchman, of all people.

"You're . . . ?" His reply was just as ineffective and came almost in the same breath. Blood of the Saints! The commandant's granddaughter, of all people.

"What are you doing here?" both asked as one.

Manuela jerked herself to a sitting position, one hand pulling the gown to fall about her at the same time. Had she found the strength, she would have stood.

"Lieutenant Saint-Denis, you're no gentleman," she hissed. Humiliation and anger smothered the earlier fires of passion. Loathing sharpening her voice, she went on in a rush, "This is my grandfather's stable, and I have every right to be here without fear of being molested."

"And you, Miss Ramon," Louis shot back, not

82

liking her implication and feeling like a fool for having thought her to be a maid out for a romp in the hay, "are not the proper young lady I believed you to be."

Manuela's arrogant pose—identical to the one she had shown all during dinner—set Louis on edge far more than her words. Only moments earlier she had been naked and willing in his arms, returning his kisses with wild abandon. Was she less than she pretended?

Giving vent to his suspicion of being tricked, he said in steely tones, "What proper young lady would be swimming half-naked in an irrigation canal in the morning and then be traipsing around in like state in a stable in the middle of the night? It seems obvious that you were hunting exactly what you found—an unsuspecting man to succumb to your charms. It's a good thing that I put an end to this farce while we were still in the kissing stage. How did you know that I was here?" By then he had sat up and pulled his robe together, his hands jerkily tying the belt after his cutting words.

Her mouth opened in disbelief at his scornful attack, Manuela leaned enough to plant a stinging slap on his cheek. Damn the man for his spying on her while she swam, for his insulting remarks, for his unbearable conceit! How dare he think that she stooped to search for a man's kiss and embrace ... and just any man's at that—even a Frenchman's?

For the insufferable man to suggest that she knew he was in the stable, that she would not have stopped their frantic embrace before it led to ... Energy rushed to her legs then and she scrambled to her feet, hands going to her hips, eyes flashing warning signals to the Frenchman staring up at her in wide-eyed surprise.

"You're the one who owes an explanation," Manuela pointed out, anger forging her words into barbed arrows. "But I will say that I came here for a reason and that it had nothing to do with you, Lieutenant."

Louis straightened up and got to his feet, determined not to give in to the wish to rub at the smarting cheek. Her slap had squelched his anger, made him realize that he had allowed wounded pride to replace reasoning—a weakness he had long recognized in himself and fought regularly to overcome. After all, he was the intruder at the *presidio*.

Manuela packed one hell of a wallop, Louis mused. Not that he hadn't deserved it, conscience made him add. Come to think of it, he admitted wryly, calm, sweet-tempered women had never held great fascination for him. He liked knowing that mysterious fires lay banked within feminine curves, fires that could blaze sweetly for a lover as well as fuel tirades against real or imagined injustices. Full of spirit himself, he had found he admired it in others—when it was not given free rein, of course.

Charmed all over again after his reflections, Louis watched the object of his thoughts flip her hair over her shoulders and boldly return his stare. She was still the most beautiful young woman he had ever seen, no matter that the black cloud of hair tumbled in disarray about her face and shoulders there in the shadowy stables. His mind riffled through the images of Manuela that he had already stored: first, nearly naked at a distance in the stream that morning; then, dressed in high style and at closer proximity in her home that evening; and now, up close in a thin sleeping gown in the stable. Even in the half-light, he could see the moist, swollen lips he had savored, could see the provocative lift and fall of dark-tipped breasts beneath clinging silk. Which picture rated highest?

"Who is Zorro?" Louis asked, narrowing his eyes to gauge her reaction. Even he had not believed she had come to find him. His need at the moment to salvage his pride had triggered that ridiculous accusation. "I heard you calling his name when you came in, and I apologize for having accused you of seeking just any young man — and especially me. Can you forgive me and also tell me about this Zorro? Obviously he wasn't here."

The way the lieutenant had ignored her slap impressed Manuela. She had not known whether to expect retaliation or more angry words, but she had not shrunk from either. Having trained herself to court outward composure ever since her frequent confrontations with the nuns at school, she had to admit that she admired the way he had reined in his emotions after first expressing his anger. Toadying men, both young and old, had always made her suspicious of what actually went on in their minds. Louis Saint-Denis seemed to be straightforward, and she found the trait refreshing. Not that he should have been so frank with his foolish suspicions about her ... But his apology had come out with discernible candor.

An impish sparkle in her eyes, Manuela fought against the smile that threatened to turn up the corners of her kiss-swollen lips.

"I accept your apology." She would show him that she too could be direct, when it suited her. "Zorro happens to be my pet."

"What kind of pet do you keep?" Was that a flash of mischief in those captivating eyes? "Is he handsome and does he walk on two legs?"

"Yes, Lieutenant Saint-Denis. He's all of that, and more."

The smile took over Manuela's countenance then. The lieutenant looked so different without his formidable gentleman's clothing. Her quick look took in the silk robe hugging broad shoulders and nipping in below the belt at the trim waist and hips, the bare, unusually well-shaped limbs beneath. That same overpowering masculine scent of him still tickled her nostrils, still swayed her in a decidedly mysterious manner.

"Where is this Zorro, Miss Ramon?" Jealousy that some young man had already wormed his way into her affections struck Louis with the sharpness of a knife's blade. What was bringing that devilish smile? Had she figured out that he felt an extraordinary attraction to her? Did she know how the feel of her body and her response to his kisses affected him?

"Zorro," Manuela called in the sweet voice to which the parrot always responded. "Zorro, come to me." She kept her eyes on the Frenchman, still sizing him up. What was there about him, other than his apparent candor, that intrigued her? Was it only the knowledge that he had initiated her into the art of kissing? Her cheeks felt warm at the daring reminder that only a brief time ago they had been locked in an intimate embrace.

A squawk and a flapping of wings signaled Zorro's descent from the loft. Before Louis could do more than dart a look upward and open his mouth in surprise, the parrot had landed on Manuela's outstretched hand.

"So your pet is a parrot," Louis remarked, a detectable note of relief in his voice, a grin spreading his mouth into boyish delight at the unexpected news.

"Yes," she responded, forcing her eyes from their intense study of the young man to rest with fondness on the bird. "I came to retrieve him before he set the pigeons to such a clamor that they awakened Grandfather. He has threatened to kill Zorro the next time he disturbs his rest. I doubt he would actually wring his neck, but he might send him away."

Louis took a step forward then, his heart heavy from the realization that he had been completely unjust in each of his accusations. He did not know where she had gained so much expertise in kissing and arousing a man, but obviously she had not come to the stable that night for such a purpose.

"Please forgive me again, Miss Ramon," he said, a hand lifting in pleading. The use of such formality after their earlier intimacy seemed ludicrous, and he added, "Could we be on a first-name basis after this ... midnight encounter?"

"Why not?" Manuela replied, wondering at the way a feathery rush of feeling swept her spine at his labeling of their strange meeting. She stepped back to prevent the outstretched hand from touching her again. The splinter in her foot pricked at her just then, and she winced.

"What's wrong?"

"My foot hurts. I must have picked up a splinter from the ladder." When he took another step

87

toward her, she hastened to add, "It'll be all right until I get inside to some light."

"I insist on looking at it, Manuela." Letting her name roll from his tongue lifted his heart in some inexplicable way.

"Please, Louis, no." How strange that his name feel so easily from her lips—and he a man she hadn't known existed until that night, one she knew so little about.

Manuela turned to leave the stables, recoiling when she saw the aisle was so narrow that their bodies almost touched again. The space between them seemed fraught with unspoken words. The careening thought of his touching her again in any way wrecked her recovered poise. Her pulse jumped crazily. What was wrong with her? Their physical contact held no meaning, had been accidental, a veritable comedy of errors. Tomorrow he would be the spying French lieutenant, she the proper granddaughter of the Spanish commandant who held him under "house arrest."

Wondering what brought Manuela's serious mien, Louis stepped back to allow her to precede him down the straw-covered path there in the stable. Moonlight peeking in at one of the openings singled her out for a minute space of time, and his breath hung in his throat at the sight of her loveliness in the yellow silk gown. He could not abide the thought that she was leaving him, that she might not ever again speak with him in the same casual way. Had the kisses affected her not at all?

"Please," he said when they had reached the door and she continued to limp, "let me see about your foot now that we're in the moonlight."

Midnight eyes probed his before Manuela

leaned the hand not holding Zorro against the door jamb and lifted the paining foot to rest across the shin of the other leg. She watched him stoop and stretch out his hands to cradle her foot. Though she had instinctively shied from his touching her again there inside the stable, she was unprepared for the avalanche of warmth spreading from his hands to her foot.

In a spot of pure moonlight, Louis peered and probed gently at what appeared to be a protruding object in the blood-stained spot on the soft underside of the dainty arch. The small foot seemed lost in his large hands. He tried not to notice the way the skirt of her nightgown whispered against his arm and reminded him of how she had felt in his arms.

"Could this be the monster?" he asked when he felt her flinch at his gingerly exploration.

"Yes." Her breath barely sustained the sound of the simple word. Why was a purely human act of kindness overpowering her?

Manuela almost lost her balance when Louis squatted in front of her and propped her foot against his knee. Evidently bored with the night's happenings, Zorro flapped his wings and soared up to the balcony outside her bedroom. To steady herself for what would likely be a painful process, she transferred her hand from the door jamb to the silk-clad shoulder below. At once she knew she had made a mistake. A new barrage of erratic heartbeats played havoc with her breathing.

Deftly Louis plucked with thumb and forefinger at the tiny shaft of wood, not surprised that she made no outcry when he removed it.

"Now the pain should go away," he told her, not

ready to relinquish his hold on her. That her hand still rested upon him pleased him in a way he could not fathom. The daintiness of the ankle and the artful swell of smooth flesh above it seemed somehow as tempting as any part of her. Before he had time to marshal his thoughts, he grazed the top of her arch with a kiss.

"Don't, Louis," Manuela whispered, afraid he would look into her eyes and read there the foolish devastation that his daring kiss had created. She jerked her foot free and removed her hand from his shoulder. Both movements satisfied her brain. Both set up protests within her body that made no sense at all. Her pulse had gone crazy.

"Good night, Manuela," Louis said after straightening up and gazing down at her with an unfathomable expression in eyes gone silvery in the moonlight. A harsh inner voice told him to back away, urge her to go inside before he made a fool of himself. Another more insistent voice begged him to pull her close, to—

"Thank you, Louis, for removing the splinter," Manuela remembered to say before whirling away in a flurry of yellow silk and flying black hair to step toward the courtyard. Every instinct of self-preservation screamed at her to escape while she could. If he were to touch her once more, she sensed some dark, hidden part of her might . . .

Louis watched her hurry with a slight limp down the path toward the *hacienda*. Not until she disappeared inside the house did he turn away. With questioning heart and leaden steps, he went to find his bed.

Because of the strange happenings that night

in the stables of San Juan Batista, Manuela Ramon and Louis Saint-Denis were more than just slightly older and wiser, as people generally are for having lived through another twenty-four hours. They were different.

Part Two

"A lovely being, scarcely form'd or molded,
A rose with all its sweetest leaves yet folded."
— Lord Byron

Chapter Five

Manuela fretted over the next three days at the despised enforced confinement within the *hacienda* and its walled courtyard. She could find no acceptable way to get into the stables and sneak off for the habitual rides and swims. The three Frenchmen and their Indian friends seemed to spend an inordinate amount of time in and about the long building, evidently concerned about their horses after the long trek southward.

If only Carlos would return from the blasted hunting trip, she fumed at intervals. Her twin could serve as escort and allow her some freedom.

At night after going to her room, and making sure Zorro was properly caged, the tempestuous young woman tried to shove aside the plaguing memory of what Louis had termed their "midnight encounter" of three nights ago. A brief, private exchange before the noon meal on the day afterward had left her mind clogged with questions, questions to which she had not yet found answers.

"Last night never happened," Louis had told Manuela in *sotto voce* as they had stood with the near-deaf Doña Magdalena in the foyer awaiting the arrival of Diego and Domingo.

Manuela's eyebrows had shot up in doubtful query as she mouthed, "Why not?" Her face warmed at the way his gaze had lazed across her face and traced the shape of her lips while she spoke. The intimate wanderings had reminded her forcefully of the long kisses they had shared.

"Both of us would be in trouble," was all that Louis had gotten out before her uncle and grandfather appeared.

The two were back then to the formalities of that first dinner. From that moment on, an invisible field of tension had splayed out between them. Its force seemed a paradox, in that it served both to bind them together and force them apart.

The Frenchman returned to addressing her as "Miss Ramon." She had no choice but to follow suit and forget he had asked her that night to call him "Louis." Why couldn't they have announced that they had met by accident in the stables and become friends? That the details of the "accident" needed to remain secret she could understand, but to pretend they were still strangers seemed ridiculous.

Feeling that her pride had been trampled, and that one of questionable status was ignoring her, Manuela had assumed her original haughty demeanor and had refused to reward Louis with more than cool courtesy. When he accepted her icy behavior with apparent indifference, she puzzled. At each successive meal, he seemed to lose another degree of interest in her, no longer bothering to try to draw her into conversation as he had on the first night he had dined with the family. Had she been wrong to think that he had ever found her attractive?

Not that she cared what the French spy thought of her, Manuela repeated to herself each night in her room. In vain she tried to escape into her reading of poetry and venturing into the private fantasy world attracting her ever since she had mastered the reading of French. Somehow, though, the memory of the ecstasy of the oh-so-real kisses in the stables refused to dissipate.

Louis Saint-Denis might have been the wrong one to initiate her into the pleasures of the flesh, she told herself with a shrug for fate's warped sense of humor, but he had done a thorough job. She felt as if one of the dust devils out on the desert had sucked her up, whirled her about, then dropped her from a dizzying height. How could anyone be the same after such an awesome experience?

Despite her willing that it be otherwise, Manuela was no longer a dreaming sixteen-year-old, content to abide in a fantasy world. Now that she knew something about the physical delights awaiting lovers, her passionate nature yearned for more. Not from the Frenchman, she would deny when the handsome, angular face with the mysterious, silvery eyes loomed to mind, but from the Lover she had dreamed of for so long. She wished for him to come to her now. She was ready — no, eager — to get on with the next chapter in her life, the one that would be filled with ardent caresses and heartfelt promises of love eternal. From the right young man, of course.

On the third morning after the arrival of the French lieutenant, Manuela sat beneath the umbrella shade of the transplanted chinaberry tree in the patio, her needlework resting on her lap.

She watched Eblo climb the ladder at the end of the long stable to tend the pigeon cote perched on its roof. The old Pueblo Indian appeared to be taking the invasion of his stables as calmly as he did everything else, she reflected.

Eblo and the commandant's grandchildren had become friends after Carlos and she had come to live at the *presido* four years ago. Now that Manuela was subject to a dueña's demands, she missed those earlier, carefree days of following the Indian about while he cared for the horses and the pigeons.

She reflected that Eblo's main interest in life seemed to be the pigeons and that his greatest pride came from having trained them to fly messages between San Juan Batista and other forts. Recently he claimed to have had one reach the great distance to the cote atop the government building in Mexico City and then return to San Juan Batista with a reply.

Abandoning the despised needlework on the bench beneath the umbrella-shaped tree, she walked through the rose garden to stand looking up at the old man's loving ministrations to the soft-voiced birds. It was almost time for the noonday meal, and the entire morning had dragged.

"I heard a lot of men talking in the stables earlier. What was all the commotion about?" Manuela called over the courtyard wall to Eblo.

"Captain and Frenchmen hunt birds after *siesta*. Choose horses and guns." After the quiet reply, Eblo continued to run his forefinger lightly over the feathered heads vying for his attention within the cage.

"I'll be going also, won't I?" Whenever Eblo

chose to keep her from learning something, she fretted, he reverted to the choppy language he had used. He could speak as well as she when it suited him.

To Manuela's disappointment, both Diego and Domingo had spent all their spare time with the Frenchman ever since his arrival. They seemed more interested in conversing with their "guest" at each meal than with her, she fumed. Damn the man! Ever since his arrival only four days ago, he had wrenched their lives into a different pattern. Nothing about the situation was fair.

"Don't know," came Eblo's reply.

The old man began backing down the ladder with care. One leg was bent permanently at the knee, and he never moved fast. Eblo had recounted to the inquisitive twins how Diego had found him left for dead after a big battle with the Pueblos up in Colorado and had ordered him cared for. Ever since, before Carlos and she had even been born, he had devoted himself to the commandant and his family. He cut his eyes to the young woman with a look indicating that he knew she was unhappy with his answer.

"You know that Grandfather has always allowed me to go hunting with him, Eblo. Plan to saddle Nightstar for me. If he didn't give the order himself, it was likely an oversight."

Even if she had to ride sidesaddle on her own horse, Manuela was determined to get outside the walls. Three days was too long to stay inside. Perhaps Diego would refuse to let her shoot with outsiders along, but she would content herself with being allowed to ride with the group.

Having learned that Eblo nearly always sided with Diego in such matters, Manuela flounced back toward the shaded bench. With indrawn breath at its fragile beauty, she watched a scarlet-throated hummingbird flit from one magenta hibiscus to another near the fountain. On wings moving so rapidly as to deny her a clear view of their color and shape, a second hummingbird hovered among the now-folding blue blossoms of the morning glory trailing across a far wall. At the sound of the first noontime bell, both zipped out of sight over the walls of the courtyard.

Something within the black-haired beauty sighed when the tiny hummingbirds disappeared from her sight. As she walked toward the *hacienda*, the throaty calls from the pigeon cote struck her as sounding unusually sad. The beauty of the well-tended beds of roses, verbena, and poppies divided by meandering stone walkways was lost on her. For no recognized reason, she kicked angrily at a pebble in her path, barely aware that it landed with a splash in the stone fountain.

Her secret wish that the French intruder not be present at lunch that day was not granted, and Manuela found herself forced to go through the motions of politeness. The only time she did not have to face Louis was at breakfast, for Doña Magdalena and she were accustomed to eating that meal at their leisure after the men had left for the business of the day. On those occasions in the past when Manuela had wanted to have private visits with her grandfather or her uncle, she had made it a point to rise early and join them. Such opportunities were no longer available now that Lieutenant Saint-Denis was present at the Ramon table even at breakfast, a fact she had learned from questioning Juanita.

"No, Doña Magdalena," Louis was saying during the noonday meal when Manuela forced herself back to the present, "there are no fine private homes in the French colonies as yet." Pleasure adding sparkle to his pale eyes, he let them wander about the large dining room with its hand-carved furniture of mahogany, its linen-draped table with attractive appointments of porcelain, silver, and crystal. "Even the governor and the commandants don't enjoy such luxury as you have here." With a polite smile at Manuela, he added, "And we have almost no lovely young ladies to grace our tables."

"Pray tell why not," Manuela said, intrigued in spite of her resolve not to converse with him unless it became absolutely necessary.

Odd, she mused, how, unless he was wearing blue, his eyes were a definite silvery gray. Today he wore a coat of a pale, creamy color that made his brown hair appear darker than she had at first thought. Odder, and far more disturbing, was the rising memory of the texture of his hair beneath her exploring hands that night in the stable. She lowered her eyes to dispel the unbidden thought.

"New France has no true settlements of size, merely forts. Our population consists mainly of soldiers, only a few of whom found wives in the last shipment of women."

Louis pondered the veiling of the black eyes fixed upon him. Would he ever be able to watch those heavy-lidded flutters without being fascinated? Did she have any idea how difficult it was to sit in her presence at each meal and fight down the urge to talk only with her, look only at that beautiful face?

"Shipment of . . . do you mean to imply that women are 'shipped' like cattle or horses?" At his absentminded nod, Manuela went on, venting her anger at the obvious injustice to her sex. "How degrading. Why would any woman allow herself to be so handled? Surely the French cannot be proud of such practices." Her indignation pushed her into sitting straighter, taller.

"Manuela," Diego intervened, seeing that his granddaughter was on the verge of becoming overwrought, "I'm sure our guest doesn't have a hand in setting up the policy, and it's not our place to criticize the actions of his countrymen."

"I heartily agree with the principle, Diego," Louis interjected. The two Ramon men and he had spent the greater part of the three days since his arrival talking and exchanging ideas. They had established a comfortable, first-name basis. "How can Louisiana ever become a successful colony if she has no families? Such is impossible without wives for our men."

Even teeth flashed whitely in Louis's tanned face as he favored all seated around the table with a dazzling smile.

"Then the women are sent over as mere brood animals," Manuela retorted, ignoring Doña Magdalena's nervous clearing of her throat, irritated at the way Louis seemed to exude charm so easily. "Do the French practice none of the romance their writers proclaim? I've never heard anything quite so disgusting. When the young women arrive, are they auctioned off, Lieutenant?" Her lips closed upon his title with the twist of disapproval.

"Not quite," Louis remarked, amused at her anger, which was turning her black eyes into fiery battlegrounds backed by velvet, but also amazed at her concern for the welfare of women in general.

Not many so young and privileged would have given thought to such matters, Louis reflected. Mayhap sixteen was truly a mark of maturity here on the frontier. With studied casualness, he had pried the information from Diego the morning after the "midnight encounter" that Manuela had become sixteen only recently.

Already concerned as to the commandant's probable reaction to any young man's having spent even a few moments alone with his granddaughter, Louis had made all kinds of promises to himself when he learned Manuela was so young. No matter that she had at first seemed delicious temptation. She suddenly became forbidden fruit.

Solemnly he had vowed that he would do nothing to encourage further meetings in private. He would be polite but reserved, he had promised himself. He would give up his earlier plan to learn all about her, to know her thoughts. Ever would he keep in mind that he had come to New Spain for the purpose of setting up a trade route between the northern provinces and the new fort he had built on the Red River before setting out from Louisiana. He would do nothing to shake the commandant's apparent faith in him as an officer and a gentleman. His was a business venture, nothing more. All these things the ambitious Louis Saint-Denis put uppermost in his mind.

Such resolves sounded lofty, bordered on the noble, when the tormented young Frenchman formed them mentally, even when he voiced them to an openly doubting Medar. To his consternation, Louis found that he lived for mealtimes because he could see the black-haired beauty then. Each time he came to the *hacienda* and saw her, he fought furiously against the desire to hold her again, kiss her, learn more about her. Taking his cue from her icy reaction to his whispered announcement that they must forget they had ever met in the stables, Louis had been most almost grateful for social conventions giving him a way out. Though he did not actually feel comforted that they were never alone, he conceded there was a measure of safety in numbers. More privilege than that he dared not allow himself.

Discarding the momentary mental ramblings, Louis went on to explain to the one crowding his thoughts there in the dining room, "The young women are housed within the forts with families already having quarters until the bachelors call upon them. A manner of courtship follows before the couples are actually wed. Actually, we've had only one group arrive, though our governor has petitioned the Crown for more."

"Sounds like a sensible arrangement for those settlers and soldiers wishing to marry and rear a family," Domingo said, looking up from his plate. He glanced at his niece to see if she was calming any from the quiet answer. Her face appeared flushed, but she no longer glared across at the Frenchman. He shifted his eyes to the young man beside him, saying with good humor, "As for those like me—and obviously you, Louis—the business of marriage holds little appeal. From what you've already told us, you've been rather too busy with your fur trading and dealing with Indians to do much courting."

"Let us not embarrass our guest," spoke Doña Magdalena quietly but firmly. "Some matters are best left private."

"You are most kind, dear lady," replied Louis, "but I'm not at all embarrassed to discuss my state of bachelorhood. As the youngest of twelve children, I greatly endorse marriage and large families, but I've never found the one I thought could be happy sharing my rather unpredictable mode of living."

Even as he conversed, one part of Louis's mind dwelt upon the mysteries of Manuela's charm. He was sorely pressed to decide if she looked more beautiful in the casual morning dresses she wore during the days, or in the elegant gowns, complete with elaborate *coiffure*, she appeared in at dinner. Fighting for supremacy were those breathtaking images of her in the half-darkened stables in the yellow silk sleeping gown, black hair mussed and falling down below the tiny waist to brush her curving hips. Relentlessly the list went on: With sultry eyes picking up moonbeams and starring for him alone, with moist lips puffed and too kissable to leave a man sane. Knowing his thoughts were leading him into the mire of despond that he allowed himself to wallow in only late at night when he was alone, he cast them aside and admired the way the pink gown she wore today brought out the deep rose of her full lips.

"A noble gesture," Manuela replied with a noticeable tone of derision.

For some reason, Louis's sudden, lengthy scrutiny—the first she had noted since the night of his arrival—summoned a flush to Manuela's high-placed cheeks, rearranged the rhythm of her

105

heartbeat. Impatient at herself for noticing where he was looking, she tossed her head, hardly aware that corkscrew curls of shining ebony bounced and jiggled upon her shoulders.

Why, she scolded, had she let the man's remarks and actions upset her? He was nothing to her; she was nothing to him, else why had he chosen to pretend that the "midnight encounter" had never taken place. Until word came from the message sent to Governor Anya in Monclova, he was a mere French officer held in a Spanish *presidio* against his will. Probably he would soon be transferred to the prison in Monclova, or one in Mexico City, and hanged for spying—which was what he deserved. She bit into a spicy corn fritter with relish.

By the time the maids brought dessert, Manuela had made up her mind about going along on the hunt, saying to Diego, "Eblo tells me we're going to shoot birds this afternoon." With an air of single-minded concentration, she selected an orange from the large bowl in the middle of the table and began peeling it. The first spurt of oil from the fruit peel jumped in midair to add a biting scent to the atmosphere. "We've not been riding in a week, and I'm looking forward to an outing."

"We hadn't planned on taking the ladies," Domingo replied, obviously feeling sorry for his father, who seemed at a loss for words.

"That hardly requires planning, Uncle. You know how I nearly always go along." She sent Domingo no more than a flitting glance.

Manuela well knew that all eyes were upon her. She added to the little pile of orange peels with tapered fingers, sniffing appreciatively at the pungent odor and keeping her eyes on the fruit.

Turning toward Diego at the head of the table, she announced in tones hinting at martyrdom, "There are so few times I'm allowed to go beyond the *presidio* walls nowadays that I shudder at the thought of missing such a chance."

Manuela lifted her great eyes then to her grandfather's, giving him the full benefit of their beautiful, heavy-lidded pleading. Her lovely face had taken on just the proper hint of woefulness as to suggest that the true depths of her sorrow remained hidden.

Louis studied the young woman across from him with undisguised admiration, not only for her beauty but also for her artifice. What man could resist such an aptly rendered plea? For a second, he entertained the thought that she might well have rehearsed it. He watched small white teeth sink into a slice of orange and felt an instantaneous urge to touch the corner of those lusciously pink lips where a fat drop of juice rested. And, he realized with a pang deep and wrenching low in his belly, not just with his finger. He thought he had conquered the frequent thoughts of what it would be like to kiss her again, and here out of nowhere came the crushing desire.

"Truly it must be painful to remain inside when you long to ride about," Louis heard himself intervening for her.

What was wrong with him, an inner self chided Louis. Had he forgotten his vow to stay away from the commandant's granddaughter? There would be that safety in numbers he counted on at mealtimes, he reassured himself. It wasn't that he was making plans to be alone with her.

107

"I sincerely hope, Diego and Domingo, that you've not decided against taking Miss Ramon along because of the presence of my men and me," the Frenchman added. "I assure you, she would in no way detract from the pleasure of the hunt."

Oh no? came Louis's relentless private voice. Squelching such warnings, he wondered if Manuela could ride well, then voted for "not very likely." Maybe he would get a chance to touch her, or at least ride beside her if she became frightened when the guns went off. He wished she would show her gratitude for his intervention with at least a covert glance from beneath those fascinating eyelashes, but she seemed intent on nothing beyond eating the fruit. Not since that night when she had thanked him for removing the splinter had she bestowed a look of admiration upon him. Had he imagined that she had found him attractive and worthy of her attention that night?

As everyone at the table seemed to expect, Diego broke the silence. "Very well, Manuela, you may go along."

Thoughtfully Diego examined her face while she sat docilely dabbing at wet lips with her napkin. He tried to imagine what it would be like to be a young woman confined by the rules of society, rules that he had never taken time to examine until Manuela had begun kicking up such a fuss. The problem was more than he could fathom. Actually, he confessed, Manuela herself was more than he could fathom.

Not having had any daughters and not having seen any of the signs of rebellion in his late wife that he suspected resided within his granddaughter, Diego was often baffled by the lovely but spirited child-grown-into-young woman sitting at his table. But always he loved her, loved her in a way he admitted secretly that he had never before loved anyone. The knowledge that soon – and from what Domingo had confided since returning from his journey southward, sooner than he was ready for it – some man's suit for her hand would have to be considered plagued his heart.

"Thank you, Grandfather," Manuela responded upon hearing assent to her wish. "You're always such a kind and understanding man." She rewarded him with a bright-eyed smile, impulsively blowing him a kiss in a charming way adopted when she was a small child.

Returning to her attack upon the orange, Manuela fumed on the inside at Louis's attempt to intercede for her. Probably he had received the scar on his left cheek from interfering in some affair that was no concern of his. Without looking up, she sensed that he had not removed his eyes from her face since making his little speech. What made him think it was his privilege today to gaze upon her so openly, as though she were present for his personal perusal? She did not need his attention or his help.

In fact, Manuela reassured herself, she did not need anything from the arrogant Frenchman. Her suspicion over the past three nights that she was different than before their encounter in the stables no longer nagged at her. She had been mistaken. There was nothing different about her, nothing changed in her life except the annoying presence of Louis Saint-Denis. Once he left the *presidio*, she would be as contented as before to wait for her Lover to come sweep her away.

With all her conscious thought, Manuela wished that Louis would soon be gone so that her life could fall back into its old, comfortable patterns. When a secret voice chided and nigh sniggered, she squashed it, rating it of no more importance than the discarded orange peels already shriveling on her plate.

Chapter Six

In three directions the undulating sandy soil fell away from San Juan Batista: northward to the Rio Grande, eastward to the Gulf of Mexico, southward to the major settlements and Mexico City. Toward the west it climbed slowly and steadily toward the foothills of the Serranias del Burro, the beginning of the majestic range of mountains traveling the length of New Spain. It was in those foothills that Diego had found the headwaters of the Santa Rosa River and diverted them through the old riverbed to the *presidio,* and it was along that irrigation stream that the hunting party planned to travel that afternoon in June of 1714.

The sun had already spent its intense radiance. A pleasant coolness in the air played about the faces of the riders as they prepared to set out from the *presidio.*

As usual when riding and hunting jaunts took place, Doña Magdalena had pleaded a headache and had asked Domingo to assume responsibility for his niece, leaving Manuela the only woman along with the hunters. Louis, at Diego's suggestion, had asked both of his countrymen, Medar Jalot and Sgt. Phillipe Penicault, to take part in the hunt. Although no one had invited him, Eblo was also along, as the old Indian generally was when Commandant Ramon ventured outside the *presidio.*

Domingo watched the Frenchman with secret amusement when Manuela joined the group gathered outside the stables. Medar and Phillipe had never before seen or met her, and they seemed as awed as Louis. It was obvious that none of the three had seen a fashionably dressed equestrienne for quite some time, especially one given the freedom to concoct her own costume.

Manuela, having been allowed by Diego in the pre-dueña period to order her own design to be made, had chosen a heavy black silk for her riding costume rather than the more popular blue taffetas and twills. Instead of following the traditional style of voluminous skirt to conceal the wearer's leg hooked over the second, lower horn of the sidesaddle, she had ordered long, wide-legged breeches to be gathered fully like a skirt onto a waistband.

To cover the portion of leg exposed while on the saddle, Manuela had asked for soft leather boots. They fit snugly up to just below her knees. Also black, they sported a rather high heel, plus jet buttons and loops up the outer sides of her legs. Not only was she more comfortable when riding in her unorthodox outfit, but also she enjoyed more freedom of movement when on the ground, not being burdened by the extra yardage required in the conventional skirt. Even Doña Magdalena had admitted, after her first horrified protests, that except upon close examination, one could hardly tell the lower section of the habit consisted of breeches.

Domingo assisted his niece in mounting Nightstar, the handsome white stallion with a small slash of black on his nose that Eblo had trained for Manuela the year she had come to live at San

112

Juan Batista. With a wink of approval for her charming costume, Domingo handed her the reins. Shortly the party was riding out from the *presidio* toward the foothills beckoning in the hazy, purplish distance.

"May I compliment you on your riding habit, Miss Ramon?" asked Louis after the riders had traveled for a brief time. He had recovered from the shock of seeing Manuela in an even more beautiful state than ever and had reined in beside her. "I've never before seen a hat quite like yours, and I find it perfect."

Louis eyed the black narrow brim edged with braid and the low, flat crown that perched atop her small head, revealing ebony braids coiled low on her neck. The slanted eyes met his with a playful look of surprise as they cantered along.

"*Merci, monsieur,*" Manuela said, hoping to shock him with her use of French. From his slackened jaw and widened eyes, she gathered she had succeeded. She worked to hold down a little giggle, feeling heady and wonderfully alive. With more warmth than she had shown him since right after he had removed the splinter from her foot that night in the moonlight, she added, "The hat is one my brother outgrew. I doubt if many young women would be guilty of wearing a man's castoffs, but I happen to like it. It shades my eyes against the glare and has chin ties to keep it from flying off."

Openly Manuela watched the angular face to see how the French officer would react to such vulgar statements. With careless ease, she controlled the frisky Nightstar, who, like his mistress, was eager to taste the freedom beyond the fort. One gloved hand caressed gleaming withers.

113

Nightstar's whiteness proved a startling contrast to the black of his rider's hair and costume.

From the moment of meeting her, Louis had sensed that Manuela Ramon was an original and that nothing about her would be ordinary. He noticed that the only relief in all that blackness was a white blouse worn beneath a short, unbuttoned vest, a blouse open enough at the neck to reveal a gold chain with a cross nestling against her glowing skin. Generally associating black costumes with mourning or with older women, he had to admit that it was a perfect complement to Manuela's unique coloring.

Louis also noted that he had been in error to suspect she was less than an accomplished equestrienne. At first he had found it hard to believe that the sleek white stallion was indeed the mount chosen for the slender Manuela, but when she mounted and gained instant control with a commanding wrist and a quiet word, he knew she was where she belonged. Never had he ridden beside such an impressive sight as the young woman upon the handsomely arrayed horse.

Manuela's sidesaddle was a work of art such as Louis had never seen, except upon the few times he had glimpsed the ladies of the Court cantering in Parisian parks. Hand-tooled silver covered the saddle horn completely and edged each flap and outer detail of the glossy black leather. Although the single stirrup was of wood, its top side was covered with a wide, inlaid silver band as ornately carved as the strips used on the saddle itself. Unless his eyes were deceiving him, Louis decided that the hardware on the bridle also must be made of silver, so readily did it

114

jangle, shine, and flash in the afternoon sunlight.

"*Parlez-vous français?*" Louis asked, not truly shocked by her frank explanation or by her use of the French words. He had somehow come to expect the unexpected from the beautiful young woman.

"I don't really speak French, Lieutenant," Manuela confided with youthful frankness. Something about being out in the open made her feel more comfortable with Louis. And there was no one hanging onto their every word. "I do read it quite well, but I've never had the opportunity to speak it and acquire an acceptable accent. The nuns were adamant about their students' learning to read French but seemed unconcerned about teaching actual discourse."

Strange that he should seem interested in anything about her other than her body, Manuela mused with pleasure. None of the young men seeking her favor had done anything other than compliment her on her looks. Though the Frenchman had done a world of ogling at that first dinner, he had seemed not particularly interested in her since their meeting in the stables — until today. She did not bother to wonder why his renewed attentions were pleasing her.

"Perhaps I might be of service. I've no claim to being a great teacher, but I could coach you on the accent — with the permission of both you and your grandfather, of course."

So she had been educated at a convent, Louis thought. No wonder she appeared so intelligent and different from any other young woman he had met in years — she was. He felt somehow cheated that he knew so little about her, other than that she was impetuous . . . and possessed a

115

passionate nature.

"I might prove to be a poor student, Lieutenant, and disappoint you."

"I can't imagine your disappointing me . . . in any way."

"But one must be prepared for such things, don't you think? Nothing is as it seems—people included."

"That's quite a statement coming from one so young . . . and beautiful."

"Would you measure wisdom merely by the number of years, or by the shape of a cheek?"

He laughed, delighting in their repartee, but delighting equally in his first chance to bask in her full attention and be free to watch her facial expressions. "If I've been guilty of either," he assured her playfully, "I'll guard against doing so in the future. Coming to San Juan Batista and then meeting you have led me to view many things in a different light."

"Ah," she mocked, pursing her lips and angling her head in teasing challenge. Her gaze moved over his lithe form and lingered a moment on his pale eyes. "The lieutenant must not be finding my grandfather's hospitality pleasing."

Stunned at the overwhelming desire to kiss those pouting lips, Louis threw caution to the breezes and said, "Perhaps I seek hospitality from a fairer Ramon than the commandant."

All at once, Manuela sensed she had lost control of the conversation. Her feelings of disappointment and rejection upon his telling her that their "midnight encounter" must be forgotten still chafed at her pride more than she had realized. She had no desire for him to learn that the memory of those kisses yet lingered. Her eyes sought the foothills up ahead.

Cantering with an energy as noticeable as Nightstar's, Diablo seemed to sense his now-quiet owner had his mind on something other than riding.

Laying a hand against the frisky animal's withers, Louis leaned forward to scold, "Diablo, calm down. I'll give you your head before we return."

"Diablo? Is that the name you call your horse?" Manuela asked, relieved that he had not pursued the earlier topic of conversation.

Catching the eyes of her grandfather upon her from up ahead, Manuela lifted a hand in a way that let him know she was all right. As was her custom, she had started out riding alongside him, but somehow today she had fallen behind after Louis had begun talking with her. She returned her attention to the handsome young man beside her, noting that he was as neatly groomed as he had been at each meal. His knee-length riding pants were brown, as were his stockings and low boots, but a striped brown jacket and tucked shirt of blue gave his habit a rakish air.

Eyes round with wonder while she studied the powerful black stallion, Manuela teased, "Is he really a devil?" What had happened to her earlier wish that he be gone? She could not remember having such fun bantering with a young man.

"He can be," admitted Louis wryly. "But I think the real reason I called him that is his spirit."

"Then you admire spirit in a horse?" It must be the light blue shirt that made his eyes the color of the dazzling, cloudless sky today, Manuela

117

thought when he looked at her searchingly.

The two horses seemed to have synchronized their gait, she reflected while he seemed to be giving her question thought. They were moving at almost the same speed and rhythm across the gently rolling sand dunes. Like a mysterious counterpoint, the sound of sand-cushioned hoof-beats drummed in steady cadence. The air rushing to bathe her face bore a hint of refreshing, earthy fragrance, and she lifted her head to savor it more fully.

"I admire spirit in horses and in people also," Louis said, grateful she hadn't cut him off after the ill-timed remark about seeking her hospitality. He wouldn't make such a mistake again, he promised himself.

What was bringing that vibrant glow to her face, he puzzled, and the secretive smile directed ahead at some private vista? All he could see was desert and the nearing foothills. Louis decided there was something different about her, but he could not pinpoint it.

"So that you might become the master and conquer that spirit, *monsieur?*" When his tanned brow creased in a thoughtful frown, she added with a touch of daring, "As you have so obviously done with Diablo?" To her surprise, she found that she wanted to learn his thoughts—about that matter and others as well.

"I wouldn't use the word 'conquer.' I've not conquered Diablo," replied Louis after a moment. "Perhaps 'channel' is more accurate—channeled that spirit into a vessel to serve better both the owner of the spirit and those he wishes to please."

Damn! She had a way of keeping his mind

118

honed, Louis admitted to himself. Not to mention the spice she added to his emotions! When he was around her, he found no time to ponder when and what Governor Anya might reply to Diego's message about the French intruders. A full week had gone by since he had appeared in the *plaza* outside Diego's office. Late May had turned into early June.

Up ahead Eblo raised his hand and the riders slowed, breaking off private conversations and musings. They dismounted shortly and tethered their horses to some scraggly bushes and wind-whipped mesquite trees. Diego gave quiet suggestions to his guests about the best ways to go about flushing the birds in the absence of hunting dogs. After removing their guns from their saddle holsters, all moved forward silently.

Louis, disappointed that Domingo had assisted his niece to dismount, looked around to see if she was at a safe distance, only to find her walking up ahead beside her grandfather with the same cautious steps as the men. Not until then did he realize her riding "skirt" was actually breeches.

Was there something new in the world of fashion he had not heard of? Louis wondered with amusement. Not likely. Fashionable ladies wearing long breeches? Even more unlikely. A scant six months ago he had met the last ship from France at Fort Mobile, and nothing so scandalous was reported from the fashion scene in Paris. Walking behind her, he admired the slim, rounded hips and found that the view was far more enticing than when only hinted at by billowing skirts over *panniers* — though he had to confess the full breeches concealed more than

119

they revealed.

Smiting his well-laid plans to put such memories to rest, images of the way Manuela had looked that night in the stable rose to taunt Louis. Could he ever truly forget the sights of those graceful legs ascending and descending the ladder? Or the way her careless drawing up of her silken gown had shaped the rounded but slender hips for his secret viewing there in the half-light? Remembering how closely he had come to sending his hands to trace the shape of her while she lay sprawled against him brought a slash of fire down low, a fullness to his throat, and an undeniable warning.

Louis bade his mind put away thoughts of Manuela and return to the present. He noted that the sun hid suddenly behind the mountains on the horizon, allowing a mauvy glow to bathe the patch of scraggly grass and weeds, bushes, and low trees. The riders had left behind the wind-shaped mounds of sand with their sentinels of torch cacti and their sparse, low vegetation.

They were now in the rocky, green section leading to the foothills up ahead. Here the stream they had followed took on the look of a young river. Snow melts and spring rains in the mountains had sent extra portions into the old bed, even creating an audible current as the water rushed over the rocky base.

Stepping aside after a quiet exchange with Diego and watching the men go on ahead, Manuela loosened the chin strap of the small black hat. With it resting across her shoulders, she gazed down at the clear water, fascinated as always by the jumble of earth colors in the large rocks on the bottom of the stream and its banks.

She loved the rocks best when they were wet, somehow imagining that the colors were then more like nature intended: the grays, the tans, the oranges, the blacks sometimes threaded with patterns of white, the mauves, the mottled browns – she could never decide which were her favorites.

Staccato gunshots sounded from up ahead then, sending fish in sporadic forays among the rocks serving as camouflage until the sudden, carrying bursts of noise invaded. Twisting her head to admire the speedy birds' lightning-quick flights, Manuela watched a flushed covey of quail, rising low and seeking safety, dart for cover in distant bushes. She could imagine the fluttering, whirring sound they made, the eager press upon the trigger after a hasty sighting, and experienced an instant of a seasoned hunter's thrill. To the accompaniment of shouts and laughter from the men, a number of the full-breasted birds dropped into the tall grass and weeds along the way.

Manuela noticed that both Louis and Diego turned at the same time then to look back at her, neither seemingly aware of the other's action. No longer caring that she had not been allowed to shoot that day, the vision in black smiled and waved a carefree hand before returning to her dreamy inspection of the murmuring stream below.

Sniffing at a sudden quickening of cool air that always signaled the beginning of the night breeze, which lived in the mountains and only occasionally visited as far as the *presidio*, Manuela moved to stand on a rocky, protruding ledge. From her perch there in the shade of the foothills, she could see far down the path they had traveled.

In the distance, the sun still shone on San Juan Batista and its walls, the waning rays reflecting mirrorlike in the silver cross atop the church. Luxuriating in the freedom she always felt outside the *presidio,* Manuela sat and lifted her face to the gentle wind. The smell of nearby trees and running water satisfied some secret longing. She breathed deeply and closed her eyes in a kind of ecstasy.

The men had never been out of sight or calling range, but even if they had, Manuela would have had no fear. She often sneaked off to that very spot atop the large, flat boulder, dressed in Conchita's clothing and riding the bare back of a stock horse.

The hunters had good luck with a second covey also, but gave up on a third since twilight was fast approaching there in the shadows of the mountains. Louis and Medar led the group at quite a distance as they returned to where Manuela waited.

"See how lovely, Medar, even as she sits watching the water." Louis spoke in low tones to his friend and valet. His eyes showed his joy as he gazed at Manuela in the diminishing distance. "On the way here, she actually spoke with me in a friendly way. I had feared she would never be civil again. I'm not sure she understood why I warned her we mustn't let our meeting in the stables be known. This afternoon, she's all a man could wish for."

Not even to his trusted valet had Louis confessed that she was the swimmer he had seen that first morning—or that he had kissed her in the stables and been kissed back. Somehow, he preferred to keep that knowledge private.

"I saw the two of you, and so did her grandfather," Medar answered with grimness.

Medar had no wish to encourage Louis in breaking his vow to keep his distance from the Spanish beauty. Any day word could come from the commandant's superiors, and, as suspected spies, the Frenchmen could be hauled into a true prison . . . or shot. The friendship building between Louis and the Ramon officers might be the only thing to save their lives, and the Frenchman's open mooning over Manuela wasn't going to set well with her grandfather. Hadn't Louis himself pointed that out time and again? Was there more than the admitted infatuation with the young beauty? He prayed not.

"Even Diego and Domingo could tell our talk was innocent," Louis defended. "I was happy to let her see that I may be a despised foreigner, but that I am human."

He handed his gun to Medar and straightened his cravat while they walked toward Manuela. With practiced hands, Louis smoothed at his hair. He had in mind that if he were one of the first to return, he might be allowed to assist her in mounting Nightstar. Such a courtesy would in no way suggest he was seeking to break his vow to stay away from her, he consoled himself.

While she was contemplating scrambling down the bank for a wildflower peeking from beneath a rocky ledge, Manuela heard voices becoming louder. She rose quickly to carry out her plan before it was time to leave. The incline was steep, but the depth was no greater than the irrigation ditch near the *presidio*. A man as tall as Louis could have stood in the stream and been barely hidden from a brief distance.

"Miss Ramon, where are you going?" called Louis, fast approaching the boulder. Everything seemed to be working out perfectly, he exulted. The others were not yet to the stream. He would walk with her to where the horses were tethered and be the logical one to help her onto her horse. He could touch her again. All at once, his heartbeat quickened. His head seemed to become lighter. Without his realizing it, Louis's walk resembled a swagger.

Before rising from the rock, Manuela had watched the Frenchman make the little adjustments to his clothing and hair. She had looked away to hide her smile. He was, as she had always heard her grandfather and uncle say Frenchmen were, vain and egotistical. At his question, she turned toward him, noticing his cocky walk right away. Did nothing daunt him? What if she had been the one to whisper that their meeting in the stables had no meaning, must be forgotten? Would his pride have sagged?

"I'm going to pick a wildflower to take back to the *hacienda,*" Manuela replied. "I like to press them and use them to make pictures for gifts."

Even as she spoke over her shoulder, she was moving toward the rocky bank.

"No, no!" Louis called, hurrying to reach her side. "You might fall and hurt yourself. Allow me to fetch it for you."

Too vividly he recalled her experience on the ladder. By that time, Louis was beside her and had almost reached for her arm to restrain her before he realized that to do so might seem improper to her grandfather and uncle coming

124

toward them.

"Show me where it is." Louis leaned to look where her eyes seemed to be directed.

"You are too kind, Lieutenant," Manuela protested, aware of the approach of the remainder of the party. "I'm quite able to get the flower for myself."

Annoyed, she turned and put one foot down on the side of the bank. His insistence seemed to suggest she was incapable of doing such simple things for herself, Manuela huffed inwardly.

Her irritation underlining her words, the suddenly haughty beauty replied, "I can get the flower without your help. It's right beside a rock below me."

"Where?" Louis asked, too overwhelmed by her nearness to note her rebuff. This time he took the liberty of putting a protective hand on her arm as he too set one foot down the bank.

For some reason she could not determine, then or later that night when she tried to understand it, Manuela felt as if her skin had been branded through the silk blouse. With an indrawn breath, she jerked her arm free. The sudden movement was just enough to throw both of them off balance. They teetered for a second before losing their footing and falling against the steep bank.

Manuela grabbed at a large rock and managed to keep from rolling down into the water. Louis was not so lucky. By the time the others had rushed to the side of the stream, he was lying awkwardly in the shallow water, his clothing and hair thoroughly doused and disarrayed. Never had he felt such a clumsy dolt.

When Manuela fathomed what had happened, she looked over her shoulder from where she clung to the jutting rock to see how her would-be protector had fared. The realization of their ridiculous states, and how funny they both must appear, touched off peals of laughter, laughter that reached Louis's ears as the cruelest punishment of all.

Only the swift movements of the agile Domingo saved Manuela from loosening her hold on the boulder and joining Louis in the water. Once her uncle did reach her and help her regain her footing, she squelched the laughter enough for him to lead her safely back up the incline. A quick brushing of debris from her costume, and she was as good as new, suffering only a slight bruise on her elbow.

Both Medar and Phillipe rushed down the bank to aid Louis. Fighting to control their own laughter at their superior's predicament, they were held back from helping him by his muttered threats. With as much dignity as he could muster, Louis rose under his own power. He could not prevent their climbing closely beside him as he scrambled up the bank under the watchful eyes of the now-silent Manuela and the others.

Having no desire to look into those slanting black eyes for fear he would see vast measures of scorn and derision, Louis busied himself with brushing off the water and dirt clinging to his hair and clothing.

Diego motioned for the others to walk on toward the horses and came to stand beside the disheveled young man, saying, "That was quite a spill you took, Louis. I saw what happened, and I realize you were trying to prevent a similar fate for my granddaughter. For your attempt, I'm grateful, as I'm sure she is also."

Diego could no better understand Manuela's attack of laughter than Louis. Through instinct he sensed that it was her unpredictable reaction, more than the fall itself, that brought the pained look to the handsome face. Not once since the Frenchman had arrived a week ago had the commandant glimpsed a single flaw in the outward show of composure ... until now.

The older man confessed to being baffled. He removed his hat and swiped at mussed, gray hair before setting it back on his head. During their talks about what kind of future Louis might have after Governor Anya sent the long-awaited reply, the young man had always appeared nonchalant, every inch the confident officer on a legitimate mission. Why would a young woman's bit of laughter affect him so?

When Louis continued to pick at his clothing and wring water from his long hair, Diego asked, "Did you suffer any major injuries?" Ignoring the sodden coat, he put an arm around Louis's shoulder and urged him toward where the others were mounting.

From somewhere nearby came the muted calls of night birds seeking shelter in the approaching darkness. Louis found their sounds strangely raucous, mocking.

Turning to look into the concerned dark eyes close to his, Louis replied in a low voice marked with self-deprecation, "Only to my pride, Diego. Only to my cursed, damnable pride."

Chapter Seven

Louis asked to be excused from dinner with the Ramons that night. When Manuela next saw him, the following day at noon, he had pulled himself together admirably, acting as though nothing unusual had happened.

Covertly Manuela watched Louis for signs of anger or resentment directed toward her but found none at all. The only noticeable change was that the gray-blue eyes watched her with a new guardedness. Both Diego and Domingo had counseled her privately about her unseemly outburst, but upon her confession that her laughter was directed toward herself as much as the lieutenant, neither had felt inclined to continue the conversation.

The next few days took on a sameness as Manuela yet chafed at her confinement and at Carlos's prolonged absence. He had promised to return within three weeks, and nearly two had already passed. Not only did she miss her twin's companionship, but also she longed to learn about his adventures in the mountains and to hear his thoughts about the Frenchmen's daring intrusion.

A kind of bothersome brooding became a part of her daily routine. When would the vexatious

Louis Saint-Denis be gone? her conscious self asked. She shut out questions asked by her unconscious, for they followed far different patterns.

Troublesome thoughts flitting about, Manuela sat one morning in the courtyard creating a picture from dried flower petals and leaves. Without warning, Doña Magdalena appeared at her side there beneath the chinaberry tree, something she rarely did. Usually she contented herself to sit in her upstairs bedroom or the living room and look out at intervals from her reading or plying of her own needle to check on the activities of her charge.

"A lovely picture, my dear," Doña Magdalena said, stooping to see it more clearly. The art of pasting dried flower petals onto a frame-stretched fabric background to form a picture was the only handiwork she had been successful in leading the restless Manuela to enjoy. Not for the first time, she noted that her grand-niece was uncommonly good at it.

"Thank you, Aunt." Manuela patted the bench beneath the tree and said with easy charm, "Sit with me."

Cocking her pretty head, Manuela looked into the little boxes of dried petals and leaves beside her. She shot a keen glance down at the frame resting across her lap, then selected a deep yellow petal and tried it in a blank spot. Liking the result, she dipped it in paste and applied it with a gentle touch. The project showed her partiality for yellow as well as a talent for blending form, tone, and texture.

"Lieutenant Saint-Denis is inside, Manuela. Your grandfather and he have discussed the possibility of his helping you with your French," Doña Magdalena said in a dry, whispery rush, her disapproval of the project showing in her voice. "I told them I would ask your opinion of the matter."

"I don't recall your caring much for my opinions of things that are ordinarily in your jurisdiction," Manuela retorted, suspecting the older woman of deviousness. She remembered well the *dueña*'s derogatory remarks about her reading French works. It seemed clear that she did not care to see her charge learn any more French than she already knew. "But since you've asked me, I believe I will accept the kind lieutenant's offer."

With finality Manuela placed one last fragment of stem on her picture and propped up the frame, leaning as far back as possible to gain more perspective. Doña Magdalena did not often give her choices. Manuela suspected that a prod from Diego had led to the one just offered.

"After all, Doña Magdalena," she said while tilting her head and squinting critically at her latest creation, "I've nothing else to do."

And so it was that, during his second week at San Juan Batista, Louis Saint-Denis joined Manuela and Doña Magdalena in the library of the *hacienda* for an hour each morning. Louis still found the young beauty's very presence overwhelming, but he had at last learned to conceal her effect on him. Never did he allow her to catch him while he admired a flawless cheek or the glistening braids she often wore in a thick coil at the base of her neck with her casual morning attire. The sideways, heavy-lidded glances she sent his way so casually during recitations al-

130

most did him in more than once, but he kept to his vow not to make personal remarks.

Doña Magdalena, no longer open about her disapproval of her young charge's being drilled in the language of a country long known to be the enemy of Spain, sat stiffly beside the single window in order to work her needle in the strong light. She seemed to pay no particular attention to what the young couple were saying or doing.

Seated side by side across the room behind the library table, Louis and Manuela centered their outward interest on the books open before them. He would lean toward her to read aloud a passage, then wait for her to repeat it, trying his best not to watch the lovely mouth form the phrases with any interest beyond that of a tutor. Patiently he would make suggestions and have her repeat it until both were satisfied with her recitation.

Sometimes her efforts were ludicrous, and Manuela would burst into delighted laughter, laughter so spontaneous and contagious that Louis could not help but join in with a huge smile or sometimes a deep chuckle. At such times he reminded himself that his pupil was only that. Studiously he tried to ignore the racing of his pulse at a careless brush of her arm against his or a sudden, soul-shattering peek directly into his eyes.

"Here's a song, Lieutenant," Manuela exclaimed with an arresting lilt in her voice one morning while thumbing through the volume he had chosen for that day's reading. "It's about a cavalier," she began, pausing to make out the rest silently before continuing, ". . . and the ladies he leaves behind."

Black eyes collided with the gray-blue, seeking to read what lay therein. Was the Frenchman, Manuela pondered, a type of cavalier who liked keeping the fairer sex in quandaries? She had accepted that the "midnight encounter" was to be wiped from her memory, but verbally accepting and the actual carrying out of the action were two different pieces of fruit. She rated the doing as a lemon. Lemons sometimes gave her hives.

"It is not your reading that needs practice," he admonished softly. "Let me hear you say the words."

Louis hoped his voice sounded authoritative. It was hard to concentrate when she looked at him in that sleepy-eyed way. The scent of roses accompanied her each day and permeated beyond his nostrils into varied parts he dared not examine. He sometimes suspected he breathed her fragrance in and out with such regularity that she was becoming a permanent part of him. The olive skin with its tones of ivory always seemed to glow from some inner source of radiance. Despite his resolve to maintain a dignified distance, he felt more drawn to her each day.

Small wonder. Each day tortured the young man with tantalizing new views of Manuela's charms: the thick half-circle of sooty lashes above flawless cheeks as she concentrated on the contents of a book, the gentle rise and fall of full breasts as she breathed, the flash of perfect little teeth when she smiled or laughed, the impulsive wave of graceful hands when she became excited or nigh carried away with her recitations—all such seemingly normal actions played bloody hell with his senses and noble vows.

Each day there in the library, Louis wondered

why he did not put an end to their sessions. Each night alone in his quarters, he suspected he knew the answer and so refused to entertain the question at those soul-searching times.

"I believe I like the melody," Manuela said after giving a satisfactory interpretation of the lyrics of the simple song she had discovered. "Perhaps it would sound good on my guitar."

A casual flip of her hair, unbound that day in careless profusion, sent a perfumed strand of silky black to brush Louis's shoulder. Eyes closing in that heavy-lidded way that mesmerized him, Manuela hummed the notes as if testing them. She slanted her gaze his way then. Catching a pained look in the gray ones so close, she asked with mock seriousness, her voice privately husky, little more than a whisper, "What's wrong, Louis? Was I so out of pitch?"

"No, no," Louis replied in a suddenly hoarse voice, a hand moving jerkily to straighten his ruffled cravat. When Doña Magdalena allowed that it would be proper for them to be on a first-name basis, Louis had exulted at his unexpected good fortune. Manuela's icy resolve seemed to melt a fraction at each tutoring session, but now he was wondering if such a thing was desirable. Hearing her say his name so intimately always threw him off guard. "It's just that . . . that I had no inkling you might be a musician."

"I'm not really," she confided in that open, innocent way he had come to expect. "Carlos learned to play from some of the soldiers at the barracks, and he taught me a bit about the guitar." Manuela hooked laughing eyes toward Doña Magdalena before adding in a conspiratorial whisper, "Sometimes he and I join in the

Saturday-night *fiestas* over in the *plaza*."

The secretive smile and the devilish lights leaping in her slanted eyes charmed Louis anew. Having watched one of the impromptu *fiestas* in the *plaza* outside his quarters, he was beset instantly with visions of Manuela taking part in some of the spirited Spanish dances, black hair flying about her face, hands clapping a steady rhythm, graceful body swaying to a guitar's seductive melody.

"Will you play and sing for me sometime?" Louis glanced over at Doña Magdalena to see if she was hearing and disapproving, but the *dueña* seemed intent upon nothing but her needlework.

"Perhaps, but I'm better at dancing. Carlos is the real musician."

After she spoke, Manuela felt an unsettling warmth steal over her face and neck, one she had come to expect from Louis's close-up appraisals during their learning sessions. His eyes seemed to be sending out secret messages that she longed to decipher. Did he sometimes recall their "midnight encounter" . . . as she did? She could not remember when his intent looks at her shifted from what she had at first deemed ogling, but she realized that she no longer categorized them that way. Whereas she had at first resented his scrutiny of her face and body, she now accepted it as some unvoiced bit of flattery. Disjointed thoughts crowded her mind.

Feeling a sudden need for distance between the pale-eyed Frenchman and herself, Manuela rose, saying in a half-strangled voice, "I think I've had enough lessons for today."

Louis stood and watched her leave the library. The whispering sway of full skirts caught in at the tiny waist and the bounce of black hair falling in a shimmering curtain down her back became another of those haunting images stacking up in his heart. No. Stacking up in his mind, he corrected.

Conchita was putting away laundry when her mistress, with flushed face, entered the bedroom and went out onto the balcony without her usual small talk. She heard Manuela murmuring to Zorro, heard the parrot's uncanny replies.

The maid checked to make sure the monogrammed handkerchief she had discovered in the laundry that last day Manuela had gone swimming was still at the bottom of the pile in the drawer. At first she had been puzzled at the appearance of the gentleman's handkerchief with the strange monogram, but before she had had a chance to question Manuela, the Frenchman's valet had provided the answer.

Conchita's mouth spread into a pleased smile as she recalled how Medar Jalot had approached her in the *plaza* on the second night after arriving and had asked which maids made it a habit to swim in the irrigation stream. The charming Medar soon had Conchita giggling at his witty accounts of life in Paris. When he attempted to hold her hand and steal a kiss, she had slipped away from him with a knowing smile and a promise to return to the *plaza* on the following evening.

Amused at the turn of events, Conchita hugged in silence what she believed was known only by her: that, unbeknownst to Manuela, Louis had secretly watched her swim on the morning of his arrival, and that, believing her a maid at the *hacienda*, he still had no clue to her identity.

"What brings such a smile to your face, Conchita?" asked Manuela when she wandered back into the room. "Has Medar been back to walk with you at nightfall over in the *plaza?*"

Conchita tossed her head and laughed, pretty teeth flashing in the dark, olive-skinned face. "What if he has? He's the most entertaining man I've ever been around."

"He's quite handsome, too, from what I remember of the day of the hunt." She watched the maid blush and straighten the already perfect white cap atop the fat black braids crowning her head.

"These Frenchmen!" Conchita exclaimed, pausing to let out a long sigh. "They seem to know all the right things to say to a woman to make her feel special."

Just as Manuela had chosen not to confide about her meeting with Louis in the stable, Conchita kept back her real feelings for Medar. She longed to confide all she knew but felt the time was not right. How she wished that Medar had sought her out for some reason other than to find out the identity of the swimmer. Not that he ever spoke of it again after that first night ...

"It's been two weeks since the Frenchmen and their Indian friends came. I wonder how much longer they'll be here?" Manuela asked. "I find it hard to believe that Governor Anya hasn't sent for them by now." Deep in thought, she pursed her lips.

"You'd miss having Lieutenant Saint-Denis as your tutor, wouldn't you?" Conchita had heard the sounds of laughter coming from the library over the past several mornings. Manuela's unusually perky spirits and a new sparkle in her eyes had not gone unnoticed, either.

"Not at all," denied her mistress, wondering at a sudden skip in her pulse. "If they would leave, I could go back to riding and doing what I please instead of having to stay cooped up all day." The words rang hollow, even in her own ears.

After *siesta* that afternoon, Diego and Domingo sent for Manuela to meet them in the library. With her customary exuberance, she greeted them with hugs and kisses, then looked puzzled when they asked her to sit with them.

"Manuela, my dove," Diego said, sitting on the chair behind the long reading table where Louis and she sat each morning during the tutoring sessions. He leaned back and fitted his long fingers together at the tips, seemingly intrigued at the little cage they made. Becoming aware that both Domingo and Manuela gazed at him expectantly, he went on. "The time has come to speak of your future."

"Yes, that's right," Domingo said, rubbing his forehead with one hand and looking at the books on the shelves rather than at his niece. Their leather bindings and gold embossments seemed to captivate him. "We want you to know that Father and I have nothing but your best interests at heart in all that we say and do." He cleared his throat.

"I've always known that," the perplexed young woman replied.

Why was Domingo acting so strangely? Manuela wondered. Her hand brushed impatiently at an imaginary stray curl on her cheek. It wasn't like him to avert his eyes when speaking to her. Her mind was like an airborne kite, dipping and diving but finding no resting place. She fixed questioning eyes on her grandfather's solemn face, hoping to find answers there.

"At your age, you must surely be thinking of marriage," Diego said.

The words seemed forced from somewhere deep inside Diego. At her age—what was he saying? he chided himself. She was still a child, only recently sixteen, still his darling girl. He watched the adored face and recalled its beloved features in a haze of swirling memories, running from when he had first held her as an infant at Carlos's and her christening, through holiday periods during her school days, on through the four years since she had pleaded for Carlos and her to leave school and live with him, up to this past year when he had watched the pretty girlish features turn into those of a beautiful young woman. He sensed he was torturing himself and sought to squelch such unproductive ruminations.

"Someday, of course, I hope to marry and have children," Manuela replied hesitantly and with noticeable accent on the first word. "I assure you that I have no such plans for now, Grandfather. First I must wait for the right man to come along, one I can love and who will love me."

Confused, she studied the two lean faces, both averted now. Why did they seem so fixed? What was the reason for this talk? Uncomfortably she shifted her weight on the chair.

"Sometimes it's best for marriages to be arranged, my dove," Diego began after he cleared his throat and tugged at an earlobe with a thumb and forefinger. He swung his gaze back to her face. "Domingo, upon his recent trip, was given a letter asking for your hand, and it's that letter we wish to speak to you about."

"Letter? From whom?" Manuela's brain searched for a name and face standing out among the few young men she had seen over the past year. She could come up with nothing. Her heart, like that of a bird sensing capture, raced with unfamiliar, agonizing fear. A wily alertness crept into her eyes.

"The man has long admired you," Domingo added, finally turning to give his niece his full attention. "He has honored you, as well as both Father and me, by seeking your hand in marriage. He's a true Spaniard with good background."

Diego hastened to add, "You'll recall our earlier conversations about the need for both Carlos and you to marry Spaniards. To chance your being cast forever into the class of Creoles, my dove, is unthinkable. You've been born into the rank of upper class and reared in it. After I'm gone, there'll be no one to guarantee your status unless you marry one coming over from Spain. A proper marriage is a must ... for all gently reared young women." A hand smoothed at his gray hair while his probing eyes held Manuela's.

"Who is it? Don't treat me like an imbecile! Tell me who it is," she insisted, aware of the truth of his words and impatient at his repeating something she had heard too often.

Yes, Manuela remembered that her social rank-

139

ing in Mexico would be affected by an improper marriage. However, such mundane matters had not played a major role in her dreams of being sought out by her Lover. Had not played a role at all, an inner voice reminded her. The romantic part of the sixteen-year-old young woman balled up into a potent, defensive weapon, ready for instant discharge.

"Don Gaspardo Anya, our governor." Diego's voice was flat, lifeless.

For a few seconds the only sound in the library was Manuela's harsh indrawn breath.

Fueled by that explosive pocket of revered, romantic dreams, invectives rushed from Manuela's lips: "Governor Anya! That horrid old man, half-dead from gout? That old man with the sour breath who revolts me by planting a kiss on my cheek each time he's around me?" She glowered at a startled Diego, then at a disbelieving Domingo, and started the process all over again. "Whatever are you two thinking of even to tell me of such a proposal? You must surely know how I despise—no, *loathe*—the governor." Her voice grew consistently louder. "I would rather think of bedding an Indian than that pudgy old man!"

Manuela saw both men's heads jerk at the last bold statement, saw them exchange horrified looks.

Before they could reply, she went on, "What am I that you would consider marrying me off to such a pitiful example of manhood? You both say you love me? Bah! You say it, but you don't show it. Is this the way you look after my 'best interests'?"

Manuela stood then and, with hands on sway-

ing hips, approached Diego where he sat behind the table, openly stunned. Leaning over to bring her face close to his, she threatened in the no-nonsense voice of a determined young woman, "Mark my words, Grandfather. I mean no disrespect toward you, but I'd rather die an old maid than enter into marriage with that old goat!"

The last word came out like one of blasphemy. As Manuela straightened up, she jerked her head aside to add a noisy, spitting sound. If the two needed to see total revulsion, she would show it to them, she exulted upon seeing the new waves of shock upon their faces. Anger sizzled in every vein. The fear of never realizing her dream of a powerful, romantic love attacked every cell in the manner of an earthquake. She trembled, felt shaken, felt she might crumble into a million pieces. The two kinsmen might love her, might think they acted from wisdom, but no one would choose her husband for her! She must await her Lover.

With growing amazement, Diego had observed the storm brewing in the black eyes glaring at him, had watched his cooing dove turn into a feminine hawk with barely concealed talons. If she had ever shown such a blatant display of temper in his presence, he couldn't recall it. He was more than a little awed at the tempest he had unwittingly stirred.

Where on God's earth had she seen the unlady-like, spitting gesture? Diego wondered. Surely not in his household. For just a moment he wondered if his allowing her the same freedoms granted her twin upon their return from the convent had been wise.

The befuddled grandfather reminded himself

141

that he had truly not known the depths of Manuela's feelings for the governor. As far as he could tell, she had always acted politely and discreetly when she had been around him, both at the *presidio* and at the governor's mansion in Monclova. He admitted privately that her lusty objections did indeed have possible grounds, and some almost-forgotten part of him admired her courage in voicing them. There were times when her tenacity and frankness reminded him of himself when he had been a youth and willing to die for his principles.

No longer young and idealistic, the commandant was, perhaps, too aware that Governor Gaspardo Anya was Domingo's and his immediate superior. He had been tempted from the very first to ignore the man's request or send a refusal without having told Manuela about it. However, his desire to see her wed to one born in Spain and his need to keep his son and himself in the good graces of the governor had won out.

Now, Diego felt nothing but disgust for himself. He tented his fingers again, noticing how wrinkled and frail looking they appeared. Grimly he acknowledged that it would take all the skill he could muster to work out what loomed as one of the greatest problems he had ever had to resolve.

"Manuela," Diego said, omitting the term "my dove," which he normally would have added. It did not apply at that moment. "I had no idea that you would have such strong feelings about this matter. Perhaps we should think on it and come up with some way to discourage Governor Anya's suit."

"Yes," added Domingo, his heart shrinking a

little when Manuela turned tempestuous eyes toward him. "That's a promise. We'll give the matter serious thought. We don't wish to upset you." His own shock and dismay at her fiery show of unhappiness was as great as his father's. "Most young women would be eager to become the wife of such a powerful man, and we had hoped that the news might please you."

Domino found that, even to him, his words sounded false when they spilled out into the room. He had the grace to grimace and shrug a shoulder at his clumsy handling of what had evolved into an even worse situation than he had anticipated. If only he had had an inkling of Manuela's true feelings about the governor. . . .

"Never will I be pleased to marry one not of my own choosing," Manuela pointed out with vehemence. Could her stormy eyes have created thunderbolts, they would have.

As soon as her final announcement richocheted around the emotion-charged room, Manuela turned to leave. Both men marked the determined, passionate look on her proud face.

"I promise you that your wishes will be honored, my dear," Diego said.

Her grandfather's quiet statement halted Manuela in her tracks, cooled her raging temper. She angled her head, openly doubting what she had heard. Her breathing settled down, and her knotted shoulders relaxed a degree. She turned to face the two men again, expecting that Diego had more to say.

"Domingo and I will not discuss this matter with anyone until we have had more time to consider what action to take." Diego's voice seemed fraught with a tightness threatening to strangle him. He cleared his throat and, despite the lack of relief, went on. "The final choice concerning your marriage should and will be yours."

Diego's efforts to conceal his troubled heart failed. His solemn face and constrained voice showed concern about how he might handle the upcoming task of telling his superior that Manuela would not become his wife. Had he ever before faced a political situation as delicate as the one facing him now? He knew well that it would take far more tact than he had heretofore been forced to exercise. His face blanched at the thought of Governor Anya's probable wrath ... and possible acts of retaliation.

Quelling personal fears and doubts for the moment, Diego added, "If anything happens to me before you are married, I charge Domingo, as your next guardian, with the responsibility of seeing that my promise is carried out." He rose. There was nothing more to say.

Then Domingo assured both his father and his niece, "I accept that charge. We'll work this out, Manuela. Trust us."

Humbled by Domingo's and Diego's promises, as well as by the terrible lines of anxiety transforming the older man's countenance, Manuela rushed to her grandfather's side and buried her face against his shoulder. His arms took her in.

After a long silence, she lifted her head to include Domingo in an encompassing, thoughtful look. The inner aftermath of quiet had set up disturbing new obstacles to consider and resolve. No matter that on the verbal level she had won. Inside, she recognized an entrapment fashioned from qualities intrinsic to her nature.

Her eyes both wise and sad with instant, unwanted knowledge, Manuela murmured contritely, "Thank you, Grandfather and Uncle, for understanding. I love you both more than you can know. Thank you."

Chapter Eight

That night, long after those in the commandant's *hacienda* had retired to private rooms for
sleep, Manuela murmured "good night" to Zorro
and latched the door to his cage. When she let
the cloth cover fall, she felt woefully alone. She
could hear the gentle strains of a guitar from
somewhere over in the *plaza* and felt the poign-
ancy of a particularly moving passage calling to
something deep inside her troubled heart. How
she longed to talk about her new problem with
Carlos. If only he would hurry back . . .

Manuela did some mental arithmetic. Having
departed a few days before the Frenchmen arrived two weeks ago, Carlos must be nearing the
presidio. He should already be at the last campsite he had told her his Indian companions and
he would make before ending the hunt. Having
camped last year with Eblo and him at the very
spot, she would have no trouble finding it.

A plan in mind, Manuela rummaged around for
Conchita's borrowed uniform. After pulling on
the black skirt and scoop-necked blouse, she
quickly plaited her hair into one long braid and
slipped into low-heeled shoes. She reasoned that
with adequate moonlight to travel by, she could
be at the campsite within two hours. Once he
heard her woes, Carlos would accompany her
back, and she could be safely in her bed long

before sunrise. Their two heads had always seemed better than one. Already her burden seemed lighter.

Counting on the unsettling meeting in the library to have both her uncle and grandfather ready to fall asleep early, Manuela eased down the stairway and across the patio without seeing or hearing anyone.

"What are you up to?" came a voice demanding an answer as soon as she stepped inside the darkened stable.

"Eblo!" Manuela exclaimed, pressing her hand to her thundering heart. "You frightened me." She looked toward the shadows, still not seeing him. "I thought you would be asleep."

Or mayhap visiting whoever had entertained him that night two weeks ago when she had come seeking Zorro, she added silently. A blurred image of Louis as he had looked in the shadowy stable tried to form, but she forced it down. Eblo moved then, but she would not have known it had she not been looking in his direction.

She peered until she could make out his solemn features in the dim moonlight filtering through the stable vents, then explained, "I must speak with Carlos, Eblo. I believe he and his party have reached the lower campsite by now. It's only a short ride away, and I plan to ride out to find him."

"He'll hunt there only a day or two before he'll be coming in. Surely you can wait till then to speak with him." No taller than she, Eblo was beside her then, his voice low but firm. "Can't you at least wait until tomorrow? If he's not back by then, I'll go with you the next morning to find him. You don't need to ride out tonight."

147

"Don't try to stop me," Manuela said imperiously. "My mind is made up." When she saw no change in his expression, she implored, "Please, Eblo, you can't know how important it is that I speak with him tonight. Tomorrow might be too late." Her voice was weighted with an urgency too genuine to be ignored.

"The commandant won't like learning of a night ride. It is a foolish act for you. I cannot permit it."

"If I told you that the futures of my grandfather and uncle are at stake and that I can't make such a heavy decision without at least discussing it with Carlos, would you think then such a ride was unwise?"

The true picture of what their superior could do to Diego and Domingo if they angered Governor Anya by allowing her to refuse his proposal had nagged at Manuela ever since Diego had assured her that she wouldn't have to marry a man she didn't choose. Since then, the problem had claimed her full attention.

Manuela had heard too much frank talk during her four years at the *presidio* not to understand how the Spanish conducted their affairs in Mexico. The governor could strip her grandfather and uncle of their positions and, perhaps, take back the land and costly gifts Diego had received over the years for his service and loyalty. Domingo made no secret of the fact that once his father stepped down as commandant, he wanted to take his place, a position for which Diego had been grooming him over the past few years. She had an idea the governor had no mercy in his heart. She doubted he even had a heart.

Unless the right actions were made, it was in

Governor Anya's power to destroy the two men she loved with such intensity. She knew that if he desired, he could manage to do so within a matter of days. Since her show of temper in the library, Manuela had discovered she could not give priority to her private dream of waiting for her Lover to appear. To contain the roilings of her heart and mind was torturous. Her need to talk over the anguishing possibilities with her twin consumed her.

"Please, Eblo," Manuela urged.

Eblo read a misery in the shadowed eyes such as he had never before seen there. It was unlike her to plead with anyone; that much he knew. Ordering, coercing, or haughty retreating were her usual methods. Without another word, he limped off to fetch Nightstar and a sturdy stock horse for himself and began throwing on their gear.

"No, not the sidesaddle," Manuela protested. "I can make much better time in the one I used before I had to change to that ridiculous thing." When he left without further talk to do her bidding, she decided she had been given back a degree of authority and added, "There's no need for you to go along with me."

The Indian was not so easily daunted. Making no reply, he continued to saddle the mounts.

"Did you hear—"

"If old Indian not go, young missy not go," he interrupted quietly, slipping into his old speech pattern and ignoring her shocked look at his high-handed statement.

Even in the half-light, Manuela saw the determination on his weathered visage. She held back her tongue.

Only the disturbed pigeons seemed aware that anything unusual was taking place that night. The two riders mounted, walking their horses a piece before giving them their heads. As Manuela had predicted, the late-rising moon lighted the path. The night air was cool and soothing to her face, and Nightstar's rocking gait calmed her.

Soon after passing the spot where the recent bird hunt had taken place, they entered the sparse forest marking the foothills. Just as she had squelched thoughts of Louis Saint-Denis earlier that evening upon hearing the plaintive music, Manuela did so again when memories of that first time they had talked tried to surface.

Due to the narrowness of the trail and the shadows' obliteration of their view up ahead, the riders slowed their climbing pace. The comforting thought that she would soon have the counsel of her twin lifted Manuela's spirits at each passing interval. Together they would find a way to prevent Governor Anya from seeking revenge upon Diego and Domingo when he learned of her refusal to marry him—unless he had been told already and had taken steps. She shivered.

"No campsite ahead," Eblo said, reining in and waiting for her to catch up. "Must have stayed high in mountains longer."

Manuela's hopes plummeted. "The last time you and I were along, Carlos stopped one night not too far up the mountain. He must have found the wildcats plentiful there and delayed leaving. We've made such good time. Surely we can reach there in a short while."

The impulsive young woman did not wait for the Indian's approval. At a slight pressure from her legs and a loosening on the reins, Nightstar shot ahead. He cantered beneath the trees, climbing with apparent ease to the open plateau that separated the foothills they had just traversed and the mountains looming ahead. Once there, away from the disconcerting trees and shadows, he took the freedom his mistress granted and plunged into a full gallop.

Left with no choice, Eblo followed. A man of lesser self-control would have at least muttered an oath at the negative turn of events. Eblo merely set his face in even grimmer lines and leaned forward over his horse to make sure he did not lose sight of the headstrong young woman.

An hour later, Manuela reined in the winded Nightstar and announced, "There's no one here." The moon was high in the sky now, and, even in the more densely forested, mountainous area, gave off a ready light.

"Where could they be?" she asked after they had dismounted to rest the horses and had led them to dip their noses to drink from the gurgling stream rushing downward over its rocky bed. "Guava and his brothers came along with Carlos. Would they have chosen another place to make camp?" Her face showed her frustration and weariness.

"It's late. We return now," was the short reply.

Eblo kept his head cocked to one side while they waited for the horses to drink. His seasoned eyes darted among the trees reaching down to the edge of the water while he appeared interested only in the actions of the animals. Upon first dismounting, he had checked the blackened rocks stacked to serve as a cooking place on previous hunts. They were warm. Indentations in the scanty soil on the edge of the stream told him that horses had watered there recently.

The call of a hawk owl came from behind them—too close behind them, Eblo realized, for their noisy approach would have sent the night bird scurrying to higher ground long before their arrival. He was relieved to see that Manuela appeared too involved with her inner thoughts to have registered the sound as being out of the ordinary. Even as he waited for the inevitable, he did not warn his charge, for fear she might innocently do something to endanger them further. Pretending not to have noticed anything unusual might allow them to leave as swiftly as they had arrived.

Willing that she do his bidding without question, Eblo said, "Come."

Ear-splitting shrieks and yells froze Manuela in her stance before she could lift a foot to her stirrup. Her long braid flipping, she jerked her head to stare in disbelief at Eblo as the old man limped to stand beside her.

"Keep quiet," he ordered in a whisper. "Quiet!" he hissed when she seemed about to move her mouth in reply.

At first Manuela hung onto the hope that the Indians on horseback rushing toward them might be those hunting with Carlos and that they were either misguided or were being led by Carlos to play a trick on Eblo and her. The prayerful wish died aborning.

Eight Indians were crowding around them and, judging by their fierce looks in the moonlight and their drawn spears, they were not in a playful mood. With horror, Manuela noted that dark red paint striped their faces and that they wore

152

only brief coverings over their loins. Their saddles seemed no more than rickety contrivances made from tree branches, then covered haphazardly with deer hides.

Eblo raised his hand and spoke in his own Pueblo. When the men merely laughed and responded in another tongue, he tried two more languages before he found one in which they could communicate. He pressed closer to Manuela's side, and she could feel the coldness of the knife blade he held concealed in the hand resting between them. Outwardly the old man appeared to be addressing the party with calm observations and explanations. His manner helped Manuela to control her wild fear. After that first disbelieving stare at the Indians, she had kept her eyes down and heeded Eblo's advice.

"They speak no Spanish," Eblo told her after another exchange with the Indians. They had not moved or put away their spears, but they seemed willing for the two to talk. "I told them you were intended of great Frenchman, that we got lost on the way to meet him. They say they'll not set us free until their chief gives permission. They will expect big reward if what I say is true."

When Manuela jerked up her chin and seemed ready to denounce his claim, the old Indian hissed, "Quiet. They hate Spanish soldiers. Never tell about your grandfather. Trust me." His eyes bored into hers, insisting that she obey him.

Manuela caught her breath. Eblo was frightened. She could read it in his eyes, even though his face seemed a mask of unconcern. He was not at all sure his explanation had satisfied their captors. He was lying to her, and she had no choice but to pretend to believe him.

"What will they do with us?" she whispered, her voice as uneven as her heartbeat. The decision to seek out Carlos now seemed horribly foolish; she should have paid attention to Eblo's warnings. All at once, she wished she had taken Louis into her confidence, maybe even asked him to come along.

Eblo never had a chance to answer. The Indians ordered them to mount and struck out on a narrow trail along the side of the mountain, Manuela's horse led by one man up near the front of the party and Eblo's by another farther back. Finding it difficult to hang on to Nightstar without holding the reins, Manuela clutched at the saddle horn and his mane for safety and balance. She found her control easier to maintain by concentrating on hanging on to the horse and locking up her disjointed thoughts about what lay ahead.

Manuela had never been higher than the campsite where they had been captured, and she was surprised at the increasingly cold air as they climbed toward the ridge. The Indians chose to travel at a fast clip, and the rushing wind soon had her chilled throughout. Biting at her lower lip, she clamped her teeth to hold down their clattering. It was hard to call up anything pleasant, but she did manage to be grateful for having often ridden straddle-legged, even bareback. The added thought of how she might have been faring had she been on a sidesaddle seemed to restore partial belief in her sanity.

The Indians did not slow their hurried pace until after sunrise. Having crossed a ridge and begun a descent by then, they stopped at a

154

stream to rest the horses and allow them to drink. Someone pushed Manuela into some bushes to relieve herself while her captors stood embarrassingly close by. Then a couple of grunting Indians led her to the water and motioned for her to drink. She stared at the peculiar way their hair was cut short above one ear and allowed to grow long over the other, the long side resting on a naked shoulder after being doubled up and tied with leather. The ones she was near seemed not much older than she.

Dizzy and weak from the grueling all-night ride, and still stiff from the cold, Manuela stumbled and would have fallen into the icy stream had not one of the young men grabbed her. Instinctively she yelled and slapped at the hand touching her, then deliberately set her teeth in the despised arm. No doubt surprised at her painful attack, the Indian recoiled and lost his footing, ending up in the water. Not until he jumped up and slapped her across the face with force enough to knock her down into the water did she feel the slightest remorse. Even through her pain, she decided the act far outshone the punishment.

Manuela brought a trembling hand up to her mouth, only slightly surprised to find blood upon it when she withdrew it. Her knees were smarting from her fall upon the jagged rocks, but she would not give the suddenly hooting Indians the satisfaction of seeing her pull up her full skirt, now wet and dirty, to examine the injuries. The Indian whose arm she had bitten stared at her with open hatred, darting occasional angry looks at his gesturing, boisterous companions. What were they laughing about?

she wondered as she regained her footing and splashed to the bank.

To busy her hands Manuela plucked leaves and twigs from her hair, trying with little success to re-plait the raveling ends of her long braid. She thought she could hear Eblo's voice in heated conversation nearby but dared not look. Figuring the less attention she drew to herself, the better, Manuela kept her eyes downcast until the one she had bitten grabbed her arm and led her back to Nightstar. He muttered what sounded like threats as he roughly hoisted her up into her saddle.

Manuela found that traveling at such a fast pace beneath a searing June sun was even more taxing than the trip of the previous night. Leaving the mountains behind, the Indians zigzagged across sandy dunes topped by clumps of low cactus unlike any she had ever seen. She surmised from the position of the sun that they had traveled north or northwest all day, although she was perplexed as to which direction the night journey had taken.

A few mesquites and low, round bushes helped to break the monotony of cacti and unending ripples of reddish brown sand, Manuela reflected with little appreciation. The inner sides of her legs were raw from where they had rubbed so long against leather, and the outer sides bore numerous cuts and gashes from the slapping limbs of low trees and underbrush on the mountain trails. Her head ached, both from the glaring sun and her swollen jaw, but she made no voiced complaints. Deep inside a more serious hurt assailed her with increasing persistence: Only her stubborn will had brought about this calamity both Eblo and she were enduring. All of it was her fault, and she had no earthly idea how to turn the situation around.

Manuela's suspicion that her life and that of Eblo might be at stake grew stronger after the third rest stop brought more cruel blows to her face. The Indian bearing her teethmarks in his arm motioned for her to drink from a filthy skin of water, and she spat in his face and refused. He showed open delight in taunting her and planting a new slap. While his companions watched and jeered, he added another blow.

When Manuela noticed that the repugnant water container looped around her tormentor's neck appeared to be the innards of some animal, a wave of nausea joined the pain of the humiliating slaps. Across the hazy horizon she searched for an answer but saw nothing other than a tempting mirage of low trees in the distance.

Once the group mounted again, red mist enveloped Manuela's mind, ebbing and waning until she lost all sense of time and place. Her semiconscious state allowed her to register that just before sunset her captors led her to what she had believed to be a mirage. There truly were low trees, a large clump of them, and she could smell a tantalizing freshness that could be coming only from running water.

Before she was rudely gestured down from her horse, Manuela took in her first close-up sight of an Indian camp. Covered with skins, the cone-shaped constructions, some large and some small, sat in haphazard fashion among the trees. Several blazing fires with fat clay pots nestled in their edges sent lazy trails of smoke meandering upward. Near the fires, women in short leather tunics stood or squatted in small groups while naked children tumbled in play nearby.

Manuela's knees buckled when her feet touched the ground, and she groped unsuccessfully for Nightstar to steady herself. She knew the Indian who reached to catch her was her tormentor, for the swollen, bloody marks from her teeth on the dark red arm stared up at her. It was the first time she had been close enough to set another brand, but her wish to do so faded into oblivion. Total blackness claimed her.

Chapter Nine

Only when gentle hands lifted Manuela's head and brought a cup of water to her parched lips did she regain partial consciousness. At first she had no recollection of where she was, no idea how long she had been lost to what went on around her. She almost called Conchita's name.

A peep through her lashes confirmed what nudged at her sluggish brain: She was indeed an Indian captive. The one offering her the welcome drink was a young woman with a round, flat face of the same coppery hue as those of her captors. Though inscrutable, the strange face lacked that air of ferociousness so visible in the painted ones of the men capturing and bringing Manuela and Eblo there.

"Where am I?" asked Manuela, wincing with pain from the motion of her jaw. "Where is Eblo?"

Quick, exploratory movements from her now-freed hands told her that her face was swollen. In the dim light coming from the open flap and the small, circular opening at the top, she could tell she was inside one of the conical houses, lying upon a cushioned mattress of an undefined material.

"Where is Eblo?" Manuela repeated. She realized then that her lips must be swollen also. Her voice did not sound right.

The Indian woman jumped back as though

159

startled and left the tent with an incoherent murmur. Manuela drifted back into near oblivion until she heard a masculine voice coming from what seemed far away.

Kneeling beside her were two men. She saw the woman standing behind them near the flap.

"Missy," came Eblo's familiar voice. "You're safe. You have been lost in darkness, but now you return before the sun rises. It is good omen."

"Where are we, Eblo? How long have we been here?" Manuela asked through puffy lips, deliberately ignoring the figure beside him. "What is going to happen to us?" She tried to move and sit up but found she could do no more than entertain the thought. Never had she felt such exhaustion.

"We are in camp alongside Rio Grande, far northwest of the *presidio*. A hunting party of young braves brought us here yesterday after forcing us to travel all night. You are in young chief's tepee." He leaned closer to peer at her distorted face.

"When can we go home?" The last word and all that it conjured up in her mind almost brought tears to her eyes, but she did not allow them to surface.

"Soon," whispered Elbo. "Sleep now." His leathered face seemed to exude compassion. He turned to say something to the Indian with him, and they left.

The next time Manuela was aware of the world came the following afternoon. She opened her eyes and stared at the strange framework of tall branches stuck into the ground in a circle and leaning together in the center. Animal skins covered the form smoothly to the apex of the cone.

At the top where the limbs met, there was a small hole through which she could see daylight. She remembered Eblo's words; she was in a tepee in an Indian village. With an effort she raised her head. The sooner she could maneuver, the sooner she could return home, she reasoned. With that fortifying thought, she struggled to sit up.

The young woman attending her earlier appeared from the shadowy recesses of the tepee and laid firm hands on her shoulders, pressing her back down against the mattress.

"Where is Eblo? I want Eblo to come," Manuela said in a forceful voice. She licked her swollen lips. "I want to go home."

The woman left and returned, not with Eblo but with gourds holding food and a steaming liquid. Seeing no utensil and realizing just how famished she was, Manuela accepted the larger bowl and sipped at its contents, trying not to imagine what they might be. To her surprise, the taste was quite good, though bland to one accustomed to red peppers used freely in seasoning. The small chunks of meat suggested wild game, not one of her favorite foods. The hot drink had slimy, greenish leaves in it that hinted at tea, but the repugnant, sharp odor and bitter taste caused her to return the gourd to the watchful Indian woman. Almost immediately she produced a container of water, which the spent young woman drained right away.

Worn out by the unaccustomed activity, Manuela lay back against what she realized was a soft deerhide covering other skins to form a thick mattress. Again she asked, "Where is Eblo?"

Until she sensed the presence of men in the

tepee, Manuela was unaware that she dozed. Warily she studied the two Indians accompanying Eblo.

A man at least as old as Eblo stood beside the slight, familiar figure. She noted that the stranger's gray hair was worn in the same strange way as that of her abductors. Beaded bands folded up the longer hair on the left side, yet it still fell below his broad shoulders. Colorful feathers stuck out at intervals down its length. On the right side, the hair barely reached the top of his ear. The ear, from the outer rim down to the lobe, held several perforations looped with thin copper circles graduating into ever-increasing size, the bottom one as large as her wrist. The old Indian's forbidding appearance set Manuela's heart pounding faster.

Her eyes darted to the younger Indian on the other side of Eblo. His hair, as black and coarse as the other's, was dressed in the same unique fashion, but across his forehead he wore a headband heavily embossed with silver beads, tiny shells, and turquoise stones. A single white feather, lengthy and tipped with red, decorated his long fall of hair. Only two hoops dangled from his exposed ear. Something metallic, shiny, and about the size of the end of her thumb, dangled from a cord around his neck. She suspected it to be a gold nugget such as she had seen soldiers wear for jewelry.

Eyes made darker and more feral by the dim light inside the tepee seemed to be piercing her own, and Manuela felt a decided tremor rush over her. If she could have sunk deeper into the mattress, she would have. Well-corded arms, at repose yet emanating unleashed power, lay crossed against his smooth coppery chest. When she dared look lower, she noticed that beneath his breechcloth, he wore clinging, fringed leather leggings, a covering doing little to conceal the muscular thighs. There was a stimulating but frightening sense of the untamed about him that she could not define, had no wish to think about.

"You are well?" asked Eblo, his voice jerking Manuela back into passable sanity. His eyes traversing her wan, swollen face, he knelt beside her.

Manuela nodded, gingerly touching her jaw. "When can we leave, Eblo?" Her words sounded half-strangled.

"Not until a reward is paid." At her stare of disbelief, he went on. "Mescaleros make demands from your intended."

"How would anyone know where we are?" Manuela asked, trying to sit up straighter and escape the scrutiny of the young Indian watching her with such a disturbing intensity. "And who is my 'intended'?" Her voice became sharp.

"Old chief is Mescatonika." Eblo gave a deferential nod to the gray-haired man standing beside him. "His son is called Mescatonaza." He looked up at the powerful figure still staring down at Manuela with the unsettling gaze.

"What have you told them about me?" She remembered Eblo's warning that she should not reveal her true identity. "Who are the Mescaleros? I've never heard of them."

"Mescaleros are of Apache family. Apaches live north of Rio Grande and follow buffalo across plains. Mescaleros live off the mescal plant, that big cactus we saw after we crossed the mountains. They follow where it grows." He seemed to

163

have forgotten her earlier question and spoke rapidly, as though he feared he might not be allowed to finish. "Years back, Spanish promised them they could stay in land of mescal, but soldiers from Santa Fe do not honor promise anymore. Soldiers keep pushing them back to our side of Rio Grande where mescal is dying out."

"Why were we kidnapped and brought here?"

"Young bucks acting wild. Made mistake."

"Mistake?" The word shot out from between her enlarged lips, and she fought not to glare at the strangers.

"They think Mescatonaza need new wife. First wife not give son. Want new blood." Eblo kept his eyes averted while imparting that information.

"Spanish blood?" Manuela asked, awed at the cunning irony of the Mescaleros' plan for revenge against those who were forcing them south of the Rio Grande. "Then that's why you told them I was promised to a Frenchman of great wealth?"

No matter what wild threat she had made to Diego and Domingo, Manuela's skin crawled at the thought of being forced into marriage with the Indian watching her. Better to be the plaything of old Anya than that savage, she thought with a shudder at either possibility.

"What do we do now? How long before they learn—"

"Patience, Missy. Soon someone will come." The old Indian seemed to believe what he was saying.

The young chief spoke to Eblo then, and Manuela thought she distinguished a phrase. The heavy beat of her heart seemed to lose a degree

164

of its foreboding.

Not believing her ears, Manuela whispered, "Did he mention Lieutenant Saint-Denis?"

Just her saying the name seemed to lend a much-welcomed normalcy to the bizarre situation. She realized then that thoughts of the Frenchman had ridden close to the surface of her mind during the entire ordeal. If Louis were here, she thought with unreasoning longing, he would know exactly what to do. Brushing at her hair with shaking hands, she darted a puzzled look at Eblo.

"Mescatonaza has wandered in Land of Tejas. He has heard of the fearless lieutenant." When her black eyes seemed intent on forcing him to continue, Eblo said hesitantly, "I told them you are intended of Saint-Denis." At her indrawn breath of protest and disbelief, he continued in a rush, "Your great beauty and spirit lead young chief to want you for his own, but he admires and fears Saint-Denis as he does no other white eyes. Keep thoughts inside; I beg you." His eyes did not toy with niceties; they ordered her to obey.

Raising her head haughtily, Manuela opened her mouth to denounce the entire plan and to demand that Eblo petition the old chief for her release on the grounds that she was the granddaughter of a Spanish commandant. When she felt the young chief's eyes washing over her with ever-increasing interest, she thought better of it and lay back against the mattress.

Something about the way the young Indian held his head made her suspect he might be understanding what was being said and that he waited to hear more. Despite what he must have told Eblo, did the imposing Indian understand

165

Spanish? How was it that the name of the French lieutenant seemed to create such apparent respect?

Manuela was relieved to see the old chief motion for the men to leave then, for fatigue had overcome her in one debilitating swoop. Troubled and frightened, she closed her eyes in a strange mood of gratitude for just being alive.

With a start, Manuela awoke. It was night. A faint smoky scent filled her nostrils. Had a guttural, animallike noise sounded nearby? She saw a star through the hole in the top of the tepee and realized she had been dreaming of San Juan Batista. With a shock she recalled that Louis Saint-Denis had been in her dream world, along with Diego, Domingo, and Carlos. What he was doing there, she had no idea. The dream was as elusive as the star overhead.

Maybe to let her thoughts wander would give her courage, Manuela reflected. She tried to visualize what must be happening back at the *presidio*. Surely search parties were already on their way to rescue her. Could Carlos and his party have witnessed the abduction and gone for help? But how could anyone track the erratic path the Mescaleros had taken? And how long would it have been before those at the *hacienda* learned she was missing?

Manuela's cheeks burned with shame at her willful disregard for others at the time of her departure. How foolish she had been to think that the greatest problem in the world was how to deal with Governor Anya's marriage proposal. She cast a wary eye about the dark tent, unable to spot her usual attendant. Cautiously she sat up and crawled on the carpet of animal skins toward the half-opened flap, only to sit back on her haunches with renewed fear.

Just outside sat a figure she recognized instantly. Mescatonaza sat cross-legged on the ground, his naked back partially turned toward the opening. The bright light of the moon almost directly overhead reflected the sheen of his copper skin and outlined his strong profile. The young chief seemed intent on watching a fire dying out across the way. If he were aware of her movements inside, he made no outward show of it.

On the far side of the open area Manuela could see what appeared to be a group of men sitting upon the ground. A strange sound, halfway suggestive of a dog baying at a full moon, came from that direction, soon followed by others just as alien. Laughter and raised voices floated on the evening breeze. They became too muffled to be distinguished above the suddenly persistent trills of a nearby night bird and the intermittent calls of tree frogs and crickets.

Returning to her mattress on stiff and sore legs, Manuela wondered if perhaps the presence of the young chief in front of the tepee was the only protection she had against an invasion by the obviously excited group across the way. She pressed her hands over her eyes to help hold back the tears of frustration threatening to wash away her resolve to maintain self-control.

Had tears helped her when as a small child she had begged to be allowed to leave the convent's dormitory and return to her home? she agonized. No. The nuns had scolded her and withheld her breakfast at those times, telling her that God never asked more of his children than they could endure. Tears, they said in pious voices, were a sign of one's weakness in accepting the burdens sent by the Lord.

The young Manuela had trained herself to hold back the salty release—at first to have her breakfast restored, then later to gain whatever prize was being refused. In time she gleaned a wisdom not explained by the sisters: While others might waste precious time and energy on crying, Manuela set her keen mind at work instantly on figuring out a logical way to gain whatever it was she desired. The weakness of others soon became one of her most effective strengths, though she preferred to refer to what she did as using charm.

But, the confused young woman reflected with complete honesty there inside the tepee, the present dilemma was unique. She had never before had to fear that her body might be used against her will or that her life might be forfeited if she refused to do as she was told. With gratitude, she realized she had not had to face again the one who had slapped her so cruelly. A feeling of nausea tugged at her, and she swallowed painfully. She became aware of the unpleasant smell and the discomfort of the soiled clothing she had worn ever since the night she had left—was that two days and two nights ago, or was it more?

All at once Manuela visualized her spotless dressing room with the copper bathtub back at the *presidio,* the stacks of neatly folded clean chemises, drawers, and stockings. The acrid animal odor of the skins upon which she lay overwhelmed her, and she tossed about restlessly. Somehow there must be a way to escape this alien world.

No matter how incredible a plan had appeared upon first examination, she lay through the night exploring each possibility. Each time she peered toward the entrance, she could see Mesca-tonaza sitting there like some watchdog. Or, she corrected upon seeing the feather in his hair outlined against the flickering fire, like some vulture. Close behind that thought came the question: Where was Louis at that very moment? Despising herself for allowing herself to think of him, she closed her eyes and prayed someone – anyone – would come soon.

The Indian woman was in the tepee when Manuela awoke the following morning after a dreamless sleep. After repeated gestures to herself and the pronouncing of her name with exaggerated syllables, Manuela gained a partial smile from the woman and a recognizable version of "Manuela."

Not until after the prisoner ate a goodly portion of the tough pone of bread proffered did the Indian make similar efforts to give her own name.

"Nomee?" asked Manuela after listening and watching the lips in the flat, round face form the name. When a pleased look flashed for a moment on the coppery visage, Manuela repeated it and pointed to the Indian. "Nomee."

The Indian motioned for her charge to follow, and Manuela stepped outside the tepee for the first time since her arrival. It was early, and there was little activity. She thought she saw a brief movement of the deerhide covering the entry of the adjacent tepee, but no one came out. Her skin prickled at the feeling that someone watched her intently from the shadowed tent.

Nomee motioned for her to follow and led the way past last night's camp fires, on through the main open area, past the roped corral of horses. The sandy soil muffled their steps in the early morning sunlight.

"Nomee," enthused Manuela when she spied their destination, only then understanding why the Indian carried such a large pile of garments over her arm. "How wonderful to be allowed to take a bath!"

Manuela's innate enthusiasm seemed rampant at that moment, and she smiled her gratitude at the confused woman. She had never before seen the Rio Grande, but she had heard so much about it that she was hardly surprised to see that it lay some distance below the sloping bank, its sluggish, rusty water suggesting great depth out in the middle.

With a cautious look around, Manuela allowed Nomee to help her remove the soiled black skirt and blouse. She waded out into the river. As soon as she reached a spot deep enough, she ducked beneath the surface and rubbed vigorously at her body and her hair. Having heard that Indians were not keen on submerging their bodies for cleansing purposes, she was surprised that she was allowed to bathe.

From where she knelt at the water's edge and washed Manuela's discarded clothing, Nomee watched with a steady eye. She made no move to join her ward or assist her. When Manuela completed her bath and arched to float on her back, she thought she glimpsed a look of surprise on the normally stoic face.

A blanket awaited Manuela when she emerged, and she reveled in its warmth, in her own cleanliness. All at once, such simple pleasures took on new meaning. She was alive and relatively unharmed. A sun was rising. Laughter, something she had thought lost forever, bubbled inside and she gave vent to it, again noticing Nomee's perplexed expression. Her swollen face and lips tried to protest being used in laughter.

"Nomee," Manuela called when the woman gathered up the clothing she had washed, "you don't know what you're missing. Why don't you go into the river?"

She gestured toward Nomee's brief tunic as though to remove it, then toward the water. Nomee shrank back as if horrified at the suggestion.

"Don't you like to swim?" Manuela made strokes in the air. "Like a fish?"

Manuela waggled one hand to suggest a darting fish. When Nomee continued staring, no longer even trying to hide her consternation, Manuela laughed again. Were all Mescaleros as devoid of a sense of humor as her solemn keeper?

The clothing Nomee gave Manuela to wear was much finer than that she herself wore. There was no shift or chemise to replace the one Nomee insisted on taking to wash, but the buttery soft deerhide of the tunic she slipped over Manuela's head felt almost as good. Better, Manuela decided when she recalled how unclean she had felt before the bath. A brief strip of the skin had been stitched into breeches too brief to show beneath the tunic. After donning them, she waited for another garment. Surely her legs were not to be left exposed from well above her knee!

Nomee made no additional offering other than low-cut moccasins. Manuela looked down at the intricate patterns of beads decorating the rounded neck of her tunic and saw that they matched those on the toes of the moccasins. She tugged at the short garment, noting the fringing across its bottom edges. No matter how much she pulled on it, it fell far short of covering her knees. Bemused, she wondered what those at the *presidio* would think of her appearance — especially the pale-eyed Frenchman.

Eyeing her own clothing spread out upon the rocks to dry, Manuela shrugged her shoulders in resignation and attempted to dry her hair with the blanket. Nomee then handed her a wide-toothed comb obviously made from bone. Choking back her first impulse to fling it onto the sand, she accepted the crude comb with a grim smile and attacked the snarls and tangles.

When Manuela had restored a semblance of order to the long mass of black hair, Nomee called her name and started off for the village over the crest of the bank. Manuela gave a soulful look at the river and followed, already regretting the loss of her brief freedom.

There was more activity among the tepees on their return trip. Manuela saw a number of children playing down at one end of the large open area and marveled at how much their happy voices sounded like those of any group of children caught up in their games. A few camp fires were showing life.

Several women moved about, keeping their heads down but casting curious glances at the equally curious young Spanish woman in their midst. One or two old men sat cross-legged before their tepees, smoking slender pipes and half-dozing in the warmth of the rising sun. She noticed again the strange, lopsided hairstyle the Mescalero men affected. Furtive glances told her the Indian she had bitten was nowhere in sight, and she let out a sigh of relief.

Just before they reached the tepee she occupied, Manuela saw a young Indian holding a shiny piece of metal and using some kind of instrument on his face. For a moment she was puzzled until she recalled having once surprised Eblo in the stables making similar motions. He had explained that he was plucking out his beard. Upon his announcement that Indians did not desire hair on their faces, Manuela had wondered aloud if they thought it strange that the Spanish men usually wore beards. Eblo had made no reply.

Out of nowhere an instant picture of a clean-shaven, angular face set with gray-blue eyes appeared. Her mind took the liberty of forming more images of the handsome Louis Saint-Denis. Her throat suddenly tight, Manuela shook her head to clear the taunting memories. As quickly as they had appeared, they receded.

Interested in the activities of the awakening village and fearful she might be shut up once again inside the tepee, Manuela was in no hurry and walked at a leisurely pace. From up head, Nomee turned back to call her name, making hurrying motions with her hands. It was then that Manuela saw what had prompted the woman's sudden concern.

The young chief, Mescatonaza, his arms crossed before him, stood before the tepee she had used, his bronzed shoulders and chest gleaming in the sunlight as he watched her approach. His only garment was a breechcloth. The beaded headband accentuated the piercing brown eyes, eyes that raked over her body boldly, bringing a touch of heat to her face. His look strayed then to her bare arms and legs, on to her firm breasts straining against the snugly fitting tunic.

Mescatonaza conferred with Nomee in a deep, compelling voice and, much to Manuela's consternation, the young woman left. Covertly she studied the face of the Mescalero, even while she gathered courage to ask to stay outside. When she made her silent plea, he shook his head and motioned her inside, following right behind.

"Why must I stay inside?" Manuela asked, vexed that she could not communicate with her captors. Like a free-roaming animal suddenly caged, she cast wary eyes about the darkened interior in search of a second exit, tossing her unbound hair in agitation when she located none.

Powerful hands reached to grip her forearms. Her black eyes snapping disapproval, Manuela shrank back from his touch as far as the grip allowed. Even when he removed the firm hold, some mysterious inner force leapt from his commanding eyes and held her immobile. From around his neck he removed a necklace of small silver beads and placed it around her own. With a tenderness she never would have suspected he possessed, he lifted the great fall of hair to allow the metal to touch her skin. His fingers lingered a moment longer against her soft neck, and she trembled all over, in much the same way as a young bird might upon realizing it lacked sufficient strength to flee a predator.

"No." Manuela shook her head vehemently, the necklace, still bearing the warmth of the giver, searing her flesh in a disturbing, insidious way.

174

"I don't want your jewelry." Hesitantly she lifted her hands to remove it, only to have them caught lightly but firmly in his. "Please," she implored, not sure what the offering signified but not wishing to encourage any kind of bond with the Indian looming above her. Her heart threatened to jump up into her throat.

Firm copper-toned hands held her small olive-tinged ones captive. Manuela glanced down at the prison his larger ones formed and shivered. Mescatonaza's touch induced a host of contradictory feelings—both alien yet familiar, both threatening yet reassuring in some way. She knew she could kick those bared shins, but she too vividly remembered the painful slaps she had suffered on the trail when she had tried to inflict pain on one larger than she. Her entire being became still, circumspect.

As though approving her latest tactic, Mescatonaza murmured something she could not understand and freed her hands. He then pulled a heavily beaded band from the belt holding up his breechcloth. Placing his hands on her shoulders, he turned her around. She could feel the heat of his body encompassing her; she could hear his breathing above all other sounds; she could smell his animallike virility. Her every pore screamed awareness of the near proximity of their half-naked bodies in the shadowy tepee. She fought to hang on to her decision to remain calm.

Jagged images of Louis and her in the stable that night made demands on her brain. Louis was the only other young man to place her in such a vulnerable position. Would the heavily breathing Indian chief retreat upon her request? Would he care that she was innocent? Had she ever before appreciated the honorable way Louis had treated her that night? Had he not been a gentleman –

Mescatonaza interrupted her wild thoughts. Deftly he placed the band taken from his belt across her forehead and tied it across the back of her head. She wanted to scream at the touch of his hands but clenched her teeth instead. While he twirled her slowly back to face him, she could feel the penetrating heat of his eyes. They wandered knowingly over the waist-length cloud of hair, then each curve and contour so blatantly revealed by the scanty costume. The fiery eyes apparently approved all that they saw. She thought she saw a flame flicker somewhere in their knowing depths just as they climbed to her mouth.

Manuela could not interpret the pained expression upon Mescatonaza's countenance or the slight tremor of his lips. With effort, she swallowed at the growing lump back in her throat, tried to ignore agonizing patches of gooseflesh popping up all over. She knew only that she felt she might be a hunter's catch turning on a spit over a blazing fire. Trembling, seeking escape from those compelling eyes, she lowered her eyelids. Her heartbeat roared in her ears, and her hands felt moist and clammy.

Uppermost in the shallow-breathing Manuela's whirling mind was the thought that a scream or a wrong movement might bring death sooner than it could bring relief.

Chapter Ten

The first morning after Manuela and Eblo set out in the night to find Carlos, the sun burst upon San Juan Batista with its usual June glory. Also as usual, the servants stirred first in the morning cool, making their regular contributions to the welfare of the residents in the *hacienda*.

Juanita fussed over the fire in the huge stove in the kitchen, urging it to hurry so as to boil the water for coffee, then sending the kitchen maids to prepare the table. She smothered a yawn behind her plump hand and tried to remember what time in the night she had heard Conchita enter their quarters. Medar's attentions to her daughter had not gone unnoticed.

By the time Juanita had the food prepared, Diego, Domingo, and Louis were sitting in the dining room sipping coffee and easing into the new day. Nothing suggested anything out of the ordinary had taken place on the previous night. The men always had the dining room to themselves, since both Doña Magdalena and Manuela took breakfast at a later hour.

Conchita was late going to her mistress's room that morning. Having dallied until quite late the night before in the moonlit *plaza* with Medar, she moved without her usual quickness. The sun was rather high when she stopped by the kitchen to eat a hasty breakfast before taking up coffee to

Manuela and beginning her duties. With steps as light as her mood, she climbed the stairs. She smothered a giggle triggered by a remembered joke Medar had whispered in her ear just before kissing her good night.

As soon as Conchita took in Manuela's empty room, the undisturbed bed, and the nightgown still lying where she had placed it the previous night, she let out a scream heard even in the kitchen wing. Within a few minutes the news had spread throughout the *presidio*.

"Gone? Where could she have gone?" Diego's words exploded all over the hysterical Conchita when she burst into his office with her announcement. "When did you last see her?" At her unintelligible reply, his eyes leapt to those of the two men in his office. "Where can she be?"

Domingo and Louis had jumped to their feet upon the maid's news. They now added their own garbled inquiries. Conchita could give them no further information, only more shrieks and tears, and they sent her back to the *hacienda*.

The men rushed to the stables to speak with Eblo and found he was also missing, as were Nightstar and Eblo's usual mount.

"Is this like your granddaughter to ride out in the night with Eblo?" Louis asked. It seemed obvious now that the two were together. At least she wasn't alone, he reflected.

"No," replied Diego, his tone sad. "She has always been high-spirited, but she has never gone off like this."

"I want to help search for her, but I feel I must ask if you have any idea why she would do such a thing?" Louis found himself holding his breath while awaiting an answer. When Diego only looked grayer and sadder, the Frenchman turned to Domingo for an answer. "Surely you must know if she was unduly troubled over something. Won't you tell me what you believe sent her running?"

Domingo sighed before replying. "We need all the levelheaded help we can get, Louis. If you're volunteering, you've a right to know what I think is troubling her." He exchanged looks with Diego before continuing. "Yesterday Father told her of a marriage proposal from an older man, one she finds repulsive."

Louis's already troubled heart pounded harder. The beautiful, spirited Manuela married to one not of her choosing? To one too old to fulfill the expectations in those starry eyes? Not that it was any of his business, but how could her grandfather—

Diego's somber voice intruded. "I promised Manuela that I would refuse the offer and not force her into marriage with anyone not of her choosing. I thought she believed me." His lean face seemed longer now that his mouth drooped. A restless hand worried at his moustache.

"Father," Domingo said, seeing the guilt and concern draining color from Diego's features, "she did believe you. I'll bet she decided to go out to meet Carlos and had no idea that she wouldn't find his party and him easily. Don't fret. We'll find her . . . unharmed."

"We must form search parties," Diego announced, motioning for a stable boy and asking him to fetch horses. The commandant eyed his "prisoner" thoughtfully and said, "Thank you, Louis, for offering your services. It will be best if you lead a party of your own. Perhaps toward the

179

high mountains to the north, since you're familiar with Indian languages and might run into some independent tribes." He turned to Domingo. "You know where Carlos might be hunting and you could head that way. You're probably right about her trying some foolhardy plan to join him and talk over everything that has taken place in his absence."

"That sounds the most likely explanation," agreed Domingo. He turned away to give orders to a private about who should be included in his party and what weapons he would take.

"Sir," Louis said quietly to Diego, "if you think she might have run into hostile Indians, I suggest taking along a horse and some goods for bargaining."

Louis's mind tripped over the horrible thought that she might really be a captive, but he had been in the world of Indians too long to forget caution and common sense. There was the possibility, remote as it might seem.

"The only logical explanation is that she left here with Eblo hoping to reach Carlos at his campsite," Diego remarked.

Diego seemed as intent on convincing himself as he was his listeners. Since when could one apply the term "logical" to the actions of the spirited Manuela? an inner voice scoffed. As she had shown yesterday, she entertained all kinds of secret thoughts and dreams, not one of which would fall into the category of what he might deem "logical."

Wishing he believed the words as stoutly as he spoke them, the commandant added, "Probably Domingo will have found them by noon and brought them back home before dark. We might be getting upset over nothing."

"I can take Medar and ride into any Indian camp, Diego," Louis said with conviction. He could not allow the older man to fall into false complacency. That Manuela and Eblo might have fallen into the hands of Indians deserved serious consideration. "I'll fare better not to have a number of men with me — or so I've found in the past. If you are short on supplies here at San Juan Batista, I have extras in my quarters that I'll take along."

"Your counsel is welcome," replied Diego, giving the young Frenchman a keen look. "And I must accept your offer of the goods since we are rather short at this time."

Diego looked away then, embarrassed to admit a shortcoming at his *presidio* — and one the sharp-eyed Louis must have already noted. A part of his mind registered what the Frenchman had innocently revealed. Those numerous packets he had seen unloaded from pack animals into Louis's quarters contained more than a fastidious officer's wardrobe. A piece of the puzzle concerning Louis's appearance at San Juan Batista fell into place. He had come to initiate some kind of trade with the Spanish. As quickly as the bizarre idea hit him, it frittered away. Manuela's safe return was all that mattered at the moment.

The able commandant reverted to doting grandfather, and he said, "I have no goods, but I do have a fine stallion you can take along, just in case . . ." His voice dwindled. The thought of revengeful Indians holding Manuela brought a hint of nausea.

Within an hour the three search parties had

left the *presidio*. Inside the church outside the walls, Father Dermoza and a number of women knelt in prayer for the safe return of the commandant's granddaughter. Later, in the small private chapel off the courtyard of the *hacienda*, Doña Magdalena and the household servants crowded before the altar with tears and supplications.

Diego put little faith in finding a trace of Manuela on the way to the capital of the sparsely populated province, but he thought a foray in that direction should be made. Marauding highwaymen had been known to rob and kidnap travelers with disturbing frequency. He waved a solemn farewell and led his group of soldiers toward Monclova to the south. He had already decided that if he had to travel all the way to the capital, he would speak with Governor Anya about the French intruders ... and about Manuela's desire to marry one of her own choosing.

Louis and Medar rode westward along with Domingo's party until it was time for the Frenchmen to leave the path to the central foothills and head north for the mountains. Domingo continued westward.

Leading a packhorse loaded with goods selected from those Louis had brought from Mobile, plus the spirited stallion from the Ramon stable, the two Frenchmen reached the foothills before dark and ran across traces of a recent trail. When they came to a spot alongside the river that showed signs of a recent camp, they stopped for the night and carefully explored the area.

"Not only the signs of a recent large fire, but

182

the damaged underbrush makes me think a goodly number stopped here," reported Louis when he returned to where Medar fed twigs to a hesitant blaze. "Several large rocks have been turned over in the edge of the stream since the last rain."

The troubled gray eyes watched the flames lick hungrily at Medar's offerings. What kinds of hardships was Manuela having to endure? If anyone dared harm her . . .

"Medar," he said, a noticeable fierceness in the deep voice, "we have a hell of a task awaiting us if Indians really have taken Manuela and Eblo. I've spent some time visiting with Eblo in the stables and learned that he has stayed by the commandant's side ever since a war with the Pueblos some twenty years ago. He seems more Spanish than Indian now, and I doubt he'd be much help with his own people."

"Which tribe would be foolish enough to incur the wrath of the commandant?" Medar asked, as aware as Louis of the seriousness of their search.

He had watched the pain grow on the face of his employer and friend ever since they had left the *presidio*. When Louis confided what seemed to have upset Manuela enough to cause her to ride off in the night, Medar had realized that Louis's concern went much deeper than that of one in the throes of an infatuation. How much deeper, he had not yet determined, and he felt sure that neither had Louis.

"Hard to tell what Indians think when temptation rears up in front of them." A vision of the beauteous Manuela ripped at the calm he had fabricated to blanket his fears. "You know I've not been south of the Rio Grande before, and I've

183

only hearsay to go on about which tribes frequent this area."

Deep in thought, Louis squatted in Indian fashion, his well-worn leather shirt, long pants, and moccasins giving him the look of a woodsman rather than a French gentleman. The fur trappers in Louisiana, the *coureurs de bois,* had taught him how well such garb lent itself to long days and nights in the wilderness. A leather thong tied his long brown hair back upon his neck. His pale eyes flashed angrily in the flickering flames of the camp fire.

"We must find Manuela, Medar!" The words burst out with the force of an oath.

"We will, my friend. I've not seen you fail at anything yet."

Convinced the fire was on its own, the wiry, capable Medar set about preparing their meal from the provisions given by the army cooks, more than a little disturbed at the way Louis continued to stare into the flames and brood.

Long after the fire had died down, Louis lay upon his blanket and stared up through the trees. Tantalizing memories of flashing black eyes, full red lips, and shining hair filled his thoughts. Little French phrases Manuela had uttered in her charming way, musical spurts of laughter, the melody she had sung only yesterday in the library — all echoed in his ears. The fragrance of roses, which always seemed to accompany her, was as real to his nostrils as the current smells of the forest and the curling wood smoke.

The rough texture of his blanket only served to remind him of the velvety touch of her hand that time he had first met the sloe-eyed beauty and had brought it up to his lips. He could not forget the way her body had felt against his later that night in the stable, or the feel of her fiery lips beneath his. . . . Manuela. Within the two weeks he had known her, she seemed to have become as much a part of him as his breathing in and breathing out.

Louis tried to see beyond the stars overhead, to plead with whatever saint might be receptive to guide him to her before it was too late. Was God on his side? An agony such as he had never known squeezed at his heart. Was it because he recognized that Manuela might be more than a tempting piece of forbidden fruit? He put away the troubling thought.

Several false starts delayed them the next morning, but by midday Louis felt they were on the right track. He had spotted a dim trail leading up to the ridge of the mountains and, trying to place himself inside an Indian's mind, decided such a route would be logical if one were trying to camouflage his path. Grimly he led the way, ever aware that even as intent as the Indians must have been on deceiving any would-be followers, he was more so in his determination to find them and see if they held captive a black-haired beauty and her companion.

Fearful that he would lose sight of the tenuous trail if they traveled after nightfall, Louis pulled up beside two enormous boulders and conferred with Medar. They would have to stop for the second night high on the mountainside without benefit of a water supply.

Without knowing why, Louis sensed that they were on their way toward finding Manuela, and his heart gladdened. At the first light of morning, they would once more climb toward the summit and hope that what they sought would be within sight – an Indian village or at least a smoldering camp fire.

Chapter Eleven

In the Mescalero village beside the Rio Grande, Manuela was standing transfixed before Mescatonaza after receiving his unwanted necklace and headband when a shadow appeared at the flap of the tent. A harsh phrase jerked the young chief to attention. The compelling eyes released their hold on the frightened young woman.

Mescatonaza moved away and turned to stare boldly at his father as he entered the tepee. Following the old chief, Eblo limped inside.

"Eblo," murmured Manuela, her voice trembling.

Though Mescatonaza had not touched her since tying the beaded headband around her forehead, she experienced a sense of deliverance when he stepped back from her. To her relief, the mysterious force seeming to surround her had dissipated. A giddiness claimed her, and she wondered if it might not have come from her boundless gratitude for the interruption. Never had Eblo's weathered old face looked as good.

Eblo carefully eyed the granddaughter of the man he so revered before speaking to her. "Today you wear the skins of a princess. What have they done to you?"

"They've done nothing but let me bathe. I didn't know the clothing was for a princess. I'm wearing it only because mine is being washed," she replied, self-conscious about her exposed legs. "Are you being treated well, Eblo?" She realized she had been too groggy earlier to ask about his welfare.

"Horses and Eblo fine." He cut his eyes toward the young chief before asking, "Are they treating you well?"

"I've not been harmed," she assured him, only too aware of the tenuous situation at the time of the older Indians' appearance. What would have happened had they not arrived when they did? Again she felt the weight and warmth of the silver beads around her neck. They might as well be some kind of leash, she agonized. "Will they talk with you about our leaving for home?"

"Not until seven moons have passed."

Manuela searched his face, then dared to look into those of the Mescalero chiefs. No messages anywhere. Her stomach felt hollow. No signs that any thoughts churned behind those impassive eyes. Their very cleverness at concealing the workings of their minds added to her fears.

"Be true to self," Eblo said in that low, commanding way he had exercised at earlier visits. "All will get rewards." His eyes bored into hers. His voice dropped even lower. "Do not chew leaves."

As if he knew what Eblo was saying, Mescatonaza touched his arm then and evidently ordered the conversation ended, for the three men turned and left her alone. With a long, shuddering sigh, she sank upon the mattress and covered her face with her hands. Why did Eblo think she might chew leaves? Did he think she might seek out poison so as to kill herself? Surely he knew

188

her better than that. How long could she keep up the mask of courage when on the inside she quaked like a coward?

Nomee came with a gourd of the same hot liquid offered at each meal. Manuela shuddered at the peculiar smell but tried to take a few sips, repulsed by the muddy green color and the slimy leaves at the bottom. A sharp image of the tea served at the *presidio* flashed before her and, desiring to hold only a solid porcelain cup of fragrant liquid, she threw the crude container with its awful brew out the open flap.

"Don't bring anymore of that vile tea, Nomee," Manuela snapped when the Indian woman turned shocked eyes her way. "I may be a prisoner, but I don't have to drink or eat what you bring."

Watching Nomee scramble outside to retrieve the container, Manuela reflected that even though the Indian had not understood the words, she had gotten the message. She moved to stand in the entry, surprised to find Nomee gone and no one guarding it. She stepped out into the sunlight and looked around the camp. Across the way she saw a group of women squatting in a circle and started over to see what they were doing. She made it past the third tepee before an Indian appeared and stopped her with a steely grip on her arm.

"Stop it," Manuela ordered, twisting to see who was jerking her into the shadows.

Her heart hammered in protest. It was the Indian from the trail, the one whose arm she had bitten! Her free hand went to protect her face and the bruises still sore from where he had slapped her. She sucked in a breath when she

189

saw a snarl curling his lips. Beady eyes held pinpoints of what seemed pured hatred. When she struggled, he jerked her arm behind her and slammed her body forward against his, holding her against his near-nakedness and laughing in a way both threatening and gloating.

"Leave me alone," she hissed, lifting her free hand to strike him. He merely held her more tightly and caught the hand in midair as though it were no more than an airborne leaf, muttering guttural words obviously loaded with venom.

A second voice joined in then and Manuela turned her head to see Mescatonaza facing her captor, unintelligible words spewing from his lips. She felt herself freed so quickly that she stumbled against the young chief, catching onto his muscular arm to keep from falling. Warily she watched as the two men continued to make a heated exchange, relaxing only after the angry warrior had stalked off.

"Thank you, Mescatonaza," she murmured, rubbing at her shoulder and arm and moving away from him. When he pointed with meaning toward the tepee she had just left, she walked toward it without protest.

Either Mescatonaza or Nomee stayed near Manuela the rest of the day as she half-dozed on the mattress of animal skins. Just before sunset she moved to sit before the opening, watching the women build up the smoldering fires across the open area. Earlier she had heard the sounds of horses entering the camp.

At first she had dared to believe rescuers had arrived, and, for no known reason, her thoughts centered on Louis, but she gleaned no support from the carrying sounds. It seemed clear that what she had heard was the return of a group of Indians she had seen leaving the village earlier that morning.

Nearby Nomee drove stakes into the ground around a small fire and stretched a thick square of animal hide over them. She poured water into the sagging middle and added small limbs to the flames. When the water sent up steam, Manuela saw her drop in what seemed to be little round stones. Puzzled as to what Nomee was doing, she did not figure it out until the young woman returned with hunks of fish and added them to the bubbling water. Their evening meal was evidently being cooked from the heat of the stones in the water. With interest Manuela saw her take what looked like a small potato, or some other kind of root vegetable, and slice it before putting it alongside the fish. The aroma soon had her mouth watering.

Across the way Manuela could see the warriors and hunters gathering around the large fire where she had seen them in the darkness on the previous night when she had awakened. From packets tied at their waists, they took small portions of some substance and put it into their mouths, chewing vigorously for a few moments. Then they seemed to settle the material in the sides of their mouths and move their jaws in the way of cows chewing their cuds. She found the entire process strange and disconcerting.

Even more puzzling were the actions of the men after they had been gathered for an hour and the sun had set. Some rose and howled like animals, setting off gales of laughter among the others. From where she watched in secret, Manuela felt repulsion join her growing uneasiness.

She stared as a couple of Indians hopped up and performed frenzied dances of no set pattern. Another let out a high-pitched yell and circled their fire with increasing speed until the shocked young woman thought he would surely fall into the flares if he did not slow down. The settling darkness cut off most of her view, but she could still see their exotic movements when they moved close to their fire. She shivered from an unnamed fear. Although she had easily spotted her enemy from the trail, she did not see the young chief Mescatonaza in the group.

"Thank you, Nomee," Manuela said when the Indian brought her food.

Gingerly she looked into the vessel and back at Nomee. Was she to eat it with her fingers? She made motions to indicate her needs, but Nomee seemed not to understand and left to dish up additional portions and carry them into the neighboring tepee, the one Manuela had decided must be Mescatonaza's. Was Nomee his wife?

Between mouthfuls of food, Manuela continued to gaze across the way toward the gathering of young men. She could see the forms of women as they carried food to them, and for a brief time their noisy activity slowed. By the time she had eaten as much of the bland fish and crisp vegetable as she could hold, they had again become active.

A drumbeat sounded across the way, faintly at first, and then with maddening rhythm. A number of men rose and formed a circle around the fire, their voices chanting in an alien cadence, their coppery bodies shining in the firelight as though greased. At each increasing decibel of their chants, Manuela sensed a corresponding

192

rise of the feeling of evil permeating her soul. If she could ever get back to her grandfather's *hacienda,* she vowed never again to chafe about the demands of society.

Not bothering to wonder why such inane thoughts washed over her, Manuela gave in to them. She wondered if she would ever get the chance to speak the French that Louis had been so patiently teaching her. The image of the Frenchman as tutor evolved into one of Louis as charming dinner guest, then into the one who had first kissed her and stirred up all manner of hidden passion. And she could not forget the tenderness with which he had removed the splinter from her foot.

Oh, Louis, a distraught little voice deep inside the young Spanish woman cried, *I need your help.* She glanced at her bare legs, became aware of the hardness of the ground upon which she sat, and dared to wonder what her fate would be.

A masculine form loomed at the tepee's flap, and Manuela caught her breath in fear, unable to identify him until he spoke.

"Are you well this night?" Eblo asked. For the first time he had come alone.

"Eblo," she said with relief. "I wondered if I was going to see you again today." She stood and welcomed the old man inside.

"Did Zaaro harm you?" When she looked puzzled, he went on. "The warrior from the trail who tried to take you this morning — he is Zaaro."

"No harm done," Manuela replied. "I wasn't aware that he was trying to take me away. Mescatonaza saved me. Why would this Zaaro try to harm me again? He slapped me hard enough on the trail." Her jaw smarted as she recalled his

193

blows, and her pulse raced at the unsettling news that the Indian might wish her even more harm.

"For a woman to fight a man in front of his friends is forbidden, but for one to bite him and draw blood is a declaration of a feud. He is set on avenging himself by bringing greater shame to you."

"Mescatonaza won't allow it, will he?" She quivered with renewed fear.

" 'Tonaza may not always be near to rescue you from one as bent on revenge as Zaaro," Eblo pointed out, glancing across the way at the boisterous group. "I've learned that Zaaro comes from a tribe north of the river, and that he's a troublemaker. It was his idea to kidnap us."

Figuring that Eblo's visit might be cut short at any moment, Manuela was ready to drop the subject of Zaaro. "Where do they make you stay?" she asked.

"Beside the corral with the horses."

"Have you food?"

"Yes, if you call boiled mescal root food." His voice indicated food was the least of his concerns.

"Mescal root? The cactus?" Manuela asked, realizing when he nodded that what she had deemed a vegetable in the stew had been mescal. "Then they really are called Mescaleros because of their liking for the mescal plant," she mused. She wanted to talk about anything except her worries; it was good just to be able to speak with someone.

"Mescaleros use every part of the cactus. They dry the roots and pound them into flour and make a kind of bread. They take the leaves and braid them into ropes to use for handling horses

194

and to weave baskets and litter carriers." In the reflected light from Nomee's fire outside the entry, he studied her face. "Have you drunk any of their mescal tea?"

"Is that what that is?" Manuela asked with a half-laugh. "I tried to drink some that first night but I gagged." When he appeared amused, she went on. "Today I threw out the gourd, tea and all."

"Good."

"Why? Is it as poisonous as it smells?"

"Not poison to kill the body; poison to the spirit."

"How can it be poison to the spirit, Eblo?" He had always seemed so wise and amenable to Spanish customs. Was he reverting to his Indian ways?

"When chewed or brewed and drunk, the mescal leaves lead the spirit to wild ways, ways not pleasing to the gods, especially to the God we worship back at the *presidio*." Peering at her disbelieving eyes, he went on in a near whisper. "Have you not heard and seen the young bucks across the way?"

Wrapping her arms around herself in horror as what he said penetrated her mind, Manuela whispered back, "Yes, I've been watching them since before sunset. Are mescal leaves what they take from their pouches?" She recalled the way they had popped the substance into their mouths and then sat around chewing. "Are they drunk, like from too much wine? Is that why they have been acting so strange?"

"It's worse than drunk, Missy, much worse. It's—"

Like a sudden clap of thunder, a deep voice

195

from the open flap hurled what sounded to Manuela like warning words, preventing Eblo from finishing his sentence. Mescatonaza had ducked beneath the flap and now stood inside. Eblo rose and replied briefly to the young chief before bidding Manuela good night and leaving as unobtrusively as he had appeared.

The silence in the tepee was tense as Manuela made out the Indian's features in the dim light. Was he too under the influence of mescal leaves? She inched backward away from him, thinking she could not bear it if he touched her. The eerie sounds from the group around the large camp fire seemed to grow louder, more ominous.

When she could retreat no father, Manuela stood staring with as much hauteur as she could muster. She hoped he noticed that she had removed the silver necklace he had placed around her neck earlier that day. If she could have reached it where it lay near the mattress, she would have flung it at him. The handsome face of Louis Saint-Denis flashed into clear focus then, and she felt strengthened. If only he . . .

Mescatonaza's presence cut off her thoughts. Facing in her direction, but with his features blotted from the darkness behind him, Mescatonaza stood with arms folded. It seemed a mountain of time eked past before he whirled about and left. Suddenly spent, Manuela dropped to the mattress of animal hides and closed her eyes, praying for rescue, praying for sleep.

Sleep finally gentled her mind. She dreamed of days of freedom, days in which she had swum in the lake, walked in the sunshine, laughed with her family . . . and the French lieutenant. The

196

appearance of Louis in her dream surprised her. She moved and flung out an arm in careless abandon, only to awaken with pounding heart. She had touched a warm body.

Manuela bolted upright, a scream forming in her throat. A big, heavy hand captured her mouth while the other pinned her arms and forced her back down to the mattress. She could feel strong limbs and bulging muscles and knew it was a man nearly naked. Zaaro! Zaaro must have slipped past whoever was supposed to be guarding her. She realized that Nomee's fire outside the tepee had burned out. The only light came from the overhead moon and the faraway flickers from the fire where the young Indian men had gathered.

Manuela writhed and flailed her bare legs, but a more powerful one fell like a log across them, imprisoning her completely. Her eyes searched desperately in the darkness. His face was so near she could hear the ragged rhythm of his breathing, could feel the insidious brush of air against her skin. Everything inside her quaked. After a pretense of giving in, of lying motionless, Manuela tried to roll from beneath the man. She managed to catch him off guard enough to end up half on top of him, yet still his captive.

He spoke then but the only word she could understand was her name. "Manuela" came out distorted but recognizable. The voice was deep and surprisingly gentle. Becoming more accustomed to the darkness, she could see him shake his head. For some unexplained reason, she again slowed her futile struggles and waited, acutely aware that her skimpily clad body lay pinioned atop his, that one heavy leg held hers to his, that her breasts lay crushed against his bare chest.

The crazy thought that she had once before been entrapped in a similar way zigzagged across Manuela's brain. But Louis Saint-Denis had been no Indian savage, she reminded herself. Her heart seemed ready to burst from within, and she realized the loud, erratic breathing was her own. Whatever the Indian had in mind to do to her, she would fare better to conserve her strength.

"Mescatonaza. 'Tonaza," her captor whispered, still shaking his head as though scolding a child. Tentatively he loosened the hand across her mouth, again murmuring, "Manuela."

A stray beam of moonlight pierced the opening at the top of the tepee then, and Manuela saw his face, saw it was Mescatonaza and not Zaaro. Her protector was beside her, not her enemy, she consoled herself. In a flash, her brain denied such a title. The young chief was also her enemy. She let out a frustrated sigh at her confused mental state.

Giving no thought to why the Indian chief had chosen to appear where she lay sleeping and then subdue her when she awoke, Manuela released part of the crippling tension and gave in to an overwhelming sense of relief. Friend or foe, at least Mescatonaza had not slapped her. As if a truce had been reached, he freed her mouth and hands.

"Why, Mescatonaza?" Manuela whispered, her voice hoarse and still strained from fright. "Why would you come where I was sleeping?" The trust shining in her eyes was lost in the darkness, but not that riding in her voice.

" 'Tonaza. Manuela," were his only words. He

198

pointed at himself, then at her. His hand moved to smooth her tousled hair back from her face and seemed to get lost in the silky mass. For just a moment, she felt as much a prisoner as when he had first forced her down on the mattress.

Strange sensations coursed through Manuela's veins along with her racing pulse. She sat up quickly and pulled at the brief tunic where it lay bunched up around her hips, embarrassed at the intimacy their bodies had shared, frightened all over again. When he made no move to stop her, she peered at him where he lay watching her.

" 'Tonaza must go," she said, adopting the shortened form of his name as he apparently wished her to. Fright made her voice barely manageable.

In answer, the Indian sat up and opened a pouch fastened to his breechcloth. In a placating tone, he spoke to her while removing something from it and offering a substance to her on the palm of his hand. When Manuela shrank back, he brought some of the material up to his own mouth, then proffered it to her again.

"No," Manuela declared. "No, I will not chew your filthy mescal leaves. Get out of here." Her voice was no longer low or hard to control. She had been wrong. He did mean her harm. Her mind had been playing cruel tricks on her. "Get out right now or I'll scream for Eblo. I'll scream till the entire village wakes up." She stood up and backed away from him.

Mescatonaza rose then and started for the opening. She could see his near-nakedness silhouetted against the dying camp fire across the way. She chose to ignore the defeated angle of the massive shoulders, just as she ignored the hand reaching toward her in apparent supplication. It seemed to the terrified young woman that he stood like that for a long while before he finally left.

Manuela wondered if her heart would ever resume its normal beat. She glanced up through the opening in the tepee as she paced its confining circle and sent all the prayers she had ever heard zinging upward. What was happening to her? Where was that world she had thought she despised? She longed to sample its joys again. Would someone rescue her before she was lost forever to the unsettling world of the Mescaleros?

As soon as the word "someone" formed, Manuela altered it to "Louis." Would Louis be coming to save her? The thought of seeing his handsome face and hearing his deep voice brought an agonizing lump to her throat and scalding tears to her eyes.

It was then that she realized that each time she had envisioned her rescuer, it was the Frenchman she thought of, not her brother, her uncle, or her grandfather. Or even her dream Lover. A hand flew to her mouth. Whatever did that mean?

Chapter Twelve

Louis and Medar rose with the sun the morning after their night on the mountainside. By noon they were following the tenuous trail across the sand dotted with mesquite and cacti.

"We must be heading toward the Rio Grande," Louis remarked when Medar rode up beside him. "There seems to be little game this side of the mountains but lots of the cactus called mescal."

"So?" Medar asked, wondering where Louis's thoughts were leading. For quite some time, they had been seeing the small cacti and its rounded stems covered with numerous jointed tubercles.

"So I'm thinking that the Indians we're tracking are Mescaleros, a branch of Apaches fond of mescal."

"Then why would they be in the mountains, and why would they be foolish enough to kidnap someone from a Spanish *presidio?*"

"For one thing," Louis pointed out, "they might not have known Manuela and Eblo came from San Juan Batista. For another, they chew mescal leaves that cause hallucinations, so they might not recall what they do from day to day. I've heard they actually believe they're reincarnated animals while they're under the influence of the cactus leaves."

"They're likely to be irrational, then?" Medar asked, his keen interest in medicine and healing whetting his interest. "I've heard of drugs that can bend a man's mind, but I can't conceive of anyone's choosing to take such a concoction." Both were silent for a while. "How is it we've not run into any Mescaleros before?"

"Probably because we've not been in desert areas where the cactus grows in great numbers. I heard from an old trapper that at one time there were several tribes on the other side of the Rio Grande but that the Spaniards in Santa Fe kept chasing them farther south after they had the Pueblo uprising some time back. Seems the Mescaleros can get so juiced up on mescal when they go into battle that they're hard to defeat—and impossible to parley with."

Louis's jaw set in a grim line after he spoke, and he withdrew into silence. The thought that Mescaleros might be holding Manuela and forcing their insidious habits on her lashed at his sense of outrage. What was building inside him as he sought to find the commandant's granddaughter? Was what spurred him on more than what he had previously termed his feelings for her—a mere fascination for a beautiful young charmer? He did not care for the direction of his musings.

The sun had reached the meridian when the Frenchmen spied an Indian camp in the distance. Their plans already made, Medar and he paused behind a large clump of cactus to carry them out.

After checking the goods on the packhorse and rubbing down the stallion brought from the Ramon stables, they remounted their horses and rode onward. Louis now wore the finery that he had learned over the past eight years would impress Indians and intimidate them. With amusement he glanced at the well-muscled calves filling the white stockings below tight knee breeches.

Louis summoned a smile at the thought of the name he had heard many Indians used when referring to him: "The one with the handsome leg." He had seen more than one chief make two somewhat parallel lines in the dirt, one curved outward to simulate a bulging calf, and then point to Louis, signifying that such was the Frenchman's identifying mark among Indians. If the red-skinned men, who generally had lanky calves, chose to set great store by the way his heavily muscled legs appeared and suspect he might possess uncommon strength, then why not take advantage of it? He had learned to garner any and all aid coming his way and be grateful.

Manuela had willingly stayed inside the tepee all that third day, dozing off and on. After her encounter with Mescatonaza the night before, she had been unable to close her eyes until after daybreak when Nomee took up her vigil. The afternoon sun warmed her prison, and for the first time she understood why the Indian women wore such short tunics. The heat was stifling.

With little interest, Manuela sat up that afternoon and combed her hair with the excuse for a comb Nomee had given her, then braided it to get it off her neck. She had just finished the task when she heard a commotion in the camp. Wondering if the nightly party was starting early, she lay back on the mattress, trying to figure out

203

if the absence all day of 'Tonaza and Eblo was a good sign or a bad one.

Excited calls and the sound of horses approaching roused Manuela. From the noise, she figured all the children and most of the Indians in the camp must be converging upon her tepee—or on Mescatonaza's or his father's close by. She scrambled to her knees and inched over to the flap, which had remained closed all day, sitting back upon her legs in shock at what she saw through the crack. Had her wishful prayers been answered?

A smile upon his handsome face, Louis Saint-Denis, in elegant dress and with carefully curled hair, sat astride Diablo as he talked with the braves gesturing toward the tent of their chief. Beside him Medar rode, leading a packhorse and a prancing stallion that she recognized as one from her grandfather's stables. Nomee backed to block the entry to her tepee, or she would have dashed out with wild cries. Her rescuer had arrived!

Instinct warned Manuela to rein in her tongue, though, and she waited to see what would happen when Mescatonika and Mescatonaza came from within their tepees. Her heartbeat thudded and thundered. Both hands went to her mouth to hold it silent when she recognized Eblo standing at ease between the two Frenchmen. Tears of thanksgiving tracked down her cheeks.

Louis, with a knowing glance toward the tepee with the woman guarding its entry, dismounted and called out to the chiefs. He used a version of Apache that he had found upon entering camp was understood. Eblo had rushed to meet him, imparting welcome information about Manuela's well-being on the way across the camp. The Frenchman's spirits swelled all out of proportion to the simple facts he had learned. Suddenly he felt as tall and strong as any two Indians put together. His chest expanded, as did his smile.

From her peephole, Manuela watched Louis greet both Mescatonika and Mescatonaza with a flourish of his plumed hat and with words sounding like their language. What he was saying she could not imagine, but hearing his voice was working all kinds of magic inside. The chiefs seemed awed and kept eyeing him and his elegant clothing, even while responding to his speech. Small wonder! she exulted. For where was there such a handsome, dashing young man as Louis Saint-Denis at that moment? The sight of him in the afternoon light quite dazzled her eyes and mind—and, though not admitted, her heart.

"Honored chiefs," Louis said, speaking slowly while his mind searched for the proper words in the tongue they could understand. "I have come to reward you for keeping my intended safe from harm and to take her back with me." Carelessly he waved toward the stallion and the goods draped across the packhorse, saying, "A fine stud for your mares and some French fabric and beads for your women should show how grateful I am. Lt. Louis Saint-Denis honors his true friends, Mescatonika and Mescatonaza of the Mescaleros."

The two chiefs crossed their arms, exchanging looks that did not quite conceal their surprise. The rays of the westward sun reflected off their copper earrings.

Louis went on in grand manner, "Your hospitality will be noted by my Spanish friends as well." Looking pointedly at the tepee from where Manuela was watching and wishing she could understand what was being said, he asked, "Now, great leaders, may I see my promised bride? I wish to greet her and chastise her for being so impatient to welcome me that she becomes lost in the mountains. Such a flighty bird must have her wings clipped."

Manuela saw Louis look in her direction and heard his strange words, but she had no idea why the Indians gathered around him laughed. She noticed that Mescatonika gave a halfway smile, but that Mescatonaza held the same frozen expression he had shown ever since greeting Louis and Medar. A row of gooseflesh crawled up her spine. Had Louis failed?

A nod from the old chief must have told Nomee to open the flap, for the next thing Manuela knew, she was being led into the open toward Louis.

"Manuela," Louis said when he saw her, rushing to take her into his arms and hold her close.

Quivering softness melded with solidity, setting off an avalanche of feeling in two racing hearts. Louis felt Manuela trembling. When he tried to tip her face to look into it, she kept it buried in the front of his ruffled shirt. His first glimpse of her in the brief leather tunic with her hair braided down her back had stolen his breath. She was so beautiful, so dignified, even when dressed like an Indian maiden. No, he corrected himself when he recalled the elegance of the leather garment, an Indian princess.

No wonder that rascal Mescatonaza had tried to freeze him out with his cold, unblinking stare,

Louis reflected. Eblo had been correct in his whispered suspicions that the young chief meant to make Manuela his bride that very night, despite probable repercussions once "the one with the handsome leg" arrived to claim her. All about the camp Louis had noted signs of an upcoming celebration – braided circlets lying in a pile near the main fire, small but whole animals being roasted on spits, fresh white paint on the faces of the warriors, the numerous earrings studded with turquoise dangling from the ears of the chiefs.

Louis dismissed such worrisome thoughts and held Manuela even closer, delighting in the feel of her scantily clad body against his, rejoicing over something not identified. Thank God he had arrived in time.

"Come, my intended," he said in Spanish loud enough for anyone to hear. "Do not fear to look upon my face just because you know I'll punish you for your foolishness."

Manuela jerked her head up then. What was Louis talking about? What had Eblo told him? Mescaleros could not understand Spanish. There was no need for pretense.

She tried to free herself from his arms while asking, "Louis Saint-Denis, have you lost –"

Louis brought his mouth down on hers, shocking her and ending her protests. After a brief yet resounding kiss, he whispered against her lips, "Eblo suspects the young chief understands Spanish. Play along." He pushed her away at arm's length then, grasping her forearms. "I thought I had lost you and I was sad. You will never again take it upon yourself to journey into the night in search of me."

The deep voice was stern and commanding; only Louis' bright eyes revealed his true thoughts. Manuela was safe, more beautiful than he had remembered. He had found her. Nothing else mattered.

"Perhaps you are wise to instruct me so," Manuela faltered, not liking the role-playing or the giving in to his blatant mastery.

Had it been necessary for him to kiss her so thoroughly to show their supposed relationship? Manuela wondered with a flare of temper. Even with Medar and the Indians looking on, she had felt that earlier, wild inner stirring from the touch of his firm mouth on hers. No matter that she tried to break the lock of those pale eyes on hers, she failed. Probably she should have expected such theatrics from the cavalier Frenchman, she mused with a surprising lightness of mood. Her mind seemed fuzzy and determined to play tricks on her. An erratic rhythm had directed her heartbeat ever since he had taken her in his arms. All she wanted was to get out of there and go home ... with the handsome Frenchman whose fiery looks were devouring her.

"Have the Mescaleros treated you well?" Louis then asked, praying her answer would be the correct one. If they had dared harm her ...

Like an arrow finding its target, Manuela's gaze shot toward Mescatonaza. The memory of his visit to her tepee the previous night stretched between them like a taut line. What purpose would be served to confess that he had snuggled beside her as she slept, then caressed her and tempted her with mescal leaves? No real harm had been done.

Deliberately she snipped that tenuous thread

forever by shifting her attention back to Louis and replying for all ears to hear, "Yes, my intended. I have been treated well here in the village of the Mescalero chiefs."

Her eyes hooked toward the young chief then. A vulnerable look she could not define lent the stern, coppery countenance an air suggesting suffering. Mescatonaza did seem to be comprehending the exchange between Louis and her, she realized. How had Eblo figured that out when she had discounted her own earlier suspicions?

"I'm truly sorry for the trouble and grief I've caused you, Lieutenant," Manuela added now that she sensed their talk was being understood. She lowered her lashes and tried to look demure and contrite.

"We'll be married as soon as we return," Louis told her, still in the unnaturally loud voice. "I will take stronger measures with you then to see that you always obey me in the future."

As though tired of her presence, Louis released her then, slapping her lightly on her behind before turning to the chiefs with casual conversation. Inwardly he was amused at the black fire shooting at him from beneath thick, sultry lashes when he had struck her and made the high-handed threat. The sight of the fixed curve of her tantalizing lips as she fought to play the required passive role delighted him further. Her attempt to appear docile almost brought a smile, even as he exchanged news of varied Tejas tribes with the sullen-eyed chiefs.

At Louis's signal, Eblo and Medar quickly made the transfer of the stallion and the packets of cloth and beads to Mescatonaza and Mescatonika. Hand in hand, Louis and Manuela led the way to the roped corral. Long before the sun set, the party had mounted and was riding out from the Indian village beside the Rio Grande.

Manuela did not even think to ask for the clothing she had worn upon arrival, so eager was she to get started toward home and put the experiences of the past three days and four nights behind her. Only when she mounted Nightstar and realized her legs were bare did she give a single thought to her appearance, and it was naught but a fleeting one. Away. The only thing of importance now was to get away. She could not seem to breathe in enough fresh air.

With Medar bringing up the rear and leading the packhorse carrying only their camping gear now, Eblo led the group. Manuela followed closely behind the old Indian at a fast clip, not noticing that Louis seemed to be trying to ride alongside her. A kind of shock seemed to have washed over her after she found herself on Nightstar and realized that freedom was truly hers once more.

No one was prepared for the wild dash of a frightfully painted warrior from behind a thick clump of mesquite, one who flung a spear toward the fleeing party after yelling heated words. Manuela heard the quivering sound just as Louis pulled up beside her, jerking her head around in time to see the spear strike his thigh. A quick look over her shoulder told her the attacker was Zaaro, and she knew with a sickening fear that he had meant the weapon for her.

"Keep moving!" yelled Louis when Eblo seemed ready to turn and pursue the Mescalero racing his horse toward the village in the distance. "I'll be all right. There was only the one

210

Indian, and he seems ready to end his quarrel. We don't need to chase after him and stir up the whole tribe. Let's keep on making tracks."

Slowing Diablo, Louis reined him in behind Manuela's Nightstar. Gingerly he tugged at the embedded spear, managing, after a painful struggle, to free it and toss it aside. He searched a pocket for a handkerchief.

"Take off your cravat and stuff it in your breeches," called Medar from behind him. "I'll have a look at your leg as soon as we get some more distance between the village and us." Silently he prayed the tip had not been poisoned.

They traveled at top speed until there was no more light. They had reached a low grove of mesquite shading a sinkhole of brackish water. Quickly Eblo set up camp and got a fire going while Medar and a now-alert Manuela prepared to dress Louis's wound. By then it was throbbing and giving him fits. He stretched out his long body on a blanket without protest.

"Was it necessary for you to cut away my favorite breeches?" Louis teased Medar good-naturedly after the talented valet, in the light of Eblo's blazing fire and with some help from Manuela, had inspected and cleansed the deep gash in the outer portion of his thigh.

When it had become evident that there was no further way she might assist Medar, Manuela had joined Eblo at the campfire. The depth of Louis's wound troubled her. She listened to the banter between the two men while Medar apparently helped Louis change into the leather pants and shirt he had worn on the trek across the mountains.

Medar never looked up from the task of repacking his ever-present medical bag as he replied in like tone, "Complaints. All I ever get from you are complaints, Louis Saint-Denis. You wouldn't have liked wearing breeches with a gaping hole in one leg." He rose and returned the bag to his gear.

Hearing the men's teasing tones end, Manuela felt new gratitude for their timeous appearance. When Medar joined her by the fire where she was warming her hands against the chilly night wind reaching down from the mountains, she gave him a grateful look. Then a sober one claimed her face.

"Medar," Manuela asked in a low voice, "do you believe Louis's leg will be all right? Could you tell if the tip was poisoned?"

So much had happened over the past few hours that her head felt dizzy, and she doubted her pulse would ever again be normal. If her rescuer were to suffer serious harm for his having dared come for her . . .

"I won't be able to tell about the poison until tomorrow," Medar replied, "but if there was none, then I think he'll have no more than a slight limp for a day or two."

Manuela had impressed the valet and sometimes-doctor with her interest in Louis's wound and her ability to assist him in cleansing it. He would have guessed that a young woman of her upbringing might suffer an attack of vapors at such a bloody sight, Medar mused. How wrong he would have been.

"Louis, that spear was meant for me," Manuela said lowly after Medar asked her to leave the camp fire and go keep Louis company while the evening meal was being put together.

She moved to sit on the edge of the blanket where Louis still rested. Her eyes searched his features for assurance that he was going to be well soon. In the pale light coming from the camp fire, his face seemed devoid of that tanned, ruddy glow she had come to associate with his good looks. Was it pain that made his lips compress, his nostrils flare noticeably with each breath. Guilt and compassion tore at her.

"I feel terrible that you were made to suffer because of something I did," Manuela confessed. His eyes were intriguing, silvery beacons there in the wavering light. His well-shaped hands lay at rest across his broad chest, and she saw the gold of the ring he always wore reflecting a soft glow from the camp fire. More than once as he had tutored her in the library back home, she had admired the ring and its scrolled initials set in the diamond-shaped crest of gold. She shifted her gaze to where Medar and Eblo were making motions and noises that indicated a meal would soon be cooking.

"You tried to tell me something about that earlier while we were still riding," Louis said, propping himself up on one elbow. "Why do you think the Indian meant to hit you? My guess is that Mescatonaza sent him to get me since I was the one who took you away."

He did not doubt the sincerity of her belief, but he did doubt the basis of her suspicions. Why would anyone wish to harm such a beautiful, defenseless young woman?

"When we were on the trail being taken to the camp, Zaaro, the Indian who wounded you, touched me, and I bit him. His arm still hasn't healed." Manuela lowered her lashes. His stare

213

was too full of doubt. "You can ask Eblo if you don't believe me." When Louis made no reply, she went on. "From what Eblo told me of the way Mescaleros feel about having women attack them in front of their friends, I made a lifelong enemy. Eblo warned me he would be after me." She met his gaze full on then. "So you see, he had reason to want to kill me, and it's my fault that you were hurt. I'm doubly sorry, for you could have been killed."

His pain lessened since Medar's ministrations, Louis smiled his forgiveness and said, "Manuela, you can't know that spear was intended for you, but even if it was, you had no control over the matter. Please give it no more thought. I'm not afraid of this Zaaro. Rest assured that after the fine gifts they received, his chiefs will refuse to let him seek further vengeance."

Louis hoped he had been able to hide his surprise at her aggressive behavior against such a formidable enemy as a Mescalero brave. It was hard to believe that the cultured young woman was capable of such rash action, and yet he viewed her act as admirable, one used in self-defense. He saw that what he had suspected were old bruises on her face actually were. He doubted that many young women would have refrained from telling right away about such ill-treatment and demanding retribution there in the village. Sweet Mother! She had even more hidden fire than he had imagined.

What else did he not know about the raven-haired beauty? Louis wondered. Raging within was the desire to know all about her. Now that he was with her once more and no family member or *dueña* was privy to their conversation, he hungered to ask all kinds of questions, to hold her close, to whisper—Blood and thunder! Was he out of his head?

Unable to bridle one question tearing at him every since he had started out to find her, Louis asked, "Manuela, what led you to leave in the middle of the night that way?"

Manuela slid him a sidewise look, wondering if she should be honest. Recalling his brief accounts on the ride from the village about the other search parties led by the concerned Diego and Domingo, she decided she could not dissemble. After all, had it not been for him and his knowledge of Indians, she might at this moment be taking part in that wedding ceremony both Eblo and Louis had told her was being planned in the Indian village. Briefly she recounted Governor Anya's proposal and her reaction to it.

With self-scolding tones, Manuela added, "I know now how foolish I was. I never intended to cause so much trouble. I'll be forever grateful for your finding me and getting me away."

"I'm sure you felt you were doing what you had to at the moment," Louis assured her, touched at the pleading for understanding showing in the lovely slanted eyes. She was so young, and yet . . . "Rescuing you seems a fair way to repay your grandfather and uncle for their many kindnesses." After digesting her account of why she had fled, he said, "If you had reached Carlos, you would have felt better to be able to talk it over. Is that right?"

When he compared her version to Diego's, Louis had to admit it seemed to fit her character—or at least what little he knew about it. More and more he was learning that there was

215

far more to Manuela Ramon than met the eye.

"Your twin and you are very close, I take it."

"Oh, yes," she answered, a smile lighting her face. "Carlos probably would have told me I was worrying over nothing, that the governor wouldn't dare retaliate against Grandfather or Uncle, and I would have believed him."

Louis mulled over her statement before asking, "Do you mean that you fear the governor will be vindictive because you refuse to marry him?"

Manuela nodded, her long braid flopping against her back as she explained, "He's known to be a very selfish man. Even though Grandfather finally promised me that I would never have to marry a man I didn't love, I realized that night that I could never get away with refusing the governor, not if he truly wants me as his wife. He's the kind who makes everyone who crosses him sorry." The remembered misery of the night she had fled came rushing back and stamped a picture of anguish on her pretty face. "So you see," she went on after a pause and a flip of her hands outward, wrists and palms upward, "I don't truly have a choice. I can't bear to think of the demotions and disgrace both Grandfather and Uncle might suffer because of me." When the handsome face seemed to demand more explanation, she added, "Besides, I've not met the man I can love, though he might just be a figment of my dreams."

Black eyes met silvery gray ones head-on. The two on the blanket seemed caught up in private, inner dramas. Unformed desires to let heartfelt words and queries bridge the brief distance between them quivered like the gut strings of a guitar lying in a gentle breeze. One might wonder forever if he had heard that haunting whisper of ethereal music, or if he had only imagined it. Had a question been asked? Had an answer been given?

Medar and Eblo brought over plates of food then, and all five sat cross-legged to eat the hastily prepared stew. Louis found himself sneaking looks at Manuela as she sat with apparent ease upon the ground in her brief tunic and shorts and ate with appetite as lusty as the men's. She seemed to have shed her sadness over the problem of the governor's proposal and slipped into a mood of joy at having been rescued. Her laughter pealed frequently at Medar's ridiculous, entertaining tales of life in the wilderness of Louisiana. In the dancing firelight, her exquisitely molded features seemed, to the admiring Louis, more defined than before her disappearance, more mature somehow.

Louis concluded that her eyes seemed larger, wiser, the upward slant of the outer corners lending her an even more exotic look now that her hair was drawn back severely into the heavy braid and her body was covered so briefly by the Indian tunic. The soft deerhide clung to her breasts like a second skin, and Louis felt stirrings within as he watched the tantalizing mounds ripple when she laughed or when she made a sudden gesture while talking in that animated way she had. He tried not to stare at the slender ankles and beautiful legs so blatantly yet innocently exposed—just as he tried not to think of their having been gazed upon by the Mescaleros. Or coveted for his sensuous pleasure by the apparently unscrupulous Governor Anya.

Louis rejoiced upon seeing Manuela so obviously happy to have been rescued. His mind told him again and again that something about her was very different from that vision in yellow he had first seen on the staircase in her grandfather's *hacienda* a bare three weeks ago. Could the brief period of her kidnaping have marked her in ways not noted upon first seeing her earlier that afternoon in the Indian village? Or, an unruly part of his mind dared ask, was the difference merely in the eyes of the beholder?

Chapter Thirteen

Getting an early start the next morning, the foursome made no stops until they were far into the mountains. Medar kept careful watch over Louis, noting how his color paled by mid-morning, but realizing that to put more distance between the Mescalero village and themselves might be more important than pausing for a rest. He had seen the murderous look on Zaaro's face when he hurled the spear, and he had no desire to see it again.

The sun was directly overhead when Eblo paused to point at a tumbling mountain stream and question Louis. "Here?"

"A good spot to water the horses while we rest a bit," agreed Louis, his voice showing the strain of the morning's hard ride. "Medar might find something for us to nibble on."

He turned a pain-wrenched face toward his valet, who was already rushing to help him dismount.

"No, I can manage," Louis insisted, ignoring the proffered hand. He sneaked a look in Manuela's direction, but she was intent on stepping down from Nightstar.

"While Eblo takes the horse to water downstream, I'll check your bandage," Medar replied, his medical bag in his hand and a worried frown on his brow.

"Tell me what we need from your supply bag, Medar," Manuela said, "and I'll prepare us something to eat." She came to stand beside the Frenchmen, her eyes taking in the drawn look on Louis's face. An unexpected rush of tenderness turned her heart upside down. "You're in pain, Louis. You should lie down and let Medar see to that wound."

He seemed as intent on wearing the masculine mask of superiority as Carlos at those times when he was ill or wounded, Manuela thought with amusement. What was it that gnawed at men and led them to pretend they were invulnerable, even those as seasoned as the tall, lean Frenchman? For that instant, she felt more mature than any of the three escorting her home.

Medar gave Manuela brief instructions about the food supplies and watched Louis stretch out upon a little patch of grass near the gurgling stream. The self-taught doctor deftly helped him pull down his breeches to expose the bandage.

"It's been bleeding," Medar murmured, hoping that the flow might be a good way to drain off any poison. "It seems feverish," he added, not liking the hardness and redness surrounding the gash.

"Here," said Manuela, suddenly appearing beside them with a cup of water. "Let me cleanse it before you put on a new bandage."

She was unprepared for the sight of Louis's exposed lower body there in daylight but knew it was too late to back away without calling undue notice to her actions. Actually, she told herself as she touched a wet cloth to his thigh, seeing Louis in his white underdrawers was no different than seeing Carlos in his. Then why is your face flushing, something within teased, and why is your heart dancing a doublestep? Was it because she was remembering their "midnight encounter," when he had so gallantly ministered to her foot?

"Your touch is much lighter than Medar's," Louis said with a grin, watching the heavy lashes veil her eyes in that sultry way that charmed him. He could not decide if he preferred seeing the flush on her face or feeling the brush of her soft hands on his skin. For sure, he was recalling their night in the stable, and his memory had nothing to do with splinters or feet. "Let him fix the food while you put on the fresh bandage."

Manuela nodded agreement but made no comment. She kept her eyes on her work, while Louis enjoyed the view. He admired the swell of firm breasts pushing against the deerskin with each breath, the purse of sympathy on rosy lips. Her nearness seemed to offset some of the throbbing from the wound. His heart swelled with an undefined fullness. Holy Mother! She was even more beautiful up close.

Stealing a glance from beneath her lowered lashes, Manuela saw him watching her with more interest than was called for. What was he thinking? She became aware of her brief Indian tunic as she knelt beside him and covered the cleansed, raw spot with fresh cloth from Medar's bag. When she finished and sat back upon her legs, he continued to lie still.

Chiding herself for noticing how close to his manhood she had been working, Manuela asked, "Do you need me to help you pull up your breeches?"

When Louis gave no answer, Manuela again

tried to rank him in the same class as her brother. With determination, she leaned over to grab his waistband, only to be thwarted when his hands covered hers and held them in midair. A prickling brushed up her spine.

"No, thank you. I can manage," the prone Louis replied, his deep voice gone thick and husky without warning.

One quick movement and Louis had released Manuela's hands. He then hoisted his hips and eased up his breeches, achingly aware of her bemused gaze. Was she so innocent that she didn't know what her touch in those nether regions could do to a man? The memory of her lips beneath his yesterday at the Indian village swept away physical pain. He lay back with eyes closed, his breath coming out heavily. The pulsing in the wound seemed to have spread to all sorts of places.

"While you rest your eyes," Manuela said lightly, "I'll see if I can help Medar."

If Louis wished her to stay by his side, he wouldn't have closed his eyes, Manuela told herself. The look on his face was definitely one of discomfort. She added a reprimand for having succumbed to a feeling akin to quivering jelly at the enforced intimacy of the past minutes. He must have been more exhausted than she realized, she thought while she walked over to join Medar and the returning Eblo.

"How is the lieutenant?" Eblo asked, looking first at Medar and then at Manuela when she joined them down beside the stream.

"He's weary," she replied, glancing over her shoulder and noting he still lay just as she had left him.

"The wound seems clean enough," Medar added. "It's deep, though, and pains him."

The trim little Frenchman arranged sliced sausage and slabs of cheese on thick corn cakes and handed them on small wooden trenchers to Manuela and Eblo. Then he went over to his employer, carrying food for the two of them and whistling a carefree melody.

The rest stop revived the animals as well as the wounded Louis. Though the afternoon ride seemed less grueling, all four welcomed the approaching twilight.

Eblo, agreeing with Louis after a quiet exchange, pulled up beside a large stream to make camp. They had crossed the summit and were almost back down to the plateau where the Mescaleros had seized their captives. If Louis were to enjoy a good night's rest and suffer no complications, all agreed that they could make it back to the *presidio* long before dark the next day. Everyone's mood seemed to have lifted.

Manuela sat cross-legged upon the ground, not far from the crackling fire Eblo had started soon after the travelers had stopped for the night. The old Indian had already slipped into the woods and had clubbed a fat rabbit hiding in a hollow tree. Cleaned and dressed now, the pink meat lay ready for turning into stew.

Propped up on one elbow beside Manuela, Louis lay sprawled and relaxed, resting his head upon his opened palm and watching the activity.

On the other side of the fire, Medar was adding various ingredients from his supplies to the rabbit in the cook pot. Eblo and he had quite a conversation about which seasonings he should use in the stew, the Frenchman opting for dried

223

herbs. When the old Indian shook his head and produced a handful of dried red peppers from his saddlebags, Manuela and Louis exchanged amused glances.

Medar turned to the young couple resting nearby and listening to the little argument with open interest. "What about it, Louis? We'll let you decide. Do you prefer my regular seasonings, or are you becoming addicted to hot peppers?"

His eyes resting upon Manuela's curving lips, Louis replied, "I suspect I'm beginning to like hot peppers more every day. Go ahead and spice up the stew."

Medar shrugged eloquently, then took the peppers from the half-smiling Eblo and dropped them into the cook pot with a flourish.

"I love a camp fire. The smell of the smoke and the colors of the flames fascinate me," Manuela confessed in a dreamy voice, aware that Louis was giving her his full attention now that the cooks were involved in their own private conversation across the way. Basking in the warmth from the camp fire and the feeling of security there in the circle of light, she stretched out her bare legs and crossed one moccasined foot over the other, leaning back with her arms extended behind her as a prop.

Louis had been unable to take his eyes off Manuela's face until her arms and legs made the fluid movements there beside him. Seeing the firm young breasts pointing upward beneath the leather as she leaned back so freely and gracefully brought an aching down low. Her long, olive-tinted legs were added temptations, and he fought to move his thoughts into safer channels. What was it she was saying . . . something about how she loved a camp fire? Curiosity saved the moment, and he sat up, ignoring the stab of pain in his thigh.

"How is it you know so much about a camp fire? I would have thought a young Spanish lady would know little about such things." Hoping the uncertain light camouflaged his boldness, Louis admired the arched body, the lithesome legs, and the tilted head. When she faced him and blinked in that heavy-lidded way, he felt his pulse quicken.

"When Carlos and I left our schools in the City of Mexico and came to live with Grandfather, we were only twelve," Manuela replied, her voice soft with reverie. The thick braid swung when she lifted her head to search for stars through the overhead trees. "He left us pretty much on our own, and we roamed as far as we could and still get back to the *presidio* before dark. Then when it was time for Carlos to learn to hunt, it seemed only natural that I be allowed to go along." Still looking up at the darkening sky, she took a deep breath. "I think I fell in love with the night sky the first time I slept in a blanket roll in these very mountains." She flexed a knee and left it up, savoring the welcome feeling of being safe . . . and free.

"So that explains your riding as well as a man," Louis commented, still admiring the graceful pose, the perfect profile. He added quickly before he lost his nerve, "Of course I already know that you swim as well as a man." His heart warned him. Why had he stirred up that unsettling vision of her half clad in the water?

Manuela bolted upright, pulling her legs in and turning to face him. "Your good manners are

225

slipping, Lieutenant," she chided. Her quick movement flung her braid forward over her shoulder and her hand absently caught it, the fingers playing along its thickness. A sudden crackle from the fire seemed to play up the tension between them.

"I prefer that you call me 'Louis,'" he said, stung at her reversion to the more impersonal term. But wait. Was that a spark of mischief in those midnight eyes, or was she truly offended? Knowing which he hoped it was, he plunged ahead to ask, "How was it you came to swap clothing with your maid and be swimming—"

"Louis Saint-Denis," she interrupted him in a mocking tone, her hand flying to her open mouth, her eyes wide, "you're destroying all my ideas about your being a dashing cavalier. Would you invade a maiden's privacy?"

Manuela could tell by the look on his face and the spark in his eyes that he was enjoying putting her on the defensive. Having spent the past four years around a teasing brother had taught her to hold few idealized pictures of herself, but she confessed she was glad it was dark so that he might not see the hot flush washing over her. She knew too well that the wet chemise had hidden little that morning. When she added that incident to the one in the stable, she had no false illusions left that Louis could ever view her as a properly brought up young woman. Whereas such thoughts would never have entered her mind before the kidnapping, they now nagged at a sense of propriety she had not known she possessed. What was there about him that played havoc with her preconceived notions? Or were new notions replacing old ones?

"I might invade one maiden's privacy, if I thought I could get away with it," Louis admitted, sliding her a flirty look. "Frankly, I enjoyed watching you swim."

That Manuela could be so free and easy with him brought a smile so wide it almost pained Louis's face. He was close enough to see the heat suffusing her skin and thought the effect delightful. A chuckle from deep within surfaced, and he forgot about his injury and slapped his thigh. What started out as a sound of pure joy ended up as a half-strangled moan of pain when his hand found its target.

Realizing he had slapped his wound in an unguarded moment, Manuela laughed and said, "That serves you right for spying on unsuspecting young women, you rogue." Her initial embarrassment erased, she asked with obvious puzzlement, "How was it you came upon me that day?"

Briefly Louis explained about his scouting ahead for his traveling party. He could not resist confessing how he had thought the swimmer to be a maid and that he had asked Medar to find out who she was. No, he assured her, he had not recognized her from his place on the bank of the irrigation stream.

"You truly didn't know who I was until..." Manuela stopped. New washes of color flooded her face there in the golden firelight.

"Not until you threw yourself at me in the stables," Louis teased, loving the way she flushed all over again at what must surely be a memory of their impassioned kissing.

For a moment, Manuela stiffened. Then she detected the merriment in his voice and sneaked a daring glance his way from beneath half-lowered lashes. She found the laughing, silvery eyes watching her irresistible. So he liked to tease, did he?

"I seemed to have had more purpose in my fall than you had in yours," she countered. Devilment danced in her black eyes. An image of the way he had looked lying in the stream that afternoon of the hunt became clearer. She let out a giggle, her teeth flashing prettily in the glow from the flames.

"*Touché,*" Louis conceded wryly. "I've wondered if I'll ever be able to forgive you for laughing at me that afternoon. I could have been injured for life, and all for the lost cause of plucking a flower for a very ungrateful young woman."

Listening to the delightful sounds of Manuela's low giggles and drinking in her close-up beauty, Louis realized that to joke with her so intimately was healing the imagined wound to his pride. He felt like a schoolboy without a care in the world. The young woman beside him was easy to talk with and heartbreakingly vibrant, not at all like the icily polite Miss Ramon with whom he had shared those first meals at the Ramon *hacienda.* That hint of defrosting that he had glimpsed during their tutoring sessions seemed a fact now. She was everything that he had suspected she might be from that very first introduction: beautiful, charming, witty, delightful company. And no child, he assured himself. Calendar years be damned.

"Now that you've had time to reconsider, will you forgive me?" Manuela asked. Heavy-lidded black eyes roved his face as she awaited his reply.

"Meet me in the stables some night, and I'll

tell you," came Louis's low-voiced challenge designed only for her ears.

Manuela felt the heat of his gaze, heard the implied invitation in the husky reply. No matter that she wore Indian garb and that her hair was an untidy braid; she had never felt more grown-up, attractive ... desirable. Here was a young man who dared tease about something she had viewed as somewhat shameful, who treated her as an equal, and who had rescued her from a despicable situation. A kind of bravado seized her.

"I'll release my parrot the minute I get home," Manuela said, laughter pushing her voice to varying musical pitches.

For no reason that either could have explained, both then rocked with laughter, his deep rumbles almost drowning out her merry peals.

Medar and Eblo, from the other side of the fire, watched the two bubbling with laughter and wondered what had been said. Too busy with making coffee and tending the stew, and doubting that any intrusion would be welcome, they merely shrugged, grinned at each other, and carried on with the task of preparing the meal.

"What have you done with my garter that you snitched that morning?" Manuela asked when they sobered, intrigued that he might still have such an intimate piece of her apparel in his possession. She felt a wild headiness, a new sense of her womanhood, and both sensations showed in the slanted looks she gave him in the firelight.

"I'll never tell," Louis remarked with a boyish grin, fighting to keep from eyeing that shapely leg where the yellow satin had no doubt ridden.

Her mouth was so tempting to look at that he was glad he won that battle. The firelight bathed the olive face with fresh loveliness. Did she know how alluring she was, how tempting her scantily clad body?

"Then I'll never return your handkerchief," she replied.

Swishing her braid, Manuela turned to watch the fire when she realized the looks he was giving her were attacking her in an unsettling yet delightful way. Only after she spoke did she recall that she had no idea what had happened to his handkerchief after she discarded it that day. If she knew Conchita as she thought she did, ... All of a sudden, though it made no sense at all, she wanted that handkerchief to hold in her hand. She made a mental note that one of the first questions she would ask Conchita would be about its whereabouts.

Louis lay back again with his head propped in his hand. In spite of the pain in his thigh, he acknowledged a puzzling truth: It had been ages since he had felt so young and excited about what tomorrow might bring. Maybe it was good that he didn't know all about Manuela, he mused, because each new facet he discovered seemed to make her all the more unique and desirable. Something within told him that he could live a lifetime and not know all there was to know about the magnetic young woman sitting beside him, though he suspected that to do so held a precious priority. What does that mean? a sneaky inner voice asked. A sobering thought jarred him: Was he, perhaps, falling in love?

A sudden call from the darkness jolted those

around the camp fire out of their varied states of complacency. Had Zaaro returned to complete his revenge against the young woman who had caused him to lose face among his fellow braves?

From the shadows on the other side of the camp fire, both Medar and Eblo reached into the saddlebags piled nearby. Medar tossed Louis his gun just as horses approached the campsite.

Manuela's eyes grew large with fright at the nearing sounds of hooves stomping on the rocky soil, of limbs rustling and snapping in the darkness. Recalling Zaaro's cruel blows, she moved closer to Louis, who had risen to his knees. He had saved her once . . .

Three horses came into view then, and she gasped. "Carlos! Oh, Carlos, you found us." Before the horses had stopped, she was laughing and dashing across the ground to her brother, reaching eagerly to be taken into his arms as soon as he dismounted.

"Manuela, you goose," Carlos scolded after giving her a bear hug and pushing her away to look into her face. "What ever possessed you to go traipsing off in the dark? Were you trying to find me? When Uncle found me yesterday and accompanied us home, everyone was going mad trying to figure out where you were. No one could imagine what had happened to you."

Louis noticed that only a soft fullness about Carlos's mouth gave away the fact that he was not quite as old as his voice and looks suggested. A darkening of his smooth olive cheeks and chin showed a man-sized beard already grew beneath.

The two Indians with Carlos nodded to the surprised party when Carlos introduced them, then moved to tether their horses with the others down near the stream. Louis watched with a nagging twinge of jealousy while Manuela stood looking up at her twin, offering the requested explanations.

After giving Eblo an affectionate pat on the shoulder and saying something to him under his breath, Carlos took matters into his own hands and introduced himself to the two Frenchmen. When it was time for Louis to shake his hand, he found Carlos's grip firm, gentlemanly, his direct looks from black eyes much like those of his grandfather and uncle. He checked to see if the eyes slanted upward at the corners, not surprised to see that they did not. There could be no others like Manuela's.

As though she could not get enough of his company, Manuela followed Carlos about, offering explanations and answering his numerous questions. Not that the brother seemed to mind, Louis noted with an interest that nettled him. Hadn't he already been told that the twins were unusually close? He was being downright foolish to resent being left out of their conversation, or so he kept reminding himself.

When Manuela ended her story by telling how Louis had ridden into the Indian camp in his finery and had bribed the chiefs into letting him take her away, Carlos bowed his head formally toward the Frenchman and said, "The Ramons will be forever indebted to you, Lieutenant Saint-Denis." A new, more positive assessment of the foreigner seemed to be taking place behind the polite visage.

Louis acknowledged Carlos's thanks in similar manner, noting how the young man, like his sister, showed far more maturity, both in looks and actions, than any sixteen-year-old he had ever met. From what inner source of strength did the Ramon twins draw? Or was the characteristic something peculiarly Spanish?

There was much for the devoted sister and brother to catch up on and fast talk flew between them, both before and during the eating of the evening meal.

"I'm sorry I caused so much trouble," Manuela told Carlos for the fifth time, or so it seemed to Louis, who was lamenting privately that all of her attention had focused on her brother since his arrival. "Do you think Grandfather and Uncle Domingo can ever forgive me?"

"Why would you ask such a question?" Carlos countered, his quick smile assuring her. "All they'll need to hear is that you're safe and almost back at home." He studied her face and her clothing then, apparently seeing them for the first time. "What is this costume all about?" Brother and sister exchanged amused looks, as if nothing either did ever genuinely surprised the other.

Then Eblo filled Carlos in on Mescatonaza and his plans to marry Manuela, the account bringing a stormy mien to the young man's smooth, olive face. Once the complete story had been recounted, he appeared more at peace, though he did fix a stony stare upon Louis during the telling of the part about Manuela's being presented falsely as the Frenchman's intended bride. Like his sister when she had first met Louis, Carlos had made little pretense at hiding his disapproval upon finding a foreigner, no matter what his rank or honors, forced into his presence.

"Now I think it's time for me to return to the *presidio* to let everyone know you're safe, Man-uela," Carlos said. He inclined his head toward his companions, and they went to fetch the horses. "You should be getting there sometime after noon, don't you think?" he asked Eblo. When the old Indian nodded, he said, "There'll be enough light for us to retrace our tracks, but I approve your waiting until daylight to travel." He stood and stretched, looking down at his sister with a fond smile and a mischievous glint in his eyes. "Girls need more light than men."

"Girls!" Manuela squealed, rising to punch Carlos playfully on his broad chest with her fists. "If I'm a girl, then you must be a mere boy. At sixteen I became a grown woman, and I didn't need special considerations even before that."

"Matter of opinion, little sister," Carlos shot back, grinning and ducking from her new attack. "Have a safe journey, all of you." His eyes went to Eblo and turned serious as he said, "God's speed. We'll see you tomorrow."

After a hug and a few whispered words from Manuela over in the shadows, Carlos and the two Indians left.

Later, while Eblo kept first watch and the others lay down to sleep, Manuela found it hard to calm down after Carlos's visit, and she tossed restlessly in her blanket roll. Seeing him after such a long absence was too good to be cut so short, she fretted. She had much to talk to him about. Her thoughts darted in a thousand directions, not helped any by the night noises rising in intensity at each passing hour.

From far up the mountain, she hard a hawk owl screech and remembered hearing a similar sound the night Eblo and she were captured. Her mouth went dry when she recalled that upon first hearing Carlos's call tonight, she had feared it was Zaaro coming to get his revenge. Then the memory of Mescatonaza in her tent flooded her mind, and her face burned.

What were those alien feelings he had stirred inside her body? Could it mean that she had something evil within that had been tempted, however fleetingly, to answer savagery? Just as Manuela rolled over on her back and stared up at the star-filled sky, she heard Louis move in his blankets nearby and, for no discernible reason, felt reassured. Her eyelids closed, and she felt sleep embracing her.

Dreams eased Manuela's sleep, taking her by the hand and leading her to her favorite escape. For the first time since her capture, Manuela saw the garden of Love, the one she had so often read and dreamed about, and eagerly entered its gates. All around were beautiful roses bathed in moonlight: white, red, yellow. She heard someone enter the garden, and she became, somehow, a yellow rosebud. Was it the Lover coming to claim his own? Looming out of nowhere, the dark figure of the stern-voiced Keeper appeared and stood before the one who had just entered, refusing to let him pluck the bloom of his choice. Manuela longed to see who had come for her, to push aside the one separating them, but she was attached to a stem.

Powerless in the dream, voiceless, Manuela cried out silently to the Lover to choose her, take her, at least let her see his face before he heeded the Keeper's orders to depart and learn suffering before he returned to claim her. Who needed more suffering? Had they not endured enough pain just through waiting to be together?

The sleeping Manuela turned restlessly in her blankets. For a second, a moonbeam sliced the darkness covering the garden in her dream, and she glimpsed the face of the questing Lover. She saw dark hair upon a proudly held head. The face was lean and handsome with a laughing mouth, and the eyes were dark-fringed and pale, crinkling silvery, worshiping looks her way. Her pulse skipped crazily. It was Louis Saint-Denis. Manuela shivered in disbelief. A Frenchman as her Lover? That couldn't be. The rosebud trembled upon the captive stem, tried to become smaller, sought to wrap her petals closer around her . . .

"Stop shivering in your blanket and wake up," came Louis's voice close to her ear. "Eblo's fire will warm you."

Manuela's eyes popped open. The familiar voice with its deep timbre was real, as real as the damp, hard ground on which she lay. It was daybreak and a fire was already crackling. Fearful that her eyes might reveal what she had been dreaming, she closed them again, making a small sound to let him know she was awake.

When she heard Louis move off toward the stream, Manuela opened her eyes to watch the way he carried himself. Even with the slight limp from the spear wound, he moved with a lithe grace she had not often observed in a man. His leather shirt stretched across broad, proudly held shoulders, shoulders that accentuated the trim hips encased in snug leather breeches — and, she thought with an indrawn breath at such wayward thoughts, she knew exactly how muscular those thighs were, how firm that flesh was below his linen. . . . A little tremor ran through her as she recalled how grand he had looked in his finery when she had spied him through the crack of her tent that afternoon in the camp of the Mescaleros. He had seemed every inch a cavalier.

"Are you well today?" came Eblo's quiet voice from near the camp fire.

"Yes, thank you," Manuela replied, sitting up and casting away her disturbing thoughts. "I was too excited to sleep much." She brushed at her mussed hair and went to stand by the fire, holding her hands out to the welcome warmth.

"Excited about going home?" Eblo asked, darting a questioning look her way.

"What else?" she parried with a defensive tone she did not understand.

Home, Manuela mused as she made ready for the day's ride. That was where she longed to be. Things would fall into their proper places there. For the first time that she could recall, she would welcome the orderliness, the routineness of living, the return to the world of the remote *presidio*.

When Medar asked Manuela to dress Louis's thigh while he helped Eblo put out the fire and get the horses ready for the journey, she was tempted to refuse. A quizzical look from the gray-blue eyes quelled her misgivings, and she realized she was letting a foolish dream flavor her decisions. What utter nonsense. Louis and she had become friends during their relaxed conversations and teasing. Her help was needed.

"Your bragging that you'd be well soon proves to be fact, Louis," Manuela said from where she knelt beside his prostrate figure. She had removed the wrappings and cleansed the wound, reminding herself that tending to Louis was no different than tending to Carlos. "The wound is healing far more noticeably today."

Manuela tried not to notice the way Louis's skin felt beneath her fingers as she moved them to test near the mutilated tissue for hardness. When she felt none and saw no new redness, she allowed her eyes to meet his. Such an intense look reached from those silvery orbs that she felt captured by it, felt she was impaled as firmly as a bird on the end of a spear. A stillness imprisoned them: she with her fingers still on his thigh, he with his breath stolen.

"You're so beautiful in the dawning," Louis said the moment his breath returned. He had slept little. Thoughts about what she might be coming to mean to him had swirled and bedeviled. "If you only knew—"

"How is our patient today?" Medar interrupted just then, climbing toward them from the direction of the stream and leading the horses.

Manuela's hands moved jerkily to apply a clean bandage, and she stood before replying, "The hardness around the wound is gone, and he says the pain is far less." Medar had come to stand beside them then. She tucked the vial of medicine in the bag he opened for her. "I believe he'll live," she joked. She had come to like the little valet and his ready wit.

"More's the pity," intoned Medar, stroking his goatee as if deep in a black mood. "He can be an absolute despot when he's well and his normal self."

"Do you mean he's been showing his better side since he was injured?" Manuela shot back, rising

238

to the bait and sending a playful glance at Louis now that he too was standing. "I never would have guessed that was the best he had to offer."

Louis was looking at her in a way she could not interpret, and she realized that when he had called her "beautiful" only moments ago, it had seemed that the word had held far more meaning then when others had spoken it. How could that be? she wondered, especially when she knew she looked so unkempt, so unlike her normal self.

"Take it from me. I've been with him twelve years, and I ought to know." Medar grinned knowingly at the two who were busily eyeing each other without seeming to.

"If you want someone to put you in the worst possible light, Manuela, ask one you'd think might show a bit of loyalty," was Louis's retort. He hated the idea of leaving the place where she had been so open and easy with him. "This man hunts ways to make me look disreputable."

"Does he usually succeed?" she asked, walking over to where Eblo held Nightstar for her. Without looking, she knew Louis was watching her every moment. That same fluttery feeling that had come over her last night when he had gazed at her so intently was stealing over her again, the one that made her feel bursting with delicious feminity and energy. "I doubt you need much help from anyone."

"Do you see what you've done, Medar?" Louis demanded in a teasing, blustery voice, easing up into Diablo's saddle carefully to keep from jarring his thigh. "You've set the princess against me, and once we're back at the *presidio*, I'll have no way to redeem myself. 'Tis a cruel world for lowly soldiers traveling in a foreign realm."

With open interest, Louis watched Manuela climb upon Nightstar and try to pull down her brief tunic. A devilish grin quirked the corners of his mouth and sparked the pale eyes beneath thick brown eyebrows. There was no way she could conceal those lovely legs, he reflected with full appreciation for the view. A perverse thought sobered him. Once they returned to the *presidio* today, everything would be different. She would revert to being the so-proper grand-daughter of the commandant guarded by her *dueña*. After today, everything would be different. Louis's heart plummeted.

Princess, Manuela mused, savoring the flattering term, not recalling that what she wore was the finery of a Mescalero princess. All she could think of was that Louis was the only one who had ever called her that.

She lifted her chin in mock indignation and called over her shoulder, "I've seldom seen a grown man weep so at his lot. Perhaps you should prepare a petition listing your grievances and present them at court, lowly, mistreated soldier that you claim to be."

Before urging Nightstar to follow Eblo, Manuela treated herself to a last look back at Louis. Her eyes softened. Pink lips became a thoughtful rosebud. What was causing that solemn look on his face? She much preferred the ready smile, the flash of teeth, and the sparkling eyes that had seemed so much a part of him these two days and nights on the trail.

"If I follow your suggestion, will you read them?" came Louis's voice after a spell of scarce talk among the four riders.

Surprised, Manuela twisted in her saddle.

They had been on the trail for awhile and, her thoughts tumbling, she had not realized Louis was riding up beside her. It made no sense, but something about the way he looked at her told her that he was referring to her inane remark made when they were leaving camp, something about his needing to submit a list of his grievances for her consideration.

Manuela's heart skittered crazily as she met the handsome Frenchman's piercing look. With a daring smile, she replied, "Try me, kind sir. Try me."

Chapter Fourteen

Manuela's homecoming was a passionate mixture of tears, hugs, and half-hearted scoldings, plus numerous prayerful thanks to the limping Lieutenant Saint-Denis and his valet, Medar Jalot. Before nightfall, Diego had insisted that Louis and Medar move into the downstairs guest wing of his *hacienda.*

"I'm taking no chances that the one who brought back my beloved Manuela doesn't heal properly," Diego assured Louis when he tried to demur. "Your knowledge of how to get a message across to the Mescaleros is worth more than I can ever pay." The remembrance of what Carlos had related about Mescatonaza's plans to marry Manuela the very night that the Frenchmen had arrived still tore at the doting grandfather's heart. "Domingo and I talked over this matter as soon as Carlos returned to let us know that you were on your way back. We'll consider it an insult should you refuse."

No one seemed to recall that Louis and his two companions were officially prisoners there at San Juan Batista.

A silent observer over the past few minutes, Carlos recalled how much thought he had given to the French lieutenant on his way back to the *presidio* the previous night. In spite of his resolve to despise the man because of his nationality, he had found him downright likable.

To his surprise, Carlos found himself saying, "Grandfather is right, Louis. Everyone will rest easier knowing that you're nearby in case your valet needs assistance." He sliced a crafty look at Manuela when Louis at last gave in and agreed to move into the downstairs guest wing.

"I saw the way you looked at the Frenchman," Carlos told his twin late that afternoon when they had settled onto comfortable chairs on the balcony outside her bedroom. He had given her time to bathe, dress, and get her hair arranged. "And the way he looked back, too." He turned laughing eyes her way. "Am I right to suspect a romance there?"

"Of course not, blockhead," Manuela denied, wondering at the heat flooding her cheeks. "He's nothing but a French officer spying on us here."

Manuela's derogatory words did not rush out as they had when uttered before the kidnapping. They seemed to catch in her throat. Beneath her pillow lay the monogrammed handkerchief she had urged a teasing Conchita to produce. Contradictions seemed to be invading her from every angle, she fretted. She turned to scold Zorro for nipping at the leaves on a potted pepper plant there on the balcony.

"Hot pepper, Zorro," she said with force. "Stop it, please. You'll be sorry."

Stretching his yellow-ringed neck and fluttering an outside wing feather of green, the parrot mimicked, "Hot pepper! You'll be sorry! Aargh!"

Properly impressed, as was the doting Manuela, Carlos muttered, "That bird's uncanny. He can say any damned thing he sets his mind to, can't he?"

"Not much different from some people I know," she quipped, holding out her hand for Zorro to light. When the bird ignored the invitation and flew up to the balcony rail to walk its edges away from them, Manuela turned back to her brother. "We don't have long before dinner, and I want to hear what you think I should do about the marriage proposal from the governor."

"Grandfather spoke with Anya when he was over checking to see if perhaps Eblo and you had ridden to Monclova to talk with him about the suit. I gather he told him there would be no joining of our two families."

Manuela had the grace to look chagrined. "I caused everyone so much trouble, when all I wanted to do was find you and talk. I did act like a dotty lizard, didn't I?"

"Not really. You've always been like that pepper plant you warned Zorro about—nice to look at, but full of fire." His voice held no accusation, merely acceptance. "I can see why you would have panicked, though," Carlos assured her staunchly when the slanted eyes revealed a trace of pleading. "Marriage is harnessing up for life, and I agree with your reasoning. The way I see it, we'd best take a long look at our partners before it's too late. I know how you moon over some handsome stranger, for you've told me more than once." Before saying more, the slim-faced young man looked all around to make sure they were the only ones on the balcony. "I believe Grandfather and Uncle Domingo were wrong to ask you to accept the governor's proposal."

"But, Carlos," Manuela insisted, fixing him with a grave look, "think of what the governor can do to them. What if he is so angered at being turned down that he takes away their commissions and their holdings? You know how vain the old fool is. I couldn't stop thinking of that possibility, and I had no one to talk about it with except you. Don't you agree that I can't be thinking of myself alone now? My family shouldn't be put into a position to suffer just because—"

Carlos broke in harshly, his voice deepening into a resemblance of Diego's when the old man was being firm. "You're wrong when you think you must consider their positions, for they're men accustomed to fending for themselves. Besides, men don't like for their women to make sacrifices for them."

"Why not? They often do for us," Manuela retorted, puzzled at what sounded like a superior tone from the one who had always treated her as an equal. She smoothed at a shoulder ruffle serving as abbreviated sleeves on the pink dimity gown.

"Because it's a man's prerogative, that's why."

"Says who? Women have some special rights too, don't they? Where do you get your ideas?" she argued in defiant tones. She sat up straighter on her chair.

"From paying attention to what goes on around me, which is where you should be getting yours instead of from those books and poems you're always reading," he chided, reaching to tug at a curl that Conchita had formed only minutes ago.

Manuela continued to send him a belligerent stare.

Seeing a petulant look about her mouth, Carlos added, "Because you're my twin and unlike any other female I've ever known, I think you've every right to choose who'll be your husband. Grandfather would have never told you that if he hadn't meant it. I know I intend to choose my bride."

Manuela heard his words but felt cheated, somehow, that Carlos had offered no panacea for what loomed in her mind as a possible tragedy. Had their sixteenth birthdays, not quite two months ago, rent that invisible bond of twinship in some way? They talked on, the lifelong camaraderie allowing all kinds of thoughts about their futures to be tossed back and forth. Whatever else the kidnapping had done, it had sobered Manuela and had made her realize that life might be more than something that waits around a corner. It was the now as well.

Diego and Domingo didn't invite Louis to meet with them in the library until two mornings later. By that time, the Frenchman had regained his vigor and could walk with no more than a slight limp. Despite Louis's objections, Medar, as well as the Ramon men, had insisted that the wounded young man take his meals in the guest room to conserve his strength and hasten his recovery. With uncharacteristic gray moods, Louis had fretted at the confinement, not eager to examine how much of his misery might be caused from his not getting to see Manuela for two whole days. Her loveliness haunted him, whether asleep or awake.

"To see you looking fit brings pleasure, Louis," Diego remarked after the three men had settled upon chairs around the library table and indulged in small talk, cups of coffee in hand.

Domino echoed his father's remarks and repeated their fervent thanks for Louis's remarkable rescue of Manuela, adding, "Father and I feel that we should apprise you of the news from Governor Anya in Monclova."

"Yes?" Louis asked, accepting a second cup of coffee from Diego. "Has he replied to your report of my appearance here?"

His own Sergeant Penicault had visited Louis earlier that morning and had reported what was being talked about among the soldiers. Commandant Diego had met with Governor Anya while in Monclova to check on the whereabouts of Manuela and Eblo, but no one could glean a hint of what had been discussed. That the governor had replaced Diego's Sgt. Santo Guerra with Sgt. Jose Benitez before Diego ever left Monclova fed one piece of gossip: Anya had the known practice of coercing soldiers into flapping their tongues about their superiors. Now that he was assigned to the *presidio* at Monclova, Sergeant Guerra was likely being led into talking freely about the activities at San Juan Batista.

Though Louis was aware of the unrest among Diego's soldiers at having lost their longtime sergeant and had even considered how the presence of his men and him at the *presidio* might figure into the matter, he gave that problem little thought there in the library that morning. Uppermost in his mind was the hope that the Ramon men would tell of the governor's reaction to the rejected suit for Manuela. Wondering how the situations would be resolved had plagued him far more than the healing wound.

Diego looked into the contents of his cup, took

247

a sip of the hot brew, and answered, "Yes, he knows that you're here as a prisoner. The day I was there was one of the first that he was well enough to spend time in his office since your arrival some three weeks ago." His voice sank a bit when he went on. "You see, Gaspardo suffers from gout and dyspepsia and sometimes has to allow his duties to pile up." After a deft wipe at his thick, gray moustache with a practiced forefinger, he said, "Actually, he seemed as doubtful as we that any real harm has resulted from your journey. Governor Cadillac's obvious concern for Father Hidalgo's plea to reestablish his mission in Tejas seems commendable. Though Gaspardo breeds horses on his holdings west of Monclova, he made no comment about your wish to purchase horses and cattle. He did mention that he might send for you to come to Monclova for questioning, but he made no firm plans."

"Of course no one could have known that you would return wounded," Domingo spoke up. "We were thinking that mayhap you might feel up to the journey in the next day or two, if the governor were to decide he wished you to visit with him."

"At your service," Louis announced, sitting up straight and replacing his cup on his saucer with care. Did the news indicate that Governor Anya had gracefully accepted Diego's refusal of his granddaughter's hand?

With difficulty, Louis pushed down the desire to ask outright about Manuela's plight. After all, he assured himself, what these Spanish people did in their private lives was no concern of his. His goal was to gain access to men in high places who could grant trading rights between his newly established Fort Saint Jean Baptiste on the Red River and Spanish settlements south of the Rio Grande. New Spain had gold and silver; New France did not.

When both of the Ramons continued to drink coffee and made no reply to his offer to do whatever they asked, Louis said, "I'm able to travel now if it pleases you—"

"No, no," Diego interrupted with a genial wave of his hand. "I doubt the governor will ever give the matter of your presence here another thought. There's no need to rush your convalescence. He seemed caught up in the excitement of a *fiesta* being planned to celebrate his birthday in a few weeks. Join us at the table tonight and see how your strength holds up."

Louis had not missed the way the eyes of the commandant and his son had glanced off each other throughout the conversation. Their smiles were easy, but something about their stiff countenances in between the smiles made him suspicious that all was not as well as they would have him believe. Did it have something to do with Manuela and the governor's proposal? Scolding himself for entertaining such ridiculous thoughts when his mind should be concentrating on his own uncertain plight, he took another sip of coffee and waited.

"I trust the governor was understanding about Manuela's sudden decision to ride off into the mountains to find Carlos," Louis remarked after much soul searching about how he might best broach the subject.

"He was, and . . . he wasn't," Diego replied. He sent Domingo a quizzical look. A forefinger and thumb traced the outer shape of his nose. As if his mind had suddenly shown a certain answer, he leaned back against the chair and said, "Damnit, man, you've as much right to know what went on as Domingo and I. You're the one who risked your life to find her and bring her back safely." Disappointment riding his voice, he went on. "The governor won't accept the refusal."

Louis set the cup and saucer back onto the library table with a clatter, his mien making no secret of his displeasure. Not that the future of the commandant's granddaughter was his business, he told himself when a wary alertness seemed determined to warn him. It was his own future he had best be concentrating on.

Leaning forward, Louis asked, "Exactly what does that mean for Manuela?" When the Ramons exchanged looks again, he said, "I'm not trying to intrude into a family matter, gentlemen. It's only that while on the journey back, Manuela did speak with me about her reasons for running away. I found that her version fit yours exactly. Her concerns about possible recriminations sounded genuine. How do you know she won't try taking matters into her own hands again, if the proposal still hangs over her?"

Teeth flashing beneath his silver-streaked moustache, Domingo smiled as if secretly amused and said, "We don't. My niece often reminds me of a colt being gentled to halter and bridle. Too much force might break the spirit, yet the training must go on." Fondness for Manuela softened his black eyes as he talked. "Father and I both hope that when she goes to Mexico City for the season, she might meet a suitable young man with whom she can find happiness. She's had little opportunity to move in social circles here in this remote area and is therefore quite the innocent."

Diego sent a restless hand up to smooth back a lock of gray on his forehead, then added, "The governor puts us all in an awkward position by refusing to accept Manuela's decision. He says that she's too young to know her own mind, that he will tender the offer until she reaches seventeen next April. He'll let the matter lie and expect no further answer until that time."

Louis digested the news with trepidation. From what he had learned, Governor Anya was accustomed to getting his own way in all matters. That the older man would retain even this slight hold on the spirited young beauty bothered him in a way he found baffling. Nothing about Manuela Ramon was his problem, he reflected again.

Without as much heart as he normally would have shown, Louis joined in the new topics of conversation that Diego and Domingo initiated then. The Frenchman acknowledged fatigue upon Diego's timely inquiry and returned to his room in the guest wing. Before he fell asleep, he sought to hone his mind in preparation for the possible confrontation with Governor Anya. Memories of heavy-lidded black eyes slanting in a lovely olive face kept clouding his mind.

Louis had not been gone long from the library before Diego and Domingo sent for Manuela. They had allowed her the past two days to spend as much time with Carlos as she wished, hoping that by doing so they were letting her recover from the ordeal of the kidnapping.

"The governor can't refuse to accept my answer, can he?" Manuela asked once Diego had told her of his meeting with Gaspardo Anya on the day after his disappearance. She rearranged the full skirt of her white cotton gown and sat up straighter against the back of the chair across from her grandfather. "Carlos told me you had seen him and that you had spoken about the suit, but I assumed he would have to take my refusal as final." Black eyes flashed to two pair of like hue. She read compassion but no capitulation.

"Summer is nearly half gone," Domingo assured his niece. Trying for a tone of enthusiasm, he went on, "Before you know it, it'll be September, and Doña Magdalena and I will be going with you to the City for the season. Who knows what might happen between now and next year when you become seventeen? Let's look upon the interval as a kind of reprieve and make the most of it. We'll go to the *fiesta* in a few weeks and have a grand time. By the way, the governor asked that you dance for his guests ... and knowing how you love performing, I accepted. I hope you like the idea."

Shrugging her shoulders and agreeing to dance, Manuela dropped troubled eyes to her hands, knotting now in her lap. Her uncle was right. She loved dancing. She tried to turn her thoughts toward having a costume made and working out a new routine for the upcoming *fiesta*. What else was there to do but hang onto Domingo's words and hope that some miracle or work of fate would save her? The real and imagined retaliation that Governor Anya could heap upon Diego and Domingo haunted her anew.

The time Manuela had spent with Carlos over

252

the past two days had reinforced her desire to seek love before agreeing to a marriage. Her twin was as much a rebel against class-based society as she, but a glaring difference had reared up during their lengthy talks. His seeming lack of the deep, caring kind of love she felt for their grandfather and uncle had shocked her, even pained her when she first recognized it during their recent talks. Whereas her brother seemed convinced that only his and her interests deserved first consideration, Manuela could not put aside her concern for Diego and Domingo. Had Carlos changed ... or had she?

"When we go to the City, will I be going as the governor's fiancée?" Manuela asked, her gaze flitting from one beloved face to the other. She needed to know her status.

"No, my dove," replied Diego. "You'll go as a young, unmarried Creole woman, a first-generation Creole at that, one eligible for a suit from a Spaniard. With your beauty and charm, plus the plenteous dowry your father left you, you'll likely be showered by all kinds of marriage proposals from handsome Spaniards."

Manuela made some kind of acceptable reply, though she knew not what. She left the library as soon as she could, her heart and mind troubled all over again.

Not that it was her business to know such things, but Manuela could not help but notice that no mention had been made of the plight of Louis and his men. Did that mean that Governor Anya had chosen to ignore the Frenchmen's illegal entry into Spanish territory? It seemed strange to her that even after nearly a month had passed since their arrival, the governor had not yet sent for the intruders to appear before him.

Manuela did not deny that thoughts of the handsome Louis had whirled through her mind ever since he had come for her at the Mescalero village. Carlos's teasing comment about his suspecting a romance between the two had not left her thoughts as readily as her quick denial had spewed forth. Even when she tried, she found she was unable to analyze her feelings for the Frenchman.

For sure, the brooding young woman mused, she could not forget the probing way he had looked at her during their long conversations on the journey back, or the way her pulse had fluttered from his nearness and attention. Honesty demanded she admit those mornings spent with him as tutor had offered as much heady excitement as knowledge of how to speak French. She no longer pretended she had buried the memory of their impassioned kisses in the stables. That tantalizing memory kept building up more and more, each time more sizzling than the time before. What did all of that add up to?

Full lips set in a pretty *moue* and black eyes flashing with self-mockery, Manuela recalled her parrot's echoing words: "Hot pepper! You'll be sorry."

Part Three

"A rosebud set with little willful thorns."
— Alfred Lord Tennyson

Chapter Fifteen

That afternoon while others enjoyed *siestas,* Manuela sneaked from her bedroom to the stables. She felt she would suffocate if she did not get out into the open for a spell.

Not many would have recognized the black-haired young woman with the thick braid wound about her head as the commandant's grand-daughter, for she wore Conchita's outgrown uniform, the one she had asked for to replace the one left behind at the Mescaleros' village. Within a short time, she had saddled a stock horse, and had ridden toward the irrigation ditch. Anticipation of gliding through refreshing water amidst dappled spots of shade from overbrush along the banks reigned and calmed her heavy thoughts.

Soon a slender arm reached with easy grace to pull itself through cool water. Eyes shut, Manuela floated facedown and drifted in her own wake, imagining she was entering another dimension as the water caressed and soothed her all over. The other arm stroked forward then, slicing a new watery path. Again she gave in to the feeling that she was in another world, one without cares or demands. A flutter of feet lifted her chemise-clad body back nearer the surface, gave her a chance for a blind gulp of air.

While she had been on the way to swim and sort out her feelings, it had never occurred to

Manuela to wonder why at Diego's latest unsettling news she had entertained no desire to speak with Carlos. It was as if she already knew what his thoughts were and that they would offer her no comfort, no resolution. For the first time in her life, she sensed she was truly on her own. Had that girlish side of her evolved into womanhood during the frightful kidnapping? that questioning part of her asked there in the stream. Another forward pull with the first arm—

"Whoa," came a masculine voice close by. Too close. "Head-on collisions might cause terrible injury . . . even to a water nymph or a princess."

Manuela's feet sank, sending her head to surface and her heart to attempt the same feat. Her eyes jerked open. Her mouth followed suit. She recognized that it was Louis Saint-Denis's voice coming only a few feet from her, though she had not heard it over the past two days. When instinctive feminine indignation at finding anyone swimming in what she deemed her private territory tried to take over, it fizzled into bone-tickling amusement and a kind of titillating pleasure she did not care to examine. She was still unsure as to what Louis meant to her.

How was it that the Frenchman showed up at the oddest times? Raking water from her eyes with her hands and then sending them to tread water, Manuela laughed into that water-splashed face no more than an arm's length away. Her husky musical notes of laughter blended with the small gurgles of stirred water. She saw again the heavy, brown eyebrows, noticed for the first time the tiny laugh marks beside the full mouth. Not for the first time, she wondered about the tiny scar on his left cheekbone. The overhead

258

bowl of bright, cloudless sky turned both the water and his gray eyes into a rich shade of blue. Louis's answering smile dazzled her, did crazy things to her pulse.

"I thought you were still a patient being held in seclusion," she said, short of breath for no discernible reason.

Beads of water clung to the tip of her straight little nose, the curly ends of her thick eyelashes. A drop of water rolled to claim a space in one of the slanted black eyes. For a moment, her view of the handsome face suffered a globular distortion. She blinked, and the drop of water glided on across her eye. Manuela could again see the real Louis. Nothing showed above the water but the tanned, smooth face and the lazily treading hands and arms. Was he naked? Her heartbeat found a new, more stepped-up rhythm.

"Sh—h—h," replied Louis, sending a forefinger to tap against his pursed lips, angling his dripping head this way and that to suggest that intruders might be somewhere nearby. At each movement, he pretended to search the banks. "You never know what manner of spies or thieves might be lurking about."

"True," she answered with mock solemnity, blinking her eyes to shed more of the droplets clinging to her lashes. Before entering the stream, she had unbraided her hair, and it floated about her like some dark, wet nimbus encircling a goddess. "I've heard that spies come this way from as far away as New France."

"Not really?" asked a suddenly round-eyed Louis. Her teasing delighted him almost as much as had the surprising sight of her entering the stream a few minutes earlier. A light-headedness had taken over and led him to swim down to join her.

Until Manuela blinked, Louis had almost persuaded himself, after the two days of not having seen her, that he had imagined the sultry movement of those slanted eyes could be as fascinating as he remembered. If only he *had* made it up, he moaned inside. Even in the cool water, banked fires were sending out warning sparks down low. "Whatever could they be traveling so far to spy upon? Is there much gold around this area?"

Manuela flashed him a droll smile, then imitated his earlier action of checking the banks for suspicious characters. Dainty chin in the water, sparkling eyes fixed on his face, she told him in a private voice laced with mischief, "The sand. Spies come to cart off the sand."

Even as he watched and listened to her there in the water, Louis could not believe his good luck at running into Manuela. He had realized that he was completely well after awakening from his morning nap and polishing off the food on the tray Medar brought. The earlier visit with Diego and Domingo had innervated him, made him eager to get back into the middle of things. He could think of little but to get out of the confining *hacienda*, breathe fresh air, and stretch his limbs. No one had been about when he had slipped to the stable and saddled Diablo.

Upon reaching the irrigation canal and stripping down to his underdrawers, Louis had welcomed both the escape from his previous heavy thoughts and from the napping Medar on the cot back in the *hacienda's* guest quarters. The sound of hoofbeats and splashes upstream had surprised him as he rested from a vigorous lap out in the center, for he had assumed that all at the *presidio* were enjoying their customary *siestas*. When he swam silently in the narrow bands of shade from overhanging willows to investigate, his heartbeat had jumped around in an absurd dance—and had not settled down yet, he noted.

To learn that Manuela also was slipping away during the normal *siesta* hours made Louis wonder if fate had led him to tie Diablo some distance downstream from where he had spotted her swimming that day of his arrival. It seemed obvious that she had no idea that anyone else was swimming. Whatever the reason the two had ended up in the stream together, Louis approved. Over and over.

Quelling his thoughts and going on with the farcical exchange, he asked, "Pray tell, princess, why would spies be after the sand?"

"To turn it into gold, you base ignoramus," she replied in a mock-serious tone, loving his calling her "princess" as he had on that last day on the way back home. At his uncomprehending stare, she added with a new glint deep within the black eyes, " 'Tis said the philosopher's stone is south of the Rio Grande, and that if one finds it, he can transform grains of sand into grains of gold. Spies come in droves to search for it."

"Aha!" Louis said with a wide grin of appreciation for her impish imagination. He did not think he had ever seen anything prettier than those dancing eyes, those teeth flashing whitely there in the sunshine. "That makes perfect sense. Then these spies must be alchemists at heart, obviously up to no good. We must join forces and be alert. Why, we must be in the midst of more gold than the world dares dream about."

261

"We mustn't tell."

"I can keep a secret."

A pert grin showed Manuela's pleasure at Louis's joining in her playful mood, then she asked, "Can you win races as well? I'll bet I can beat you to that willow drooping into the water up there."

Louis barely had time to note the destination and nod before she had darted in the direction with fast, gliding motions. When they reached the tree, he told himself he had allowed her to win by an arm's length; but secretly he wondered if she hadn't outswum him. Winded, he noisily flopped down at the edge of the water and fell back against the bank.

"You're a mean swimmer," he said between gasps as he leaned back on his arms. He watched her clutch a willow limb arching over the stream and move in rhythm with the wake they had created. Being laid up had taken its toll, he admitted to himself. His pulse must think he was still swimming.

"Carlos taught me," Manuela replied with a proud smile and a special glow in her eyes. She remained in the water and kept her hold on the dipping willow limb, knowing that if she went to sit beside him, the chemise would be little more than a second skin. A hurried peek at the pink spot on his sprawled leg told her that his wound was almost healed. Her first sight of so much exposed masculinity brought secret tremors. His wet underdrawers kept him from being completely naked, but still ... She fought not to think of how she had lain against that muscular body that night in the stables and ...

"Your twin and you must be very much alike."

"I thought we were until recently," she admitted, a woebegone expression flitting across her face for a second.

Feeling all powered up from the brisk exercise in the water, as well as from the sight of the beautiful young woman, Louis said what was on his mind. "It's pretty obvious that you're not alike in all ways—and I confess I'm damned glad you aren't." He let his eyes flick across her shoulders and the tops of her breasts showing as she still bobbed lazily in the water. She looked good enough to eat.

"Are you flirting with me?" Manuela asked, cocking her head and letting water drop from her ears, first on one side and then the other. Her eyes never left his face.

"I believe I must be." Louis had not realized he was until that moment. As it had on previous occasions, her candor shocked him. "None of your menfolk would approve, would they? They would likely accuse me of not being a gentleman and of taking advantage of their courtesy to me."

Manuela turned over his words in her mind. He really was the most handsome young man she had ever been around. That he wore only underdrawers seemed not to bother him at all. He reached to swipe a wet fall of hair from his forehead, the movement setting up a fascinating play of muscles across the dark-furred chest. This time the memory of how that solid hunk of flesh, those manly arms, had felt when she lay across him that night in the stable would not disappear. She tried to ignore it . . . and failed.

"Would they be right?" she countered, once she could trust her voice. "Would you forget you're supposed to be a gentleman?"

"No. I *try* to be a gentleman at all times. However, if I wanted to take advantage, I could grab you right this minute and kiss you and—"

"But you've no interest in doing that, have you?"

The minute the words came out, Manuela wished she had not asked. Her cheeks felt hot. Crazy pieces of that dream on the trail in which his face had loomed as the face of her Lover had been trying to get her attention ever since they had met in the water. Admitting that there had ever been such a dream made her feel foolish, almost shy. What if he could read minds?

"Should I lie and say 'no'?" Louis thought she seemed too intent on his answer for him to deny the truth. Was she blushing?

"I wouldn't know. I don't pretend to know the ways of gentlemen."

"Sometimes it's hard to be one, especially around such a temptingly beautiful creature as you, Manuela."

"My, but you know all the ways to turn a lady's head, don't you?" She returned his flirty look. "Suppose you were one of those young gentlemen that Uncle tells me I'm sure to meet in Mexico City this fall. How would you be expected to act?"

"I doubt we would be dressed as informally as now," he remarked wryly. Thinking about her moving in society in the company of ardent young men ruffled Louis's ebullient mood. He had not forgotten her confession that night on the trail about how she hoped to meet the man she could love. Would she find him in Mexico City? Something wrenched at his heart.

Manuela tipped back her head in laughter,

sobering to glance back at him and say, "You're right, Louis. We would most likely be at a ball at the viceroy's palace, all decked out in finery, our hair combed and styled." She studied his near-nakedness, adding, "But I can't imagine a man there being half so handsome as you." When he continued to bathe her with warm looks, she said, "Of course I realize from having grown up with a brother that I shouldn't make such remarks to a young man, or else he'll become even more conceited than he is already."

"Am I conceited?"

"Yes, you are."

"Why would you say that?" He could not hide the little dent to his pride made by her answer.

"Oh"—Manuela hedged a moment while collecting her thoughts behind half-lowered lashes—"I believe it's from the way you always seem so sure of yourself." She met his injured gaze full-on then. "I doubt you could have rescued me from the Mescaleros if you'd not felt that way. It must be wonderful to have such confidence in your thoughts and actions."

"I don't always have that confidence." He could not categorize all that she had said as traits of conceit, Louis assured himself. The last statement had come out like a compliment. Those sleepy-eyed looks of hers were fanning ever-heating flames.

"I don't believe you. Nothing seems to daunt you." She could see a new spark deep within the gray-blue eyes.

"You do." When he spoke, Louis knew how true the words were.

"I do?" she echoed. "Why? Are you afraid of me? Don't you like me?"

"I wish I knew how to answer." When she kept watching him from where she bobbed and floated beside the willow limbs as if awaiting more explanation, Louis said, "Maybe it has to do with your being so beautiful and so young." And, the passionate part of him added, that you can't be around her without wanting to touch her, kiss her.

"Sixteen isn't young," she scoffed. "Not when you think about how most young women are already married at that age, not just then coming under the care of a *dueña* for courting period . . . as I am. Would you like me better and feel more comfortable around me if I were an old hag?" Rosy lips pounded while widened black eyes showed clearly that even she could never envision herself as old or ugly.

No longer trying to fight down the building urge to kiss the black-haired beauty, Louis rose and entered the water then, reaching out his hand to her and coaxing her to follow him back near the bank where their feet could touch bottom. That Manuela had acted as though mesmerized throughout his bold actions came as something of a surprise. He had halfway expected that she might skitter away, make some kind of objection.

When Louis claimed her hand and led her to the edge of the water, Manuela felt again the overpowering sense of being all woman and desirable, the one that she had first experienced while with him on the trail. No part of her chose to protest his obvious intent. Something about the way his pale eyes squinted and sent hungry looks hovering about her mouth made her lips tremble, just before his captured them.

Great waves of warmth encircled Manuela, right along with Louis's arms. All sound and feeling seemed to have bunched up inside a sphere containing only the two of them, she reflected. Everything seemed magnified: his breathing and her own, the roar of erratic heartbeats deep inside her ears, the answering rhythm from his firm chest. The delicious smells of trees in summer shade, of cool water on a hot day, and of some fragrance distinctly masculine rewarded her nose. For a moment she thought she might be tasting the very essence of the handsome young man kissing her with such devastating sweetness, and she tightened her arms around his neck. No longer did she have to wonder at the ways of kissing, so thoroughly had he initiated her that night in the stables.

Somehow they ended up lying on the upward sweep of the bank beneath the arching willow branches, lips and bodies entwined there in the shadowed space meant only for two. Louis teased the sweet inner shape of her mouth with his tongue; hers answered back. Honeyed teasing turned into serious messages.

Louis watched through passion-weighted lashes as Manuela's eyes fluttered open. For a moment, he thought he saw eternity within those deep pools of black velvet. A shiver already begun inside wracked him as it surfaced, sapping his arms of strength. A wave of weakness such as he had never known before washed over him, and he recognized it as the aftermath of unabiding awe. How was it that no other young woman had ever affected him as Manuela Ramon did, had done so from the first moment he had watched her walk down the staircase in her grandfather's *hacienda?* Was he falling in love — or had he done so unknowingly upon that first sight of her?

When she opened her eyes, Manuela startled at finding those silvery ones watching her during their kiss, probing far into her secret self, seeking as if to plumb her very soul and search out things she herself knew nothing about. She glimpsed a kind of reverence touched with surprise in those widening, dark-edged gray irises, a kind of acknowledgment she could not understand. Dazed, she wondered if she might not be dreaming.

Why would Louis Saint-Denis be torching her soul with a look of the same intensity as his kisses? A part of Manuela seemed still out floating in the water, so ineffective did her limbs feel. Why did she have the sensation that she might be drowning, might not ever be saved? Her brain seemed to be as dappled as the space there beneath the airy willow limbs, for she realized that she had no wish to be rescued from this new kind of capture. One soft hand wandered from its hold about his neck and fingered a private path through the dark hair to his ear, then on to his cheek. She sensed there was more to be savored than the delicious mouth.

Long before they had exchanged those mind-boggling looks, Louis had been achingly aware of Manuela's wet body beneath the thin chemise. Holding her next to his nakedness, he could feel the luscious breasts soft against his bare chest, could feel the flat little belly conforming to his lean muscles. Her mouth was the prime target, though, and he fought against seeking further intimacies that might frighten her and lead her

268

to refuse him the nectar of her mouth.

Not long after he found himself on the ground with that irresistible body lying halfway across him, much as it had been that night in the stable, Louis lost sight of original, gentlemanly good intentions. The elusive, purely masculine part of him, which had unknowingly initiated Manuela's feeling of being totally female, took over. Louis was all loving male now, fully aroused. From past dalliances, he knew well that he possessed more than adequate charm and expertise to win the object of his ardor. Ever racing pulses fueled those inward flames.

Her mouth and tongue still belonging to him, Manuela moved her second hand to Louis's other cheek, thrilled at the feel of the cupped, manly face. When his fingers trailed with tenderness across a shoulder and slipped aside the wet chemise, she burned with new warmth and something akin to expectancy. The touch of his hand at the side of her breast set off even more searing tremors, and she feared she might lose her breath. When his fingers stole gently upon the swelling mound and discovered the now-hardened peak, Manuela did lose her breath. Inside she was a raging furnace, one she feared might explode any second. She struggled to free her mouth, to stop the spinning world, to drink in air.

Louis, his heart threatening to run away, moved his lips to kiss a path across the closed eyes, the perfect nose. The sight of her face and full lips all blossomed with passion tore at him in a way he had not expected. He could feel her breath upon his face as she struggled to correct her breathing. A shadow, not one from an outward source, dampened his passion.

The lovely face was not the face of a young woman passing a summer afternoon with a mild flirtation. Neither was it the face of one to whom a man could make love and savor the experience as just one of life's little special pleasures. There was something different about Manuela. Hadn't he sensed it from the beginning? There was more to her than a delectable body, though for the life of him he could not imagine why he had to be having such thoughts at that particular instant.

His hand upon her breast and his lips pressed against her pulsing temple, Louis lay still. Their rapid breathing seemed the only sounds in their private little spot. Obviously aroused, Manuela seemed as eager as he to explore further into the delights of passion. He had already noted the innocent threshing of her hips and legs while they kissed and fondled. What was gnawing at him, he agonized, sending him to examine their passion? Did it have something to do with his earlier, devastating look into her eyes and soul? Why did he feel that he would be losing more than he would gain by continuing their wild embraces? The answer no longer could be denied.

"Manuela," he whispered in tones suggesting midnight. Jumbled thoughts and feelings were wrecking the proud Louis Saint-Denis he thought he had known so well. "You're beautiful. Your skin is like a rose petal."

A pleased smile served as Manuela's reply.

When she continued to lie motionless with eyes closed, Louis's hand moved to return the straps of her wet chemise to the satiny, olive shoulder. He might not ever know what held him back from claiming what he sensed could be his, but he realized that he had no choice. Something more powerful than desire controlled him now.

Manuela opened her eyes then. A relentless chill followed the path his hand took as it left her breast. Why had Louis stopped his caresses? The feeling was not much different from the one experienced in the dream when the rosebud had been left on the stem. Had the dream been prophetic? Was the handsome Frenchman the Lover for whom she had waited ... and was he turning away? She had never before allowed the thought to form fully. No longer could she hold it back, Knowledge of what Louis meant to her stomped through her mind, kicking away every obstacle in its path, demanding recognition.

"Manuela," Louis whispered. "I love you. I think I have since I first met you."

"Oh," Manuela gasped, tears adding fresh magic to her eyes. "I love you too, Louis, but I didn't know it until this very moment."

With renewed eagerness, trembling lips met in a gentle kiss of promise; loving hands traced patterns of ecstasy across wet backs. Thundering heartbeats matched up harmoniously there in the hungry embrace.

Louis lifted his mouth far enough from hers to ask, "What will your grandfather say when I ask for your hand?"

Manuela's face showed her surprise.

"You do realize I'm asking you to marry me, don't you?" Louis asked, smiling to realize she was only then putting together what he was saying. Mother of Jesus, but she was beautiful! "Will you be my wife and go back with me to live in Louisiana? I have only a crude fort to call home right now. I'll be receiving a grant of land

271

upon my return and can start a house. It's just a wilderness now. We don't have any settlers around Fort Saint Jean Baptiste yet, but someday it might grow to be a large town and—"

"Louis Saint-Denis," Manuela interrupted. "You don't know much about me if you don't know that towns and society hold no attractions for me. I have ever longed to love and be loved by someone who would take me to a world belonging only to the two of us. What you're saying makes me only surer than ever that I do love you. Oh, yes, I'll marry you." This time, she initiated the searing kiss.

"I'll speak to Diego within the hour," Louis told her when the kiss ended. "I'll be happy to report to him that I have conducted myself as a gentleman around you—and if I don't leave now, I'll be lying. Will you take my ring as a token of our betrothal?"

Murmuring, "Yes," Manuela watched as he removed the gold ring and placed it on her finger. "It's beautiful, Louis, but it's far too big for me." She examined the initials deeply carved into the diamond-shaped surface of gleaming gold, noting that tiny acorns sat at the top and bottom angles. "How will you mark the sealing wax on your letters if you give it to me?"

He brought her hand up to his lips and kissed the finger wearing the too-large ring. "I've a regular stamp I can use, princess. I've never before allowed anyone even to try it on, and I'll like knowing you have it until I can get you a ring to fit your pretty finger."

When Manuela sighed her acceptance and offered him her lips, Louis gathered her close again and kissed her fiery lips with renewed passion.

"If that's the way a gentleman kisses a lady, I might become quite fond of gentlemen," she said when he ended the kiss and seemed to have run out of words. A curious air of testing stretched between them. His eyes held the strangest look, one seeming to show both pain and query.

"I hate the thought that some other man might touch those lips," Louis told her, rising and stepping toward the water. If he had ever needed a good cooling off, he knew it was right then. "I believe Diego can find no fault with my proposal, especially since you said that he promised you might have the final say about your marriage."

"I can tell everybody likes you," Manuela assured him, already picturing herself in his arms in his Louisiana wilderness. She tingled all over. Where was there a more handsome man than the one she gazed upon, the one whose ring she wore as a sign of his love for her? "Grandfather will be proud to give us his blessing."

Once Louis forced himself to go into the stream, he turned back to say in what he hoped was a teasing voice, "I know now why spies come to this desert area, and it has nothing to do with the sand."

Manuela sat up and flipped wet tresses behind her ears, tilting her head to emphasize her question. "Why do they come then?" She loved his wit, thought about how lucky she was to be marrying a man who liked playing little games as she did. She felt she might be glowing all over.

"To find a beautiful young princess named Manuela. She's the treasure."

After Louis had swum all the way back to where his clothing and horse awaited around a bend, a shaken Manuela sat beneath the willow branches and pondered. Her mind might as well have been back in the *hacienda* taking a *siesta*. Nothing she could think of made any sense at all. She wondered if her brain might be of no more substance than the clouds hovering over the distant mountains. Feeling not at all foolish, she brought the gold ring up to press against her lips, then pinched her arm. No. She wasn't dreaming.

Letting out a laugh of pure joy, Manuela headed with light steps and heart for her clothing and her horse. Her Lover had come! Happiness would be hers at last. Nothing could stand in the way of such a marvelous work of fate. She would make sure of it.

Chapter Sixteen

Colonel Diego Ramon squared his shoulders to a finer angle and drew himself up to full height there on his chair. Probing black eyes glared from beneath gray brows pinched together in a forbidding straight line. Shades of similar disdain and formality had laced the answer he had just boomed out.

Sitting on the other side of the handsome desk in the commandant's office, the young man posing what had seemed to him an acceptable question paused in surprise.

"Why are you so opposed to my marrying Manuela?" Louis asked, puzzlement threading his voice and sobering the previously beaming face. "Hear me out, Diego. I love—"

"It matters not to me how you feel about my granddaughter," the older man said in even frostier tones. The wrinkled but still firm hand resting on the top of his desk clenched. "Never will I give permission for her to marry any but a true Spaniard. She knows my feelings about this matter. Based on what I've learned about you these past few weeks, you might well be the fine, upstanding young man I believed, but—"

When Louis leaned forward from his chair as though to interrupt, Diego unclenched his hand enough to point an accusing finger at him and continued at a faster pace, "Please hear me out, sir. No matter what our past relationship has been, you're a foreigner, one on a mission that smacks of trickery to set up some kind of trade agreement between your Fort Saint Jean Baptiste and the Spaniards in Mexico. Had we had a more able governor in Coahuila, you would have already found yourself shipped off to Mexico City to face Viceroy Alencastre, the Duke of Linares."

"I've never objected to being transferred from San Juan Batista," Louis remarked in what he hoped was a reasonable way. "In fact, my mission is, as you suggested, twofold; but it isn't two-faced. Governor Cadillac showed good faith as a true Catholic by sending me to investigate the needs of your Father Hidalgo. If the priest felt the need to write for aid from the French, then we had to assume he was desperate. I confess that I hoped, along with our governor, that once I arrived and met with officials, some kind of trade agreement could be reached. You know that my passport plainly states our desire to purchase cattle and horses. If I recall correctly, your only comment about it was that such matters are out of your hands. Even Domingo seemed interested, I did not pursue the matter, as I didn't wish to displease you."

"True," admitted Diego, the hand on the desk relaxing as the Frenchman related the facts. "My son and I often disagree about what he deems the enforced fealty to the Crown. But that has no relevance here." Though Louis's request to marry Manuela had surprised and angered him, the commandant admitted to himself that he might have unwittingly contributed to the present dilemma. "Perhaps it would have been better all around if I had escorted your men and you on to the fort in Monclova that first day."

"May I ask why you didn't?"

Diego looked down at the ornately tooled leather covering the top of his desk. Why hadn't he? The simple truth seemed to be that he had taken such a liking to the young man and was so hungry for news of the outside world that he had neglected his duties as commandant for a brief time. He made no reply, so crazily did his mind whirl. When the matter of Louis's brave rescue of Manuela tried to claim his attention, he squashed it.

Uppermost in Diego's mind rode the long-conceived plan for Manuela to marry none but a Spaniard. How foolhardy for Louis to think for a moment that he would bless a union destined to take his beloved granddaughter far away into what could be no more than primitive wilderness ... beneath the French flag, at that! Squeezing the old man's heart further was the thought that such a marriage could mean he might never see Manuela again.

"Then you don't plan to discuss my suit with Manuela at all and learn her feelings for me?" The question pained Louis in every cell, for he suspected what the answer would be. He was surprised that his usually ticklish pride had not a single dent from the adamant refusal to consider allowing Manuela to marry him, a foreigner of obvious inequality to the proud old Spaniard. It was the young man's heart that lay shattered.

"No. There's nothing for Manuela and me to talk about regarding this matter."

Silence and an oppressive heat claimed Diego's office there in the waning afternoon sunlight. A thickening burned at the back of Louis's throat, and a heaviness crept up and down his legs and arms. The original purpose of the entry into Mexico lay buried beneath raw pain. What did it matter whether or not he made a contribution to New France? The vital question now was how could he live without the black-eyed beauty by his side. Surely when he could talk with her, Manuela would reassure him that something could be worked out. After all, hadn't he seen before how easily she charmed her grandfather into giving in to her wishes?

Diego cleared his throat and settled back against his chair, saying in his best commandant's voice, "I think it best that I send you over to Governor Anya this week. Nothing can be gained by your staying here until he sends for you. You told Domingo and me this morning that you're well enough to—"

A rap at the door followed by the sound of Sergeant Benitez's call interrupted just then.

After Diego rose and called through the door for him to enter, the sergeant did so.

Sergeant Benitez saluted and awaited permission before saying, "Commandant Ramon, an official escort has just arrived from Fort Monclova to transport the French spies to the prison there." Well-trained, the sergeant did not allow himself to sneak a look at the French lieutenant. "May I present the orders, sir?"

"By all means," remarked Diego, reaching for the folded document with the familiar seal marking a patch of thick wax. "In the future, Sergeant Benitez, refrain from being so formal. Here at my *presidio*, I like things a bit more relaxed, the way Sergeant Guerra ran them for me over the past

278

five years. The Lipan tribe have been with me from the beginning, and I have no wish to see them treated as anything other than desirable citizens of San Juan Batista. They're accustomed to running their private affairs. I've already heard more complaints over the short time you've been here than I ever did while Sergeant Guerra was in charge."

With a smart salute and an angry set to his thin lips, the heavyset sergeant left.

"This order says that the Indians accompanying you may stay here at San Juan Batista for awhile or return right away to Tejas," Diego told the keen-eyed lieutenant watching from across the desk. "Which do you prefer that they do?"

"Let them return to their people. My own soldiers will be coming to seek me out before winter. It's likely that some of the Assinais they've been hunting with on the Colorado will be with them." Louis's heart lurched. Did his going to Monclova mean he would never see Manuela again?

"How many Frenchmen can we expect?"

"Fewer than twelve," Louis responded, surprised that he could converse normally when, on the inside, chaos ruled. "Though Governor Cadillac's orders tell of twenty-four, I left twelve back at the new fort on the Red River to make improvements there. I lost one on the journey to a mangy rattlesnake."

Diego clamped his lips shut to keep from easing into a comfortable talk with Louis about the often heart-wrenching duties of officers. Damn! Even now he felt the young man's personality pulling at him. The intelligent eyes seemed crowded with confusion . . . and a hint of plead-

279

ing. For a moment a spot of light slanted across the scar on Louis's left cheekbone, and Diego wondered how it was that he had never gotten around to asking how it had gotten there. There had been so much to talk about with the bright young man . . .

"Governor Anya insists that you three Frenchmen leave immediately with his soldiers," Diego said once he could focus again on the situation of the moment. This was no time to be softhearted. "Domingo is still out with a party on a routine check along province boundaries. I'll say 'farewell' for him . . . and for the rest of my family. Your men and you may have an hour under guard to get your personal belongings together."

Louis stared at the old man he had come to revere and think of as his friend. Everything was happening so fast! Was fate to be so unkind as to prevent even one more glimpse of Manuela? For one accustomed to being in control, he was dumbfounded. He felt as if someone had sneaked up from behind and knocked him from a cliff. He was still falling, had no view of his destination.

His throat full, Louis swallowed and asked, "May I request a moment with Manuela?"

"Don't make this any harder for either of us, Louis. My affection for you is genuine, but my duty toward my granddaughter far outweights any other consideration. I think for me to shake your hand and leave you under the guard of the governor's men is the best way to end our relationship."

While talking, Diego had come from behind his desk to face the now-standing Frenchman. The weathered old hand reached out in a kind of apologetic friendship but clasped with a deter-

280

ACCEPT YOUR **FREE GIFT**
AND EXPERIENCE MORE OF
THE PASSION AND ADVENTURE
YOU LIKE IN A
HISTORICAL ROMANCE

Zebra Romances are the finest novels of their kind and are written with the adult woman in mind. All of our books are written by authors who really know how to weave tales of romantic adventure in the historical settings you love.

Because our readers tell us these books sell out very fast in the stores, Zebra has made arrangements for you to receive at home the four newest titles published each month. You'll never miss a title and home delivery is so convenient. With your first shipment we'll even send you a **FREE** Zebra Historical Romance as our gift just for trying our home subscription service. No obligation.

BIG SAVINGS
AND **FREE** *HOME DELIVERY*

Each month, the Zebra Home Subscription Service will send you the four newest titles as soon as they are published. (We ship these books to our subscribers even before we send them to the stores.) You may preview them *Free* for 10 days. If you like them as much as we think you will, you'll pay just $3.50 each and *save $1.80 each month* off the cover price. *AND you'll also get FREE HOME DELIVERY.* There is never a charge for shipping, handling or postage and there is no minimum you must buy. If you decide not to keep any shipment, simply return it within 10 days, no questions asked, and owe nothing.

mined farewell when a grim-faced Louis took it. "Thank you for your kindness and hospitality, Commandant Ramon," Louis said, his eyes asking for the older man's understanding.

His features stern, Diego nodded, smoothing his moustache as he led the way outside where six soliders stood at attention. With no further word to Louis, he informed the corporal from Monclova that the Frenchmen were now in his charge. His shoulders held with their usual military beating the commandant left the *plaza* and headed for his *hacienda* on the other side of the wall.

"Louis and the other two Frenchmen are gone?" Manuela echoed in horrified tones that night when she came down for dinner and asked Louis's whereabouts. Dismayed at their calm announcement, she frowned at Diego and Domingo. The breathless anticipation of seeing Louis and receiving Diego's blessing that evening on their planned marriage winged off in the way the hummingbirds zipped from the courtyard over the walls. A kind of wary waiting ruled, set her on edge, and made her cautious. "Where and when?"

Inside Manuela the question "Why?" screamed for an answer. Had Louis asked for her hand as he had told her he would? Or had he decided that to do so would be a mistake and dashed back to his fort in the wilderness of Louisiana? She could think of no reason why Diego would have refused his permission for them to wed. If she wasn't to live in Mexico, there was no need to worry about social class and marry a Spaniard. Louis had told her more than once that in New France, no class distinctions ruled, that the few settlers shared a noticeable bond. Had she only imagined those declarations of love that afternoon? Her heart lifted to recall that his crested ring lay hidden within the folds of his handkerchiefs upstairs in her bedroom. As her thoughts careened, the hand holding her fan clenched upon the ivory handle.

Calling out fond greetings then, Carlos and Doña Magdalena joined the trio in the living room to await dinner.

As soon as she could, Manuela asked Diego and Domingo again, "What happened to the Frenchmen?"

"Father says that Governor Anya sent for our 'prisoners' to be brought to him at the province capital," Domingo replied when Diego still seemed hesitant about answering. "His soldiers came and took Louis and his two men away before my scouting party and I returned at dusk."

"Was Louis well enough to make the journey?" Doña Magdalena asked, thinking, as was Manuela, of the half-day's time required to reach Monclova. She sat on the sofa from which Diego had risen upon her entry into the room. Once he eased back down beside her, they exchanged solemn looks. "This was his first day to be up and out of his room. Why did they have to travel at night? He'll be exhausted." With a noisy clack, she opened her fan and moved it rapidly before her face.

Manuela eyed her great-aunt askance. Since when had she had warm feelings for the Frenchman? Something was wrong. She could feel it.

Her eyes flitted from face to face but found not a single expression to give her solace.

Diego assured his fretting sister-in-law, "Yes, Louis met with us in the library this morning and seemed fine, said he was ready to get on with living. I'm sure he'll stand the journey without problems."

"Do you want to hear what I've learned over at the barracks about why Anya had him chained to his horse?" Carlos asked, pacing over near the door opening out onto the patio.

"Chained?" Manuela shrieked, aware that both Diego and Domingo watched her every movement. Did they suspect she loved the Frenchman? It helped a little to note that Doña Magdalena appeared as shocked and disapproving as she. "Why on God's earth would the stupid man have Louis chained? He isn't a criminal. He isn't out to do us harm. What have you heard, Carlos?"

"One of the privates is kin to one of the soldiers who came for Louis and his men, and they exchanged a few words while the prisoners were making ready for the journey. It seems that you were right, Grandfather, in suspecting that the governor swapped sergeants with you to pick yours about what's been going on over here. Sergeant Guerra has no doubt talking freely of what he's learned over the past five years at San Juan Batista, none of which seemed to interest the governor. But when the sergeant told *all* about happenings over the past three weeks—"

"*All?*" interrupted Domingo and Diego at the same time.

"What does that mean?" Manuela jumped in to ask before either of the startled men could. "Quit

283

being so dramatic, Carlos. What was there to tell?"

"The talk is that Governor Anya suspects Louis is the reason that you tried to reject his suit," Carlos replied with an injured look from her accusation. "He's learned that the French lieutenant lived in the quarters for visiting officers until he was wounded and moved here into the *hacienda* a few days ago. Then some dolt told about Louis's private mission being the one that succeeded in rescuing you, Manuela. From what I learned, the old man must be literally frothing at the mouth with jealousy." Only then did he note how tense his sister had become.

"Can this be true, Grandfather?" Manuela asked. Finding out exactly what had happened to Louis after they parted at the irrigation canal in mid-afternoon was proving to be as hard as accepting that he was gone. Inside she was panicking, but she found it somewhat comforting to learn that he hadn't left of his own accord or because Diego had ordered him to.

"A corporal with five soldiers came soon after *siesta*. He did not say a word about the governor's being upset, just indicated that the matter of interrogation was routine. I told Louis 'good bye' and came inside. I heard nothing of his being taken away in chains until Domingo came in and told me. None of this was my idea," Diego explained to the four anxious faces watching him with varing degrees of disapproval and horror on their faces.

"I can't imagine Louis's having to endure chains," Manuela said, her voice low and sorrowing. "What a despicable action for Governor Anya to take! I knew he was vile, but—"

"Enough of angry words," Doña Magdalena scolded her charge. "I too am bothered that such a charming young man should be subjected to such treatment, but I realized that we women must accept the ways of men in their world, as they do in ours of the home."

"Accept?" Manuela retorted. "What do you mean 'accept'?" Black eyes flared with sparks of indignation. How much dared she tell about the afternoon's wonderful discoveries? The memory of her losing her temper with Diego and Domingo that afternoon in the study warned her. The action now seemed childish, unworthy of a young woman loved by one so brave and stalwart as Louis Saint-Denis. Besides, what good had come from her having revealed her true feelings about not wishing to marry Governor Anya?

With all eyes on her, Manuela went on. "How can any of you *accept* this unjust action toward Louis? Surely you feel that you know him quite well. You've spent the better part of three weeks visiting and dining with him, learning that he's no spy. I've heard you talk about the passport he carries. Don't you believe that he truly came here to petition in favor of Father Hidalgo's wish to rebuild missions for the Tejas? He could have set the Indians he brought with him against us, but he didn't. What can you be thinking of to sit back and accept such injustice toward one you've befriended, one who risked his life to save Eblo and me from no telling what kind of treatment from the Mescaleros?"

"I believe my sister made some good points," Carlos spoke up, walking to throw an arm around her shoulders. Like Manuela, he too sensed there was unexplained tension in the room, and it

285

involved more than just his twin. He sent anxious looks to Diego and Domingo. "Shouldn't we do something to help? Do you suspect that his having Louis brought in chained means that Anya plans to throw him in prison?"

Manuela almost gave in to tears at Carlos's mention of prison. How could she bear to think of Louis being confined to a cell? What agony he must be going through. Her heart swelled with renewed indignation as she listened to the casual talk among the three Ramon men. It was plain all disagreed with the governor's action, but none seemed to think a solution was possible.

No matter how carefully Manuela studied the guarded faces of her grandfather and her uncle, she could not determine what they were hiding as they conversed. Had Louis gotten a chance to talk with Diego about their betrothal? It appeared to her that he had not. If he had, and if Diego had greeted the news of their love with his blessing, as she felt sure he would have, wouldn't he have tried to delay Louis's removal to Monclova, or at least sent Domingo to follow and make certain he was treated fairly?

Ending the conversation about the Frenchman, Diego coldly pointed out, "As we all know, there's a ruling from the Crown that no trade will be allowed between Mexico and any other country but Spain, and that any foreigner will be arrested upon suspicion if apprehended within our borders. I may be the one at fault for not having sent the French lieutenant over to Monclova when he and his men first arrived."

But Louis came here chiefly on a mission of mercy, Manuela agonized secretly. His visit had something to do with trade only in a minor way.

Even if she didn't understand all the reasons he had come, she sensed they would be logical. The man she loved was honorable; she was certain of it. Some instinct told her just as certainly that to remain silent about their newly declared love was the wisest course. Not until she learned what was causing the almost visible vibrations emanating from Diego and Domingo would she reveal her determination to wed Louis Saint-Denis in the church outside the *presidio* walls.

After a miserable dinner hour, in which everyone tried to speak of cheerful topics and none succeeded, Manuela excused herself and went up to her room where she poured out her heart to Zorro. The parrot cocked his head and seemed to listen.

"Hot pepper!" Zorro said, obviously liking the sound of his latest utterances. "You'll be sorry!"

Manuela smiled wanly then, the ridiculous reply jolting her from her mood of dejection over the plight of the young man she loved, the one who had taught her the magic of flirting . . . and kissing. All at once, an idea streaked to mind. When she was sure that all had retired and no one was about to see, she slipped out to the darkened stables.

"Eblo?" Manuela called when she opened the door from the patio. When his form appeared from the shadows, she told him what cruelties Governor Anya might be inflicting on the two who had risked their lives to rescue them from the Mescaleros.

"What can we do?" he asked after her voice died away and the only sounds were the occasional shifting of horses' feet inside their stalls.

"First, you can send this note by carrier to the

viceroy in Mexico City. I wrote two in case one pigeon doesn't get through. Do you think there's a good chance that at least one of the messages will reach the palace pigeon cote?"

Eblo nodded emphatically. He took the tightly rolled pieces of paper and asked, "What does message say? If we're going to go behind the commandant's back to do this thing, I need to know what you're up to."

Her heart lifting at Eblo's apparent willingness to help Louis and her by acting without Diego's permission, Manuela told him, "I've written that Governor Anya is falsely holding as a spy a French envoy here on a religious mission. I explained that harsh action against the man will cause the Tejas to rise up against all the northern provinces."

"Is this true?" Eblo asked, drawing back at the implication of her words. "Did you learn this from the Assinais coming here with Saint-Denis? Black Eagle and his men are angered that Saint-Denis has been taken away, but I don't think—"

"No, it isn't true," Manuela assured him. "Or at least if it is, I've no way of knowing. I made it up in the hope that Viceroy Alencastre will send someone up to stop Anya's unlawful seizure of the Frenchmen. If anyone other than those under Anya's orders can talk with Louis and examine his passport, they'll see what Grandfather and Uncle did—that he is what he seems. I've heard Uncle talk of trouble between the viceroy and Anya, trouble having to do with Anya's ignoring orders from Mexico City when it pleases him. If the viceroy can catch the governor in a wrongdoing that might cause any kind of trouble with the Tejas or even the French, well . . ."

Eblo shook his head in puzzlement. Manuela's mind was delving into matters that he knew were not her territory – or his. However, his sense of obligation to Louis and Medar for having rescued them from the conniving Mescaleros sat a notch higher than any other at the moment. The old Indian well knew from eavesdropping at the Mescalero village that had Spanish soldiers been among those in the arriving search party, much violence would have taken place; Manuela and others from the *presidio,* as well as he himself, would likely have been killed or worse.

Limping off into the darkness toward the ladder at the end of the stable, Eblo already had in mind the two pigeons to send on the journey to Mexico City.

With a fervent prayer that what she had set into motion would prevent further punishment for the dark-haired Frenchman she had come to love with such passion, Manuela sped back across the dark courtyard.

Both Conchita and Manuela wore serious looks over the next weeks. Neither could get properly interested in the new gown Manuela had forced herself to design for her performance at the *fiesta* in Monclova. Hoping to count Louis among those watching her dance, Manuela had chosen strips of green and yellow silk to be sewn into a voluminous skirt of wide stripes. When Inez, Conchita's cousin, the most talented seamstress among the household staff, brought the skirt for a fitting, Manuela smiled her pleasure. Louis would love it.

Twirling before the mirror in her bedroom and

admiring the way the strips of silk rippled at the slightest movement, Manuela clapped her hands to a remembered melody and watched the skirt bell out from her dancing feet.

"It'll be perfect, won't it?" she asked the two appreciative servants. "Inez, I want a yellow ruffled petticoat to wear beneath, one so full it'll flare along with the skirt." Humming beneath her breath, not admitting even to herself that she was counting on Louis's being one of those watching her dance, Manuela asked, "Did you know that Carlos has agreed to play his guitar as the lead during my dance?"

Conchita replied with a knowing smile, "No one will hear the music. All they'll think of is the way you look as you dance."

Manuela rushed to give both Conchita and Inez giant hugs, saying, "What would I do without the two of you? I sometimes get butterflies thinking of dancing before the governor and all the people at the *fiesta*. But when you tell me such wonderful little lies, I get excited thinking of what a thrill it'll be to have such a grand audience." For the first time in days, the old sparkle showed in the huge slanted eyes.

The sewing went on. The day before those at San Juan Batista were to leave for Monclova, the gown was complete. As an addition to the colorful costume, now topped with a low-cut bodice of green silk with a narrow strip crossing over slender forearms to serve as sleeves, there were short drawers of the same yellow silk. Green ribbons held them just above the knees. Even Doña Magdalena confessed that, though gaudy, the gown was perfect for the spirited dance Manuela would perform.

Domingo went ahead to Monclova two days before his father and the other family members left for the weekend of festivities. Though both Diego and he had dispatched messengers regularly over the past three weeks to learn what was happening to Louis and his men, none had returned with more than gossip filched from uncaring soldiers. Neither Diego nor Domingo discussed their growing concern outside their offices. It seemed clear that the Frenchmen were being held incommunicado in prison cells.

"Which birthday do you suppose Governor Anya is celebrating?" Carlos asked Manuela. They had been traveling on horseback since mid-morning, and up ahead rose the encompassing walls of the fort outside the small town of Monclova. "His ninety-ninth?"

Manuela grinned at her handsome brother's exaggeration and replied, "Not quite. Doña Magdalena said he's older than she and that she believes it's his fiftieth." She knitted her brows then and asked, "Do you realize that's only four years less than Grandfather claims?"

Manuela guided Nightstar around a patch of cactus edging the narrow road, glancing back to see if the small carriage occupied by her great-aunt and Conchita was still in view. Even through the cloud of dust kicked up by the team pulling the vehicle, she could see the corners of the large trunk holding their clothing jutting from where it was tied onto the rear. Thoughts of all the dust that had been sifting into the carriage on the journey and how fractious Doña Magdalena must be by now made her glad all over again that she had insisted on riding Nightstar.

Poor Conchita, mused Manuela. The cheering thought for both her maid and herself over the past weeks had been that once in Monclova for the *fiesta*, they would be able to gain news of the Frenchmen who had become so important in their lives. When Conchita had learned from the soldiers over in the *plaza* that the men were in prison, the young women had despaired.

Eight soldiers from the *presidio* accompanied the group, four up ahead and four behind the carriage. Highwaymen were scarce in northern Mexico, though they bothered travelers along the southern sections of the King's Road to the City with frequency and ferocity. Diego had ridden alongside his grandchildren for most of the way but had gone on ahead now that Monclova was so close.

"I'll bet Francesca will be glad to see you," Manuela said. "When we were last here in the spring, she was turning into quite a beauty."

"Francesca Anya will never be a beauty, and you know it." Carlos shot her a disgruntled look. "Maybe you're hoping the great Figaro will be at home this time." He winked at her and added, "Just think what you'll miss if you don't get to claim him for your stepson. He must be at least ten years older than we are." With a careless flip of his hand, Carlos went on, "And of course there's always the second son, Felix. You two would truly make a pair."

Accustomed to his teasing, Manuela managed to send her twin a haughty stare. What he was saying about the two Anya sons coming close to being her stepsons pained her more than she would have Carlos know. Some restless voice had kept reminding her over the past three weeks that the governor's suit had not truly been resolved, that there was still no guarantee that she might not have to marry him unless Louis gained his freedom along with Diego's approval.

In the young woman's eyes, Governor Gaspardo Anya was revolting all by himself as a prospective groom. His two leering sons with their weak chins and bulging eyes had always repulsed her. She hoped Figaro had not come up from Mexico City to help celebrate his father's birthday. The last time she had been around him, he had tried to kiss her and fondle her breasts, and she had cursed him and walloped him with her fist. To think of having to endure the presence of either Figaro or Felix as members of her family were she to have to marry—

"What in the world has you in such a sour mood?" Carlos asked, interrupting her troubling thoughts. Keen black eyes assessed her with concern. "Are you afraid I forgot I'm to play lead guitar for your dance tomorrow night?" When she made no reply, he asked, "Are you concerned for the welfare of the handsome Frenchman?"

"Yes," Manuela snapped, angered at his flippant mood. She could find little to lift her spirits other than the thought that she might get to see Louis. Inside a pocket of her black riding costume, she could feel the reassuring weight of his ring concealed in the monogrammed handkerchief. "You and Conchita tell me you've heard Louis is in prison. What if that were you locked up? Wouldn't you expect me to be worried about you?"

"But I'm your brother. Why would you be so upset if Louis Saint-Denis is in prison? What is he to you?"

The afternoon sun had brought a touch of pink to Manuela's face beneath the broad-brimmed hat, but the heat washing beneath that olive skin now had little to do with the sun. No one else had asked that question.

"Carlos," she said in a voice that he had to lean from his horse toward Nightstar to hear, "I'm confiding only in you. Louis and I are in love. He asked me to marry him and return with him to Louisiana."

Carlos pursued his lips and let out a low whistle. "Then that's why Grandfather and Uncle have been wearing such long faces."

"I don't believe they know it," she pointed out. "Louis must not have had time to approach Grandfather about our wish to marry before Anya's soldiers came for him." At her twin's increasing look of puzzlement, she went on, still in the private voice. "We met by accident at the irrigation canal on his last afternoon and discovered we were in love. He was to have told Grandfather all about us when he returned to the *presidio*. I had hoped that night when I came down to dinner to learn that our wishes were to be granted. Instead, I learned Anya's men had taken him away . . . in chains." A fullness in her voice suggested there might be tears in the downcast eyes.

"Why haven't you told me this before?"

"I felt I had to keep it secret."

"Even from your twin?"

Manuela looked at Carlos with eyes far wiser in the ways of love than those staring back at her, saying, "What good would it have done?"

"You always said that you had to talk over everything that troubled you with me. What's changed?" He felt a twinge of guilt at not having noticed earlier the mysterious sadness deep in her eyes. His interest in playing his guitar, racing his horse, and wrestling with the Indian youths living outside the walls of the *presidio* had kept him occupied since his return from hunting. He had thought Manuela caught up in the making of her gown and the perfecting of her dance routine. "I realize we've not been together much lately except when I was playing for your dance, but—"

"Don't blame yourself, Carlos," Manuela interrupted to say. "I couldn't talk about it until I'd accepted what I must do."

"Do? What can you do? You know we've heard the man's in prison, that Grandfather's messengers have been refused permission even to talk with him through the door. Uncle Domingo said that the governor has never given Louis an audience during the time he's been here. If he ignores prisoners long enough—a favorite trick of his, I hear—they die from diseases floating about in that hellhole of a prison. I hate to tell you this, but there's nothing anyone can do."

At Carlos's announcement of what Conchita had also heard was likely to be the fate of the Frenchmen, Manuela winced. Full lips trembled for a moment before settling into a determined shape that went well with the strong, upturned chin. A womanly wisdom gleamed from the black depths of her eyes as she motioned for Carlos to ride even closer. They would be at the governor's mansion in minutes. In detail, she told her twin what she planned to do to save Louis's life and how he could help her.

When their horses clattered across the carefully laid round stones of the huge courtyard leading to the governor's stable, Carlos was still sending shocked but admiring looks at the proudly lifted face of his beautiful sister.

Chapter Seventeen

Before dinner that night in the governor's mansion, Don Gaspardo Anya greeted all of his guests from San Juan Batista with courtesy. Private, unpleasant talks on the previous day with the earlier-arriving Domingo about his imprisonment of the Frenchmen, and with Diego that very afternoon, might as well not have taken place. Exhilarated at the first sight of the beautiful Manuela since Easter, Gaspardo denied to himself that only a short time ago he had felt even older than the fifty years being celebrated on the morrow.

"More lovely than I dared recall," Gaspardo murmured upon taking Manuela's politely proffered hand and lightly kissing the smooth skin. Gone were hateful thoughts of gout and creaking limbs. The sight of the young beauty set both his blood and mind into a heady race. Were those haughty, slanted eyes sending him messages? The thought of claiming that tempting body quickened his pulse. "All look forward to your dancing for us tomorrow evening, but none so eagerly as I."

"I'm honored that you requested me to perform," Manuela replied. It was not easy to hide the repulsion that the touch of his lips and moustache upon her hand fed to greater heights. She saw the remembered thick lips beneath the enormous black moustache salted with gray.

Though she admired the trim moustaches of Diego and Domingo, she had always recoiled at a peculiarity of the governor's. Above the center of his top lip, the hairs from his wide nostrils seemed to be growing down to form a part of the moustache. The untidy moustache appeared to form a nest for the drooping nose, an oddity that Manuela somehow viewed as unsanitary, even repulsive.

With exaggerated good manners, Gaspardo proceeded to make sure that all of his family greeted each guest there in the spacious receiving room. Manuela was relieved to learn that Figaro, the elder son, had been unable to travel from the City, where he served as aide to a court judge, to help celebrate his father's birthday; but Felix was there.

At twenty-two, Felix displayed inordinate pride at being appointed his father's assistant. The young man showed that one day he would look like his father; his body was short and thick, already spreading into rounded edges that would not have to swell much more to be termed plain fat. At least Felix Anya had some space between his moustache and his ugly nose, Manuela noted. Unlike Figaro, Felix had never made advances toward her, so she was glad she could give him at least one mark of approval for his appearance. Not that it counted for much, she reminded herself. Inner amusement brought an added sparkle to her eyes to match the pasted-on smile.

"We're happy you could come for the *fiesta*," Marthe Anya remarked once Manuela and she had a chance for words alone. Gaspardo had taken over entertaining the men near a serving table at the end of the long room, one holding wine decanters and silver platters filled with tiny biscuits and nuggets of goat cheese. "My brother-in-law has looked forward to your visit." Her round face wreathed with a pleasant smile, the plump woman eyed the lovely visitor's tiny waist and graceful figure without a visible trace of jealousy. "You've become such a beautiful young woman, Manuela. How well I recall when I came here from Seville two years ago that you were no more than a pretty girl."

Manuela murmured her thanks for the compliment and made a comment on Marthe's new gown before asking about the other members of the family. Outwardly listening to the vivacious Marthe's glowing accounts of the progress and health of the governor's three daughters and her own Celia as well, Manuela remembered how it was that the plain-faced Marthe had come to act as mother to her nieces and hostess for her brother-in-law.

Widowed by Gaspardo's younger brother, and with a child from that marriage, Anna had accepted Gaspardo's frantic invitation to bring young Celia and come live in Mexico. His wife, Isabel, had died giving birth to a third daughter. Manuela thought it strange that although some seemed to pity Marthe because she was not yet thirty and already widowed, she appeared contented in the governor's mansion.

"Look how Francesca sidles up to Carlos every chance she gets," Marthe whispered with amusement. "Gaspardo has teased her all day because she couldn't make up her mind which gown to wear tonight and which to save for the *fiesta* tomorrow. I told him to let up on her, that a fourteen-year-old girl needs to act giddy every once in a while."

Amused that her remarks to her twin had not been too far off the mark, Manuela turned to watch Francesca dimple up at Carlos and turn red at whatever he said. Across the room she saw Doña Magdalena sitting with the younger girls near a small table, obviously enjoying telling them some incident from the years of her past social life in Mexico City.

Felicia Anya, at whose birth Gaspardo's wife had died, was only two and seemed determined to outshine the silver-haired lady. Her sister Fiona and her cousin, Celia, both of them eight, acted just as determined to hear out what must be one of Doña Magdalena's interesting tales. Each time Felicia whirled about and fell dizzily upon the tile floor to gain attention, the eight-year-olds pretended she did not exist. Manuela smiled to see that the spirited little girl's antics were beginning to draw warm looks from the normally stern-faced Doña Magdalena.

"Felicia is still a little charmer, isn't she?" Manuela asked Marthe.

"She's my love," Marthe replied with a doting smile. "Of course my Celia is my first love," she amended as if she feared she might have insulted her own child. "And I've come to feel that both Fiona and Francesca are as dear to me as if they had been my own. The four girls and I have a good time."

Hearing the deep love threading through Marthe's soft words, Manuela wondered if the Anya girls knew how lucky they were to have one so obviously contented at mothering looking after them.

The time flew as Marthe, in her role as unofficial hostess of the mansion, made everyone welcome and comfortable. Dinner was almost pleasant, marred only when Manuela would look up and catch Gaspardo's bold gaze marching across her face and fashionably bared shoulders. She could hardly wait for the evening to end so that she could return to her bedroom and find out what Conchita had been able to learn about the Frenchmen.

"The prison is that long building at the far end of the *plaza?*" Manuela asked after listening to Conchita's findings. Along with her family, she had visited at the mansion often and knew the layout of the fort well. "Were you able to get inside?"

"No," Conchita replied in woeful tones, relating all that Manuela had asked her to learn. She added, "There are two guards at the entry, except while one is walking the post, and both laughed when I asked if the Governor had interrogated the Frenchmen. I learned that no soldiers have come up from the City recently, though I wish you'd tell me why you want to know that. I tried not to seem too interested in the Frenchmen, just curious because they had come from our *presidio.*"

Manuela's heart dipped at the news that no soldiers from the viceroy's troops had come. Eblo's carrier pigeon must not have reached the City and stirred the viceroy to action. All depended on her now. She forced her mind back to the situation and asked, "And you say that all three are in separate cells?"

301

"Yes, and not next to each other. Louis's air vent—those holes are too small to count as windows—is the third down from the end of the building, facing the *plaza*. Medar's is the fifth, and Sergeant Penicault's is the seventh on the other side."

"Good girl! You found out a lot for only a few smiles, didn't you? I wonder how much more cooperation we can get for the coins I brought along."

Conchita looked down at her clasped hands and asked, "What is it you have in mind, Manuela? I suspect you have a plan to set the men free, and I fear for you. You've not confided in me, but I can tell you feel more for Louis Saint-Denis than you've let on." She lifted pleading eyes then to her mistress. "Why won't you talk with me about him? You must surely know that I'll help you in any way that I can."

"You've already been a tremendous help, dear friend," Manuela replied, taking a step to put an arm about her maid's shoulders. "I've known I can count on you to help me, and I'll not keep secrets from you anymore. Now that we're here and know for sure that the men haven't appeared before Anya and aren't likely to, I see that there's only one way to get them out of prison. I'll tell you what I have in mind now."

Far into the night, the two black-haired young women talked. For the first time, they confided about their burning loves for the pair of foreigners who had won their hearts back at San Juan Batista. Before they dropped off to sleep, Conchita on a cot in the dressing alcove and Manuela on the tall bed in the guest bedroom, Manuela's plan had been set into motion.

* * *

Noise and excitement filled the air all the next day. Leaving behind the confusion reigning inside the mansion as servants prepared for the night's festivities, Carlos and Manuela strolled about the vicinity of the governor's mansion there beside the fort. Citizens of the province of Coahuila had traveled from far corners to join those in the town of Monclova in taking part in the *fiesta* celebrating their governor's birthday. Donkeys and carts, as well as horses, filled all available liveries and corrals. Vendors' stalls just outside the huge *plaza* beside the governor's mansion offered all kinds of goods and produce for those combining marketing with attending the festivities. Excited barks from dogs, shouts of laughter, and the blend of holiday voices in conversation drifted from the crowd filling the market.

With outward enthusiasm, Manuela admired baskets woven of willow branches and mescal leaves in myriad shapes and sizes. They lay stacked beside a family obviously proud of their artistry. Floppy-brimmed hats with intricate patterns nestled atop each other, forming haphazard columns as high as a man's head. Thinking to bring a sparkle to his sister's eyes, Carlos clowned around, trying to find a hat that might fit better than the one he had at home. He gave up after awhile. The smile on her lips never quite reached her eyes.

Manuela paused before the numerous stalls offering the colorful produce from the area. There were pale oranges of all sizes, tangerines, and shiny lemons. Gardens had provided seasonal choices, such as squash, onions, potatoes, tomatoes, and peppers. Red peppers, yellow ones, green ones — some dried and strung in long garlands from posts driven in the ground; some freshly picked, lying in piles, all plump and shiny. Their dried stems plaited into thin ropes, fat clusters of garlic jutted from what looked like improvised horsewhips looping beside the colorful stringed peppers.

Down the way, strong smells of freshly dressed goats and chickens led the twins to forego further browsing among the markets and amble back toward the *plaza* before mid-afternoon.

While outside the governor's mansion, the revelers were finding little peace and quiet for their impromptu *siestas* beneath trees or overhanging roofs, those inside rested up for the night's faster-paced festivities. Closed shutters added shadowed coolness and a degree of quiet.

Diego and Domingo left their bedrooms before it was time for the remainder of those resting in the mansion to be up and about. Gaspardo Anya had reluctantly agreed to meet with them in the privacy of his library on the ground floor. None of the three paid any attention to a uniformed maid intent on polishing the brass doorknobs of neighboring rooms.

"Diego," Gaspardo began, "I thought I'd already explained my views on spies to you and Domingo. Such matters lie within my sole jurisdiction as governor of Coahuila. Though I may use my province's officers as advisors whenever I choose, I don't recall having asked your advice in this matter. Your interest in this Lieutenant Saint-Denis seems quite out of the ordinary." He showed his annoyance that the Ramons had

304

made it clear that the welfare of Louis was no longer to be dismissed as unworthy of discussion. "Perhaps you can explain why."

"The man risked his life to save Manuela's," Diego said. "I'm sure you can see why we owe him our gratitude."

"Gratitude, yes," Gaspardo said, a semblance of a sneer on the thick lips. A pudgy forefinger played at the side of his untidy moustache. "Beyond that, why this concern for his personal well-being, his quarters, his food?"

"The man is a gentleman and an officer in the French army," Domingo pointed out. "No matter that our kings might be opposed on certain principles of trade, it seems that we owe fellow officers our respect on grounds of simple decency. Spain is no longer at war with France, and it hardly seems proper that we would treat a French lieutenant as a common criminal when no crime has been committed."

"How can you be sure?" the governor asked.

"Have you spoken with him?" was Diego's weighted reply.

"I've told both your son and you that I haven't."

"As one with years of military experience, may I suggest that you grant him audience?" Diego inquired.

"What good could come of that?" Obvious resentment at Diego's insinuation that he himself might be lacking in knowledge of such matters deepened the furrows on his brow, brought fire to Gaspardo's beady eyes. "I may not have served in uniform, but as governor I've been privy to the ways and wishes of our viceroy. Sometimes ignoring those who occupy cells is the easiest way to maintain control. Sooner or later, they lose their zeal for whatever cause put them there."

"And their lives, as well," Diego replied, his face sad.

"Governor, if you met with Saint-Denis, you might see that he isn't your ordinary young man, that he is worth decent treatment while you're awaiting orders from our viceroy," Domingo suggested, aware that his father was angering their superior, just as he himself had done upon his earlier arrival.

Something gnawed at the fat little man, and Domingo sensed it had little to do with French spies. Was the gossip true that Anya blamed Louis for Manuela's attempted rejection of his suit? he mused. Was the governor truly gloating to subordinates that when he was through with him, the Frenchman would hold no appeal for any young woman? He hated thinking that the man might be capable of such cruelty.

"I hardly think that to bother the busy Duke of Linares with such a trite matter as three French spies is necessary. I've sent no word to Mexico City. I don't need advice from anyone as to how to handle spies." After his acid comments, Governor Anya reared back against his chair.

"You intend to let Louis and his men rot in that filthy prison, don't you, Gaspardo?" Diego asked, no longer caring that the man was becoming visibly riled. Right was right. "Without even a hearing? Hasn't the viceroy sent you the missive concerning the Crown's rules for treatment of political prisoners—or did it get lost, as some of his past edicts reportedly have done after they arrived here?"

"Perhaps I'll interrogate them next week,

though I think our viceroy sometimes assumes more powers than he was granted," Gaspardo answered after an ugly silence, no doubt sensing the threat underlying Diego's words. A self-pitying smile preceded his words. "I've not been well, you know. My health and business matters have delayed my normal procedure for dealing with prisoners."

"All we ask is that you provide decent quarters and food for the Frenchmen and let them come before you, or at least Lieutenant Saint-Denis, the officer in charge," Diego said.

"Your former sergeant told me that the man has you charmed, Diego," the governor said, a sly look replacing the earlier one of self-pity. "And your whole family as well—especially the beauteous Manuela."

Neither Diego nor Domingo made an effort to reply to the sneering governor's insinuation. Instead, they tried to take comfort from Gaspardo's half-promise to interview Louis during the coming week. Both had confidence that if the persuasive young Frenchman could ever present his case before the governor, even the doubting Anya would have to admit that Louis was no sneaking spy bent on malicious action against the Spanish. Even so, they left the library with less hope than when they entered it.

"You'll dazzle everyone as you dance," Conchita promised her mistress when she made the final touch to the shining jet hair. She slapped lightly at the high cheekbones, pleased to see a touch of pink spread beneath the olive skin.

With the setting of the sun, the noises from

the huge *plaza* outside had steadily increased. Wandering musicians seemed intent on outdoing their fellows, and jangled rhythms and melodies collided with each other as they floated on the evening breeze.

"I'm scared." Manuela stared at the image in the mirror. Her hair was drawn back from her solemn face and caught up at the crown in a gleaming swirl. A tall ivory comb set with multicolored brilliants held it in place. Below the crownlike loop, the back part of her hair fell straight down to her waist, like a shimmering curtain of ebony. The festive green and yellow silk dress seemed out of place on one so beset with inner fears, she fretted, and her eyes appeared far too large for her face.

Conchita said, "I wish I could have brought better news from what I overheard in the library. Neither your grandfather nor your uncle could persuade the governor to change his mind about his horrible treatment of the Frenchmen." At the woebegone look upon her mistress's face, she reassured her for the second or third time over the past hour, "Everything will work out fine. You'll see. Carlos has already made his visit to the prison guards, disguised as a drunken musician with a big pot from betting on the cockfights and a guilty conscience as large as the pile of coins."

Not until she stood in the center of the vast *plaza* on the raised wooden platform and heard the festive talk and laughter die away did Manuela believe that anything could work out fine. At the obvious sign of respect from the boisterous, gaily dressed audience, she relaxed. Earlier performers of a farcical drama had lifted party spirits even higher. Over with the other musicians he had commandeered from among those attending the *fiesta,* Carlos stood at the side of the dais with his guitar cradled, his smile approving and urging her on. Though everyone else stood or sat upon the ground, Gaspardo Anya and his family and guests sat upon benches out in front of the entertainment platform.

Ivory castanets in her hands, silk skirt of striped green and yellow belled out from her tiny waist, Manuela bowed her head and lifted her arms. The silence deepened. With the clappers in her left hand, she clicked the first four beats of the simple rhythm she would delineate throughout the dance. Carlos responded to her signal and rolled out the initial soft chord. Following his lead, the other guitarists picked up their parts, filling the torch-lighted *plaza* and the surrounding area with joyful, rippling melody. The dance and the music claimed all at the *fiesta.*

Her lithe body a study in emanation of rhythm, Manuela moved to the lively melody of the guitars. Graceful arms echoed the strong rhythm of the guitars with practiced ease, now moving as a pair across the green silk bodice to the left to reach for an invisible apex of an arc, then returning to the right to repeat. Gradually she added a more complicated beat from the smaller, right-hand pair of castanets, never letting up on the original movements of those in her left hand. Busy also at carrying the lilting song were her slippered feet drumming on the wooden floor in their high heels. Tossing her head to welcome subtleties in Carlos's rendition

309

of the music, Manuela felt her hair swish and dance across her shoulders and back as she dipped and turned around and around. The music and her dance were of love and gaiety, not as profound as the highly popular flamenco danced by men alone or with women as partners, but grand in its own way.

Letting a smile brighten her face when she whirled and faced the air holes up high in the prison edging the far side of the *plaza*, Manuela wondered if Conchita had been successful in tossing Louis's ring and handkerchief into the third from the end. She had been too afraid to include a note but counted on her beloved to know that the message she sent did not need to be put onto paper. The thought that perhaps Louis watched her dance lightened her mood, and the movements of the dance became more spontaneous, a change the spellbound audience seemed to sense immediately. Murmurs of awe at the dancer's beauty and vivaciousness rippled through the crowd even before the music and the castanets no longer sernaded. Applause was hearty, spontaneous, and accompanied by cheers for an encore.

Manuela bowed low, lifting her eyes to those of Governor Anya and sending him a piercing look. When she turned to bow to those standing at the sides and the back of the platform, her heel seemed to get caught in a wide crack toward the far edge. Carlos appeared quickly to lift his sister into his arms right after she tumbled to the ground from the elevated platform.

"What happened? Is she hurt badly?" Governor Anya asked when he rushed to meet a frowning Carlos and peer into the face of the one who moments earlier had transfixed him with her provocative dancing.

Manuela kept her face buried next to Carlos's neck but managed to reply, "I'll be all right. I need to lie down."

By then Diego and Domingo and the rest of the governor's party had crowded around the twins and added their questions.

"Carlos," Diego said when he leaned to examine Manuela's ankle and could see nothing in the poor light coming from widely spaced torches, "take her up to her bedroom and get Conchita to help her into bed. The poor child is exhausted." A fond hand patted at the wan cheek, the only part of her face he could see. Her eyes were closed, as if she might be in deep pain.

"I'll come along and make sure the injury isn't serious," Doña Magdalena said, a worried frown upon her face.

"No, thank you, Aunt," Manuela said, opening her eyes to send a reassuring look to her *dueña*. "Please don't let me spoil the rest of the evening for all of you. I'm terribly weary. All I want is to go to my room and go to sleep. Carlos can carry me." She lifted her head a bit to peer into his solemn face. "Can you manage to get me to my room?"

Nodding, Carlos said to those encircling them with worried expressions on their faces, "If someone will get my guitar and Manuela's castanets, I'll take her on upstairs. I saw Conchita going toward the doorway a few minutes ago when the dance ended. I'll join you as soon as Manuela gets settled for the night."

Over the group's halfhearted protests at Manuela's leaving the festivities so early, Carlos

311

strode through the crowd toward the governor's mansion on the far side of the *plaza*. Not until they were inside her bedroom did he put down his burden.

"Did it work?" Conchita whispered, eyes wide. She had closed the door as soon as the pair entered.

"Like a desert breeze brings a smile," Carlos replied, grinning down at Manuela where he had dumped her onto the bed. "Nobody will expect to see Miss Ramon till tomorrow after she's had a full night's rest. And nobody will want to disturb the poor, injured girl's sleep after the *fiesta* ends."

"I'll make sure of it," Conchita promised solemnly. "I'll be a regular watchdog at her door."

Chapter Eighteen

The doctored jug of wine Conchita had earlier left in the guards' station near the door of the prison barracks did its work. The minute she saw the soldier's head slump forward onto the desk, Manuela slipped from where she had been waiting in the shadow of a bougainvillea vine and took down the leather thong of keys.

The governor had no doubt ordered a relaxing of duties during the *fiesta* as Carlos had reported, for Manuela had seen no second guard around since midnight. The man's deep-chested snores told her he would sleep for some time. A measure of light from the sliver of moon helped her find the right keys.

The echoing grate of metal on metal seemed to be the only nearby sound in the eerie stillness, causing Manuela to peer cautiously for observers there in the cavernous hallway. She saw nothing moving, heard no more than what sounded like snores and heavy breathing from sleeping men. As she had counted on, the off-duty soldiers and other revelers had retired to places more private than the *plaza* outside the prison walls. The fetid odor noticeable at the entry assailed her nostrils with greater force with each stealthy step, and, her racing heart swelling with sorrow, she agonized anew at the imagined miserable conditions Louis must be enduring in the horrible prison.

Saying a prayer of gratitude for the good luck Conchita, Carlos, and she had had all night in carrying out her plans—and adding another of pleading to see them all the way to fruition—Manuela reached her goal. After one false try, she turned the key the right way and opened the heavy wooden door with its barred peephole. She slipped inside, her heart in her throat.

"Who is it?" Louis asked, instantly disturbed at the intrusion. The evening's noisy *fiesta* on the *plaza* outside the prison had kept him awake later than usual, and his mind protested being awakened. Though the single air vent up high let in a bit of light, he figured he must be dreaming, for at the brief opening and closing of the door, he thought he had seen the skirt and shape of a woman.

Not even in his groggy state did Louis dare hope his late-night visitor might be Manuela. Growing awareness reminded him that his ring, tied to a corner of a handkerchief and tossed through the tiny barred window earlier that evening, sat hard and warm on his finger. The handkerchief, the one he had dropped that first morning near the irrigation stream, lay hidden in a pocket, precious because it bore the scent of rosehip perfume. He had no idea how Manuela had managed to find his location and send him her keepsakes, but he knew he would not ever forget the joy surging through him when he recognized the missile clinking against the stone floor. To him, the message was clear: Manuela was in Monclova.

The entire day and night had been like no other during Louis's imprisonment. Fleetingly the events dashed through his mind while the figure stood motionless in the dark corner near the door. That morning a guard had confided that people had gathered from the entire province of Coahuila to celebrate their governor's birthday and that the main festivities would take place in the *plaza* separating the prison from the mansion. When Louis asked if anyone had come down from San Juan Batista, the soldier had turned on his heel and left.

Louis, struggling for alertness, recalled how after the sun had set and the revelers had filled the *plaza*, a new guard had come with a pail of warm water, clean cloths, and soap. He had grabbed the welcome essentials to cleanliness and set to work, surprised a second time when a packet of his clothing was thrust through the bars in exchange for that discarded. Having suffered from unaccustomed, despised filth, the Frenchman gloried in feeling clean again. His request for a razor had gone begging, had not rated any kind of answer.

Impatient fingers raked through his beard as Louis lay there on his bunk and let the memories of the evening flit to mind. At least the hair was clean now, he reflected with that same determination exercised over the past three weeks to rise above physical discomforts. Did the unexpected privileges mean that perhaps Manuela had intervened and that Governor Anya was going to relent and grant him an audience? His visitor might be someone sent to escort him under cover of night to the governor's office—but why would a woman be sent?

His mind up-to-date and honed to the moment, Louis suspected he knew now why the shadowed figure in the cell might be a woman. He recalled

315

the guard's sneering offer earlier to send a courtesan to pass the festive night with him; he lifted his head to a better angle. For a few moments, the hoarse sound of a dog's barking nearby drowned out the strains from some faraway night guitar. A piercing look told him for certain that a skirt covered the lower part of the visitor standing in deep shadows by the door.

"I told the guard I have no wish to sample the Mexican girls. Go out the same way you came in." Was that a giggle? Energized for the first time in weeks, he sat up.

"Perhaps *monsieur* will change his mind when he looks me over, *oui?*" She let her black cloak flutter to the floor. Her voice was low, seductive, and set off darts of fire in Louis's veins.

Manuela smothered her laughter, letting excitement twirl her heart into a dance with a new, dizzying rhythm. While she removed her clothing in the darkened corner, her eyes adjusted to the dim light. She wondered if he could hear the blouse, skirt, and petticoats rustling as they dropped to the floor. The feminine sounds seemed loud, as did the pulse hammering in her ears. What would he say when he recognized her?

Wanting to savor Louis's surprise, she walked toward the bunk, her eyes fixed upon the blur of his face. Even with the new, full beard, he looked like no other. As the North compels the needle of a compass, silvery eyes directed her. She could not have turned back had she wished. And she entertained no such wish.

"Manuela, am I dreaming?" Louis whispered, his eyes widening at the sight of the beautiful body moving toward him in that graceful way

316

belonging only to his beloved. Surely he was dreaming. Never a minute had passed that he hadn't longed for her, hadn't prayed to see her once more. And now ...!

Transfixed where he sat upon the cot, Louis wanted to look everywhere at once. Her bared breasts, tipped by dark circles, beckoned, sending traces of desire all over. Another step from Manuela and the undulating movement of her hips drew his gaze. Flaring from the narrow waist, their curves were the visions his hands longed to make real. The sight of the dark triangle down lower dried his mouth, set his heartbeat to a more frantic pace. One more seductive movement of the long, shapely legs and she stood before him, the tempting swell of her belly and hips right before his face.

"By the saints," Louis managed in a strangled voice, "what are you doing here?" Was he truly awake? The scent of her perfume—roses, what else?—lent him courage enough to put out his hands. What he touched was a satin-encased waist. Warm, firm flesh. Manuela was real!

"Louis," she whispered in worshipful tones, "I couldn't return home tomorrow without first loving you. Tell me I haven't—"

He stood then and pulled her close, imprisoning her words, claiming her mouth, giving in to the pent-up emotions devouring him ever since leaving her in the irrigation canal outside San Juan Batista. Her lips surrendered, even made an attack of their own when his tongue slipped beyond their silkiness and made a foray into her mouth. Great waves of need to make her his washed him into a sea of feeling such as he had never known, threatening to drown him before he

317

could find a balance. Clutching her closer, he allowed his hands all kinds of freedom. Those greedy hands pressed the curved hips to meet the gentle swell of his manhood, and as gently let them find their own natural clinging when the need to mark a pattern up the slender back took over. At each progression of his wandering hands, the mounds of her breasts pressed against his chest, insistent, begging. Her tongue met each thrust of his with answering hunger, each tantalizing action bringing him newer thrills.

Soft, feminine hands formed searing paths of their own. Up across his bearded cheeks to his ears, into his hair, down to the nape of his neck, each movement hurtling Louis back into those fascinating depths of whatever threatened to drown him. He was lost, yet at the same time saved. He was weak, yet he had never felt stronger, more completely masculine. His beloved had come to him.

Manuela swayed, the impact of her nakedness against the body of the man she loved sending her senses reeling. When his hands lovingly caressed her buttocks, her back, she thought she would surely faint. The delicious assault on her mouth warned her that she had entered an unknown world, one first glimpsed that night in the stables, and she eagerly sought the next step. Her fingers delighted in the feel of his bearded face, the shape of his ears, the manliness of the strong neck beneath, and they charitably shared their knowledge with her hungry heart.

So, Manuela exulted, to love uninhibited was to feel this fiery racing of blood, this wild beating of heart, this scary losing of breath as if being carried from the earth – and not have to squelch it, wonder at it. She had only guessed in innocence at the tempest his uncontrolled caresses on her body would create. Her youthful reckoning had fallen short. Neither time nor place held meaning for the reunited lovers there in the shadowy cell. The distant guitar might have been singing its provocative love song only for Louis and her.

Manuela recognized that something exquisite down low was brewing, building with an intensity only hinted at by previous kisses and embraces, no matter that they had been bold. His lips left hers to kiss her neck, to wander down to aching breasts, and she let out a little cry of delight at the promise of his touch. When he reached those warming swells and traced their fullness with his fingertips before settling his magical mouth on her nipples, teasing them into tighter buds, she moaned deep in her throat, her head thrown back in undisguised ecstasy and invitation.

"Touch me again, Louis," she begged, reaching for his hands when it seemed they were deserting those pulsating spots.

Her Lover obliged ... but not with his hands. His tongue and mouth recaptured first one nipple, then the other, hurtling new rivulets of delicious torment into the secret paths of her womanhood. When he sucked ever so gently, Manuela could no longer disguise the trembling tearing at her and uprooting old notions, flinging them into nothingness. A storm threatened to push her out to an unknown sea, and she hesitated at the terrifying thought that something beyond her control now moved her.

Manuela sensed that ever since that night in the stables when they had kissed so passionately, she had been different. Happily she welcomed the knowledge that an even more telling difference marked her from the moment she had undressed and gone into his arms. Once they consummated their love, he would belong to her forever, and she, to him, no matter that they would never see each other again.

Crooning endearments, Louis moved his mouth to claim the other, waiting breast. Manuela melted in a most exquisite way, acknowledging that whatever whipped at her emotions was all-powerful, would never abate until it had worn itself out. Let her scudding heart be deluged with passion, she invited in rapturous secret. Let her shaken body fuse with that of the man whisking away her breath, the one she trusted to guide her in the tempestuous ways of love, the one she planned to surrender to before helping him escape the Spanish prison. Not that she would tell him he must leave Mexico to save his life until afterward . . .

Her heart wrenched with sudden, crippling pain, Manuela hid her thoughts behind lowered lashes and clung closer to the body setting hers on fire. *Louis,* she wanted to say but couldn't because her mind was whirling and out of control, *you're the man of my dreams, the man I'll always love, though I'll never get to see you again.* Even as she welcomed him as her Lover in the way she desired, she agonized, she was bidding him farewell forever.

His gentle hands cupping the beautiful face so that he might read those exotic eyes, Louis asked when she hid them, "Do I see sadness in your eyes, beautiful princess? Are you sure this is right for me to make love to you before we're married? Are you sure?"

Surprised at his ability to do so, Louis waited, his breath and heartbeat erratic. He watched her thick lashes lift in that sensuous way that haunted him, whether awake or asleep. The meager moonlight showed him the beckoning stars in those slanted, midnight eyes, the dewiness of proffered, love-swollen lips. Yet he waited. Having loved her since first seeing her, he had accepted waiting as a condition of that love. She was so young, he tried to remind his throbbing loins. An inner voice pointed out that Manuela was already more woman than any he had ever encountered. She was *his* woman. Forever.

"I'm sure," Manuela heard a husky voice say. Could it be hers? She swallowed, but a lump still punished her throat. The beginning would only rush along their parting.

With something akin to reverence, Louis smiled at her and put out his hands to free the black hair from its combs, almost startled at its texture and perfumed warmth when it fell into a curtain of black silk, his only regret that now part of her beautiful shoulders and breasts lay hidden. The little sound of her stepped-up breathing, the fragrance of her body and hair, filled the small cell, jumbling his senses.

Unable to gauge how long they had already been in each other's arms, Manuela felt a consuming compulsion to feel all of his nakedness next to hers, to know his body as he was learning hers . . . before it was too late. Almost shyly, she reached for the buttons on his shirt; but as soon as she uncovered the first peeping curls on

321

the broad chest, all traces of shyness left. With his help, the clothing soon lay on the floor near her own.

"Come to me, Manuela, as though you're already my bride. I love you more than I'd even guessed," Louis whispered, spreading his arms to hug her close again.

"And I love you, too." How glorious to be able to whisper the words to him, she exulted, going into his arms, then leaning away to see him.

Louis smiled at her open and frank appraisal of his chest and taut belly, almost laughing at her indrawn breath and her innocent, widening eyes when they fixed upon his fully aroused manhood there in the half-light. Feeling more like a king than a prisoner, he pulled her nakedness next to his, delighting in the feel of satin curves against his turgescence, of warm, pliable breasts next to his chest. Where was there such perfection of womanhood? He sought to worship her with his hands and lips, finding each silken hollow and curve more delightful than the last, wondering how much longer he could fight against the turmoil lashing at his soul, tormenting his every cell. With murmurs of assurance and love, he eased them onto the cot, not hushing until she lay still in his arms, apparently content to entwine her body with his and return kiss for kiss, caress for caress.

Swept away at the renewed agitation inside, now that she was clasped next to Louis's virile body, Manuela tried to let him know that she had no fears, that all she wanted was to belong to him totally. Hungrily her mouth tasted his, never still, never satisfied. More . . . she wanted more. Her hands followed trails similar to those

Louis forged on her body, and she wondered if he felt the same wondrous excitement from her touch as she was feeling from his. The chest, the rigid nipples, the corded muscles of his back, the intriguing flatness of his belly, then the furred area leading down to the swollen part of him that had shocked her upon first view.

Her insides being tossed about by raging torrents, Manuela arched her hips against his, wanting him to claim her, to make her know what it was she burned for, to still the raging within, as she suspected only Louis could. When he rose above her, she thrust forward eagerly to meet his pulsating shaft, her moist, velvety petals inviting the next unknown. She felt a throbbing, searing fullness, then a blast of roaring pain. Like a bee seeking the sweetest nectar, there came an exquisite, probing hesitation ... whispered love words, imploring kisses. Next, an unbridled, rhythmic force in harmony with nature sailed her into oblivion, lifting her on an ever-rising wave of shared passion, sailing both toward eternity as one vibrating entity.

Manuela surrendered joyfully to the force sweeping her away, consuming her, thrilling her, pushing her into the eye of an exquisite turbulence where she floated away up high as one perfect being with her Lover. A last roar of silvery sound in her ears ... the pang of falling. ... Too soon, within the joined lovers and all about there in the darkened prison cell, an inevitable calm reigned.

Awed, the lovers basked in the perfect silence. Even the plaintive notes from the distant guitar had died away. Quivering all over, Manuela tightened her hold on Louis's shoulders. He lay quietly within her embrace, his face nestled between her breasts. She lightly frosted the crisp hair with kisses, unaware that tears washed her cheeks. The moments she had longed for were already memories to cherish for the rest of her life.

"I never knew what making love was all about till now," she confided. "It was wonderful. I'll love you forever."

"I'll love you forever, too," Louis whispered back. "I've a confession to make." He lifted his head to see her beautiful face, shocked to see her tears. "I've never truly 'made love' before tonight, merely the motions. My whole life takes on new meaning now that we are one, Manuela. I never knew lips could be so sweet and fiery at the same time." He sampled them playfully, then wiped away her tears. That she yet wore a brooding look bothered him.

"Mayhap you've taken a liking to things fiery since you've come to Mexico," she replied, finding it hard to tease when her heart weighed heavily.

"Must you go so soon, darling?" Louis asked when she roused herself and wriggled from his embrace, then stood and began pulling on her clothing. He watched the tantalizing curves disappear beneath a shift, then a blouse and a skirt. His hands tingled when he thought of how well they had learned that lovely body. Halfheartedly he fingered his own clothing there on the cot where she had tossed it. "We've not had a chance to talk. I must know how you got in here and—"

"Sh-h-h," Manuela whispered, a bit alarmed at the way his voice was swelling. She could feel the silvery eyes caressing her and fought down the impulse to return to his arms. Time no longer belonged to them. "We mustn't let anyone hear us." As soon as she finished dressing, she went to sit beside him on the cot, leaning into his welcoming arms but deliberately cutting short his searching kiss. "I can't tell you much, but you're going to be freed soon. If I could have, I would have freed you and your men tonight and had your horses ready for escape. To set you free now would only lead to your being tracked down and killed. Carlos could get no farther with the guards than to bribe them into giving you better food and treatment. Tomorrow you'll be released by the governor."

Manuela reasoned that there was no need to share news of further ruined plans—the messages sent by Eblo's carrier pigeons to the viceroy in Mexico City. Had that ploy worked to free him, the soldiers would have already come to take him to the capital where more humane treatment likely awaited. Her voice ducked out on her, and she swiped at a lock of hair falling across her face before finding it again. "Soldiers will escort you straight to the Rio Grande. You must ask no questions and return with all possible haste to your fort in Louisiana."

"You've done a lot of planning to get me out of here, haven't you?" Unbelieving that one seemingly so young could have accomplished so much, Louis stared at the lovely face. He leaned to kiss the closed eyelids, first one, then the other. The tickle of the curling lashes beneath his lips brought a fresh ache for her. His lips against her temple, he asked, "Even if the soldiers force me across the Rio Grande, what's going to keep me from coming back to get you?"

"I am." His caresses were heating up her blood

325

again.

"What do you mean?" He felt her stiffen. He almost shook her to make her open her eyes and let him see what he longed to see. Hadn't she told him over and over that she loved him? Why else would she have come and—

"Your life means more to me than anything, Louis."

Manuela lifted her lashes as Louis was willing her to. Love for him spoke clearly from the ebony depths, and she even managed to force a smile. Her determination not to think of what she had to do tomorrow had seen her through the entire evening. She would not weaken now. This was the last time she would ever gaze upon that handsome face, feel those adoring eyes of silver washing over her, hear that deep bass voice with its cultured cadence, smell the manly essence of him, taste the glory of his lips against hers.

Forcing herself to put away such debilitating thoughts, Manuela said, "Please believe me when I say that I love you and will forever." Then, hoping that the same ring of truth shone through her next words, she added, "But plans for us to be together will have to wait until after you've left Mexico."

"I love you too much to leave without you. What's my life worth if I don't have you?" Instantly all the things that she had come to mean to him attacked his heart and crippled it. Her somber mouth was not in accord with his memories of their night of love, and he leaned to kiss it, glad to sense from her warm response that she wanted him again as deeply as he wanted her. Heartbeat robbing him of breath, he confessed, "No matter that your grandfather is a man I revere, he will have to listen the next time I ask for your hand."

"Did you speak to him about us?" Manuela asked, not believing her ears. Her own voice almost rose to normal, and she cautioned herself to keep it low. "He never let on."

"Then you didn't know that he refused my suit, that he still insists you must marry a Spaniard?" Puzzlement rode the beautiful face lifted to his, and he wondered if the same look might not be claiming his. Why hadn't Diego told her? What must she have thought?

Manuela shook her head, her hands going up to rake her unbound hair from her face. Leaning to retrieve her combs and fastening it back, she said, "Something told me not to tell of our love, but I truly thought he didn't know. Not that it matters now." Her mind was racing. What had Diego been thinking of to deny Louis's request to marry her? How relieved he must have been that the soldiers from Monclova arrived when they did. Had he been the one to have Louis chained? She pushed away the hateful thought that everyone seemed to be against them.

"Will that change things? Can't you meet me on the far side of the Rio Grande?" His fingers outlined the shape of her face, lingered at the strong chin, then eased up to define the edges of her full lips. "Bring Conchita, for Medar confided on the way from San Juan Batista that he loves her and wants to marry her. We talked of having a double ceremony." He was so close that their breaths mingled as he talked.

With far more than her ears, Manuela heard, even memorized, Louis's declarations. His tender touch upon her face was tearing her into aching

327

shreds. With sadness for both Conchita and herself softening her voice even more, Manuela replied in grieving, husky tones, "Conchita and I can't be there. I'll love you forever, Louis, but I might not ever be able to marry you."

"Of course we'll marry; we're destined to become man and wife. Doesn't tonight prove it? You're not giving up hope, are you?" he asked, pained anew to hear the sadness in her words. If she believed them, then there was no hope, would never be any. He hugged her closer, murmuring against her hair. "Please tell me you'll not give up hope, my love. I couldn't stand thinking there's no way we'll manage to be together." Inspiration tore through him, and he pushed her back enough to look into her face. "Take my ring back, and we'll still be betrothed. I'll return next spring. Everybody will be calmed down by then."

Manuela stood, fearful that the guard would be waking soon. The herbs would last just so long. "I won't take your ring back, Louis. The most important thing is to get you out of this prison. Anyway, next spring's seems a long time off."

"Lots of things can happen between now and spring." She took a step toward the door, and he went along, his arm around her.

"Yes, lots of things." She didn't look at him while she mouthed agreement with his optimistic outlook. If she were to let him know there was no hope for them to be wed, he might do something foolish and not get away safely.

They were at the door by then, embracing and yet trying to end contact. Even when arms retreated, hands would not give up, and eyes never made an attempt. The farewell kiss was both the most punishing and rewarding either could recall.

It shook them to their very souls, left them breathless, staring into each other's eyes as long as they could see during her backward retreat down the darkened hallway.

"I was charmed when your maid informed me you wanted to talk with me privately," Gaspardo Anya said the next morning when Manuela entered his library. Along with everyone else in the mansion, he had been delighted to see her at breakfast and learn her ankle no longer pained her.

The sight of the black-haired beauty in a white off-the-shoulder gown sent his old heart to thudding and bucking around like one of the unbroken mustangs on his horse ranch near Monclova. Never had she appeared more alluring. He read a sense of mystery in the slanted eyes and wondered what made her seem more mature, more womanly than ever before. Maybe it had to do with his having seen her dance and watched that curvaceous body move so sensuously with the stirring music from the guitars. He had found it impossible to fall asleep because of the desire she had stirred with her performance. Even the young courtesan he had finally sent for had left him unsatiated, for as hard as he tried to imagine that the silken body writhing beneath him was Manuela's, his mind had not been fooled. And this morning he had awakened with gout in his left leg.

Manuela allowed the governor to kiss her hand and lead to her a settee at the side of the large room. Again she hid her repulsion at the man's moustache, tried not to notice the thickness of his lips, the roundness of the short body.

"You are kind to grant me audience, Governor Anya," Manuela said after both were seated.

"Please, Manuela, call me Gaspardo when we're in private." Her perfume tickled his nose. He had not noticed before that she wore such a sweet fragrance. Somehow he had paired spicy scents with the proud-faced young woman.

Manuela lowered her eyes and nodded agreement before getting to the reason for the meeting. "I came to talk with you about your suit for my hand."

The old man shifted his weight on the far end of the settee, clearing his throat noisily of the phlegm that always plagued him until past noon. Suddenly clumsy under her scrutiny, he searched for a handkerchief, not finding one until the third pocket. Having one of his coughing fits in her presence upset him, and he cursed inwardly at the picture he must make as he noisily tended to his needs.

"Aren't such matters best left to your grandfather and me, my dear?" he asked once he was in control again. He tried to keep his shock and disapproval of her actions from showing. After all, she was here, wasn't she? Young people did sometimes have a way of approaching things more directly than their elders, he confessed. Mayhap her answer was different from the one Diego had given. Hope cast aside disapproval, and he added, "Of course if you prefer the matter be one between only the two of us, I've no objections."

"How much does it mean to you to have me as your bride?" Manuela had rehearsed the words and was glad. They came out as staunchly as she

330

had intended. She watched the old man poke his handkerchief back into a pocket. Were his fingers trembling? Was he ill again? A flush was marching up from his thick neck and jowls to his broad face.

"Everything," Gaspardo managed to get out in a thick voice. After having ached for her all night, he could hardly believe his ears. Was she hinting that she might consent to his suit? "Having you as my wife means everything in the world to me, Manuela."

"Enough for me to name the conditions under which I'll marry you?" With no attempt at being flirtatious, she sent him a measuring look from beneath half-lowered lashes.

Smiling at her daring flaunting of convention and thinking that once she was his he could tame her, Gaspardo said, "Name them, my dear. I'll send my men to the City to buy anything your heart desires. We can be married by Christmas and—"

"Wait," Manuela broke in to say, a hand lifted in protest. "My conditions don't rest on anything money can buy. They have to do with the release of your French prisoners."

Gaspardo sat up, angered that a snippet of a girl would dare broach the infernal subject he had been forced to discuss over the past two days with the men in her family. What was wrong with the Ramons, to be so concerned over three spies? Actually, he confessed, only one. Beady eyes became smaller as his temper rose.

Had Manuela made any kind of retraction or voiced any kind of apology, the smitten governor would have known exactly what to say. But she merely sat on her end of the settee and watched him with those great black eyes fixed on him, while her hands lay clasped lightly on her lap, creamy olive against the white skirt. Her breasts continued to lift and fall in the gentle pattern of calm breathing. Artfully arranged black curls clung to her neck and spilled onto the top of her partially exposed breasts.

All at once Gaspardo could think of no reason to be angered. The most desirable young woman in the world sat before him. She could be his, to control as he saw fit. He swallowed at a sudden rush of saliva, then licked hungrily at his lips.

"Why would you bother your pretty head about the welfare of the Frenchmen?" he asked after the silence kept stretching out.

"Because I'm in love with Louis Saint-Denis."

Gaspardo jumped up then, visibly disturbed more than earlier. The gouty foot seemed the least of his aches. He limped up and down before the settee, aware that the slanted black eyes watched him with remarkable detachment.

"You say you're in love with Saint-Denis, and yet you'll consent to become my wife?" he asked once he calmed down enough to question her without yelling. "What kind of game are you playing?"

"It's not a game," Manuela remarked. "You give me your word that the Frenchmen will be given their horses and a soldier escort to the Rio Grande, and I'll agree to marry you after my seventeenth birthday next April. I must have some kind of proof before that date that they've returned to Louisiana safely, or the wedding will never take place. You must insist that the lieutenant send you a letter when he reaches Louisiana. Neither he, nor anyone else, is *ever* to know how he came to be freed."

As she spoke, Gaspardo sank back down onto the settee, next to her this time. The close-up view of her almost did him in, and he felt passion building such as he hadn't dreamed of in years. He was so busy imagining what it would be like to possess her, he could hardly think of what she was saying.

"You're young, Manuela. You don't know what you're saying. How can you agree to marry me when you say you love another?"

"Because I love him more than I love myself."

Sighing at the whims of the young, Gaspardo smiled. "If I agree to your terms, will you try to love me after we're married? Will you serve as my hostess and bear my children?"

"Yes." Manuela sat as still as a statue.

"Very well, then," the governor said, a gleam in his eye turning his smile into something akin to a leer. "We have a bargain. Do your grandfather and your uncle know about this meeting and what we're discussing?"

"No, and I don't want them or anyone else to know. We'll keep our agreement secret until nearer my birthday. That too will be one of the conditions, or I'll never marry you." Fire blazed back in the assessing eyes, and she lifted her chin a degree.

Gaspardo threw back his head and chuckled at her audacity. Who would have thought any young woman would have dared even suggest what Manuela was throwing out before him as coolly as if she might be discussing a business deal? God, but she was a determined young woman, he mused. The thought nagged at him that such a willful spirit might be difficult for an older man to break, but he set it aside. When the time came, he would conquer her. In the meantime, he would do exactly as she demanded.

"My dear, I grant all of your conditions. We'll wed at the church here at Monclova on your seventeenth birthday in April."

Swooping then to plant a kiss on the tempting red lips, Gaspardo drew back in pain and disbelief. His lips never met their goal, for Manuela slapped him hard across the cheek and jumped up from the settee.

"Is that any way to treat your betrothed?"

"As far as I'm concerned, I don't owe you one touch until I see the letter from Louis indicating he and his men are back in Louisiana." Manuela glared down at him.

Gaspardo stood and grabbed her arms, muttering with rising anger, "What makes you think I'll stand for such treatment?"

She watched his eyes dip to her bared shoulders, then to the valley between her breasts and linger there. Making no reply, she merely lifted her chin and gazed at him. The thought that Louis would be safely away from Mexico soon kept her from recoiling at the old man's gaze and the touch of his hands upon her forearms and lent her strength.

"You're right, my dear," Gaspardo said in a beaten voice. He had read a beautiful woman's knowledge of her charms in her eyes. "I want you too much to force myself on you now. One hug won't count —"

Kicking his left ankle smartly before he could pull her against him, Manuela jerked free of his hands and moved toward the door. She looked back at the doubled-over figure there before the settee. He seemed unable to put weight on his left foot.

"Then we have an agreement?" Manuela asked, one hand on the doorknob. "The Frenchmen will be safely on their way to Louisiana before sunset tomorrow?"

Gaspardo, snatching his mind from the paining, gouty foot, shot a measuring look toward his secret fiancée and grunted, "Yes."

The door closed. The matter was settled.

Part Four

"Who pepper'd the highest
was the surest to please."
— Oliver Goldsmith

Chapter Nineteen

Mexico City was a place of much social activity the year around, but even more so in the winter months. When Domingo and his soldiers escorted the party from San Juan Batista down to the capital in October, the season was bursting into bloom.

Guests at the palace of the Viceroy of New Spain, the Duke of Linares, the newcomers found themselves swamped with waiting invitations. Old friends and acquaintances of Doña Magdalena, Diego, and Domingo, as well as those of the deceased parents of the twins, had been apprised of the pending visit and seemed eager to entertain those from San Juan Batista.

"You've worn such a sad expression ever since that weekend in Monclova that I'm becoming depressed just from looking at you," Carlos scolded Manuela the morning after their nighttime arrival. "I was hoping that after all this time you'd be able to put your misery aside." They were strolling in the spacious walled courtyard behind the viceroy's palace after a leisurely breakfast. "On the trip down, you didn't seem to take pleasure even in riding Nightstar. Maybe now that you'll be going to parties and meeting new people, you'll get that Frenchman out of your mind."

"Bite your tongue," Manuela retorted. "I've no

wish to get Louis out of my heart or my mind."

"You should, sister of mine. You're not going to hear from him again. You know as well as I that he could've sent a letter by messenger before we left home, even from his fort in Louisiana. It's been nearly three months now, hasn't it?"

"Perhaps he fears word from him would get me into trouble. I gave him no reason to think there's a chance of our ever getting together." She sighed. "I had hoped the governor would hear before we left for the City, though, and let me know that Louis reached Louisiana."

"If old Anya had told that Frenchman why he was being freed, he would have probably killed him," Carlos mused aloud, ambling beside her on the cobbled path.

"That was part of the bargain with the governor, that he not tell Louis or anyone about our engagement. Conchita and you are the only ones who know." She shot a look of concern up at the beloved face, noting how fine were the olive-skinned features, how vibrant his black eyes. He was fast becoming more man than boy.

"Several people know that he proposed earlier and will be whispering that you've merely put off giving an answer."

"Let them talk. I don't care, so long as Louis is free and well." Nights of wrestling with her feelings about her lover had strengthened Manuela's resolve that her sacrifice to secure his freedom had been worthwhile. If suffering were a condition of love, she now felt she had passed all tests, for, to her surprise, she yet grieved terribly over her shattered dreams.

"Well," Carlos said with reflection, "we did

learn that some soldiers escorted the Frenchmen from Monclova the day after we left for home. Several times I've heard Grandfather and Uncle complain that they've been unable to get direct word from Anya about how the release came about. Old Anya must have put the fear of God into his soldiers, for they've not ever leaked any details."

Manuela sighed. "I've tried not to think about what took place, and I refuse to beg Grandfather or Uncle for news about Louis. Learning he's no longer in that horrible cell has to be enough." But she lied. Her mind had careened with questions, but she could not trust herself to discuss Louis with Diego or Domingo, not after she had learned that Louis had asked for her hand and been refused. She felt she no longer knew her grandfather or her uncle at all.

Old questions haunted her: Had Louis been well enough to make the long journey back home? He had seemed so gaunt that night in the prison. A sprig of hope sometimes led her to wonder if he might truly return in the spring and approach Diego again with his suit. If he did come—and how foolish she felt for even entertaining the thought—would Diego imprison him, or send him back to Monclova? Such worries always led her into remembering their glorious lovemaking, then into despair that such fulfillment could never be hers again.

Letting their minds idle and their bodies rest from the arduous trip down from San Juan Batista, Carlos and Manuela continued to wander down the cobblestoned path among the numerous plantings of fragrant, blooming roses and brightly hued hibiscus. A host of birds seemed at home in the haven; their colorful flittings and cheerful calls made the courtyard seem even more restful. Manuela recalled that upon their arrival the previous night, she had seen what she vaguely remembered after four years: the palace and its grounds covered two blocks and actually sat right in the center of the City. The thought that just outside the walls were streets, promenades, and parks, likely filled with horses, carriages, and people at the morning hour, seemed nigh unbelievable. Against the high, surrounding walls of grayed limestone, poinsettias stood as tall as the lemon and orange trees, their red leaves bunching up in their unique way at stem ends to form showy flowers.

Close by, looming above the walls, the great stone prison brooded in the sunlight, but neither brother nor sister chose to comment upon it, chose instead to note a long building forming the far end of the courtyard. It sat directly across from the back of the palace.

"All I can figure is that it must be living quarters of some sort, for its stone walls and ornate architecture seem the same as those of the palace," Carlos decided after they both had given up wondering what it was.

A pretty girl with heart-shaped face and laughing black eyes approached the visitors there in the courtyard, a fluffy white cat in her arms. Behind her came a gangling boy with the awkward step of one not yet old enough to manage his limbs as a synchronized unit.

The girl seemed in total control as she spoke and introduced her brother and herself.

"Ramona and Lorenzo de Alencastre," she told with practiced ease. "Our parents are the Duke and Duchess of Linares. And this is Nero, my pet." The haughty cat surveyed the newcomers with unblinking green eyes.

When Manuela and Carlos returned information and revealed they were twins, Ramona's wide-spaced eyes rounded.

"Wouldn't that be fun, Lorenzo!" the fourteen-year-old girl exclaimed to the brother nearly as tall as she, a charming show of small perfect teeth drawing Carlos's admiring eyes. "Maybe it's only because he's the viceroy, but Father always has the most interesting guests stay with us."

As did that of Lorenzo, Ramona's skin coloring and texture suggested the finest Castilian blood: richly olive, velvety smooth. If she had ever suffered her younger brother's gawkiness at an earlier age, Carlos mused, she had overcome it, for her actions flowed with the ease of one considered fully grown—as he was, he reminded himself, standing to his full height. A rounding of the front of her full white blouse told that her breasts had already passed the budding stage. Were she to don a low-necked gown and dress her long, dark hair fashionably, Carlos's thoughts ran on, Ramona Alencastre would have beauty and cleavage enough to catch a man's eye . . . and hold it. For some reason, he swallowed hard at the surprising thought.

Even at eleven, Lorenzo Alencastre proved as warm and welcoming as his sister, and the four visited together until it was time to go in for lunch. As at breakfast, the meal was served at the convenience of the palace guests and residents, and it happened that none but the four young people chose to eat at that time. They parted for *siestas* in their private quarters, promising to meet again later in the large receiving room downstairs for the evening's activities.

The viceroy had invited his family and house-guests to meet for a social gathering before dinner. To add spice and initiate the Ramon twins into the capital's society, he had issued a few invitations to selected people in the City.

Having come over from his vast estates in Spain only two years earlier to serve the Crown-appointed post of Viceroy of New Spain, the Duke of Linares was finding his position more demanding than he had first believed. Tempers flared among his underlings at the slightest provocation. No one on his staff seemed eager to make a decision without first talking it over with him in boring detail.

Too, he reflected frequently, there was the tedi-ous business of relegating everyone born in Mex-ico to an inferior social class. It made no sense to him that the son of a Spaniard, whether born in Spain or in Mexico, was not still a full-blooded Spaniard. Petty. The citizens of New Spain too often struck him as being petty and greedy for quick fortunes from the silver mines.

Accustomed to lavish entertaining from their years of moving in royal circles back in Seville, Fernando de Alencastre and his wife Margarethe—formally known as the Duke and Duchess of Linares in Spain—bore the social demands easily. It was their eldest daughter, Charolotte, who dealt them private troubles. The younger Ramona and Lorenzo presented no spe-cial problems.

Widowed back in Spain little more than a year

344

ago, Charolotte, childless and only twenty-one, had arrived in the spring from the estate of her in-laws near Madrid to live at the palace. It seemed evident to her parents that she had come because she had nowhere else to go, or at least no place where someone might help her find a desirable husband. Her in-laws had made it plain that in time she would be expected to marry an older family member. As headstrong and passionate as she was beautiful, Charolotte had a far more exciting future in mind.

Manuela, dressed in yellow silk embroidered heavily with gold thread, moved easily alongside Doña Magdalena that night in the palace receiving room as her great-aunt introduced her to those she had known during her years as a member of City society. Fluttering her gold-encrusted fan as Doña Magdalena had taught her, Manuela felt as if she might be on a stage. More than one bold masculine eye from across the room had chanced to meet the cool black ones of the newest beauty in their midst and covertly assess the graceful curves. So many introductions followed that Manuela found it impossible to keep them straight.

"Viceroy Alencastre both honors and pleasures me by allowing me to escort you into dinner on your first evening at the palace," Leon d'Espinoza told Manuela after initial exchanges of pleasantries. His dark eyes caressed her face.

Quickly recalling that the now-retreating viceroy had introduced the dashing young Spaniard as his aide, Manuela noted the young man's admiring gaze and summoned a polite smile. "I shall look forward to dining with you." Why was it that his good looks pleased nothing but her eyes? she asked herself after they became separated in the throng of chattering people. She welcomed a moment of solitude.

"Having fun, Manuela?" Domingo's voice came from behind her as she stood in a quiet spot near a window alcove off to one side of the huge receiving room and stared into the busy street below. Dark had not taken over yet, and she could see the carriages leaving down the long driveway after having deposited those invited to dine at the palace.

"I had thought the viceroy was having dinner only for the ones staying in the palace," Manuela replied after turning to give her uncle a solemn-faced nod. The long-forgotten sight of the numerous street lamps had fascinated her on the previous night as they had approached the City and then followed the main thoroughfare to the mammoth palace. While gazing outside just then, she had watched a lamplighter set his flame to the dishes of whale oil atop those guarding the wide boulevard outside.

"The Duchess and he decided at the last minute to invite some friends so that Carlos and you wouldn't have so many new faces and names to digest at once."

"They're very kind, aren't they?"

Domingo agreed, then added, "I was hoping that once we got here, you'd wear some of those old, dazzling smiles. For you to have a good time is the main reason we came, you know." More than once after learning of Louis's suit, Domingo had been tempted to intervene for her and suggest to his father that perhaps to entertain Louis

346

Saint-Denis's suit would not be detrimental. After all, Manuela had never seemed to aspire to ordinary goals, had never indicated she cared to live any kind of life other than the quiet one enjoyed at the *presidio*. No doubt that what ailed his beloved niece was love for the handsome Frenchman, but what could an uncle do against a domineering grandfather? Besides, Louis was back in Louisiana now, and it seemed unlikely that he would return and risk a second imprisonment.

"I know. Already I'm feeling better," she lied. She brushed at the wisps dangling in front of her ears, then checked the angle of the pearl-encrusted comb gathering black curls at the crown of her head. Three fat sausage curls fell from that pretty point down her back, their ebon sheen contrasting against the yellow of her gown. Conchita had made it her business on the first day in the City to learn the latest in hairstyles from the personal maids in the palace.

"Don't worry about your looks, Manuela," Domingo assured her. "You're the most beautiful young woman here." Not for the first time that night, he noticed her creamy yet olive complexion and thought what a picture of perfection she made with her great, slanted eyes and daintily sculpted features.

"I've heard that the viceroy's elder daughter is the most beautiful woman in the City," she teased the doting uncle. "She wasn't with her parents and the younger children, so I've not yet met her."

Domingo chuckled and sipped from his wine glass. "Believe me, you'll know when Charolotte is in a room. She always arrives late."

"You've met her then?"

"Oh, yes," Domingo answered, a knowing look taking over the handsome face, a smile sending the trim moustache up one side. "I escorted her to some parties when I was last here."

Manuela tried to read something into his reply and his look but could not.

A buzzing and turning of heads over near the arched entryway into the enormous room caught their attention. A beautiful young woman with reddish lights in dark, elaborately coiffed hair stood behind the majordomo and seemed to be talking with someone out of sight in the entryway. Her dress was lustrous wine-colored taffeta, embroidered with gold and sparkling brilliants. Manuela did not think she had ever seen such a daring neckline, or such a lush figure. She made no protest when Domingo took her arm and guided her in the direction of the latecomer.

"That's Charolotte now. No telling who's her escort tonight. She may even be married again by now. When I was last here, talk was that her father's aide, Leon d'Espinoza from Seville, seemed the likely winner of the beauteous widow. I've been lazy and catching up on my rest all day rather than current gossip," Domingo whispered as they walked among the guests. "I want you to meet her before she gets hemmed in by her many admirers."

Just as Manuela and Domingo neared the step leading up into the entryway, she heard the young woman say to a person still not in view, "Would you be a darling and fetch my shawl from the side courtyard? I threw it on a chair while we were out there."

Charolotte evidently saw the handsome Captain Domingo Ramon from the corner of her eye then and hurried down the step amidst rustling taffeta, saying in what Manuela thought must be the throatiest voice she had ever heard, "Father told me last week that my dashing officer from the North would be arriving soon, Domingo, but no one told me you were already here."

Domingo took the proffered hand and bestowed a lingering kiss on its smooth top, lifting his head and eyes then to pay its owner homage. "What a warm welcome, Charolotte. And from one who was only too glad to see me leave back in the summer."

"Naughty one," the beauty said, giving him first a pouty look, then a flirtatious smile. She flicked open her jewel-encrusted fan and hid all except her upper face. Long, a bit narrow, and widely spaced, her dark eyes met Domingo's teasing ones with practiced art.

Then Domingo turned to the doe-eyed vision in yellow beside him and said, "May I introduce my niece, Manuela Ramon? This is her first season in the City, actually the first time she has visited since she left school a few years back."

Charolotte preened a moment behind her fan as she watched the younger woman take in her fashionable, revealing gown and her lavish coiffure. Lowering the fan and dipping her head to the proper angle, the viceroy's daughter acknowledged the introduction. A slight flaring of nostrils at the base of her arrogant nose was the only sign that she might be suffering a touch of jealousy at the perfection of the palace guest.

"Welcome, Manuela," Charolotte said, her voice not hiding all vestiges of the animosity she was no doubt feeling at the sight of the younger beauty. "I hope that your stay here at the palace will be pleasant."

As the three stood talking, Manuela made polite replies, both to the imposing Charolotte and to Domingo. She had not known there were properly reared young ladies in the world who could exude such strong vibrations of sexuality, and she wondered how it was that the young widow had not already found a second husband. It seemed obvious from her inviting eyes, her large, moist mouth, and full-blown figure that the viceroy's daughter was one fashioned to please men.

"Here's your shawl, Charolotte," came a masculine voice. A man had just moved down the step from the entryway behind the viceroy's daughter. Two hands draped the length of wine taffeta around her naked shoulders, one pausing heavily for a moment on a shoulder when the speaker's eyes and mind apparently cut off normal signals to his body. Though the night was far from cold, the elegantly clad young man froze.

Domingo was the first to recover, blurting, "Louis Saint-Denis! Louis, what on earth are you doing here in the viceroy's palace?" None of the news from Monclova had hinted that the Frenchmen had not returned to Louisiana when freed. "It's wonderful to see you safe and sound."

Charolotte stared at the *tableau* before her, wise eyes attempting to take in all at once.

"Miss Ramon, Captain Ramon," Louis managed to say when his body agreed to function once more. "I'm delighted to see you again."

Dropping his hand from Charolotte's shoulder, Louis hurried from where he had stood behind her and presented himself before Manuela with a courtly bow. The unexpected sight of her raveled all self-composure and played havoc with his heartbeat. When she stood as if struck mute and made no effort to lift her hand to him, he seized it and brought the protesting member up to his lips. His face solemn and puzzled from her cold-eyed rebuff, he turned then toward her more receptive uncle. Both men tried to talk at once, neither satisfied to be the listener until both realized nothing would get explained if they kept up such action.

"And the viceroy's soldiers arrived the next night after the *fiesta?*" Domingo repeated after Louis had given a brief account of how he had ended up in Mexico City some weeks ago. "That would have been the night after we returned to our *presidio* in the afternoon. What perfect timing. Wouldn't you say so, Manuela?" He turned to his niece, aware throughout the Frenchman's recounting of his adventures that she had stood silently by his side and that Louis had been hard-pressed to keep from addressing all of his remarks to her unresponsive face.

"Perfect," was Manuela's only reply.

All the time Louis had been telling about his men and himself, Manuela had fought several internal wars and posed as many more. Uppermost in mind had been the question of how he happened to be in Mexico City. Should she have thrown caution to the winds and greeted Louis with the warmth of her love for him? Her heart had nigh burst with joy when she first heard his voice and saw his handsome features. Or should she have slapped him for his having trampled on her heart and then moved on to play similar games with the viceroy's daughter? She remem-

351

bered Charolotte's words to him about her having left her shawl in some private courtyard, so she surmised that the two had been alone before coming into the receiving room. Her temper scaled new heights as she thought of the way his hand had lingered upon Charolotte's shoulder, of the way the older woman even now gazed upon him as though he were a choice morsel on her plate, available at her whim.

Here was Louis once more clean-shaven, all dressed up in fine array, no longer cast into a prison cell, once more free to exercise his charm on selected victims. Manuela swallowed at constantly rising gorge in her throat when she thought of how young and stupid she had been to give herself to him that night in Monclova, like some precious gift. He wasn't her Lover; he was a no-good French spy out to take advantage of any who stood in his way. The hand holding her fan clenched into painful knots; the one hidden in the folds of her yellow skirt was in no better shape. How Louis must have laughed at her innocence, must be laughing yet.

And, Manuela agonized further, how he must have loved knowing that it had been her money used by Carlos to purchase him decent food, a bath, clean clothes. The cruelest joke of all he didn't know about, she realized in a moment of lucidity, and she was thankful. Never would Louis learn that she had foolishly agreed to marry gross, old Governor Anya in return for his freedom. She had no idea that her reeling inward thoughts brought new fiery lights to her slanted eyes, sent pink roses to bloom in her cheeks, and fashioned her full lips into a beguiling *moue*.

"How about you and your family?" Louis asked

both Domingo and Manuela, doubting that she would answer. Why was she so remote and angry? He had prayed for her planned visit to the City to materialize soon, had looked forward to a glorious reunion. He had thought she would be ecstatic to find that she had been right when she had assured him while in his cell that he would soon be freed. What had happened to change her from the loving, responsive sweetheart coming to him that night at Monclova? Surely she didn't think there was anything serious going on between Charollotte and him? "Are you and your family well?"

When Manuela seemed to be struck deaf and dumb, Domingo told all about those back at the *presidio* and also how the party came to be at the palace.

"How nice that Manuela will get to meet so many handsome bachelors here in the City," Charollotte spoke up, moving to slip her arm through Louis's. "I suspect she'll return to the Presidio of the North as the fiancée of some lucky young man."

"If that wasn't my original plan in coming here," Manuela said with sizzle barely hidden beneath satin tones, "it does sound promising." Her heartbeat still struggling from the initial sight of him, she watched from beneath half-lowered lashes to see Louis's reaction to her words. Was that a flush on his face there in the dimly lighted room? Was he perhaps feeling relieved and a bit ashamed that she was openly releasing him from vows never uttered from anything other than the wish to use her for his own needs?

If Lieutenant Saint-Denis needed to hear it

353

from her that she no longer put any faith in their earlier promises, he could learn it in the presence of his new love, Manuela reflected. An exhilarating thought enlightened her: Governor Anya hadn't freed Louis to return to Louisiana as he had agreed to do as part of their bargain. She no longer owed the governor anything. She was free to seek her *real* Lover—and next time she would not be so easily misled! A thought sliding in behind that one was that Eblo's pigeon must have reached the palace pigeon cote with the message and prompted the viceroy to send for the Frenchmen at Monclova before the governor could free them to return home. All of a sudden Manuela felt mysteriously light-headed, set onto a new and dangerous course, one leading she knew not where. She recognized in that same instant that she did not care where.

"The handsome bachelors here are in for a treat," Louis said dryly when the silence seemed to call for him to make some kind of reply. Even as he tried to converse normally, he had not been able to ignore Manuela's disconcerting manner of blinking her eyelashes. Each time she lowered or lifted them in that heavy-lidded way, his pulse charged anew. What was there about her that made her seem more beautiful than he recalled? She seemed more poised, more in control, even more than on that first night he had met her. What had happened to the teasing, laughing beauty who had declared she had no desire to move in elegant society? She had apparently come to regret her declarations of love for him. Was there someone else? The mere thought rent his heart, made him work to control lips gone rubbery. He must talk with her in private.

"True. Manuela has already captured the attention of every man here tonight," Domingo said, wondering at the silent exchanges going on between the Frenchman and his niece. Had the passion flaring between them back at the *presidio* evolved into something flavored more with anger than love? At first, he had feared that they might fall all over each other and create a problem for him to tackle. After all, Diego was still insistent that Manuela must marry none other than a true Spaniard.

Domingo mused that as Manuela's protector while in the city he would have found it difficult to keep Manuela away from the debonair Louis had their romance still bloomed. With appreciation for Charolotte's considerable charms, he breathed a bit easier to see that she was determined to retain whatever hold she already had on the handsome French lieutenant. Now Manuela could freely circulate in upper-class society and perhaps meet one who could offer her a desirable marriage. Sending her a doting smile, he announced, "My niece will bring much beauty and delight to the social circles this season."

At last someone new joined the foursome – Leon d'Espinoza, the handsome young aide to the viceroy – and the talk became more general, less constrained. A waiter brought a tray of wine, and all grabbed glasses as if desperate for refreshment. Carlos and Doña Magdalena came over to meet Charolotte, both surprised but openly pleased to find that the man with his back to the room was no less than the Frenchman they had thought long on his way back to Louisiana. By the time the dinner gong sounded, the unexpected meeting between Louis and those from

San Juan Batista seemed, on the surface, to have been taken in stride by all involved.

Sitting on the viceroy's right while Doña Magdalena claimed his left side, Manuela toyed with her food throughout dinner and attempted to converse with the attentive Leon d'Espinoza. She had never before seen a table provide for so many guests, nor one set in such sumptuous manner with gold plate, imported porcelain, and sparkling crystal. Individual place cards sat in crested, gold holders that gleamed in the candlelight from the several tall candelabra interspersed with mammoth floral arrangements down the center of the long table.

She noted down the way that Carlos's dinner partner was the young Ramona, and that with her hair coiffed fashionably and her gown revealing a modest display of neck and shoulders, the pretty girl was holding her own with the adults — especially with the smiling Carlos. Domingo rated the right side of the Duchess and, from where Manuela sat at the opposite end of the table, appeared to be having a grand time.

The congenial Duke seemed interested in his lovely young guest's accounts of life in northern Mexico. Next to Doña Magdalena, and across from Manuela, sat Louis and then Charolotte. Once the Duke put it all together how Manuela and Louis had come to know each other, he included Louis in their conversations, despite his daughter's obvious attempts to keep the handsome Frenchman's attentions for herself.

"Manuela was telling me that the Indians have caused little trouble in Coahuila over the past few years. Did you have cause to meet any of the tribes from that area while there, Louis?" the older man asked. "We've talked of many things these weeks, but I don't believe I thought to ask about the tribes from northern Mexico."

His pale eyes reflecting candlelight, Louis replied, "Yes, your Grace. I had reason to visit the Mescaleros over the mountains." He addressed the viceroy but watched Manuela. Was she too remembering his taking her away from her captors? His immediate goal was to get her in private and talk with her. Her obvious contempt for him was driving him crazy. The headway he had made with the viceroy concerning the possibility of trade privileges would come to naught were he to lose Manuela's love. Nothing else mattered. Not once since that night in Monclova when she had come to his cell had he entertained the thought that she would stop loving him.

"What adventure to see how the tribes actually live!" the Duke responded, leaning back against his chair to allow a servant to take away his meat plate. If he noticed the way Manuela and Louis had studied each other covertly all during the meal, he made no show of it. "I really must make a trip up that way and see that part of New Spain for myself." He addressed his aide then. "What about it, Leon? Does the idea appeal to you?"

"In all ways, your Grace," the young man replied, smiling at Manuela there beside him.

"We at Fort San Juan Batista would welcome you and your party, your Grace. Please accept an open invitation to come at your convenience," Manuela said. "You might like to know that we find good hunting in the nearby foothills." She could feel the heat of Louis's gaze on her bare skin and wished she had a shawl to conceal her shoulders and the tops of her breasts. Why was he yet acting surprised at her rebuff and sending her secretive looks? Had he assumed she would respond to his smiles and fall into his arms upon seeing him? A part of her moaned at the tempting thought of feeling that masculine body against hers again, but she kicked it into what she hoped was oblivion. "We have few guests and find that all who come offer some kind of amusement, even those not invited."

The viceroy laughed at her droll remark, saying, "Your uncle Domingo warned me that you're as witty as you are beautiful, and I must agree." Revealing that he had caught her inference, he cut amused eyes toward a startled Louis before returning his attention to Manuela. A tiny flicker in his eyes seemed to mark a discovery. "Then you found the French spy amusing during his stay at the fort?"

"Oh, yes, your Grace. He turned what might have been a dull summer into one of entertainment." Manuela loved watching Louis toy with his wine glass and look less than in control. "But," she went on after hooking a telling glance across at the wide-eyed Louis, "your family and you must have also found Louis amusing, or you would have had him locked up." Her voice rippled out in playful tones spiced with deviltry. She ignored Doña Magdalena's stern look and plastered an innocent smile on her face. A dramatic tilt of her head set the ebony sausage curls to dancing sideways. One hugged her neck and draped across an olive swell of breast.

"You're right," Charolotte spoke up from her chair across the table to challenge Manuela. "We think Louis Saint-Denis belongs here in Mexico

358

City, not back in some godforsaken fort up in Louisiana among heathen Indians. His coming here is likely the work of fate. Perhaps you at the *presidio* didn't properly appreciate our ... our French spy." Doting eyes washed over Louis where he sat beside her, clutching his wine glass as a drowning man might hang on to a twig. "Father has offered him a commission in his army, if Louis will only give the right answer."

Manuela almost lost her breath at the surprising words. A work of fate? Never! Fate had no role in the matter. She herself was the one who had had Eblo send the message by pigeon. Would fate have led her to send the man she had believed her long-awaited Lover into the arms of another?

Evidently awaiting an opportunity to change the subject, Doña Magdalena jumped in then with questions for the Duke about an upcoming concert someone had mentioned earlier. Ever the perfect host, he obliged and turned the talk to lighter matters.

Grateful for her *dueña's* interruption, Manuela lifted her wine glass to her lips to keep down a barbed question of doubt. A restless hand strayed to the curl clinging to her neck. Could Louis possibly become a traitor to his beloved Louisiana? Why should she care if the despicable lieutenant proved to be both spy and traitor? It seemed to the distraught Manuela that the sophisticated Charolotte wanted Louis for a husband and intended that he reside with her in the big-city luxury to which she was obviously accustomed. How else to achieve her ends but to inveigle her father into luring Louis with the offer of a commission in the Spanish army?

Waves of anger, swelled to near cresting with what she refused to recognize as jealousy, threatened to steal Manuela's breath and coherent thought. She sensed that the handsome Leon d'Espinoza was sending blatant, flirty looks her way as he talked with her, but she could not make her thoughts detour. Some kind of acceptable replies must have fallen from her lips, for Leon smiled and continued to speak with her.

If she had harbored secret hopes that to talk with Louis in private might clear up some obvious misunderstandings, Manuela now knew that nothing so simple would resolve her pain. Behind lowered lashes, she acknowledged there was no doubt that she had been used. That was it, plain and simple. No wonder she ached all over, felt like lashing out at everyone in sight. Hadn't Louis confessed to her once that he was ambitious, eager to make a name for himself in the New World? What better way than to worm his way into the affections of the known enemy – and especially into those of the leaders' womenfolk? Her teeth closed upon the thin crystal of her glass, the contact edging her back to sanity and the conversation floating around her.

Relieved that he had refrained from responding to Manuela's obvious baiting, Louis paid as little attention to the ensuing talk about concerts as Manuela did. On the inside, horrible thoughts that she had never meant her confessions of love careened about and brought an uneasy feeling akin to nausea. Was she as cold and calculating as she was trying to imply with her cutting words and haughty manner? He refused to believe she had found him no more than a summer amusement. How could she discharge the memories of their kisses as having no meaning—and what about the night in Monclova when she had come to him as a virgin? His arms ached to hold her again, to feel her body close . . .

The sight of Manuela with her black hair coiffed so smartly with the tall comb at the crown tore at Louis's already wounded heart. How his fingers itched to fondle that shining curl gracing her neck and bosom! God, she was even more beautiful and desirable than he had remembered. Having to watch the viceroy's aide try to monopolize her attention was driving him into a frenzy. Those slanted eyes, which had always mesmerized him, still plumbed to the bottom of his heart with each doe-eyed look in his direction. Even now as she appeared engrossed in studying the wine in her glass, her full lips in repose, Manuela epitomized all that was feminine grace and loveliness.

If Louis had ever doubted just why it was that he could not respond to the unspoken invitations from the voluptuous Charolotte or accept the generous offer the Duke had made for him to remain in Mexico as a commissioned officer, he no longer had unanswered questions. If he believed in elusive fate, and he doubted that he had ever given it a passing thought until that moment, then he believed her appearance in Mexico City was the work of fate.

Forever would he remain in love with Manuela Ramon, he reflected. She was his life. Letting out a small sigh, covered by the spatter of polite conversation around him there at the viceroy's dinner table, Louis accepted the bleak statement as utter truth. Without the hope of having her at his side, his life held no meaning.

A man of lesser ambition, of less capability of loving to the fullest, of less belief in himself, might have given up. Like a wheel being rolled laboriously uphill, Louis's mind kept turning until an idea glimmered.

By the end of the meal, when the men stood and excused the ladies to pursue their private visiting in the receiving room until they joined them later, Louis had in mind a plan to capture Manuela's attention. First her attention, he reasoned, then her love. His beloved was cantankerous but curious, he thought, escaping into his old habit of playing mental word games. Willful but wonderful.

Chapter Twenty

Manuela stared in disbelief at the couple who burst through the palace doors and joined Leon d'Espinoza, Doña Magdalena, and her the next afternoon as they stood near the front entry. With disdain, she lifted her chin and sought another spot of interest to gaze upon somewhere down the long drive. Inside, she was a churning mass of emotion, the same one tearing at her since the night before when she had first seen Louis with the beautiful young widow. Surely the carriage ordered from the palace collection would appear at any minute.

"What good luck to learn that you planned a carriage outing for Manuela at the same time Charolotte wanted some fresh air, Leon," Louis said with a courteous bow and a coaxing smile at his companion, the viceroy's plainly pouting daughter. With a courtly nod toward the stern-faced Doña Magdalena, he went on, "Surely you would prefer to remain indoors and visit with your friends who've come to call? With such a fine foursome, there'll be no need for a *dueña* on a sightseeing ride through the city, do you think?" He rewarded her with one of his nicest smiles.

Her eyes squinting against the bright sunlight, Doña Magdalena relented. "You're right, Louis. I would enjoy having a quiet teatime with some old friends. I'll entrust Manuela to the three of you for the outing." With black skirt lifted daintily, she turned to go back up the stairway into the palace.

"Really, Louis," Charolotte complained loud enough to be heard even by the approaching coachman and two footmen. "I had in mind riding horseback, not in a carriage, even if the top is open." As though unsure that her gown and hair were properly arranged, she tugged at the green overskirt and tossed auburn-tinted curls into pretty disarray. "I didn't have time to find my matching umbrella." No one made comment, though, for the clattering wheels and noise of the horses drowned out her complaints. She glared at Leon and Manuela, once the footmen escorted all into the handsome vehicle and Louis and she sat across from them on the soft leather seat. To no one in particular, she said, "I'm sure Leon doesn't welcome our intrusion on his time with Manuela. After all, he only met her last evening."

Her face flushing to a tone similar to that of her pale pink gown, Manuela pretended indifference to the activities going on around her as the foursome settled onto the luxurious seats and the footmen took their stances on the rear platform. She could feel Louis's eyes appraising her beruffled gown, and she fidgeted at the short sleeve barely covering her forearm. Her view from the carriage there in front of the palace was of the city's center, the Plaza Mayor, the very area, she recalled from her history lessons, which had once been the ancient Aztecs' temple enclosure.

Manuela looked out across the spacious though littered square, serving now as a major market place, and faked greater interest than she felt. Buildings with arcades through which pedestrians sauntered to inspect the myriad wares of the bazaars lined the south and western sides. On the north side, beside the city hall, the great Cathedral continued to grow skyward, and she tried to remember what the nuns had told her about how long the building of the mammoth structure had been in progress—nearly a hundred years?

Ignoring the gleeful smile upon Louis's face across from her, she turned for a look at the viceroy's palace behind them when the carriage began to roll upon the cobblestones. With its walled gardens and adjacent stone prison, it occupied almost the entire length of one side of the large *plaza*. She saw in the clear afternoon light what darkness had obscured on the night of their arrival: The two-storied palace gave the appearance of a fort, with small towers at the corners, evenly spaced loopholes in the encompassing walls, and two great gateways with massive double doors.

Throughout her leisure inspection, Manuela was aware that Louis watched her every movement with a look bordering on memorization. What more could he possibly want from her? That he dared push himself into her presence incensed her beyond all reason. She loathed him, had been a fool to have thought he was her long-awaited Lover!

"Up ahead among those monasteries and convents is the Convent of San Francisco," Leon told Manuela after the carriage had traveled a block or so down the wide street beyond the *plaza*. "Isn't that where you said you attended school?"

"Yes," Manuela replied soberly, her thoughts already scampering within the confining convent walls. Were young girls still sitting in obedient, silent circles before the black-garbed sisters in bleak classrooms? It seemed only yesterday that she had worn drab uniforms and supped on bland food offered as fare for the soul rather than meager sustenance for growing, lively young bodies, and she felt a slight shiver of repulsion race along her spine. Straining to see down the street beyond the brooding convent walls, she asked, "I seem to recall that this is Goldsmith Street, reputed to be the most beautiful in the city."

"And small wonder," Charolotte spoke up. "This is where the smiths work their magic with gold and silver and precious stones brought over from Spain." She waggled a ring-bedecked hand in front of Louis's face, then across for Leon to see, smiling to watch the colors sparkle from rubies and diamonds.

"The shops along here turn out all kinds of goods," Louis told Manuela once they were continuing down the wide street toward their destination, the Alameda, the city's largest and most popular park. He wished she would favor him with a direct look from those bewitching black eyes, but she seemed to be ignoring him as deliberately as she was ignoring the viceroy's aide. He tried to take some comfort from that observation, but when he realized that the young Spaniard was actually good-looking and persona-

366

ble, he could not find much to be cheered about. Was Leon to be one of those fortunate enough to be allowed by her grandfather to court Manuela? Longing desperately for her to acknowledge his presence, give him a direct look of some kind, he went on. "They sell saddles, ironwork, furniture, candles, not to mention all the imported goods from Europe and Asia."

"I know all about that," Manuela retorted, wanting Louis to see that she recalled something about her former life in Mexico City, that she did know more than what she had learned at the remote *presidio*. He must think she was some kind of ignorant *mestizo*, she fumed. "Carlos has gone today along with Uncle Domingo to meet with Mr. Gustov Ortega, the man who manages our late father's import warehouse. Someday Carlos will be taking over the business, I'm sure. In fact, he might stay on in the city and begin learning now."

Manuela looked across at Louis then and wished she had not. He had never looked more beguiling or more handsome than in the white costume trimmed with silver. His eyes seemed mysterious echoes of the flashing metal forming the buttons on his satin vest. To see Charolotte's arm looped through his possessively brought a flash of unreasoning jealousy, and she slipped her own through the handy one next to her. The handsome, brown-eyed Leon d'Espinoza favored her with a doting smile, then covered her hand with his.

"Even for one so young, Carlos seems to have a level head for such a business," Louis remarked. "I'm sure he'll do well." When he had first arrived, he had heard that Leon was the favorite to win Charolotte's hand, but apparently that rumor had been only that. He had not been able to shake the headstrong beauty since that first night he had dined at the palace. At first he had wondered if perhaps she might be using him to make Leon jealous, but that had not seemed to be the case, not even after he had let her know his heart belonged to another. And now it looked as if the handsome Spaniard was set on winning Manuela, not interested at all in the viceroy's widowed daughter. He clamped his teeth together to keep from telling the man to go to hell, to remove his hand from Manuela's, that the beauty in the ruffled pink gown belonged to him, and that he could have Charolotte without contest.

Still fuming that Louis had forced Charolotte's and his presence upon her and further stirred her roiling emotions, Manuela paid more attention to the sights and sounds around them. She had forgotten how broad the streets were, noting that even on the narrowest, three vehicles could travel abreast; on the widest, six. They met and passed carriages that vied admirably with the viceroy's in luxurious decoration: There were trappings of silver, gold, precious stones, seats covered with quilted and embroidered cloth of gold and silk. The drivers and lackeys, as often as not, wore ornate livery to match the trim of their employer's showy vehicles.

And so many happy-faced people were about, chattering and laughing! Manuela saw that the streets and walkways were thronged with gaily dressed citizens, some idling before shops and stalls, some hurrying with purpose, their purchases in baskets or clutched in their hands or carried by trailing servants or blackamoors.

"How long will you be staying in the city?" Leon asked Manuela after Charolotte and he had discussed the merits of several young couples met in carriages, with whom the viceroy's daughter and he had exchanged waves and lengthy greetings, as close friends might do.

"Not long," she replied, not wanting to think about having to be around the arrogant Louis Saint-Denis any longer than necessary. Leon was nice enough, she guessed, but he was far from what she called an acceptable suitor—he failed to live up to the pictured Lover of her dreams. With a wrench in her heart, she reminded herself that so had Louis, now that he had ingratiated himself into the affections of the viceroy and his family as completely as he had done with her own back at San Juan Batista.

"But, darling," cooed Charolotte in specious tones, "didn't someone tell me this very morning that you came for the season and to buy your trousseau?"

"Someone has misinformed you," Manuela replied curtly, tossing her black curls and cutting her eyes at the lovely young widow.

"Then you're not engaged to marry Governor Anya next spring?" Charolotte asked. Her voice held no softness this time, and her small eyes narrowed.

Aware that Louis seemed even more intent on hearing her reply than the others, Manuela stared hard at the auburn-haired beauty. "No."

"I remember now where I heard it," the viceroy's daughter said then with a fake laugh. "I ran into his son Figaro in the *plaza* this morning, and he's the one who told me. Surely he wouldn't

369

make up such a wild tale, not being assistant to a judge and all." She tightened her hold on Louis's suddenly tensed arm.

"I can't speak for what Figaro Anya tells." With that heated announcement, Manuela returned to her study of the city as the carriage rolled along the cobblestoned street. Inside, she was trembling with new wrath. How dared the governor tell his son of their private agreement! Now that it was obvious that the old reprobate had lied to her about freeing Louis to return to Louisiana, she owed him nothing—nothing but a smart slap across his face. She forced herself to put aside private miseries. "I'd forgotten how many bells ring here. Aren't they enchanting, Leon?"

All during the day, she realized, there came an almost continuous chime from the thousands of bells in the city. Janglings from the numerous church spires called to the faithful to remind them of prayers, of the passing of time on earth, and to make amends for sundry sins and transgressions. Earlier when they had passed the many monasteries and nunneries, the tinkling of small bells regulating the routines of their inmates had reached her ears. Last night as she lay tossing and searching for sleep after the startling discovery of the handsome, carefree Louis Saint-Denis at the palace, she had heard the distant, low pealing of bells summoning nuns and friars to nocturnal devotions.

The carriage entered the Alameda then, joining the numerous sedan chairs being balanced by Orientals with swinging pigtails and the other luxurious carriages rolling down the shaded pathways meandering beneath the green-leaved trees. At Leon's direction, the driver, before going on to a nearby stable, pulled up close to a large pavilion and waited until the foursome had stepped down among the crowd of handsomely dressed men and women gathered in the park.

"Would you care for a cool drink of fruit juice and perhaps a comfit or sweetmeat before we stroll beneath the trees?" Louis asked Manuela when the two were left standing side by side, more or less alone, while a group of young couples waylaid Charolotte and Leon with good-natured banter about an upcoming horse race.

"Yes," Manuela replied, eyeing the tempting assortments on the vendor's tray nearby. That Leon had been quick to appear at Charolotte's side when their friends had approached them had not gone unnoticed, either by Louis or by her. She was not sure what was going on between the two, or apparently had at some time in the past, but she was curious. Was Charolotte set on commanding the full attention of all good-looking men, as Uncle Domingo had hinted? Not that Leon appeared disinterested in her, and yet she felt that he was as aware of every movement Charolotte made as she was of Louis's. For some strange reason, her musings lifted her mood, and she leaned to point at candied figs.

"Try this honeyed almond," Louis told her when she had had her fill of the sugar-glazed fruits. His fingers carried the comfit to her lips, and their gazes became locked. The way her eyelashes had fluttered and flirted unknowingly all through the carriage ride had turned his insides choppy. "I must speak with you in private, Manuela," he whispered.

"I'm not interested in anything you have to say.

371

You're despicable!" Even to her, her words sounded like lies. Hearing him say her name so intimately played havoc with her earlier self-control. If he wouldn't stand so near and look at her in that devastating way, she reflected, she could get her mind to think straight. It wasn't fair, the way just being around him kept her pulse jumping erratically. If she could stay out of his presence . . . But, she assured herself, she had done her best. He was the one who wouldn't back away from what was a most intolerable situation.

"Meet me tonight at midnight in the rose arbor behind the palace," he urged, noting out of the corner of his eye that Charolotte and Leon were leaving their talkative friends behind and coming toward them. "It might be a matter of life and death . . . and you do owo mc, don't you?"

Manuela broke their gaze by the hardest concentration and chewed on the tasteless almond, washing it down with fruit juice of an origin she could not have identified if pressed. What did he mean, a matter of life and death? Whose? His own? As angry and hurt as she was at the way he had obviously used her, she confessed she had no wish to see him dead. She was shocked that he would make reference to his rescuing her from the Mescaleros, but she admitted she was indebted to him.

For Manuela, the rest of the afternoon passed in one sunny haze of doubts, fears, and recriminations for all the wrong things she had done in her life. Of where the four of them walked there in the Alameda, what they saw, what they talked about, she had no recollection. Her entire being seemed focused on the garden behind the palace at midnight.

"I thought you'd never get here," Louis said in a low voice when Manuela darted from the shadows of tall oleanders and hibiscus into the rose arbor. His arms wide, his smile flashing in the reflecting light of a lantern in a far corner, he hurried to gather her cloaked figure close. Even when she seemed determined to remain stiff and aloof, he kissed her hair and held her tightly. His heart threatened to jump from his chest at the feel of her, the smell of her. Once she entered the arbor, the scent of roses had heightened, reminding him of that first time he had met her and kissed her fragrant hand.

"What is this all about, Louis Saint-Denis?" she demanded when she could catch her breath at the nearness of him, at the sight of his handsome features up close, at the feel of his body next to hers. No matter that she had intended to make him keep his distance and merely listen to what he had to say, she was all aquiver from his obvious eagerness to hold her, to regain something of that old passion they had shared back in the cell at Monclova. Was it only a few months ago? For a second, she thought she was again naked in his arms, so alive were the pores of her skin.

"I had to tell you that I love you or I would've died," he whispered, his voice taut with restraint. "To see you look at me with eyes of distrust and anger is killing me. I'd thought you'd be happy to find me here alive when you came. I can't imagine what you must think—"

"What I think is that you're a reprobate and full of deceit and that I'm a fool a second time

373

for coming here," she broke in heatedly, trying unsuccessfully to step from his embrace. Her entire body seemed on fire. He had duped her again! "I was led to believe you had returned weeks ago to your Fort Saint Jean de Baptiste in Louisiana and all the time—"

"Wait," he interrupted her diatribe firmly, not loosening his hold for fear she would flee. "It seems to me that it's in our favor that I've met the viceroy. I had nothing to do with ending up in Mexico City instead of back in Louisiana. How could you think I did? There Medar, Phillipe, and I were in prison, expecting we knew not what from what you'd told me about escape coming shortly, when these soldiers from the viceroy appeared and escorted us south. I never did even meet Governor Anya. I'm still as surprised about the whole matter as you must be. Not until I arrived and met with the viceroy did I learn that he'd received a message that Governor Anya was holding my men and me without first giving us an audience. I can't imagine how word reached him when Anya seemed determined to detain me in prison until I rotted."

Manuela relaxed a bit at his story, not sure she should let him know yet of the message she had had Eblo send by his pigeons. Inside, something sang at the thought that she had indeed been successful in getting him away from Governor Anya's clutches, but other matters pressed to be explored. "Why aren't you in a cell here? Did the fair Charolotte lay her man-hungry eyes on you and decide you'd be perfect to dance attendance on her?"

"Hardly," Louis remarked, relieved to learn of her jealousy, delighted to see the sparks fly deep in the midnight black of her eyes. Then she did still care! "No one can touch my heart, Manuela, when you have it so firmly in your control." He waited no longer to claim the trembling mouth. The sweetness of her seeped throughout his hungry soul, and his lips tried to convince her of what his words obviously had not – he loved her, adored her, desired her above all earthly rewards. Her arms pulling his head closer to hers bound him in the way he longed to be captured forever.

"What are you going to do about getting away from here?" Manuela asked when he had freed her lips and urged her to sit beside him on a bench there in the shadowed arbor. From a distant steeple, a bell chimed in sonorous tones, but she heard no noises from the *plaza* outside the palace walls. The lateness of the hour seemed to add to the magic of being with him once again. "What can I do to help?"

"Nothing," he assured her with a touch of masculine arrogance which warned her of the truth of Carlos's remark that men did not like their women interfering in men's affairs. "I got myself into this mess, and I'll get myself out of it."

A bit chastened at the knowledge that she had indeed played the major role in putting him in Mexico City and that he would not relish hearing it, she asked in properly subdued tones, "Has the viceroy truly offered you a commission to stay?" When he nodded thoughtfully, she asked, her heart paining her, "Will you accept?"

"Never will I be anything but a Frenchman, Manuela, living in New France, serving my own king." His voice was that proud one she recalled from their first meeting, and his eyes shone silver with intensity. "And beside me will be you, my wife. Such stuff are my dreams made of, and that only."

"But how can those things be?" She sent a hand to stroke the troubled brow, then let it trace the handsome features of his face. Everything seemed against their ever being together for any length of time.

"I'm not sure, but I know I've some kind of acquaintance with good fortune, or I'd never have met you. The viceroy seems an intelligent man, and he has discussed with me what he and I see as a need for the French and Spanish to get along with each other here in the New World, despite what our kings may wish from across the Atlantic. Naturally he's for helping restore Father Hidalgo's lost mission and accepts my passport stating that as my purpose for being here as valid. When I told him of the trading goods I'd had to leave behind at San Juan Batista, he seemed impressed with what I'd feared had become a foolhardy dream—to begin some kind of trade between our colonies."

"Do you think he'll allow you to return and actually set up some kind of trade route?"

"I doubt he'll put it into those words, but I've a feeling that he'd be willing to ignore any rumors about such a trading agreement, were he to decide to free me to return to Louisiana." He captured her hand and brought it up to his lips, planting warm kisses in the palm, then forging little tremulous paths up and down each finger. "Now that you've come, I feel I can conquer anything." A nagging thought claimed his attention and he asked, "What was Charolotte telling about your being engaged to Anya? I've met that son of his even before dinner tonight, but I've never before heard him speak of the engagement. I thought the final decision on that had been postponed. Every time Figaro fawned over you after dinner, I wanted to smash his face and tell him that you've made no agreement to marry his father. Why didn't you tell him to go soak his head in cactus juice?"

"Figaro doesn't bother me," Manuela denied, not eager for Louis to engage Figaro in conversation and learn too much about her secret arrangement with the governor. If he were to find out that she had interfered . . . She leaned to kiss him.

Louis murmured against her lips, "Come with me to my apartment." When she looked up questioningly, her eyes pools of sparkling midnight, he gestured toward the long, low building Carlos and she had noted at the back of the garden that first morning they had walked about. "I'm a lucky prisoner here, though not as lucky as at San Juan Batista, for I don't get to see you every day. Come let me make love to you, hold you in the way I've dreamed of."

"You know that I took more chance than I should have just to meet you here," she told him, her grief at having to refuse him plain in her tone. "Oh, Louis, what will we do? I can't bear the thought that you might end up having to marry Charolotte to stay alive."

"That isn't the viceroy's way, Manuela, my love. Actually, I think Charolotte will end up marrying Leon, the handsome aide who seems to be paying you more attention than she—or I—can stand right now. Medar tells me he's learned that they've been eyeing each other ever since she arrived, but that she likes playing the field too much to give him an answer yet. From what I can see, she's becoming so jealous of you that she might show her true colors and grab him back—if she can, after that hot-blooded Spaniard has seen you. God! The thought that he or some of those others hanging around you might kiss you—"

"Sh-h!" she soothed, smiling through tears of gratitude upon learning that he had no serious desires toward the voluptuous Charolotte and leaning against his broad chest to hide her signs of relief. "No one will ever touch me but you, Louis . . . even if I have to return to the convent."

"Never say that," he protested. "You've told me how you hate walls, and I'd see you wed to another before I'd agree for you to be hemmed away from the world." All over he ached with love and longing for the beautiful young woman in his arms, and he wondered if he truly could give her up to another. Every cell cried out for a way to claim her forever.

"I must go. Conchita met with Medar earlier out here while we were having dinner, and she agreed to make excuses if Doña Magdalena were to come to our suite. But we can't let anyone get suspicious before the viceroy frees you."

"I've confidence he will, and then I'll have to ask your grandfather again, because I'm not leaving Mexico without taking you with me. Surely he'll be impressed that the viceroy has faith in me as a decent man—even if I am a Frenchman."

No loner willing to waste the remaining precious moments together on words, the lovers pressed nearer, lips and bodies as close as the petals in the fragrant rosebuds overhead, heart-beats singing and throbbing in unison. The stirrings inside threatened to explode and lead them to give in to the overpowering wish to shed their clothing and fall into an enveloping mass of caressing limbs and bodies there upon the bricked floor of the rose arbor. His hand cupped a breast beneath her cloak, finding that even beneath the silk of her gown, it waited, warm and peaked with desire. Her hand fondled his neck before sliding hungrily down the broad back, all tensed with muscles held under control by dint of will.

Only a soulful "meow" from Nero, the pet of the viceroy's younger daughter, as it prowled about in the garden in search of some kindred feline soul in the darkness snatched them back from the brink of surrender.

"Nero the Emperor couldn't have been more cruel," Louis whispered hoarsely when Manuela turned to leave without even attempting further talk. He watched her small, fleeing figure until it blended with the darkness beside the garden entry into the palace, feeling bereft and far less confident than he had pretended to her that some kind of future lay ahead for them.

A kind of frenzied activity seemed to rule those at the palace over the next few days: parties, some in the afternoon and others at night, nearly all ending in games of chance being played until past midnight by women and men alike; concerts, both in the palace grand ballroom and in the city halls; sallies to Alameda in groups of carriages brought from the vast collec-

379

tion behind the palace stables; more trips to the park on horseback, the women decked out in their finest riding costumes, their saddles ornamented with blazes of hibiscus and roses, the men resplendent in vests embroidered heavily with gold and silver and boots sporting like trim. And never were there opportunities for Manuela and Louis to find time for more than a private word or two, except through the language of their eyes. Leon and Charolotte seemed intent on keeping the foursome just that—a foursome.

"Manuela, Carlos and I feel we've been neglecting you over the past days," Domingo told his niece one night before dinner as they awaited the arrival of other guests for a particularly large affair there at the palace. "Each time I've seen you, though, it appears that Leon is keeping you good company, not to mention Charolotte and Louis." He noted the guarded expression on her face then. "Are things going well between Leon and you? He seems to force out the others who try to swarm around you. I'm sure Father would approve—"

"Yes, Uncle Domingo," she was quick to agree, wondering how much his wise eyes noted when Louis and she were near each other. She knew that Doña Magdalena was too short of sight and hearing to discern that the Frenchman and she were once more speaking the silent language of lovers, but Domingo might not be so easily fooled. "Leon seems to be exactly what Grandfather would like me to accept as a suitor."

"Do you see him that way?"

"Not exactly," she hedged. She knew she had best not entrust her secrets to anyone, not even to Carlos now that he had taken such an interest in pursuing his own paths. Not that she minded, she told herself staunchly. She had learned when she had returned from the Mescalero village that maturity was leading Carlos and her down inevitably separate paths. "How have things been going with Carlos's sessions with Gustavo Ortega? Are matters well at our warehouse? Does Carlos think that's what he'll like doing for the rest of his life?" She seldom got in more than a few sentences with her twin, but he did indeed seem happier and more content than she had seen him since their arrival a little over a week ago.

"Yes, I believe he's ready to stay on and work closely with Gustavo. You'll recall that Father and I discussed the possibility that he might wish to do so." Domingo glanced about the huge room beginning to fill with chattering, beautifully dressed people. "Have you seen him this evening? I'm sure he'll be wanting to tell you all about it himself. It's just that he's so busy. . . ."

"Yes, and not only with learning about the import business," she remarked with a knowing smile. "I've seen the way the young Ramona Alencastre becomes a grown-up young lady in the evenings when my handsome brother is around. Do you think the viceroy objects?"

"No, I get the impression that he's rather pleased, to tell you the truth. More than once he's talked with me about how the deplorable business of a lower caste for any born to Spanish parents here in Mexico has no basis for existence, in so far as he can see. I don't believe that if he approved of Carlos as a suitor for his daughter's hand on general grounds, that he'd withhold it simply because you two weren't born in Spain. Certainly," he added in even lower tones, "Carlos would be able to provide handsomely for Ramona—should they still show interest in each other in a couple of years when it might be time to speak of betrothal."

Manuela spotted the young couple then and waved, proud to note that they made a spectacularly handsome pair. At least Carlos wasn't going to have the problem she was having, she moaned silently. He hadn't fallen in love with one of the wrong nationality. In fact, Ramona fit every one of Diego's requirements, including having been born in Spain.

"Why the heavy sigh?" came a masculine voice, breaking into Manuela's musings and causing Domingo to move away after a polite greeting.

"Good evening, Figaro," she replied stiffly. Having already run into Governor Anya's son on several occasions and not liking the last encounter any better than the first, she wished she possessed magical powers and could make him disappear. He seemed to sense that he held a secret she did not want discussed, and it gave him a decidedly boorish air. She had never liked him, not even before he had tried to kiss her and maul her last year, but now she detested him.

"Where's the handsome Leon? Don't tell me that he and the other bachelors are beginning to believe the talk that you're already engaged. I wonder who could have started such a rumor." An oily smile made him look even more like the governor than Manuela had recalled. "I'd be glad to serve as your escort, since the gossip is that you're engaged to marry my father."

"You know nothing about the matter, and I don't know why you don't contact your father and find out the truth. Really, Figaro, your idea of humor bores me." She snapped open her fan and waved it rapidly before her flushed face. Across the way, she could see Louis, handsome in deep blue coat and knee breeches, making his way toward them, and she had no desire for the two men to engage in serious conversation. No telling what Figaro would end up saying, and she had already decided she would never be able to explain to Louis about her agreeing back in Monclova to marry the governor to set him free. Not that any of that counted now, but still . . .

Leon d'Espinoza and Charolotte appeared beside them when Louis did, though, and general talk among the group kept Figaro from asserting himself. Nevertheless, his beady eyes kept sending nasty little messages to Manuela all evening.

"Conchita," Manuela confided late that night as the maid helped her prepare for bed, "I think I'm going out of my head over Louis. I believe it was easier to think him lost to me forever than to run into him here and find out he still cares for me." Tears glistened in the large black eyes. "How will he ever get freed? Even though he comes and goes like a house guest just as he did at San Juan Batista, he's still a prisoner. What does Medar say?" Conchita had told her that almost every evening while the viceroy and his guests dined and enjoyed entertainment, she was meeting Louis's valet in the garden and that they had pledged undying love.

"Things look bad, even from the usually cheerful Medar," the maid replied, her face sober and sorrowing. "He's allowed to live outside of prison to attend his employer, but Phillipe is required to sleep in a cell. I suppose they think that to lock up his sergeant is some kind of safeguard against the lieutenant's possible escape." Walking to the window and staring down across the shadowed garden, she went on. "From here I can see the window of the apartment behind the garden where they stay, and I've noticed how late the light shines through it. There's no telling what they're planning."

Manuela rose from the stool in front of the dressing table and looked in the direction Conchita indicated. She, too, had figured out which were Louis's quarters, but she had not voiced it to the maid, had not allowed herself the luxury of imagining what he must be doing and thinking out there. "If the viceroy insists on his staying here and serving in the Spanish army, even as a commissioned officer, I know it'll be the death of him. He has such pride in being a Frenchman. If only I could think of a way to help."

"There's no place to send a messenger pigeon from here except back to San Juan Batista," Conchita consoled, still amazed that Manuela's message to the viceroy had reached such a distance. "You helped in the only way you could, or the three would still be in that awful prison in Monclova. Did I tell you that I saw the pigeon cote atop the stables when Medar and I strolled outside the garden walls the other night?"

"Oh, Conchita, you didn't tell him—"

"No, of course I didn't," she hastened to reply. "I understand how ticklish men can be when it comes to their sense of pride. They like to think they're in control."

Two black-haired young women gazed desolately from their second-story bedroom in the viceroy's palace, their sad eyes fixed unwaveringly on a glowing window in the long apartment building set against the back wall. Only the depth of their love for the unseen Frenchmen equaled their concern and fears for their futures.

two blue-banded windows, paused there.
...three...bags and...sat...against the...
...with a panel...there, and...were...diverge...
...from a spread window...the long...rays...
falling across...the...back wall...over the...
depth of shade...two...for the...of...Francisco...
...and their...various years on each...times.

Chapter Twenty-one

The next day, scarcely two weeks after their
arrival in the city, Manuela was summoned to
join Carlos, Domingo, and Viceroy Alencastre in
his handsome study on the ground floor. Heavy
expressions on the men's faces suggested they
had reached some serious decision.

Manuela, halted on her way to go with Doña
Magdalena to pick up some gowns ordered from
a dressmaker near the *plaza*, settled her blue silk
skirts about her on the chair proffered and
asked, "You wanted to see me?" She addressed
her question to all three, for no one seemed eager
to speak first.

"My dear," the viceroy answered from behind
his desk, "we've had a carrier pigeon arrive from
your grandfather's *presidio* with a disturbing
message, and we've been discussing the best way
to handle it."

"Is he ill?" she asked, eyes big and frightened
as they searched the faces of Carlos and
Domingo. "Tell me."

"No, Father is well enough," Domingo replied.
"He might not be if we don't hurry back, though,
as Eblo's pigeon brought word that the Lipans
have moved away from the *presidio en masse*

386

since we left. You might not have known it, but ever since Governor Anya replaced Sergeant Guerra with his own man, Sergeant Benitez, the Indians haven't been satisfied. Benitez has a way of treating them like undesirables, when Father has never taken that attitude toward them. He and I both know how much we need them to make the fort self-supporting, plus their presence has always kept at bay any marauding bands of Indians, especially the Tejas."

"Then we must return at once with soldiers to help out, mustn't we, Uncle?" she asked. Thoughts of Diego's well-being tore at her. Her feeling of alienation dispelled, she longed suddenly to see him, to hear his familiar, beloved voice.

"To send enough soldiers to spar with quarreling Indians isn't possible right now," the viceroy replied grimly. "I've had to send reinforcements over to the western coast to put down trouble in the port of Acapulco, and I have only a couple of dozen men to spare."

"What if the Lipans stir up some tribe to join them and attack . . ." Manuela could not complete the thought, for tears welled and brought a painful knot to her throat.

Carlos rose and came to stand beside her, placing a comforting hand on her shoulder. "They have a marvelous plan in mind, Manuela. Hear them out." A sudden pressure of his fingers hinted that she might like the news, and, from habit, she reached up her own hand to rest lightly against his.

"Domingo has been adding to my knowledge of and appreciation for the considerable talents of our in-house prisoner, Louis Saint-Denis," the

viceroy said in a musing voice. Long, elegant
fingers toyed with an unlighted cigar as he
spoke. "It's his opinion, and Carlos's as well, that
if I were to free Louis and his men and allow
them to accompany the party back to San Juan
Batista, Louis would likely be able to parley with
the Lipans and win them back. They were telling
me of his success in rescuing you from the Mescaleros without bloodshed, Manuela—except a
little of his own. I must confess that I'm highly
impressed with the remarkable French lieutenant, and I've found no evidence that he came to
Mexico as a spy. I hate to think what might have
happened to him had not one of the magical
pigeons from San Juan Batista arrived with
news of his imprisonment at Monclova."

Manuela's heart lurched and then raced crazily
as the viceroy talked about her beloved and the
strange events that had placed him in Mexico
City, events she well knew she had instigated.
Was it possible that—

"However," the ruler of Mexico went on, "I had
so hoped to talk Louis into staying on here and
perhaps joining me in my mission to improve the
lot of New Spain that I've not been easy to
dissuade." He no longer pretended to himself
that he hadn't also hoped to gain Louis as a son-
in-law, but he had already noted the keen, secretive looks being exchanged by the beautiful
Manuela and the young Frenchman and guessed
that even had he detained Louis, Charolotte
never would have won his heart. He assured
himself that there was nothing wrong with Leon
d'Espinoza, except that he wasn't strong-willed
enough to handle his daughter. Oh well, worries
could be dealt with as they presented them-

selves. Right now, he needed the safety of his northernmost *presidio* resecured right away and with as few soldiers as possible. "Your uncle is a most convincing officer, though, and I'm deferring to his suggestion."

"What about you, Carlos?" Manuela asked, her voice shaky at the thought of Louis's freedom and his return to San Juan Batista. "Will you stay on here and continue to learn about our warehouse affairs?" She patted his hand still resting on her shoulder, aware for the first time that it felt more like that of a man than a boy. With a start at the thought, she twisted her head to look into his eyes.

"Yes," he replied, smiling down at her to let her know he shared her secret joy about Louis. "Uncle Domingo assures me that he'll take care of Doña Magdalena and you on the way back, and I've great confidence that Louis can handle the Indian problems. The viceroy has offered to let me move into the apartment Louis has been using, so that I'll not be having to fend for myself with nothing but a manservant."

Domingo rose, black eyes studying her with concern, and said in a caring way, "Our plans are to leave at daybreak. I'm sorry to break short this first social season for you, but I see no other way unless you care to stay on here at the viceroy's invitation until I can return for you some time after Christmas."

"Oh, no," Manuela declared, horrified at the thought of being left behind, especially now that Louis would be heading north along with Domingo and the soldiers. "I've had a lovely time and I appreciate the kind offer to stay on, but I'm ready to return home."

"Very well, then," Domingo responded without further ado. "Can Doña Magdalena and you manage to get your purchases and belongings together by daybreak tomorrow?"

Manuela did not know what she said to the three men standing politely as she left the room, but she obviously said all the right things, for they let her go with understanding nods. Her heartbeat was kicking around like crazy, and her imagination was having a joyous holiday. Louis was freed! Louis was returning to San Juan Batista with her.

Conchita was as elated as her mistress at the grand new of the Frenchmen's release. Neither minded in the least having to leave the city far earlier than planned. Both had secretly confided their preference for the slower-paced life they had known at the *presidio*. In between packing, they often stopped and hugged each other with gleeful giggles at the thought of having their sweethearts not only alive and well but also near them every day — at least for the weeks it would take to return to San Juan Batista. Beyond that lengths of time, neither dared speak or dream.

The farewell dinner that night in the palace was even more elaborate and festive than any previous celebrations. There were speeches and toasts after the numerous courses had been served and consumed by the large gathering. Several young men who had not gotten beyond exchanging a few words with Manuela in the presence of Doña Magdalena, or someone else, did their best to lure her into shadowed corners or into taking moonlight strolls for breaths of fresh air, but she fenced them off effectively. Not even Leon, looking particularly handsome that evening in lemon yellow satin with velvet brown waistcoat beneath the flared coat, could persuade her to walk with him on the side verandah opening off the large game room.

"You're so beautiful in that white gown," Leon whispered when she allowed him to bring her a cup of coffee where they sat on a settee while others yet played at cards. His eyes roved across her olive shoulders and partially exposed breasts there in the soft light from overhead chandeliers of steadily burning candles, as though trying to commit to memory her brunette perfection. "I had hoped to tell you in private what your eyes do to me when you cut them that way behind half-closed lashes." He glanced across at Doña Magdalena sitting at the nearest table, her attention apparently on her cards. "Will you be returning to the city anytime soon, or must I wait until the viceroy and I make our visit north in the spring before I see you again?"

Manuela listened with her pretty ears and tossed ebon sausage curls charmingly, but her heart heard not a word. She smiled with a kind of secret amusement deep in the heavy-lidded black eyes and replied in a voice far wiser than one would have expected from such soft, young lips, "I've a feeling that once I leave, you're going to find all kinds of reasons to get to know Charolotte even better than you seem to already. Her loveliness will soon make me fade into no more than a memory."

Leon pretended not to know of what she spoke and would not let up in his persistence to gain her promise to answer his letters if he wrote her.

Once Doña Magdalena turned from her cards to squint at them disapprovingly, for his voice had become charged with audible emotion.

Across the room, Louis missed not a single action. Had Leon or any other young man succeeded in luring Manuela out of his sight, he had already decided he would follow, no matter what the consequences. Charolotte, clinging to his arm all evening, alternated between bouts of depression and attacks of lively flirtation. Her lips as lusciously wine colored as the satin gown flowing over her lissome body, she seemed not to believe it when he told her before dinner that he had been freed, that he was leaving on the morrow, never to return. She had even dragged him over to the duke to ask him to deny what Louis was telling, but her father had merely smiled and assured her that it was all true. When she tried to protest and pout, he became the all-powerful viceroy and stared down at her icily until she turned away with a great but silent show of temper, her arm linked possessively in Louis's.

In her black silk riding breeches and the flat little hat once belonging to Carlos sitting atop her shining black head, thick braids looped neatly at its base, Manuela left Mexico City the next morning along with the party of some two dozen soldiers. Not until the group stopped for the night in the mountains did she glimpse Louis up close enough to make out his features, and that was at a second, larger camp fire across from the one prepared for Doña Magdalena, Conchita, and her by the same trio of privates attending their needs on the trip down. She had not minded, though, for she knew he was with her and no longer a prisoner.

When the third and fourth days passed as grueling trials, even to those accustomed to riding horseback for long periods of time, Manuela contented herself with the knowledge that eventually Domingo would get enough of talking and planning with the Frenchman about what they must do when they arrived back at the *presidio*. She had waited so long. What were a few more days or even weeks? Ruefully she confessed that already she had learned that her preconceived notions of the suffering demanded by love had been immature and foolish, those of a dreaming young girl. Now she felt she knew pain intimately.

"How are Doña Magdalena and you faring?" Domingo asked Manuela a few mornings later as they entered a wide valley and found the King's Road wider and less perilous. At least twice each day, he checked on the trio of women traveling in the middle of the group. He glanced at his aunt in the small carriage, amazed as usual at the composure on the finely lined face.

That Manuela seldom rode inside with her amused her uncle, for most of the young women he knew would have protested such long hours on horseback. Conchita seemed resigned to her role as companion to the older woman, though, and Manuela appeared to thrive on the freedom of riding Nightstar near them but not necessarily close enough to talk with the two inside the carriage. She seemed to draw from some inner store of happiness, and Domingo believed he knew what it was, though he did not dare let on for fear she would learn that he himself had no qualms about allowing her to marry Louis Saint-Denis. The final decision wasn't his, he reminded himself, and he had little hope that Diego was going to view the Frenchman in a better light just because he had returned to assist in getting the Lipans to come back to their homes and jobs at the *presidio*.

"We're doing fine, Uncle Domingo," Manuela responded in her usual cheerful way, casting a searching eye to the clouds darkening in the distance. "I'm wondering if our good weather is going to desert us before nightfall, though." She reined in Nightstar to canter beside him. She knew that far up ahead Louis and his men rode with twenty Spanish soldiers from the viceroy's company and that bringing up the rear were the original eight who had traveled down with them from San Juan Batista. "We've met few other travelers and seen no highwaymen, so I guess we're lucky so far."

"Agreed," he replied, no longer astonished when she came out with such adult wisdom. "I'm hoping those clouds won't become a raging storm before we get back into thick forests again."

At their position so near the Gulf of Mexico, they were vulnerable to storms that sometimes formed over the water and then moved inland with terrific force. More than once Domingo had seen protective tarpaulins attached to trees carried off by the winds as if they had been no more than bolts of sheer silk. He had hoped not to make the return journey while such seasonal storms were yet brewing out in the gulf, but now there was no choice but to travel with all possible haste. Knowing his father and their home were more vulnerable than at any time since he could recall did little to bring him restful sleep or peace of mind during the days.

By mid-afternoon, it was apparent to the entire party that they would have to stop early and make plans to protect themselves from what would likely be a long, stormy night. Having heard of some highwaymen who took advantage of such violent weather to pounce upon unsuspecting travelers as they attempted to rest and seek refuge from storms, Domingo decided that he had best share some of his worries and his duties with the capable French lieutenant.

"Louis," Domingo told him while the two watched the soldiers make shelters for the lead group and their horses, "I can't be everywhere, especially if the storm breaks as heavily as I suspect it will. Since the soldiers might balk at taking orders from a Frenchman in the event an emergency did arise, I'm going to ask you and your men to sleep close to the women tonight instead of the usual soldiers. Go ahead and ask Medar to prepare a camp fire and food for all to share. I'll be up ahead with half of my men, while Sergeant Sonchez stays with the others behind on the road. That way, if we become separated — and if the horses were to become frightened and get loose, who knows where we'd end up before finding them — each group will have a leader to keep it moving onward toward the *presidio*."

"Sounds as if you expect a bothersome night," Louis remarked, rather surprised that Domingo would open the way for him to speak privately with Manuela. Not that the past several days spent together on the trail were not necessary and enlightening as they talked of the ways in which they could outmaneuver the Lipans without bloodshed and win them back to the fort, still he had suspected that the wily Domingo was taking no chances that his niece would be available to him. He liked the assessing, approving looks the older man was sending his way. "Are you suspicious that highwaymen may be around?"

Domingo let out a sharp laugh. "I'm always suspicious of that, my friend. I've heard that the most daring of them all, Jacinto Navarro, now has a few Indians riding with him, and that he's more fearless than ever. He would likely risk all to capture the guns, ammunition, and goods in our wagons."

"Surely they'd think twice before attacking such a large group of armed soldiers, though."

"That's why I've been keeping men both ahead and behind our women and the wagons and allowing little distance in between when we travel and make camp," Domingo told him. "If we hadn't run into this storm, I think we could have felt safe; but now, I'm taking extra precautions, just in case."

Louis smiled at the capable Spanish officer and said, "You can count on me to safeguard the women, and thank you for the privilege."

Medar drafted Phillipe to help him prepare the evening meal for the women and the three Frenchmen there beneath sheltering trees alongside the only road leading northward from Mexico City. The sergeant went along good-naturedly, obviously as cheered at being

396

freed from Spanish authorities as Louis and the dapper valet. He confided to Medar that already he had a notebook filled with accounts of all that the three had endured – and enjoyed – since their arrival several months ago.

Domingo's apparent faith in them by issuing them weapons and entrusting the safety of the women to them made Medar feel, like Louis and Phillipe, that they were no longer among foreigners. As he stirred at the pot of stew, Medar wondered if the French soldiers staying behind to hunt in Tejas had already arrived at San Juan Batista and found them gone. If so, would they have come searching, or would they have returned to Louisiana? He cast a look around at the darkening woods, aware that sprinkles of rain had begun to blow against his hooded garment.

"The wind will whip up the coals and make the stew cook faster," Medar assured Phillipe, who was glancing about apprehensively. "I've peeled several pieces of that strange fruit we saw back down the way, the one with the pink meat inside that somebody called a mango. Quite tasty, just as Domingo assured us it would be." He sent a flirty wink at Conchita where she stood at the edge of the large tarpaulin draped between some trees growing close together. Already she had gotten out eating utensils and implements.

Resting inside the carriage, Doña Magdalena looked outside at the activities and shuddered at the unpleasantness of it all. She had thought that to return to the city of her former life would bring inordinate joy, but all she could do was miss the peaceful air and way of life in her brother-in-law's *hacienda* at San Juan Batista. The minute she returned, she meant to tell him of her renewed gratitude for his having offered her a home with him in exchange for looking after Manuela and teaching her the ways of a young Spanish lady. And then, she promised herself, she was going to tell him that even after Manuela was wed and gone and no longer in need of a *dueña*, she longed to stay on with him there forever. When she recalled the warmth of his smile and his unexpected hug upon their departure that morning several weeks ago, she wondered if perhaps he would not be surprised, if perhaps he might even suggest ... She felt her face flush, and she smiled.

"I can't believe we're finally allowed to talk and be together," Louis told Manuela there where they sat cross-legged on a treated rug beneath the tarpaulin erected to shelter the six of them while they ate and slept that night. They could hear the rain peppering the fabric and making little plopping sounds as it found paths through the thick-limbed trees. Low bushes and the nearby carriage kept the rising wind from doing more than teasing at their hair. She had not loosened the braids caught at the base of her neck, but tendrils had escaped during the windy afternoon and formed soft, feathery locks about her face and ears. He leaned closer, but not before sliding a cautious look toward Doña Magdalena still in the carriage. She was smiling and seemed unaware that Manuela and he were alone in the near darkness. He asked, "Are you crying?"

"It must be the smoke from the camp fire," she replied, sending a hand to brush at the telltale sparkles upon her lashes. How could she confess that just sitting with him, hearing his voice, and feeling his eyes adoring her were so much like dreams come true that she could not keep back a tear or two? Stretching her arms out behind her, she sniffed at the tempting aroma of the stew and the fresh smell of rain in a forest, wrinkling her nose in a way that charmed Louis utterly. "I'm afraid to believe it's true that you and your men are our personal guards tonight. Uncle Domingo must be having a change of heart about you and me."

Not wishing to alarm the women, Louis had not revealed all that Domingo and he had discussed as possible dangers during the night, and so he smiled at his beloved and said with bravado fed by her radiant smile, "I've a feeling that even your grandfather is going to have a change of heart about us."

Besotted, they dreamed in whispers for a brief time, and again privately in their minds and hearts while the meal was served and eaten and thoroughly enjoyed by all six there beneath the tarpaulin. Medar had surprised them with a couple of bottles of excellent wine. Even as the storm began to whine and howl through the forest and hurl daggers of rain beneath the edges of the now-undulating tarpaulin, their spirits felt no dampening.

"I agree with Doña Magdalena," Louis told Manuela and Conchita when the storm gave no signs of lessening and the rain had long put out their camp fire, as well as the ones they had seen in the distance serving the two groups of soldiers. "For the three of you to sleep as best you can inside the carriage is the only solution. At least you'll stay dry and warm that way." He pulled his tarpaulin cloak closer about him, for the gusts of wind now carried blasts of cold air along with the bone-chilling damp. "We men will roll up in our blankets here beside you." In the lantern light he saw the adoration shining in Manuela's eyes and fought a new urge to embrace her. His sensible side reminded him that he had had his share of good luck for the entire journey by being able to talk with her and share the evening meal.

A quick check on the horses beneath a second tarpaulin nearby and Louis joined Medar and Phillipe for an attempt at rest. The noise and ferociousness of the storm edged out any normal feeling of sleepiness, and he contented himself to stretch out and relax a bit.

As the thunder and lightning moved inland and ceased its violent play right above the travelers, Louis must have fallen asleep, though, for it was with a jerk that he opened his eyes just before dawn at a sudden noise. He fingered his gun lying beside him. The horses. Something was upsetting the horses.

Wide awake and alert then, Louis sensed that the whickers were coming from more than nervousness, that something alien was upsetting them. A hint of a lightening on the horizon suggested that the storm clouds might have dispersed enough to allow a partial sunrise within an hour or so. Above his head, drops of rain still fell upon the sagging tarpaulin, but they lacked the persistent rhythm of those during the height of the storm, and he wondered if perhaps most were not now coming from the sparsely leaved trees above them. Slipping his large-bladed knife from its holder beneath his left arm, he sent a searching gaze all about.

"What is it?" whispered Phillipe, already following his lieutenant's lead. His knife was already in his hand, and he too was trying to penetrate the darkness with his eyes.

Medar started to speak from his own bedroll, but gunshots from the vicinity of the hind camp, where the supply wagons were parked, burst just then. Streaks of fire from gunpowder joined the hellish noise of men's voices coming through the woods and their horses' squeals of terror.

"Let's tie the horses to the wheels of the carriage," Louis ordered, already on the run to move them.

Shortly they had the job done, despite the protesting snorts from the animals and the soft but obviously frightened queries coming from the women inside. All the time, the blasts of firepower rent the darkness, though at less and less frequent intervals.

Hoping to calm the women's fears, Louis assured through the closed carriage doors, "If we're being attacked by highwaymen, they'll be after the supply wagons to the rear. We'll be close by. Stay down." He and his men then rolled beneath the carriage with their guns and ammunition, prepared for whatever kind of defense would be needed should the marauders discover them sandwiched between the two camps.

Peering from beneath the carriage and in between the legs of the horses tugging restlessly at their reins, Louis could detect no movement in the forest, even after the gunshots and men's voices no longer rang out. He knew the woods were too wet for him to hear any telltale snapping of twigs if someone wished to sneak up on them. After a long period of silence, he noted that there was a definite lightening in the east now and that the rain had stopped. Had the soldiers run off the intruders, or had they themselves been captured?

"We can't leave here because our charge is to protect the women," Louis whispered to Medar and Phillipe after nearly an hour's silence there in the mud beneath the carriage. "I'd give my right arm to know what in the hell has gone on. I thought I heard horses traveling some time ago, but with so much mud muffling sound, I can't be sure they were actually leaving."

"I believe whoever came has gone, or been killed," Phillipe replied lowly. "What if I sneak back to see what I can find out? There's enough light now, and Medar and you won't be needing me."

Louis pondered a minute, liking the idea of the sergeant taking a look and bringing back a report. "Get on with it, then," he said, still keeping his voice down. "Be careful and hurry back."

While the vigil went on beneath the carriage, the three women inside suffered all kinds of agonies. The noisy storm, the cold dampness, and the lack of adequate space to stretch out comfortably had prevented them from finding much rest during the long night. Once the exchange of gunfire ceased in the camp behind them, they, like the men below, lay with ears tuned to the slightest noise, trying to visualize what had taken place and what lay ahead for them in the slowly approaching dawn.

Manuela eased up on an elbow to look out the window of the carriage, smiling to recall how Louis had whispered over an hour ago that he and his men would be beneath them with their weapons. Before they tried to sleep earlier in the night, Conchita had unbraided her hair and brushed it into submission, but now it hung about her face and shoulders like an unruly cloud of midnight silk. She glanced down at her wrinkled riding habit and grimaced. The only good thing about the entire night had been those few hours spent with Louis. Even though they had not been able to go off alone, she savored the intimacy of nearness to such a degree that she wasted no time grieving over what was lost. Too much had been gained.

Within a short time, Manuela saw Phillipe returning in the pale light from the direction of the rear camp. Impatient all over again at the waiting and not knowing, she eased from her cramped position on the carriage seat beside Conchita and opened the door. Nightstar's nose met her affectionate hands, and she stood on the ground, calling softly, "Louis? Can't you tell me what's going on?"

Louis scrambled from beneath the carriage then, aware that the tarp he had rolled up in was covered with mud and that he must be quite a sight. "You shouldn't be outside yet. Phillipe says the soldiers ran off the highwaymen some time ago. Until it's lighter, we should stay quiet. They think all who weren't killed are gone, but no one can be sure that some stragglers did not stay behind. They might be wounded and even more dangerous, now that the party has gone on." He gazed at the vision before him, wondering how it was that she could look so tousled and delectable under such deplorable conditions. The heavy-lidded look she was sending him made his heart turn over.

Manuela shivered from the heat of Louis's gaze and crossed her arms over her bosom, aware then that part of her trembling came from the coldish, damp air. "Shall I go back inside?"

"No," Louis replied, concerned that she seemed to be chilled. "I'll ask Medar and Phillipe to get a fire going. I can't believe we're still in danger now that it's getting light so fast." He stooped over to give quiet instructions to his men. Once they had scrambled out and started off to gather up firewood, he turned back to her. "Were you frightened?"

"Not when I knew you were here to watch out for me," she admitted, her faith in his bravery adding a special spark to her eyes. "I did worry over the welfare of you and your men."

"You must know by now that we can take care of ourselves." Her declaration of trust in him pleased him in all ways, and he felt all must be right with the world. He shed the mud-encased cloak then and walked around the end of the carriage, speaking quietly to each horse tied to the wheels.

Like a limb crashing down from a tree, a great noise and rush of movement hit the jauntily-walking Frenchman at that moment. A half-clad Indian jumped from where he had hidden nearby and grabbed Louis from behind, his arm closing like a vise upon his neck. With the pressure on his windpipe, Louis was unable to let out a sound, was almost downed by the sudden blackness threatening to overpower him as surely as the muscular red arms. Falling to the ground beneath the weight of his attacker, he managed to roll them from beneath the hooves of the horses and away from the carriage. Though he

struggled for his breath and sanity, he prayed
that there was no second Indian to attack Manuela around on the other side. And then he had
no time for thought of anything except survival.

Louis struggled in the mud to remove his knife
from its holder beneath his left arm, and once he
did, he slashed at the restraining arm at his
neck. A brutal slap sent Louis's knife sailing
beneath a horse's hooves, and he was left with no
weapon. It appeared that the Indian had none
either, and the two men wrestled silently there in
the mud, muscles knotted and straining for mastery. Within seconds, Louis had the Indian beneath him and was able to pound his face with a
couple of well-aimed blows. As if stunned, the
Indian lay still long enough for Louis to see his
face. With renewed fury, the Frenchman continued his punches to the sneering face. It was the
very Mescalero who had thrown the spear at
Manuela when he was rescuing her from her
captors, the spear that had landed on his thigh
and had caused him much pain and suffering.

Manuela heard the frightening sounds from
the other side of the carriage and rushed to peek
just as Louis and his attacker fell to the ground.
Her hand balled into a fist pressing against her
mouth to keep back a scream of recognition, she
stared at the strangely cut hair of the Indian
wrestling with Louis. What felt like prickly
mountains of gooseflesh formed along her spine.
Hacked off short above the left ear, the now-
muddy mass of hair hung low on the right side,
the thong bunching it up close to that ear having
slipped down and freed the black strands into a
tangled mop.

Zaaro! When Manuela glimpsed the eerie red

paint smeared above the savage's eyelids, she recalled the horror of the man's brutal treatment on the torturous ride during the kidnapping. Then the memory of the warrior's spear, obviously aimed at her as punishment for her attacking him and shaming him before his friends, and the uncanny way it had pierced Louis's thigh as they had ridden from the Mescalero village assailed her. What was Zaaro doing this far south of the Rio Grande? Were other Mescaleros about also, and was it at them that the soldiers had fired in the darkness, rather than at highwaymen as Louis had suspected?

Frozen at first, while the terrifying thoughts tore at her, Manuela screamed for Medar and Phillipe and rushed toward where the men lay pounding each other in the mud. She had seen Louis's knife disappear beneath the horses tied to the carriage wheels and scrambled in the mud to find it, aware of the frightened, feminine sounds coming from within the vehicle but chiefly tuned in to the guttural grunts and groans from the two struggling so intently to subdue each other. On her knees, trembling, trying to talk calmly to the frightened horses, she searched frantically. With a grim smile of victory, she let her hand close over the heavy piece of metal and rose, wiping it clean of mud on her riding skirt. Now, she thought as she watched the fight slow into a test of holding strength there on the ground, if she could only put it in Louis's hand.

Louis didn't know when Manuela came to dig for his knife, but he saw from the corner of an eye when she moved with it in her hand toward him. "Throw it near and then go back," he yelled when it appeared she was going to bring it to him.

Zaaro seemed even more incensed at the sight of the tousled-haired, muddied young woman with the knife in her hand and spat out words apparently filled with hate. The cochineal-coated eyelids gave his eyes and face a wily, brutal look there in the dawning. Zaaro's distraction upon seeing Manuela gave Louis an advantage, though, and he got off a hefty blow to the Indian's windpipe, gaining the needed second to grab the knife she flipped near his right hand before stepping back nearer the carriage.

Once his hand closed over it, Louis felt he had seized more than a weapon. A great wave of triumph for Manuela's being brave and level-headed enough to get the knife to him fed what had become a waning strength into a roaring surge of power. He rolled Zaaro beneath him.

"My God!" came the dual cries of Medar and Phillipe as they rushed to respond to Manuela's screams for help and saw Louis and the Indian in what seemed a certain death lock.

Even as Phillipe pulled his own knife and Medar readied his gun, the heavily breathing Louis plunged his knife down into Zaaro's neck and held on to its grimy handle until the blood spurting upward, then trickling downward, was coming from a sprawled form grown grotesquely still.

The six gathered close afterward, thankful that Phillipe's quick scouting of their area resulted in finding no additional Indians lurking about. Conchita helped Medar get the fire started while Doña Magdalena, strangely free of tears and any signs of having the vapors, took Manuela aside

407

and helped her wash away the worst of the mud on her face and hands. Louis, after dousing his head and hands with a bucket of water from the supply barrel on the back of the carriage, disappeared into the woods and came back wearing dry deerskin breeches and shirt.

"Are all of you unharmed?" Domingo called, riding full speed toward them and jerking his horse to a standstill with uncharacteristic force. He leapt from the saddle and ran toward his niece and aunt, his face a gray picture of concern when he spied the inert body of the Indian in the distance. "We hadn't known any of the rascals stayed behind until we heard the screams." By then he had his arms around both women and had scanned Conchita's smiling face with quiet anxiety. He let out a huge breath, and his voice was still not quite steady when he exclaimed, "By the Saints! I nearly went out of my mind before I could get here. Tell me what happened."

And they did, in great, dramatic detail. Domingo hadn't heard it all before six soldiers came riding after him with guns and sabers at the ready. He directed them to remove Zaaro's body and bury it alongside those of the four men shot in the night.

"Were they all Mescaleros?" Manuela asked.

"No," Domingo replied thoughtfully. "There was no other Indian among the dead. One man lived long enough to tell me that their leader is the notorious Jacinto Navarro and that their goal was our wagons of guns and ammunition. They had about despaired of finding a way to ambush so many until the storm appeared. No doubt even Navarro didn't realize that the Mescalero joining up with him had a private war to fight against a certain beautiful young Spanish woman."

At Manuela's and Louis's earlier accounts of Zaaro and the likely cause of his vindictiveness, Domingo had paled, and the normally healthy olive color of his face still hadn't returned. Throughout the telling, he had sat beside his niece with his arm about her slender shoulders, more relieved at each passing moment to see that she was recovering from the threatening ordeal.

"Zaaro must have spotted you riding on Nightstar for the past several days, Manuela, and made his plans to grab you whenever he could. Damn him!" Domingo exclaimed. He crushed her to him in another tight hug and rose, his face working with obvious emotion. "We'll be even more grateful to you now, Louis Saint-Denis, for again saving the life of our beloved Manuela and killing the one who dared wish her harm." He smiled feebly at Conchita where she sat beside Medar on the tarpaulin before going to Doña Magdalena standing near the fire. He put an arm around her slight figure and said to the somber-faced group in a sorrowing voice, "There's no telling what dastardly injuries that wily Indian might have planned for all of our women. I will ever be indebted to you Frenchmen, as will my father."

Medar took his medical bag and ministered to three wounded soldiers, happily announcing upon his return that two would have to travel in a wagon for that day, but that the other was able to ride. Not until mid-morning did the party once more get underway. Behind them they left five fresh graves and unsettling memories of a stormy night. This time, there seemed to be no question as to where the three Frenchmen would be riding.

Along with the three privates normally escorting the women, Louis, Medar, and Phillipe now rode. The sun was trying to peep from behind clouds yet whirling about high overhead, but its additional light was not needed to lend brightness to the smiles on the faces of Manuela and her maid, or to those creasing the faces of Louis and his valet.

Chapter Twenty-two

With her heart growing lighter each day, Manuela at last gazed upon Saltillo, the town lying ahead on the plateau that would spread gradually into the flat expanses draining the Rio Grande and lead them, within two days' time, to Monclova and then to San Juan Batista. The precious, snatched moments with Louis soothed her soul in ways she had longed for, and there were times that she dared dream that her grandfather would at last approve of his suit for her hand.

"We'll stay at the Oxhead Inn," Domingo called out to the middle group in the weary party of travelers late that afternoon. "I've sent a rider ahead for them to prepare rooms and food." All smiled and lifted arms in celebration. A good-natured shout came from where Louis and Medar rode some distance behind the carriage.

"Wonderful!" Manuela exclaimed when her uncle slowed beside her. In her enthusiasm, she leaned to pat Nightstar's damp withers. The farther north they traveled, the warmer the sun at midday, no matter that it was nearing Christmas and that the nights were sometimes quite cool. "I can hardly wait to have a nice, long bath, and I'll bet Nightstar will like having a stable with lots of hay."

"All of the animals are as wearied as we,"

Domingo replied, his alert eyes stretching up ahead where the lead soldiers rode, even as he allowed his horse to match gaits with Manuela's and stay alongside her. "I confess I'm relieved not to have run into any more highwaymen or storms. As the robbers' major targets seem to be back in the unpopulated sections along the King's Highway, I'm hoping that we've passed such dangers. With Monclova only a long day's journey away from Saltillo, we can gain consolation from knowing that we'll soon be back at our *presidio.*"

The noisy caravan sent squawking chickens scurrying for safety and brought barking dogs and laughing children to the wide street of Saltillo when they rode into town. Numerous curious merchants and chattering shoppers rushed from the stores and stalls to gawk. From behind small windows in the houses along the side streets popped faces of housewives and pretty young girls, apparently eager to see for themselves what was causing such excitement in their remote mining town.

Having stopped at the Oxhead Inn each time she had traveled to and from Mexico City, Manuela felt she was at last in familiar territory when she saw it up ahead. The long, low building of sun-washed adobe was already in shadow by the time the middle group reached it. As the lead guard of soldiers had already gone on to the military post down the street to house their horses and themselves, the place seemed a quiet, welcoming haven there in the twilight.

"Isn't this heavenly, Conchita?" Manuela enthused after they had been shown to connecting rooms by the friendly innkeeper and left alone with their belongings to await the requested bath water. Their doors opened onto a covered walkway edging the large square courtyard behind the section facing the street and containing a bar and a separate dining room. She gazed out the window at the fountain bubbling in the center of the open area, noting how the fading light made the few, late-season hibiscus blossoms surrounding it appear dark and mysterious as they prepared to fold for the night. Bougainvillea vines, without blooms in their dormancy, trailed upon the arches of the protecting roof of the walkways and created intricate patterns of dark and light laciness. Masses of low, bushy poinsettia trees at the four corners of the patio seemed to stand guard, their massive red blooms a stark contrast to their leaves of rich green.

"Truly it's heavenly here. I'm glad we're almost home," Conchita replied. "There were times when I wondered if we'd ever get this close." At Manuela's amused glance, she went on. "I'm no horsewoman like you, and besides, I have to ride in the carriage with Doña Magdalena most of the time." Her voice took on a note of compassion. "Not that I mind all that much, though. She seems as eager as we to get back to the *presidio,* and I admire the way she took the awful mess with Zaaro."

Manuela nodded, not liking to recall her fears during Louis's fight with the Indian. As at the time of his spear wound from Zaaro, she suffered a twinge of guilt that her reckless actions had caused the pain endured. She turned eagerly when serving girls appeared with pails of water.

"Dare I dress up this much for a simple meal at a roadside inn?" Manuela asked after the sooth-

413

ing bath. With Conchita's help, she had washed her hair for the first time in days. Still damp as it fell straight down her back, its healthy sheen glowed blue-black in the candlelight reflecting in the small mirror above the washstand. Her thoughts, as usual, rested on Louis Saint-Denis. Would he notice that she looked special, now that her hair was clean and shining and her body clothed in something other than a disheveled riding habit? She preened a bit, standing on tiptoe to admire the red taffeta ruffle curving across her olive-tinted bosom and shoulders.

"After weeks on the highway, how can you doubt it?" Loving eyes took in the smiling beauty. "I can just imagine Lieutenant Saint-Denis now when he sees you looking so stylish and ladylike. He'll smile all over."

Manuela felt her face flush with anticipation. Domingo had told her that Louis and he would be joining Doña Magdalena and her for the evening meal. "Will you get to see Medar?"

"Yes, he and I plan to meet at a tavern down the street." Her smile widened as she patted the black braids forming a coronet across her head. "I'll be back to help you get ready for bed, though."

"Don't bother, Conchita. I can do for myself, and you so seldom get more than a few minutes alone with Medar. Take advantage of our stopping over in Saltillo. When we reach Monclova tomorrow night, you're not likely to be so lucky as to have free time from duties at the governor's mansion. You know what a big staff they have there and how involved you always get." Grabbing the shawl of white lace the maid had laid out on the bed for her, she bade Conchita good

414

night and went next door to her great-aunt's room and rapped.

They did not have long to wait before Domingo, handsome in a fresh uniform, called to escort them into the inn's dining room where a smiling Louis stood upon their entry and came forward.

"But of course you must try the local specialties," Doña Magdalena insisted when Louis looked perturbed at the serving girl's listing of foods available that evening. "I especially like their *frijoles* seasoned with hot peppers and tomatoes. The *tortillas* filled with goat cheese and green chilies rival those of Juanita back home at the *presidio*."

Domingo smiled when she referred to the fort as home and added his own recommendations from the fare at the inn.

When all was said and done, though, neither Manuela nor Louis knew what they ordered or what was served and eaten by the congenial party. His handsome, clean-shaven face wore a perpetual smile, and she doubted he had ever looked so handsome as he did in the snowy shirt with ruffled front and elaborate cravat centered with a silver pin marked by a crest like the one on his gold ring. Though he had tried to get her to take back the ring during stolen, private moments since the fight with Zaaro, Manuela had refused, saying that until Diego gave them his blessing, she had no wish to get her hopes too high. In the glow from fat candles stuck in wall sconces in the corner where the foursome sat around a linen-covered table, his eyes sparkled with silvery warmth each time they rested on her, which was often.

"What kind of reception do you think I can expect from Governor Anya?" Louis asked Domingo after coffee had been served. The way he had been whisked away from the prison in Monclova by the viceroy's soldiers still puzzled him. From what he had inferred from the viceroy's varied conversations, the relationship between the governor and his superior was not on firm ground. Exactly why word about the French prisoners had been sent to the capital by way of pigeon had never been explained to Louis's satisfaction. It made no sense to him that Diego would have intervened, not after his vehement refusal to discuss the request to marry Manuela; yet from his talks with Eblo, he had gathered there were no trained pigeons at other *presidios* in the north. Could it be that Diego's heart had softened?

"Maybe we'll be lucky, and he'll be laid up with his gout or some other convenient illness," Domingo replied with a lazy smile. "Frankly, I don't see how the man can afford to make much of a fuss since the viceroy is all-powerful. With your passport now containing his endorsement and blessing for your proposed restoring of Father Hidalgo to the lost mission in Tejas, you're no longer subject to arrest as a spy."

Manuela breathed an audible sigh of relief. Louis would still be safe, even in Monclova, and he apparently had no idea that she was the sender of the message. No doubt the viceroy believed Diego was the one using Eblo's pigeon to report the mistreatment of a French officer and had never questioned the vague initials. Fate had been kind . . . so far.

"The entire situation was intolerable," Doña

416

Magdalena said with a toss of her silver head and a huffiness not often noticeable. "Especially now that I've seen with my own eyes how loyal Louis is to Manuela . . . and to all of us. I hate to think what might have happened to us if that Zaaro hadn't been—" She broke off, her weak eyes bright with the horrible memory of the recent fight at dawn, before she continued in a tremulous voice, "If Louis hadn't conquered him, we could have been killed. I'm not sure I can forgive Governor Anya for his high-handedness in the matter of locking up the Frenchmen as if they were rogues. His sister-in-law, Marthe, is a saint to live in the mansion and care for his children as if they were her own."

Saying good night to Domingo when he left the women at their rooms and went down to his own seemed normal and easy for Manuela, but saying it to Louis and hearing his footsteps fade on the cobbled walkway nigh broke her overflowing heart. All night she had hungered to hear him talk privately to her, as he had been quick to do the past few nights after the evening meal.

Restless and unable to make herself shed the red taffeta gown, she prowled about the room, then stretched out upon the bed, savoring the wonderful feel of its firmness. She could hear music floating from somewhere near. An occasional burst of laughter reached her ears, reminding her that others were still awake and sampling the delights of life. Impatiently she rose and resumed her aimless moving about, feeling closed in by the walls.

A peep through the window showed Manuela

that the benches near the silvery fountain were bathed in moonlight. Throwing caution to the winds beginning to dance among the bougainvillea vines, she recovered her shawl and went outside. A walk in such a protected place might soothe her, she mused as she thought back to the rigid rules required while traveling. She had not realized how much she missed such freedoms until she approached the gently singing fountain and sat upon one of the benches, lifting her head and giving the gentle breeze liberty to dance in her unbound hair and caress her face.

Not believing his good luck, Louis flicked away his cigar before moving from the shadowed veranda outside his room toward the beautiful young woman sitting beside the fountain. Like Manuela, he had not been content to remain inside when so many emotions tore at him. The closer they came to San Juan Batista, the more he feared her grandfather would yet be adamant in his refusal for them to marry. When he was being totally honest with himself, he knew that nothing about his situation had changed. He was still a Frenchman, still determined to take Manuela back with him to his fort on the Red River in Louisiana.

"Would Doña Magdalena have me drawn and quartered if I were to join you?" he asked when she turned her head toward him in apparent, pleased surprise. In the moonlight, the red of her gown appeared as an exciting new color, one both red and black and incredibly lustrous. His heartbeat jumped into new patterns.

"You can go wake her and ask," she teased,

liking the way his eyes washed over her with obvious appreciation for what they saw. Was it fate that had led her to come outside? She patted the spot beside her on the stone bench, feeling a section of hair settle across her bare shoulder from the gentle motion. "I'll tell her that I invited you to meet me here for a midnight tryst."

"I doubt even you would be so daring." Smiling hugely at her spirited ways, he sat then, inhaling the marvelous fragrance of her—both the perfume from rosehips she usually wore and that from the essence that was pure Manuela. Without even trying, he could recall that first meeting and the singular, heady scent of her, one which yet played havoc with his breathing when he was in her presence. Woman, desirable young woman. The one he loved. The one he intended to marry.

Their gazes merged into one mesmerizing look of yearning and longing, the only sounds at the late hour coming from the trickling water and faraway strings being strummed with an arresting skip at odd intervals. Odd, he thought, the uneven rhythm was not unlike that of his pulse. Unmindful that alien eyes might be watching, though he had noted no light shining forth from any of the inn's several rooms, Louis put out his hand to stroke the midnight black hair. Without quite knowing how it happened, he found her in his arms, her soft breasts through the whispering taffeta molding themselves against his beruffled shirt. The curtain of hair fanned over his arm in that way he knew he could become addicted to, and her lips received the touch of his with an almost unbearable, welcoming sweetness.

"One day soon," he promised in that velvety voice she had so longed to hear all evening, "we'll not have to sneak away for stolen kisses. I love you too much to let myself think that we might never marry, Manuela."

"Let's take the moment and treasure it," she replied with new wisdom. "I've learned that dreams don't always materialize and that we're subject to more than our own desires." How it hurt to confess her doubts about their future together, she agonized as she traced the beloved features so near with tender fingertips. "But this I know: I'll always love you."

The next kiss seared even deeper into her soul and Manuela tightened her arms about his neck. This time his tongue teased at hers in invitation, and hers accepted, following the heated insides of his mouth with a fervor that set up all kinds of flames deep inside. She clutched at the broad shoulders, then allowed her hands license to rove through the thick, brown hair and explore his ears, his neck. So dear. Each part of him seemed designed only for her pleasure, she exulted.

"I should go inside now," Manuela told him after several more devastating kisses. "If we were to be seen by the wrong people—"

"I know." His eyes silvery there in the moonlight, Louis made himself stand and reach out to her.

With his arm resting across her shoulders, Manuela walked with him toward her door. Each hesitant step brought whispering complaints from the red taffeta gown. A dog howled somewhere far away, the lonely sound echoing within seconds from another direction in tones even more mournful. Nearer, a night bird trilled a sweet treble phrase.

Opening her door, Louis looked down into the lovely face lifted to his. "Good night, my love." His words were so soft that she had to strain to hear them.

Before he could kiss her, Manuela threw her arms around him and whispered, "Please, Louis. Not just yet."

As if rehearsed, they moved as one inside her room and closed the door quietly. A moonbeam angled through the window and settled on the bed. Blind even to that subtle invitation, they kissed there by the doorway, lost to everything but the delectable feel of their mouths, tongues, and bodies meeting and declaring love.

Louis lifted Manuela into his arms and took her to the bed, lowering her with gentleness. His eyes probed hers, liking the answers sparkling there. He smiled when he turned her to unfasten the back of her gown, then planted soft kisses on each spot exposed as it rustled downward, downward. She was already breathless by the time he removed the chemise and her other garments, already sighing with longing and eagerness for what she knew lay ahead. Her compulsive little moans and movements fanned a flame down low inside Louis.

"You're so beautiful in the moonlight," he whispered when he rose to shed his own clothing. "I love seeing you in any light, but in moonlight, you're bewitching."

"I'd not want to bewitch anyone but you, Louis." Her mind taunted her with the thought that she was the one under a spell. She watched him move toward her now in splendid nakedness, awed at the wondrous play of muscles on the tall, manly frame. All at once her hands itched to touch him, caress all that made him her very own Lover. Lying back against a pillow, her hair spread out like an ebony cloud of silk, she opened her arms and pulled him close when he lay beside her and came into them. Her love, she exulted as he kissed her, was with her, was setting her on fire both inside and out. How could she dare think of anything beyond that moment?

Passion long denied surfaced and lent new heat to Louis's wandering hands. She felt that each path must be leaving visible marks of fire, and she writhed with pleasure at the way his fingers teased her throbbing breasts. His mouth left hers and found its way to those womanly mounds, kissing and taunting on the way to the uplifted nipples awaiting their share of ecstasy. A torrent of flame tore deep inside her when his tongue flicked the peaks into tight, damp rosebuds. She searched his neck and shoulders with begging fingertips, realizing that what she desired was to take all of him inside her through her very pores. Hungrily her hands traveled down the broad back, matching her caresses with those he was bestowing upon her own willing body.

Now the silkiness of her thighs was captivating him, and his lips followed the paths of his hands, delighting in the new textures of her fragrant skin. All of her. He longed to possess all of her, and he forced himself to stop the wild assault and hug her close, feel her nakedness lying all along his own. Inside, a veritable storm of fire built into thunderous proportions. How could he live and not expect to hold her this way each night for the rest of his life? His heart pounded in anticipation at all that he could imagine lay ahead if the beautiful young woman in his arms were to become his. Love. Companionship. Children. Eternity.

"I couldn't love you more if you were already my wife," he murmured just before he once again claimed her mouth. "Before whatever powers can hear, I declare we are married, forever."

"I, too, feel we're one. You're the Lover I've dreamed of, waiting for so long, Louis."

Her words spun out like magic, wrapping themselves around the ragged edges of his heart like a soothing balm. When her eyes opened in that heavy-lidded way and moonlight picked up stars in their midnight depths, he moaned low in his throat and let his mouth have its way. His tongue went home to those velvety inner reaches he had marked as his own, and his pulse danced to a haunting gypsy rhythm. Never would he get enough of feeling her silky nakedness gathered close.

A storm of desire dizzied Manuela, and she clung closer to him, breathing in the heady, masculine smell of him, combined now with the smoke from his earlier cigar, delighting in the way his hair brushed across her forehead possessively, exulting in the way his hands molded her body into hills and valleys of warm longing. A foray across her belly and down into the secrets of her womanhood stole her breath, brought a low sigh of utter ecstasy back in her throat.

She wanted nothing more than to belong to him again in the fullest sense, and her hands explored all that awaited her private worship. The furred chest, the muscled back, the hard, lean buttocks, and the strength she sensed from

423

each touch thrilled her anew at the wonder of her ever finding such a man as her Lover. When she kissed his ear and, not knowing why the impulse seized her, traced its shape with her tongue, he moaned in a way that told her how much her caresses were pleasing him. Laughing back in her throat then, her breasts rubbing against his nakedness with movements she guessed might be wanton, she planted kisses on his eyelids and worked her way down to his mouth, once more sending her tongue to sample and delight him.

Their short, quick breaths seemed the only sounds in the whole world, and she moved sensuously against him in unconscious entreaty for him to take her with him on the glorious trail to that shimmering oblivion she so well remembered sharing with him that night in the prison cell. Louis heard the incessant call of his throbbing manhood, felt the unspoken invitation from the satiny hips pressing closer, and watched the incredibly beautiful eyes star with love for him.

Manuela closed her eyes in rapture when he answered their bodies' fervent demands and made her his own again. The world seemed to pause for that moment of glorious reunion. It then rocked and whirled like a mere speck of a dust storm in eternity as their shared passion built ever higher before swirling back in on itself and bursting upward and outward, far beyond the zenith imagined. One single, shining moment flared like a million stars all wrapped up as one blaze of light, then zoomed into those mental havens reserved for perfect memories before deserting the lovers and releasing them back to the world made up of more than feeling. Heartfelt sighs, from one and then the other, crept into the tiny space between them and served as a kind of lingering finale.

After a spate of tender hugs and kisses, Louis forced himself to leave a half-protesting, clinging Manuela there in her bed and don his clothing. His room seemed a hundred miles away, and he had no heart for doing what he knew he must do, what she herself reluctantly admitted, upon his questioning, that he must do.

"Partings don't match up with loving," he whispered against her ear when she walked with him to the door. Then he looked at her lovely face and knew that with each passing moment, she became a more vital part of him. "My life won't truly begin until there are no more good-byes for us."

Her lips swollen from his kisses, her eyes starred with love for him, she replied in husky tones, "Maybe we'll find that there won't be many more, now that we know we're married in our hearts."

"Keep believing that, my darling, and it will come true."

Even the loveliness of the whispering fountain out in the moonlight was lost on the two lovers as Louis walked away toward his room. Their eyes gazed at awesome, inward beauty.

At times the next day as they headed toward Monclova, Manuela rode Nightstar without noticing when trees bordered the road or when they did not. The blue of the brilliant sky and the heat of the sun made no impression on her either. Her thoughts dwelled upon the handsome French lieutenant who, from time to time, found excuses to ride alongside her and send worshiping smiles her way. More determined than ever to marry him, she prayed that her grandfather would be more likely to listen to her pleas this time when she approached him. What need did she have of the trappings of civilization when she could have the company of her Lover forever? They were entering the gates of the governor's mansion before she had come up with any reassuring answers for her aching heart.

Governor Anya, notified by an advance soldier of the approach of the travelers, welcomed his houseguests after his sister-in-law, Marthe, had already greeted them and shown them inside the receiving room. If he disapproved of finding a stranger among the familiar faces, he made no show of it. In fact, when Domingo introduced Louis, the governor acted as if he had never before heard the name.

"Welcome, sir. A friend of the Ramons is a friend in the mansion," the governor said. "My son Felix is away at the family horse ranch, and I'm sure he'll be sorry to have missed greeting our guests." No leering looks had accompanied his earlier, cordial greeting to Manuela. Indeed, his manner was circumspect. "Have our guests' rooms been readied, Marthe?"

Her round face wreathed with the customary smile, the young widow nodded and gave orders to the servants standing nearby. "I've seen to everything, Gaspardo," she told her widowed brother-in-law in a soft voice. "You shouldn't overdo since this is the first day you've been able to walk for a good while." With obvious concern and affection, she walked to take his arm and motioned toward a plush, cushion-filled chair

426

with a footstool in front of it. "Please indulge me and sit and rest your leg while we visit."

Within a short time, Marthe won out and had everyone seated and comfortable for a brief visit before it was time to get dressed for dinner. She sent for the children to greet the visitors, showing what Manuela had noticed on the previous visit – the woman had a natural gift for mothering. Her own daughter, Celia, received no more loving attention than did the three of the governor's.

When Manuela saw the saucy little Felicia – she must be three now, she realized – cut her dark eyes at a smiling Louis and sidle over to be lifted upon his lap, her heart nigh burst. With a pretty child on his knees and his deep voice talking to her quietly with obvious liking, she could well imagine that he would be the kindest of fathers.

After dinner, Manuela watched for a chance to speak privately with Governor Anya. She wanted to get matters settled between them right away. When a servant came to request that he respond to a sentry calling at the side door, she watched him hobble away with the aid of a cane and found an excuse to leave the room.

When the governor started back down the hall outside his library, Manuela approached him. "May we speak alone for a few minutes?"

Gaspardo Anya recoiled inwardly from what he believed would be a tempestuous session such as the one that had taken place the last time he had conferred with the beautiful Manuela in private, but he nodded and went with her inside his library. Strange, he mused, that she no longer excited his blood, no longer seemed the epitome of young womanhood, as once he had been wont to see his second wife. It seemed ages ago when he had watched her dance and lusted for that beautiful body. He knew his recent illness had been more serious than ever before, but what was wrong with him now? All at once, he felt fatigued.

"Governor Anya," Manuela said, eager to get their business out in the open and clearly understood. She flounced down on a chair opposite the settee where they had sat and talked that morning. With effort, she pushed away the memory of his fumbling attempt to kiss her. She looked everywhere but at the untidy moustache above the thick lips. "You and I had an agreement, one I know that you didn't honor."

"Well, my dear," he replied in ingratiating tones, settling himself with difficulty on the settee, "I don't believe there was much I could've done after the viceroy's soldiers appeared not long after you and your family left the mansion. They took over the destiny of the Frenchmen. What would you have had me do? Override orders from the mighty Duke of Linares?" His voice took on a sharpness at the utterance of his superior's name. The same soldiers who had taken the prisoners away that day had brought with them a peppery letter of reprimand from the viceroy for his having taken it on himself to act as judge in a matter that was not his to judge. And it hadn't been the first he had received, he agonized with rare honesty. "I thought your only concern was for the safety and well-being of your French dandy lieutenant and his friends."

"It was and is," she retorted, choosing to ignore

428

his barb. "My point is that I no longer am beholden to our agreement since their freedom was due to no action on your part." When he continued to watch her from where he sat upon the high-backed settee with an expression bordering on thoughtful surprise, she went on, "I wanted to tell you that I'm refusing your proposal of marriage and that I intend to tell my grandfather about our conversation."

"Domingo explained before dinner why the Frenchmen are with him," he replied. "Letters the soldiers brought from the viceroy and my son Figaro substantiate what happened in the city. I well see the wisdom of using the talents of any who can win back the Lipans to the *presidio*. I see no reason why Diego or Domingo need be told of our secret agreement – or of any talk between the two of us about marriage." Gaspardo recalled too well the suspicious tone of Domingo's words about the rumors Figaro seemed to be spreading in Mexico City, rumors he had written his son to spread discreetly in the hopes that no suitor would approach Manuela. Everything seemed so changed, in a completely different focus, and he found it hard to explain, even to himself. With his health failing, he needed more support and respect from the two Ramons over at San Juan Batista, not less. That they ranked high in the viceroy's estimation was all too clear from today's letter; such matters couldn't be ignored if one were to remain prosperous and in office. "I release you from our agreement. Will that make you happy?"

"Yes, that's exactly what I hoped for." All of a sudden, his moustache seemed not so hideous, and his face appeared more that of a kindly old man. Her fears that he might make a hue and cry about her wishing to break off their engagement faded, and Manuela smiled at him with pure happiness. "Thank you for being so understanding."

Puzzling over the mysterious sense of relief flooding over him after Manuela rushed from the room, Governor Anya sat to collect his thoughts in the sudden peacefulness seeping over him. Her smile had struck him as being much like one coming from his fourteen-year-old Francesca upon seeing that he had handed her a coveted gift on a silver platter.

For some reason, he found his thoughts centering then on the warm, tender smile of his sister-in-law, Marthe, when she cared for him during his numerous illnesses, or when she looked to him with dancing eyes for approval of something clever one of his daughters said or did. The softness of her voice and hands as they soothed his aching brow or placed compresses on his paining foot suddenly became qualities he treasured with something akin to reverence. Never could he imagine Marthe's gentle voice dripping scorn for his attempts to be complimentary or witty, as Manuela's and other young women's always seemed to do. He did not understand at all why those few attributes of one almost old enough to be mother to the younger woman seemed far more desirable than Manuela's voluptuous breasts and tiny waist above flaring hips, or her rose-petal lips, or her tantalizing, heavy-lidded black eyes.

Shaking his head at all that filled his mind, the governor rose and made his way stumblingly back to the large room where laughter and lively talk led him. Above all the other voices, he found himself hearing only that of Marthe. And he knew that when he reached the doorway, she would lift her eyes to his face and smile in that special way she seemed to reserve only for him. This time, he knew he would smile back.

Chapter Twenty-three

The excitement of making the last segment of the trip to San Juan Batista seemed to permeate the group leaving Monclova the next morning. Cheerful notes laced the calls of the soldiers as they mounted up with a great clatter of hooves upon the cobblestones. Still traveling in between the two groups of soldiers, the women made no attempt to hide their own elation. They were going to a place more meaningful than the one often called the Presidio of the North; they were going home.

"Your smile is brighter than the sunshine," Louis told Manuela when he had convinced himself it would not seem forward to her *dueña* to ride alongside her for awhile. "And twice as pretty." Riding ahead of the carriage holding Doña Magdalena and Conchita, she wore an orange riding costume with a creamy silk shirt caught at the neck with a splashy tie of black and orange flowers. The vivid colors set off her dark beauty in a way that made him blink upon his first view of her up close. "You must be looking forward to getting home."

"Yes," she caroled with undisguised joy, flashing him a secretive look of adoration. "I'm dying to see Grandfather and Juanita and Eblo ... and Zorro. I'll bet he has moped and moaned ever since I left." The sight of the brown-haired Louis in a snowy white shirt covered partially by a handsome leather vest embroidered with turquoise and black jet beads dazzled her. She had become accustomed to seeing him in the leather breeches he seemed to prefer for long days of riding, but he had never before worn such an ornate vest. The turquoise of the bright beads reflected in his gray eyes, turning them into a fascinating shade of blue.

Manuela noted that his horse, Diablo, pranced with the same kind of repressed energy, almost a kind of expectancy, that she felt emanating from his handsome owner. Seeming to sense that the morning held a kind of special significance, Nightstar tossed his white head and mane more frequently than normal, his silver-trimmed bridle and reins jangling prettily and flashing in the sunlight at each playful movement. He acted as if he knew that his private stall lay only a half-day's journey ahead, and Manuela sent reassuring pats to the gleaming withers.

"A parrot can't feel," Louis said, hoping to get a rise out of her.

"Zorro can, and he can do far more than just mimic, too," she defended. Only when he grinned did Manuela realize he was teasing. "He knows what he's saying."

"I've liked him ever since the first night I came." His laughing gaze invited her to recall their "midnight encounter." "I hoped each night he might visit the stables again, but I was never lucky but that one time."

Manuela slid him a coquettish look. "Who knows? He might decide to visit the pigeons again some night."

"I'll keep my ears tuned," he promised. He was

not sure what caused it, but she seemed far more carefree that morning than on the entire trip north. Yesterday he had shared her apparent glow of happiness from their lovemaking in her room at the inn, but something new had been added since then. Was it only the thought of returning home and making sure her grandfather was all right, or had something happened the previous night at the governor's mansion that had lightened her heart?

"I was glad to see that Governor Anya showed you and your men such courtesy," she said after they had ridden in companionable silence a while.

"He doesn't seem as bad a sort as I'd imagined," Louis replied frankly. "In fact, I was afraid he might show hostility and even bring up the matter of asking for some kind of commitment from you. Did Domingo say anything about that?"

"Not to me." Inside, pleasure over her secret tickled her stomach. She prayed that Domingo had not insisted on discussing the question of the governor's suit for her hand and perhaps learned all about what had taken place upon their last visit to the mansion. If he hadn't, then no one need ever know of her bargaining for Louis's freedom. She knew that Conchita and Carlos would forever remain mum. "I doubt we're going to have any trouble from that quarter. Doña Magdalena said after breakfast that she's beginning to suspect the governor is far more interested in Marthe as his next wife than in me. She could be right, you know."

Louis squinted across at her, recalling that the older man and his sister-in-law had seemed especially doting during the lengthy farewells. And last night he had noted their obvious devotion to each other and the children. Manuela was looking awfully smug ... in the nicest kind of way, of course. What did she know that she wasn't telling?

Louis left her then, for he wanted no suspicious Doña Magdalena making reports to Diego that he had been more attentive to Manuela than one whose suit had been so rudely denied should be. From whatever position he rode, though, he kept an eye on his beloved.

When the landscape became the familiar one of rippling mounds of sand dotted with cacti and mesquite, Manuela strained to catch a glimpse of the silver cross atop the church at San Juan Batista. After she saw that first flash, a welcoming sparkle ahead in the overhead sunshine, she felt she was being directed in a way as mysterious as the one that apparently called Eblo's carrier pigeons home to a familiar cote.

"I see no thief has carried off the sand in our absence," Louis said as he rode up beside her again.

"I guess alchemy must have failed again," Manuela replied, her mouth forming a playful *moue* as she gestured dramatically. "Maybe to turn all of this into grains of gold would've displeased as many as it would have pleased." Her gaze drinking in the vast expanse of bright sand and low vegetation between the nearing *presidio* and themselves, she said musingly, "On that day of discovery, I felt so sure I had all the answers." She saw from a light leaping in his pale eyes that he well knew she referred to more than what her words indicated. A sigh for her inno-

435

cence of that afternoon they had spent teasing and kissing in the irrigation stream escaped her lips – and for his as well, she realized when she thought of how both had foreseen no reasons why Diego would refuse to bless their betrothal. How simple everything had seemed then.

"If my status is changed at the *presidio* and I'm not allowed my earlier freedom, how will I bear it not to see you often?" Louis asked, pain at the possibility showing plainly on his countenance.

"Surely such won't be the case." She watched his profile against the blue sky, thinking that his nose was even more perfect than she had recalled. The soft thuds of the horses' hooves against the packed sand sounded sad, and she forced a smile when he once more turned toward her. "You'll feel my love coming to you, no matter where you are."

"And you, mine." His heart lurched when he saw her eyes shadow beneath the brim of the flat little black hat. Knowing that she did indeed love him would ease whatever new obstacles lay ahead. With renewed strength, he straightened his shoulders and looked squarely at the walls of the *presidio* up ahead. He assured himself that the inordinate pride riding with him into Mexico six months ago no longer hindered whatever action might be called for to win Manuela Ramon as his wife.

"Grandfather," Manuela called when Diego strode toward her there in the patio leading from the stables to the *hacienda*. To see the beloved face breaking into a smile and then feel the familiar arms holding her close brought unexpected tears. The soft scratch of his moustache as he kissed her cheek made her feel like a little girl again. "How wonderful to return and find you're well."

"You knew I would be all right," he countered, his voice thick, his keen eyes taking in the lovely face lifted to his. "I was sorry to have to cut short your visit to the City."

"I could have stayed on at the palace had I truly cared to, Grandfather. You know I don't give a fig for all the goings on down there. I was more than ready to leave."

Diego studied her intent face and hugged her one more time, his eyes bright. Then he turned to the hesitantly approaching Doña Magdalena, his smile mellowing as he took her hand and planted a light kiss. "Welcome back."

The silver-haired lady returned the warm smile, murmuring a reply too low for Manuela to hear. "I'm delighted to be back ... home, Diego."

Diego insisted then that the two retire to their rooms for rest before spending time in lengthy visiting. With minimum protest, for they confessed to being weary, they obeyed.

Restlessly, Manuela tossed upon her bed, wondering what was going on out in her grandfather's office. Finding Zorro had not forgotten her and was yet a small bundle of green feathers with a sassy beak eased some of her tension. She was still playing with the parrot when Conchita appeared after awhile and set up a bath for her mistress.

"Have you heard any news yet?" Manuela asked, leaning back against the tub, luxuriating in the caress of water upon her skin and the fragrance of perfumed soap.

"Not about our special Frenchmen. No doubt the officers are going to talk until time for the evening meal before coming out of Commandant Ramon's office." Kneeling beside the tub where she had been helping Manuela wash her hair, Conchita sat back upon her legs and sighed. "Mama told me that all those strange horses we thought we saw in the stables belong to the French soldiers who didn't come on to Mexico with the lieutenant."

"The ones who went hunting with the Indians and were to come later?" Manuela asked, trying to recall what Louis had told them back in the summer about the remainder of his men. "When did they arrive?"

"Mama says they came a week ago and that the commandant invited them—there are fifteen soldiers and eight Assinai Indians—to rest here for awhile before starting out again for Louisiana. She was shocked to learn about what has happened to the lieutenant and his two men since they left here at the end of summer for Monclova."

"Aren't we all?" Manuela mused. "No doubt all the Frenchmen will be glad to be reunited, and gladder to find that their officer is still alive." Idly she picked up the wash cloth and let drops of water trickle down her shoulders and breasts. The olive forehead with the tints of ivory creased in deep thought. "I'll bet Grandfather was glad to see some soldiers come, even if they are French. From what I've heard, Louis and his men get along well with nearly all of the Indians. It seems unlikely that the Tejas would be eager to attack the *presidio* if they had watched these soldiers ride down here."

Conchita encouraged her mistress to leave her bath and get dressed then. Still chattering about sundry matters, but more often about their sweethearts than any other topic, they managed to reach the jewelry-selection stage by the time the first bell sounded from downstairs.

"Choose anything," Manuela insisted, eager to rush down the stairs and find out if Louis was going to be allowed to join the family for meals. In the mirror she eyed her green satin gown with its draped fold forming a mock cuff across the tops of her breasts before cornering sharply to edge her shoulders and vee daringly low in the back. Puffed sleeves fell in shimmering fullness down to just above her elbows, where bias cuffs, real this time, held the fabric close to her slender arms. The *panniers* held out the voluminous green skirt over a creamy petticoat embroidered with little nosegays of darker green satin thread.

"Emeralds," Conchita decided, opening first one drawer and then another until she found what she had in mind. "The square cut goes so well with the neckline." When she fastened the gold chain and let the large stone rest in splendor above Manuela's barely covered breasts, she smiled approvingly. Looping earrings of smaller emeralds into the dainty ears took only seconds. A loving pat to the elaborate coiffure piled high at the crown of her mistress's head, and she was ready to relinquish her claim. "You look marvelous. If he's not there, I'll see what I can find out, and I'll go give him a message myself when you come back upstairs."

"I'll bet you would at that," Manuela teased, turning her head first one way and then the other to get a better view of the black curls giving her the appearance of one knowledgeable about what was fashionable in the city. "And you would just happen to run into his valet and—"

"Never you mind," Conchita broke in. "If you don't hurry, the second bell will ring before you've even gotten downstairs. You don't need to be antagonizing your grandfather now, of all times."

With an indrawn breath, Manuela picked up her skirts and scooted, not slowing into a lady-like walk until she reached the top of the stairs. Descending in that slow, elegant way Doña Magdalena had taught her, she went down to the ground floor, ears straining above the constant whisper of her satin slippers and skirts upon the tiles to catch the musical bass sound of a certain French lieutenant. Holy Mother, she prayed, let him be there.

Louis sensed the moment Manuela started down the staircase and found that Diego's voice actually faded a bit when he at last saw her. She was no lovelier in the green satin than she'd been in the yellow silk she was wearing that first time he had seen her move so effortlessly down that same run of stairs, but she was every bit as lovely, he reminded himself with a little catch of breath. Clearing his throat and attempting harder to pay attention to what Diego was saying, Louis had no control over his pulse. It ran races of dizzying speed.

Manuela presented her hand to Louis as properly as she had upon their first meeting, but this time there was no wish to withdraw from the touch of the handsome man in black silk coat and breeches who bent to kiss the proffered hand. Oh, no. This time she welcomed the light brush of his lips, even hungered for them to trail upward and touch parts of her invisible. She blinked to hide the sudden rush of gratitude for finding him in the *hacienda*, not knowing that she was setting her beloved on fire with the heavy-lidded action.

Dinner was a happy occasion, and Manuela felt giddier at each course. Both Diego and Domingo seemed as enthralled with the debonair French lieutenant as they had during those first weeks of knowing him. Her hopes soared. Louis had once more charmed her grandfather. Surely there would be a future for them. She smiled and made gay replies to all remarks sent her way, even recalled some amusing incidents from her visit in the capital to entertain the obviously doting Diego.

For the first time in months, Manuela slept soundly that night after Doña Magdalena and she left the men talking over brandy in the library and went up to their bedrooms. The signs she had read all evening appeared too positive for her to fight the bone weariness trying to claim her, and she slept without dreaming anything she could recall the next morning.

"Domingo's and your plans sound solid to me," Diego told Louis the next day in his office. "I'm glad your men decided to stay on here a while before returning to your fort. No doubt they've told you what a disheartened bunch they were upon arriving and finding that you had been imprisoned. Only the week before had I learned that you were no longer at Monclova, but in

Mexico City." He ran testing fingers across the handsome leather top of his desk and frowned. "I'll never understand why Governor Anya didn't see fit to inform me of the viceroy's soliders' appearing after we left and taking you down to the city. The man is an enigma."

"I figured you knew all about it," Louis said. Was this the time to thank Diego for his having sent the message via carrier pigeon to the viceroy?

"Our main concern right now is not the governor," Domingo interjected. "We need to leave right away to talk with the Lipans and persuade them to return. I took the liberty, Father, of asking Governor Anya to swap sergeants with us and assign Sergeant Guerra back here. He assured me the exchange will be made right away."

"That'll help matters," Diego replied with obvious relief. "If Sergeant Benitez hadn't been so high-handed with the Indians, they never would have left. The tribe has been here with me since the fort was first built nearly fifteen years ago. Wonder how it is that you were able to reason with Anya when he has ignored my requests for the return of my old sergeant?"

"I don't know," his son answered. "He seemed a changed man in lots of ways." His fingers smoothed at his moustache. Should he tell now all that the governor discussed with him? Shooting a glance at the serious mien of the French lieutenant, he decided against delving into any matters other than the seeking out of the Lipans. "What about it, Louis? Shall we leave at dawn tomorrow, taking both my men and yours?"

"What's my reward to be?" Louis asked, swinging his probing gaze from one shocked face to the other.

"Your reward has already been given, or so I was led to believe," Diego replied. "Your freedom is your reward." Barely schooled anger laced his words, and his black eyes glittered.

"Come now," Domingo spoke, cocking his head at Louis in disbelief at his demand. "You know that the viceroy let you return with me—at my request, remember—for the purpose of helping me persuade the Lipans to return to their homes here at the *presidio* and then escorting Father Hidalgo back to his Mission of the Holy Saints. Isn't that reward enough?"

"No."

"What else do you think you deserve?" thundered Diego. "You've not accomplished either mission yet, and who knows how the Indians will react upon being approached? They might launch an attack on all of you and then come down here to strike at the rest of us." Diego fidgeted in his chair there behind his desk before adding, "I'm no coward, but I've learned that a man never knows when he's dealing with Indians."

"I do," Louis asserted calmly. He crossed his arms across his chest and lounged against the back of his chair. "As for the reward I want, I want to marry Manuela and take her back to Louisiana with me."

Both Ramons leaned forward stiffly, their eyes and mouths set in similar patterns of disbelief.

"You know my thoughts on that matter," Diego said after a disturbing silence in his handsomely furnished office. "There's nothing to discuss. She'll marry a Spaniard."

"Then I'll refuse to go along tomorrow."

443

"But you promised the viceroy—" Domingo protested.

Louis broke in. "To *assist* you in luring back the Lipans without bloodshed and to restore Father Hidalgo to the mission in Tejas, if I remember correctly. I've already assisted you by telling you what will work when you approach the Indians, and I'm not refusing to escort the priest to his old mission whenever you say you're ready for me to do so." Knowing full well that he was treading dangerous ground, he went on. "If I go along tomorrow, I'll do so only with your promise, Diego, that upon my return you'll give Manuela and me your blessing and allow us to marry."

"This is downright ungentlemanly," Diego snapped. "I can't believe that one with your background and—"

"Don't try nudging at my pride," Louis interrupted to say with a resigned shrug. "I've found that I don't have any when it comes to trying to win the one I love. You can think of me as an out-and-out ruffian, for all I care. I want to marry Manuela more than I've ever wanted anything in my life, and she says she wants to marry me." When both Spaniards continued to stare at him with varying degrees of hostility and disbelief at his daring, he went on in the same serious vein. "I have something you want, and you have something I want. Why can't we make a swap and let everybody be happy?" A smile wreathed his face then, for having spoken his thoughts had made him feel he might truly have found the way to win the hand of the only woman he would ever love.

"You'd chance being locked up again?" Diego

444

asked, amazed as he had been the day he had first met Louis at the way the young man's smile seemed to invite a like response. He denied the invitation, though, and remained stern-faced. He had not been prepared for Louis to pursue again the subject of marriage to Manuela, not after his earlier, vehement denial.

"I would." Louis's smile faded.

Domingo exchanged looks with his father before saying, "I admire a man who knows what he wants, Louis, but I don't think you understand my father's position about my dead brother's daughter." A brush of guilt at his having allowed Louis and Manuela time together on the journey home swept Domingo's conscience. His earlier hope that Diego's gratitude might soften his attitude had fled upon seeing his father's angry face. "Manuela must marry a Spaniard, or she'll no longer be accepted into the upper class here."

"From what she tells me, she has no desire to move in society here. She wishes to go with me to the fort in Louisiana, and if you talk with her, you'll find out for yourselves. I can assure you that even if we were to live elsewhere in New France, class distinction will never touch her. I love her and will take care of her always." Louis saw the softening in Domingo's eyes, felt his new friend's unspoken compassion. He forced himself to look into the demanding eyes of Diego and ask, "Sir, what will your answer be?"

Shaking his head in bewilderment at the puzzling ways of young people, Diego replied, "Without the Lipans living and working here at the *presidio*, we cannot be as self-sufficient as in the past, and therefore not as successful in our duties toward the Crown. We need their presence to discourage warring tribes from looking upon us as enemies almost as much as we need their skills. I'm forced to use my best effort when trying to parley with Night Hawk, their young chief. The way he left in the night with his people shows he has no wish to bargain. Your reputed rapport with Indians — yes, I've spoken with your men and listened to Eblo's admiring accounts — could be the deciding factor. You put me in a difficult position, Louis, and I won't pretend I'm not angry that you're sneaking in private matters with those that should be strictly business."

Rising, Louis said, "I apologize for angering you, but I take nothing back. Perhaps you'd like some time to think it over. I'll await your decision in my quarters." With a brisk but courteous nod to each of the Ramons, he left the commandant's office.

"Now what, Father?" Domingo asked after Louis's retreating footsteps no longer sounded.

"That cocksure scoundrel," Diego replied with a grudging trace of admiration in his voice. "Who does he think he is to stand before Spanish officers and make demands, demands that are both reprehensible and impossible to meet?" When Domingo made no reply, he asked quietly, "What do you think? Do you think Manuela might truly care enough for our French lieutenant to want to marry him and go far away to live in what Louis describes as no more than a wilderness?"

"You'd better ask her." Domingo was certain of Manuela's answer, but he ducked his father's questioning look.

"How can I bear thinking that she might be getting trapped into a kind of life she won't care for, or that I might never see her again?" He rose and, resting one hand in the other behind his back, wandered about the office, pausing every once in awhile to stare out a window or at paintings on the walls.

"Then what Louis tells me is true. You do want to marry him and go away to his Fort Saint Jean Baptiste," Diego said to Manuela later that afternoon after the two had talked for awhile in the library. What had happened to that impetuous, fiery-tempered girl who had stormed at him when he had told her of Governor Anya's proposal? he wondered. Beside him now sat a young woman in complete control of herself and with an air of maturity he found disquieting.

"That's right, Grandfather." Glancing down at her pink gown where her hands lay clasped in her lap, she sighed. "How many times do I need to tell you that I don't care to live in Mexico and be what you keep calling an 'upper-class lady'? I want a life totally new and belonging only to me. You know how I dislike walls and rules hemming me in. Ever since I grew up in the convent, I've dreamed of freedom from such things." An imploring hand reached toward him as he sat alongside her in front of the desk where Louis had tutored her in French those weeks back in the summer. "Won't you please give us your blessing? Without it, I can't think of marrying, and you well know that." Tears glistened on the thick, black lashes.

There was no doubt in Diego's mind that the Manuela who had spoken so eloquently all afternoon about her future was a young woman in love. Banked fires lay in her black eyes, but she was controlling them admirably.

"My concern must be only for your happiness," Diego conceded after a thoughtful pause. He recalled how it was to love so passionately, then found himself thinking about Doña Magdalena and another kind of love. . . . Pushing away that surprising thought, he went on. "I cannot allow my own fears that I may never again see you influence me too greatly."

"Of course you'll see me again," she promised. Eagerly she leaned toward him. "If you'll consent to trading even once a year with Louis and his countrymen, there'll be official traveling between our two forts, and I can come back to visit without the need for a special trip over such a distance. I heard you say last evening to both Louis and Uncle Domingo that the idea bears thought before being discarded completely, especially since the French goods are badly needed in this area."

And so it was that on that very evening, while the three men smoked cigars in the courtyard and Manuela and Doña Magdalena sat inside over their final cups of coffee, Diego told Louis that he was willing to live up to the proposed bargain.

"Only if you're successful in bringing Night Hawk and his people back with you will I consider you engaged to my granddaughter," Diego reminded the suddenly ecstatic Louis. "And there's to be no wedding until after you've taken Father Hidalgo back to his mission and gotten him settled in."

"Agreed, sir," Louis said, reaching out his hand to shake the solemn-faced commandant's. That done, he turned to receive Domingo's handshake and congratulations. "I'll do my best to look after Manuela and make her happy."

"Father, I think it appropriate that we go inside and let Manuela and Louis have some private time together out here while we visit with Doña Magdalena, don't you?" Domingo asked.

Diego harrumphed and finally mumbled, "Yes, that will be acceptable."

"I can't believe that we're going to be together forever," Manuela told Louis as they strolled among the flower beds there in the darkness. No moon had risen, and the flowers, most of them sleeping in the dormant season, seemed mere globs of shiny dark bushes in the pale light coming from the windows of the living room. She sniffed at the spicy smells of autumnal nighttime in the desert terrain. Her arm linked in his, she leaned her head against the firm muscles of his forearm.

Glancing back toward the living room and deciding that no one was paying them too much attention, Louis stopped and pulled her to stand in front of him. He looked down at her beautiful face, loving the way it lifted to his like a blossom opening to the rising sun, and kissed her. The way she clung and gave him freedom to capture her pretty mouth brought tremors deep inside. The feel of her breasts through the silken gown reminded him of their own vibrant silkiness, and he wondered if he could endure life until he could stand beside her in the church outside the *pre-*

449

sidio and vow before the priest and God to honor, love, and cherish her forever. He knew well that the two of them had already taken those vows in their hearts in necessary privacy, but he had a sudden urge to shout to the world that Manuela Ramon was his, was to be his wife for eternity.

Manuela sensed the turbulent thoughts filling Louis's brain, for identical ones controlled her own. She had learned enough about him to know that when he held her so reverently, as he was doing, that he was entertaining loving thoughts.

"Tell me what you're thinking," she urged, breaking off the kiss to hear what she wanted to hear.

"That I love you and that I'll never be happier than this moment until we're repeating our vows in church."

"I knew that's what you were thinking," she exulted. When he tilted his handsome head in query, she explained, "Because that's what I was thinking."

"I had already found you perfect, but now I learn you're a mind reader as well." He smiled at the delight on her face.

"Not really a mind reader, Louis, but I feel we share more than a liking for making love." His adoring gaze thrilled her but prompted her to add, "And I'm not perfect."

"You're perfect to me. How is it that I never knew you liked to make love?" he whispered, his voice swelling with secretive laughter. "Tell me about it."

"I will, but not till after we're married." She tossed the long curls falling down her back in mock annoyance but slid him a flirty look from behind half-closed lashes.

"The time will become eons, but at least it seems a fact now that we'll marry in that church out there."

"Only if you come back safe and sound and bring the Indians," she reminded him, leaning close again and slipping her arms around his back to hold him more tightly against her breasts. Remembrance of his brush with death during the fight with Zaaro ripped at her composure. She closed her eyes and sent up a silent prayer for his safety. When she opened them, she saw through the lighted windows that Doña Magdalena was rising from the settee in the living room, her face toward the courtyard.

"We must start back inside now, Louis," Manuela said. Her hand caressed his face, even as she turned to urge him back toward the *hacienda*. "I love you. Promise you'll return for me."

"Count on it, my beautiful Manuela. Don't forget that I love you, too." The emotion lacing his words wrapped around her heart as masterfully as his arms had held her only moments earlier.

Doña Magdalena was outside then, peering from the vague circles of light coming from the windows behind her. They called to her in musical voices there in the darkness as they walked arm in arm to meet her.

Chapter Twenty-four

Surprising both Diego and Domingo, Louis chose to take only a dozen men along to find and parley with Night Hawk.

"Your reasoning makes little sense to me," Domingo told the Frenchman after they had left San Juan Batista behind and were riding toward the Rio Grande. "If I didn't know you had so much hinging on success, I might suspect you weren't eager to persuade the Lipans to return."

Louis shot Domingo an amused glance in the morning sunshine. "We've had few soldiers in Louisiana from the beginning, and we've had to learn to find ways to get along with the Indians short of force. I find that most are as eager to live in peace as we and that to approach them with too many armed men makes them apprehensive and far less trusting of anything one might say. That Diego stored my goods intact during my absence is in our favor, for always they like gifts." He turned to note the progress of the five French soldiers, four Spanish ones, and three Assinais following the two officers before letting his eyes check on his pack horse.

"I think I have much yet to learn from you, my friend. If you can talk Night Hawk into bringing his people back to the *presidio*, I'll have no qualms about going with you and Father Hidalgo to his old mission in Tejas."

"Doesn't Diego expect to have the priest already at the *presidio* when we return?"

"Yes, he was sending Sergeant Benitez and some men to Monclova this morning so that Sergeant Guerra can trade places with Benitez. They're to go on then to the mission westward from Monclova and fetch Father Hidalgo back with them." Thinking on the sly ways in which Sergeant Benitez had obviously undermined the Lipans' faith in the Spanish at the *presidio*, which had led to their nighttime departure the past month, he added, "Getting rid of that meddlesome sergeant should help more matters than those concerning the Indians at San Juan Batista."

Not until the end of the second day did Louis spy the Indian village he sought, the one his soldiers had spotted on their trip down to San Juan Batista and told him about. Their crude shelters no more than a few animal skins stretched over skinny mesquite branches beside the Rio Grande, the Lipans, spears in hands and fierce looks upon their faces, watched the riders, hands palm-upwards in apparent friendship, come closer. A few horses stood together at a distance, necks craning as they whinnied in some kind of greeting. Children at play became silent and darted to seek hiding places near the women at work around a camp fire down by the river.

Louis halted his group and studied the brooding face of Night Hawk coming toward him there in the waning light. A second camp fire burned behind him on the bank and served as a gathering place for the dozen or so other young men belonging to the tribe. Having visited with the young chief back at the *presidio* more than once over the past summer, Louis knew that the Indian felt his duties strongly, and that, like most chiefs, he held the welfare of his people dearer than his own safety. He also knew that from their having lived at and near the *presidio* for nearly fifteen years, the Lipans were no longer as capable of living well on the land as were those tribes not trading total freedom for a more comfortable existence. It was Louis's guess that the young chief barely remembered living anywhere but at the Spanish fort.

"We come on a mission of peace, of friendship, Night Hawk," Louis called to the Indian, now standing still up ahead. He stepped down from his horse and said lowly, "Domingo, come with me, but leave your gun here. I suspect he'll come nearer talking frankly with me than with a Spaniard."

Domingo almost protested, but when he saw that Louis had no gun, he did as the younger man had requested. Instant anger at the chief's audacity in sneaking away in the dark and leaving the *presidio* a target for any wandering Tejas warriors seeking quick thrills warned the Spanish officer that Louis was right. It was best that he not talk right away.

"Stop there." Night Hawk spread his legs and seemed to dig his moccasined feet into the loose sand. His hand tightened upon the spear. "We have broken no Spanish law." His eyes pierced Domingo's set face. "You have no right to be here in our camp."

"True," Louis conceded quickly, having stopped the moment the chief had ordered it. He cut a warning look at Domingo before going on. "Neither Captain Ramon nor I are here to make any kind of demands on you or your people. Had we wanted to use force, we could have brought many soldiers along."

Night Hawk seemed to consider that a moment, then nodded. "Why you come?"

"Commandant Ramon sent his son and me to talk with the Lipan chief," Louis replied.

"About what? We took nothing that wasn't ours." He glanced toward the river where a few goats and chickens wandered along its banks, all obviously searching for food without much success. "We're free to come and go as we choose. We've taken no oath to live at any fort." He glared at Domingo and then sized up the men stopped some distance behind.

"That's why we're here," Louis said in conciliatory tones. "Commandant Ramon respectfully asks that you return to your homes just outside the fort."

"Why would we do that when the sergeant takes our food and animals from us to feed the soldiers — and eyes our young women with lust? Not for the Lipans is such treatment." With a proud, disdainful look at both the officers before him, he spat upon the sand.

"Can you prove such accusations —" Domingo began with anger.

Louis held up a restraining hand, though, and squelched the fiery retort, saying softly, "Please, Domingo. Let's hear the man out. He no doubt has grievances and must be allowed to voice them. Don't you agree?"

Reining in his temper, Domingo nodded. The Frenchman obviously respected the red man as though he were no different than he, and he puzzled over the idea that maybe that was the key to Louis's reputation for getting along with

455

the Indians. Still not sure that the lieutenant's ways would work with what his fellow Spaniards and he had always thought of as savages but admitting to a new respect for the young man beside him, Domingo determined to remain silent until urged to speak.

Within a few minutes, Louis and Night Hawk were talking calmly about the Lipans' complaints against the Spanish at the *presidio*. When Night Hawk seemed convinced that no more soldiers were going to appear from the mesquite bushes in the distance, he invited the travelers to join his people for the evening meal. Louis directed his men to water their horses and rub them down for the night while the Indian women made ready to serve the fish stew simmering over their camp fire down by the Rio Grande.

Later, after all had eaten and made small talk, the tension had receded to the point that the soldiers and Assinais felt no apprehension about setting up their private little camp back near where they had tethered their horses.

Having invited Louis and Domingo to join him and his men around his camp fire, Night Hawk lay aside his pipe and spoke. "Saint-Denis, talk is that your word is as true as your knife blade."

Louis returned his own pipe to the collection near the fire and said, "I believe you've heard right."

"If we agree to return to the *presidio*, how can we be certain that the sergeant does what you say he will?" For the first time, the chief leaned to meet Domingo's eyes. "What does the commandant say about that, Captain Ramon?"

His earlier doubts as to the wisdom of Louis's talking calmly with the Indian erased, Domingo replied, "My father has Sergeant Guerra in charge again. Had he realized all that Sergeant Benitez was about, he wouldn't have allowed it. You should have spoken with him about the matter."

"When have Spanish officers listened to Lipans?" A touch of wounded pride rode the red-skinned face.

"Beginning this minute," Domingo assured him. "My father gives his word, as do I, that you and your people can expect the same fair treatment you enjoyed before Sergeant Benitez arrived. We need you at the fort, and we believe you need us."

Night Hawk showed nothing of his thoughts but rose and bade the officers find their bedrolls. A cold night wind was rising, and both Louis and Domingo left willingly.

"They'll probably talk around the camp fire before going to sleep," Louis told Domingo when they reached their own camp. "Night Hawk will have an answer for us in the morning."

Domingo looked pensive, but an air of complacency marked the younger man's features.

"Where is Inez?" Doña Magdalena demanded that first afternoon after Louis and Domingo left San Juan Batista. She had asked to meet with Manuela and Conchita in Manuela's bedroom to talk about the gowns needed if a wedding was to take place in the near future. "Conchita, your cousin may be the finest seamstress here at the fort, but she seems not to care that we're kept waiting."

"Don't fret, Aunt," Manuela soothed. Ever

since their return two days ago, Doña Magdalena had seemed irritable and quarrelsome, not at all the normally even-tempered woman Manuela had found her to be most of the time. "She'll be here shortly. First, she was going to the storehouse to fetch some of the yard goods we brought back from the city." Smiling then at the thought of the lovely white satin Louis had instructed a soldier to bring over that morning, she walked to her bed and flipped out a length to show her great-aunt. "This is what I want my wedding gown made from."

"Where did this fine material come from?" Doña Magdalena asked, leaning down and peering to check the closeness and lustre of the thread. Her fingers caressed the heavy fabric between forefinger and thumb, and her mouth pursed in approval. "I must confess it's superior to what we found in the city, even in the finest shops near the palace."

"It came from the goods Louis brought with him to trade. He says the silks and satins from France are always superior."

Doña Magdalena remarked thoughtfully, "Yes, that's generally true. It's just that we've not been allowed goods from France here in New Spain for a number of years."

Manuela welcomed Inez then, but her heart recorded the older woman's praise for French goods. If she could coax her into talking with Diego, perhaps . . .

The four women talked in detail about styles of wedding gowns and what would look best on Manuela, their voices becoming more and more excited as the afternoon drifted by. Not once did anyone mention the unsettling thought that if

Louis did not come back from his mission to woo the Lipans into returning with Domingo and him, there would be no wedding ceremony. Manuela was the only one who bore the added burden of knowing that even if Louis made it back safely, unless he had succeeded, there could be no marriage.

The next day at the *hacienda* found the women still at their planning, though some sketches Manuela had made began to take on more decided form. When she took them down to show Diego before dinner, he made hesitant comments but seemed preoccupied as Doña Magdalena and he sat in the living room.

"You've given your blessing, Diego," Doña Magdalena reminded him when Manuela rushed back upstairs to return the drawings to her room before Juanita sounded the final dinner bell. "You shouldn't be gruff with Manuela when she's trying to share her joy with you."

Sipping at a glass of sherry, Doña Magdalena fixed her eyes on Diego there on the other end of the settee. What had been wrong with him ever since their return from the city? He seemed to avoid being alone with her at any time, and he never once had sought her out to discuss Manuela and what went on at the palace. Heretofore, the two had spent many hours each week talking about the beautiful girl and her high-spirited ways, usually ending each session with laughter and delight at her daring. Was he perhaps regretting having given permission for Carlos to stay behind in the city and learn about the import business left him by his father? His lean, still handsome face appeared to be chiseled of stone.

"I know, and I don't mean to spoil her happiness," Diego replied after a brooding sigh. His hand smoothed at his neat gray moustache. "It's just that things around here will be so changed once she marries and leaves."

Doña Magdalena laughed low in her throat. "I would've thought you might be looking forward to more peace and quiet—at least for awhile." When he still seemed lost in thought and appeared not to have heard, she went on, eager to comfort him. "Carlos will do well in Mexico City, Diego. I've not seen him any more content than when he talks of all he's learning. Have I told you that the Duke's younger daughter, Ramona, positively dotes on him, and that the parents seem to be encouraging their friendship?"

"No," Diego replied, meeting her eyes then. "I've not thought to ask you about my grandson. Diego did tell me how pleased he is to be working with Gustavo at the warehouse, and what good things the manager had to say about his quickness. By the time Gustavo is ready to retire in Spain, Carlos will likely be ready to take over his father's business without any problems. At his age, he doesn't need to be thinking of a match, though, not even to the viceroy's daughter."

"Oh, they're not doing anything but making puppy eyes at each other," she assured him, cutting her eyes knowingly. "That the viceroy invited Carlos to stay in his guest quarters sounds like a solid endorsement though."

"You women are always trying to make matches, aren't you?" he teased softly. Watching the patrician features flush becomingly, he wondered what there was about her that seemed so different since her return. Sometimes he felt she wasn't the same younger sister of his long-deceased wife that he hadn't seen in years until he invited her to come serve as *dueña* to Manuela. She seemed more alive, more vibrant somehow, more like the formerly vivacious Magdalena he had known when all of them had lived in Mexico City. and yet the artfully arranged hair shone silver, and a tiny network of lines made a claim upon the pretty olive face. The sparkle of the black eyes, he decided as he watched her struggle for an answer, somehow called up memories of that younger Magdalena.

"What's wrong with trying to promote true love? I, for one, haven't forgotten what being in love is like," she quipped, surprised at her flirty tone. Had some of Manuela rubbed off on her? she wondered as she felt the flush return with more force. "Sometimes it might need a bit of a helping hand."

Diego threw back his head and laughed. "That's what I remember about you when you were young, Magdalena," he confessed. "You were always charmingly candid."

"Was I really?" Her voice showed how much she doubted the accuracy of his memory.

"Yes, and I'm glad to see you haven't changed."

She sent a hand to test the jeweled comb rising in front of the chignon at the crown of her head, flattered that Diego had such delightful memories of her as a young woman. The smile she sent him was unusually warm. He was such a dear man. Was this a good time to confess to him that she had no desire to leave the *presidio* when Manuela left with Louis? No, she decided upon seeing his mien had become aloof again, she would find a better time.

The dinner bell tinkled then, and Manuela

rushed down the stairs almost before the sound faded. Laughing and teasing, she made a great show of having Diego offer both arms to the women he would be dining with. By the time he had seated each one, a contented smile rode his countenance.

Looking down the table into Doña Magdalena's still flushed face, he asked, "Have I neglected to tell you how happy it makes me to have you back? It was god-awful quiet around here while you were away." When Manuela tilted her head toward him from where she sat, he shifted his eyes to include her, adding a bit self-consciously, "Both of you. I'm happy to have both of you back."

While Manuela's wedding gown moved from the stages of being mere lines on paper into pieces of satin cut into matching shapes for stitching together, a different kind of coming together was being pursued near the Rio Grande.

"Domingo," Louis said the next afternoon after they had reached the Lipans' camp, "I'll ride along behind Night Hawk's people on the way back to the *presidio*. They're going to be slow, what with the children and animals along, but we've no need to be in a rush, do you think?" The two were standing at the edge of the Indians' encampment where the women and children had toiled most of the day dismantling their shelters and gathering up their goods for the trip back to San Juan Batista.

"None at all," Domingo replied. "With most of your men remaining behind and with the additional soldiers coming up from the city with me still there, the fort is well protected." Lifting a hand to smooth his moustache, he cut a grateful look at the Frenchman. "You've done a fine job. You'll be deserving your reward." A pleased look upon his face at the thought of the young lovers being able to look forward to marriage, he went on. "Night Hawk seemed very satisfied after our talk this morning. Did you see the way he almost smiled when you gave him the bolts of red cloth and the beads? I got the feeling he was almost glad we came after him, especially now that Sergeant Guerra will be back overseeing their activities. I doubt the Lipans would be making ready to rejoin us at the *presidio* had it not been for your intervention. Right off, I would have lost my temper and all would have been lost."

Louis made no comment, but a small smile of satisfaction wreathed his face as he watched some of his men assist the women and children in securing their goods on hastily fashioned slides to be attached to their saddles and pulled behind their horses. Absently he continued his whittling on a thick limb with his knife, then said musingly, "Diego must have sensed that sending that first message by pigeon to the viceroy would result in something worthwhile someday, for I can't imagine any other reason he would have tried to save my life. I remember how furious he was when I first asked for Manuela's hand—"

"What 'first message' are you referring to?" Domingo broke in to ask doubtfully. "He sent only the one that came while I was there, telling of the Lipans' leaving the fort vulnerable, the one leading to you and your men being freed to return with me." He frowned in disbelief at what

463

Louis had suggested. True, neither Diego nor he had wanted Louis and his two men held as they were in prison and had tried to persuade Anya to give them a hearing, but neither had considered going over the governor's head to report to the viceroy. "I heard the Duke mention an earlier message, but it didn't come from Father, for I asked him. I meant to inquire at Monclova, but I forgot to."

Louis told then of that first message and how it had led the viceroy to send soldiers to Monclova to escort Medar, Phillipe, and him to Mexico City for questioning. "I recall that the viceroy told me it had come from San Juan Batista, that the old Indian, Eblo, was the only one from the northern section having success with training the pigeons to carry messages so far. I'm almost sure it would have had to have had the Ramon name on it or the viceroy would have discounted it."

Domingo pondered before replying in a bemused voice, "I've a good idea that the first message was sent by a Ramon all right, but not by Diego Ramon."

"Who then?"

Domingo threw back his head and laughed before answering, "Manuela must have done it."

"Manuela?" Louis's face grew still, as did his eyes. "She wouldn't have interfered in men's affairs that way." His voice tightened with each word. When her uncle continued to look amused but made no comment, Louis asked, "You're making a joke, aren't you?"

"No, my friend. I'm almost certain she cajoled Eblo into sending the message." A kind of perverse pride in his beautiful niece's daring crept into his voice. Noting Louis's grim face, he said, "Don't get testy. She was making sure in every way she could to guarantee your safety. You should feel flattered that she cares so deeply for you."

Louis fought down his unreasoning anger. Mayhap her decision to send a message to the viceroy did show she loved him, and mayhap he was being too edgy about the genteel young woman's taking an active role in saving his life, but his male ego suffered at the unsettling thoughts. He had not needed feminine meddling to ensure his safety. He would have managed; he always had. Grasping the stick he had been whittling on, he made one huge slice and cut it in two, then threw the pieces as far as he could. He slammed the knife in his shoulder holster and burst out, "Damn! I guess I'll have to have a serious talk with my intended when we get back to the *presidio.*"

Domingo watched the square-shouldered Frenchman stalk off toward where Night Hawk and his men had gathered, ready to start back southward. A grin tugging at his mouth, the Spaniard wondered how Louis would have reacted had he told what Governor Anya had confided only days ago about Manuela's offering to marry him in exchange for Louis's freedom. If Louis didn't already know about Manuela's fiery temperament and independent spirit ... well, Heaven help him, Domingo mused.

It was late, long after midnight, when a lean figure climbed up the corner pillar of the *hacienda*'s veranda, found a handhold in the iron grill-work of the balcony, and vaulted over the railing.

As if aware that the sentry over in the *plaza* halted at the alien sound, the figure blended with the darkness and grew still for a time. Then, shadowed and silent, it made its way to the bedroom with shutters open to the cool night breezes whipping down from the foothills in the distance.

Once he stepped inside, Louis stood still to catch his breath and gaze at the heart-stopping sight before him in the moonlight. Over the past three days of traveling slowly behind the Lipans, he had tried to imagine his being with Manuela again would not have to be different just because he did not approve of the way she may have interfered. All he had to do was tell her, and she would promise never to make such a move again—if she truly had sent the message.

When the caravan did not reach the fort until long after dark, the suffering Frenchman had tried to appreciate being back in comfortable quarters, but, instead, paced up and down, venting part of his anger at having been maneuvered by a woman on a totally unsympathetic Medar.

"The way I see it," Medar had remarked with a casual shrug of his shoulders and a rare look of disapproval toward his employer, "we'd be foolish to look too hard at why we're alive and free, only at the bare fact that we are. For myself, I intend to thank Manuela for sending the message. We might have rotted in those cells in Monclova. Anyway, how else would we have ever gotten to see Mexico City?"

Sending the valet away to his own room, Louis found he could not bear to wait until the next day to see Manuela and talk with her. Now that he was here in her bedroom while everyone else was asleep, he hesitated.

Manuela stirred and murmured something, her actions sending rivulets of excitement to her unknown visitor. He walked silently over to her bed, never taking his eyes from the lovely face. Like a silky covering of ebon, her hair fanned out on her pillow, and he fought the urge to feel its warmth. A shoulder lay exposed, and with tender fingers he lifted the blanket to protect it from the night's chill. Seeing her lips quirk at the corners from the apparently welcome covering touched his heart in an unsettling way. The beautiful young woman before him was no schemer. She would know that men's matters belonged to men. Shaking his head at his ticklish pride and thinking that once he asked her about it she would be able to reassure him, he planned to leave with the same stealth used in entering her bedroom. One last look at her sleeping as sweetly as an angel convinced him that she was what he had called her more than once—perfect.

"Hot pepper! You'll be sorry!" came an ungodly voice, followed by a squawk.

Louis snapped his head toward the sound, seeing Zorro on his perch in the far corner. Having heard Manuela tell how she covered his perch at night to keep the parrot quiet and inside, he eased over to search for the cloth. Just as he located it on the floor and draped it hurriedly over the loop of framing wire, he heard another voice.

"Is that you, Louis?" Manuela sat up in bed, not believing what she was seeing. His eyes flashed in the pale light as he turned toward her. "Am I dreaming? Are you all right?"

Signaling silence, Louis put his fingers to his

lips. He had tensed upon hearing the parrot's nonsensical words, fearing that a family member might be aroused. "Yes," he whispered. "I couldn't wait till tomorrow to see you."

Manuela smiled and said in a sleepy voice, "You don't have to worry so about being heard. Doña Magdalena's is the only other bedroom on this end of the balcony, and you know she doesn't hear well. I won't even ask how you got here, I'm so glad to see you." She held out her arms to him.

"Darling," he said just before he sat upon the edge of her bed and accepted the kiss being offered. The feel of her body all warm from sleep answered hidden needs, and he hugged her close, loving the way her hair fell like a silken curtain over his arms. Her lips were as soft and delicious as he'd remembered. His blood raced in fiery veins, and his heartbeat drummed demandingly.

A few fervent kisses later, she pulled away and asked with noticeable shortness of breath, "Were you successful? Will we be able to marry?"

"The Lipans are sleeping in their houses tonight." Her smile seemed bright enough to compete with the moonlight angling through the window. "We'll be man and wife before everyone soon." The happy announcement reminded him of his reason for needing to see her, and he leaned away from her to watch her face. "I want you to tell me you had nothing to do with my being freed from Monclova."

"Why do you say that?" Her heart, already turning somersaults from his kisses, took on a heavy hammering. She reached to touch his cheek, but he moved back. It was then that she saw the slicing, silvery looks of accusation.

"Don't evade this, Manuela. I want to know if you stepped into business that didn't concern you." His voice held little of its earlier tenderness, for he was being denied what he had prayed for—a quick denial.

"What concerns the man I love concerns me, Louis. I don't see why you're upset over . . . what I did." Which one of her exploits had he learned about—the message, or her agreement with Governor Anya? Or had he found out about both? A feathering up her spine warned her that she should have paid attention to the advice coming from Conchita and Carlos.

"Tell me all about it." This time he crossed his arms over his chest, shutting her out.

"All about what?" She lifted her chin. He was behaving not at all like the Louis she had fallen in love with.

"What you did to get me out of Governor Anya's prison in Monclova. I know, so you might as well be honest—if you know how." There was no doubt in his mind now that Domingo had been right. She was the culprit, and she felt not the least bit of regret, else why was she looking so flustered?

Manuela glanced down at her hands, noting that they lay in fists against her blanket. His mentioning Anya must mean that the governor had told Domingo and that Domingo, for some stupid reason, had passed on the knowledge to Louis. Angry herself then at the way he was putting her on the defensive, she retorted, "I did agree to marry the governor if he set you free to return to Louisiana, but what difference does it make now? He never did what he promised, and, as you well know, it never happened that way."

Black eyes lifted, flashing fiery, warning signals. "That bargain no longer exists."

Louis reeled from what she was telling. "You offered yourself to that old man in exchange for my freedom?" Shock still held his heart immobile, and raw anger ruled his brain. "Why would you do such a crazy thing?"

"Get out of my bedroom!" she hissed. "You'd not understand, so why should I try to explain? Surely I don't have to answer to you about something so obvious. I'm not an imbecile, and I won't be treated as one." She drew up her knees and hugged them close. "I don't care to talk with you about this anymore. I should have let you die in prison."

"Oh, you weren't taking a chance on that," Louis shot back, sarcasm plumping out each word. "No doubt before you made the *noble sacrifice* of offering yourself to the governor, you sent the message to the viceroy and forged your grandfather's name to it. You don't leave much to fate, do you?"

"Why should I?" she parried with an indignant toss of hair for his apparent density in failing to understand her motives. Tears pricked at her eyelids, but she blinked them back. She had no wish for him to see her cry, and she summoned new anger to cloak her anguish. "Get out of my room, Louis Saint-Denis. I never want to see you again!"

Louis rose with as much dignity as he could muster and sent her a heated glare. "Gladly. I've no desire to be around women who think they need to meddle in my affairs. You probably find it hard to believe that I've managed to stay alive all these years without your fine hand arranging

470

things. Seek your legal husband from among the Spanish upper class, as your grandfather so obviously prefers. No doubt you'll find one there who likes being manipulated by a woman." Not even looking back, he stepped through the window and left.

Near dawn, after a rooster heralded the new day with annoying good cheer, Louis still tossed upon his bed. Not so angry anymore, but still tormented by the fiery exchange with Manuela, he recalled the ludicrous words of her parrot and grimaced at what might well have been a prophecy:

"Hot pepper! You'll be sorry."

Chapter Twenty-five

Manuela could not sit still late the next after-noon, and Conchita scolded good-naturedly as she tried to make the thick braids interweave neatly at the crown of the small head.

"You're going to get to see him within a short time," the maid assured her mistress, certain that Manuela's unusual nervousness was caused by her eagerness to greet Louis upon his return to the *presidio*. "Medar told me after breakfast that when they arrived in the night, the Indians gave a kind of dance of thanksgiving to be back in their homes outside the *presidio*. Everything is going just as you wished. Now the wedding date can be set, and so can Medar's and mine." She stood back to admire the jet braids looping prettily. "I'm sure you're disappointed that the men were too engrossed with talk to share the noon meal with Doña Magdalena and you, but that'll make dinner even more exciting." A smile lighted her pretty round face at the thought that she would be joining her own lover in the big *plaza* at dark.

Manuela let out a shuddering breath. Conchita would not understand the anguish torturing her ever since Louis's visit to her bedroom after midnight; besides, she did not dare mention the visit. There was no need to enlighten Conchita, her only *confidante* now that Carlos was in Mexico City, no need to tell that it was not anticipation over seeing Louis that made her fidgety, for saying it aloud would not help. It was fear, plain and simple. The thought that she was going to lose Louis scared her; that she might have already lost him frightened her even more.

What had Louis told Diego and Domingo during their day together? she wondered while Conchita chattered on. That he no longer wanted to marry her now that he had seen the way she had of over-riding all obstacles to make things go her way?

After Louis slipped from her room, and again all during the day, Manuela had agonized over her inability to wait calmly for desirable things to happen. She recognized that passionate splash of willfulness inside as dangerous, had done so ever since the night she had torn out like a fury to seek Carlos had resulted in suffering, not only to herself but also to others. But, she groaned, she had done nothing to curb it.

Not that she had ever told anyone or spent time fretting, but there were nights when Manuela yet awakened to find herself drenched with perspiration, her mind screaming from recalling that terrifying scene with Mescatonaza trying to seduce her mind and body, or of Zaaro slapping her about. Inevitably then would rise memories of Louis's wound from Zaaro's spear and his later fight to the death with the Mescalero bent on harming her. She thought she had learned her lesson, she reflected, but she hadn't hesitated in stepping in when she believed Louis's life was at stake. Was there a difference?

"Conchita," she asked sorrowfully when the chatter ceased, her slanted eyes meeting those of the caring maid, "is it wrong to love a man more than you love yourself?"

"No, of course not. If you didn't, you'd not be truly in love." She studied the troubled face lifted to hers there before the dressing table. "Are you having doubts about your love for the French lieutenant?"

Manuela looked down at her ringless hands clasped together on her lap. "Mayhap my doubts are that he doesn't love me back in the way that I love him."

"Cheer up, then," Conchita responded with a warm laugh. "I've seen the way he looks at you with those pale eyes, and I can tell he worships you."

The usual decisions about jewelry had to be made then, and Manuela had to look at her gown to remember she was wearing one of deep yellow. A plunging, veed neck did more than hint at her generous cleavage, and the small collar standing up behind her neck, encrusted with seed pearls on both sides, created a decorative frame for her solemn face. The long sleeves, puffed elaborately from shoulder to elbow, tapered closely to above the wrists.

"Jet will do nicely," Conchita announced, already opening the small drawers of the ornate jewelry case and bringing out glittering beads and combs. "See?" she asked after having set a tall jet comb in front of the braids at the crown and stooping to meet Manuela's eyes in the mirror. "The little diamonds across the curved top sparkle, just like your eyes."

When her mistress seemed unimpressed, Conchita fastened a string of shiny black beads about the slender neck, reaching with deft fingers to straighten the dangling pendant with similar diamonds encrusted in its glossy hard surface. "Right at the top of your breasts, see how it flirts and winks? The lieutenant won't be able to keep his eyes off it." Slipping a matching bracelet on an uncooperative wrist, then adding earrings that were no match for the blackness of the shining hair drawn back severely from the finely sculpted face, she announced, "You're more beautiful than I've ever seen you."

"You say that every night, Conchita," she remarked wryly. Checking her image in the mirror and seeing only her fear and doubts staring back at her, Manuela licked lips suddenly dry. "I wish I were one of the hummingbirds that visit our courtyard when it's warmer, and I could fly away out of sight."

"Why would you be so morbid when you at last have what you've wanted for so long?" Conchita did not conceal her vexation. "After all you've done to make this night happen—"

"Please," Manuela broke in, rising and kicking her long skirts out of her way so as to stride across the room unhampered. "I'd rather not think about that right now."

There was time enough before the first dinner bell for her to wander out onto the balcony, and, along with the chance to be alone with her unsettling thoughts, she welcomed the coolness of the purple twilight. Without her willing it, her eyes strayed across the walls separating the *hacienda* from the military quarters. She could see nothing but the darkening tiled roofs of buildings and the tops of carefully cultivated trees, bare now of leaves, but she sensed that Louis was beyond the walls, and a shuddering sigh escaped. What was he thinking?

That he was one mixed-up Frenchman was what Louis was thinking over in his quarters. Ignoring Medar's obvious attempts to brighten his mood while helping him get dressed for dinner with the Ramons, he puzzled over what course he should take. An inner voice warned him that he had no way of knowing what the impulsive Manuela might do, so would it matter what he might plan?

Putting aside his personal woes, Louis had talked all morning with Diego, Domingo, and the returned Sergeant Guerra about possible ways to keep Night Hawk and his people contented at the *presidio*. After a hasty meal at midday, taken after the ladies of the *hacienda* had already gone for *siestas*, the three had separated for their own private rest.

Father Hidalgo joined them afterward to meet Domingo and Louis and take part in the discussion of tomorrow's journey to the Mission of the Holy Saints. After having rested most of the time since arriving at San Juan Batista on the previous day, the priest, looking frail but hardy, had seemed to grow more animated at each plan made for his return to what he called fondly his "lost children."

"Will Father Hidalgo be joining all of you for dinner at the *hacienda?*" Medar asked, breaking into Louis's reverie.

His mouth pursed in criticism, the valet gave one final inspection of the handsome figure be-

476

fore him. He adjusted the flaring skirt of the dark blue coat to stand out more fully above the tight knee breeches, leaning to blow his breath on the crested silver buttons topping the inverted side pleats, then polish them with a soft white cloth. Earlier he had given new lustre to those on the front and at the cuffs of the sleeves. The pale blue shirt and cravat, one of several Louis had ordered made while in Mexico City, lent an air of fashionable sophistication to the lieutenant and brought a smile of approval to Medar's slim face. A handsome satin vest of a third shade of blue, embroidered in gold and magenta silk threads, retained its look of the Orient, where, the merchant had assured Louis, it was woven and then decorated by hand before being shipped to Acapulco, then to the capital.

"Yes, the priest will be there." And, his heart sped up at the thought, so will Manuela. What would she say? Had she already told her family that she wanted nothing more to do with him? When the viceroy and his handsome aide, Leon d'Espinoza, made the promised visit to San Juan Batista in the spring, would she then smile approvingly on the handsome Spaniard with the proper credentials to claim her hand? Or, if Charolotte had indeed worked her magic on Leon, as he suspected she planned to, and already had him hooked, would Manuela then smile upon another in the party? From what he had heard of the plans over the last few days in the city, the adventurous group would be large and filled with all manner of young Spaniards eager to explore the northern reaches of New Spain in the company of the all-powerful viceroy.

Not liking the direction of his painful musings,

Louis tried to feel relief that neither Diego nor Domingo had mentioned Manuela all day. On the other hand, he wondered if that might be a bad sign. He cleared his throat and brushed at his hair, attempting to quell his nervousness.

"Your lady will no doubt swoon upon seeing how handsome you look," Medar said with only a trace of teasing. For the life of him, he could not recall his employer and friend having been so visibly agitated before without his being privy to the cause. What had been gnawing at Louis ever since they left the Rio Grande on the return trip with the Lipans, and why had he not confided in him? Surely he had gotten over his ridiculous anger at Manuela for having helped them out of prison. "I don't think you'll have to remind her how lucky she is to be marrying such a fine specimen of a Frenchman."

Louis made no reply right away but merely reached for his glass of brandy and polished it off. "I can hardly imagine 'my lady,' as you call Manuela, swooning over anything," he muttered wryly. "She is more apt to cause others to do so."

"Ah," Medar was quick to say, "she is one perfect beauty, without question." Why wasn't Louis smiling while he talked about his intended, as he had been wont to do until recently? That couldn't be a note of derision he detected in his voice, could it?

"Perfect. A word that gets bandied about sometimes without its user thinking upon its meaning," Louis remarked, going toward the door. "I'm not at all sure there's such a thing as a perfect woman, Medar."

"Who would want one?" the dapper valet retorted good-naturedly. "I dare say a man would find himself striving forever to live up to a wife without imperfections. He might allow himself moments of delusion about her being perfect, mind you; but if he truly loves her, he'll admit she has faults just as he himself has." Taking his neglected glass of brandy from the side table, he sipped slowly. "I'm still testing Conchita, trying to find what her fault is," he remarked with mock grimness. No sign came that his attempt at levity was noted. "Have a nice evening," he called as Louis went outside without a backward glance or his usual farewell.

Could it be that Louis was doubting his decision to marry the commandant's granddaughter? Medar swirled the brandy in his glass and studied the lazy movement of the thick liquid intently, as if expecting to see answers floating there. Only the thought that he was meeting Conchita shortly in the *plaza* brought him back to the moment.

Louis found Doña Magdalena and the three Ramons already in the living room visiting with Father Hidalgo when he arrived at the *hacienda*. In a way, he was glad to be spared the sight of Manuela's descending the staircase in her elegant style, as he had so often watched her do. Each time, he had experienced a mysterious feeling that some invisible, eternal cord stretching between them became shorter with each step she made, and he had no wish tonight to be taunted by whatever it was that had pulled at him since his first sight of her swimming in the irrigation canal.

"Louis," Diego said after courtesies were exchanged all around and the young man came to stand beside him at the window looking out upon the courtyard. "I couldn't help but notice that Manuela and you met almost like strangers. Are you not eager to claim your reward for a job well done?" His voice was light and teasing, but his eyes studied the Frenchman with curiosity. Though Diego yet had doubts about allowing Manuela to go to Louisiana, he freely admitted, now that the marriage seemed inevitable, that he truly liked Louis, had from their first meeting. There was something about him . . .

Louis smiled and sipped his wine, hoping to divert Diego's piercing gaze. It seemed plain from the normalcy of everyone's greetings that Manuela had made no remarks about their disagreement. She could hardly do so, he realized, without confessing that he had slipped into her room in the small hours of the morning. The memory of their cutting exchanges washed over him anew.

"Never would I want to seem too amorous in front of her family," Louis remarked with a smoothness he did not feel.

"Of course," Diego intoned, not at all sure the glint in the pale eyes came from respect for propriety. "We can set the wedding date now, though, and allow the two of you to have some time together—under the watchful eyes of Doña Magdalena, of course—before you leave tomorrow for the mission on the Colorado River." Even while talking with Louis, he watched his sister-in-law as she spoke charmingly with Manuela and the priest across the room. Her deep lavender gown showed up well beside the deep yellow of Manuela's, he noted. He must remember to

480

tell her that he liked the change from her usual somber black. After all, she had long passed the acceptable two years given over to mourning her dead husband. "As Doña Magdalena was saying before you arrived, it's a shame you must leave again so soon and will miss being here for Christmas."

"Such things can't be helped." Louis was shocked that he had forgotten it was December already. All he could think of was Manuela.

"It will take time to prepare a proper wardrobe for my granddaughter, and you can use the next weeks to look forward to the ceremony upon your return."

Domingo came up to them then, asking both his father and Louis, "Has a wedding date been set yet?"

"I believe it might be difficult to know exactly when we'll return from our journey, Domingo," Louis replied, trying to tear his eyes from Manuela's profile across the room. "I'd guess it'd be close to two months, wouldn't you?"

"That sounds about right." Domingo glanced over at his serious-faced niece deep in conversation with Father Hidalgo. "Don't tell me that you and Manuela are already having a lovers' quarrel. I figured you would have much to talk about, and yet you're not even standing close."

Recalling Louis's angry outburst upon learning of Manuela's being the one most likely to have sent the mysterious message to the viceroy, Domingo smiled charitably. So, he mused, the Frenchman had erred in declaring to Diego and him that in matters concerning his love for Manuela, he had no pride. All at once, Domingo felt a twinge of pity for the one he had come to look upon as a good friend. Love could do strange things to a man, he recalled with a mental sigh for his own many assignations gone awry simply because he could not give up his freedom.

From the beginning, Domingo had suspected that Louis and he shared some kind of tenuous bond, and that one of its threads had to do with the zest for adventure in the New World. Was the French lieutenant perhaps searching unconsciously for an excuse to avoid taking a wife and necessarily curtailing some of his exploring, now that the ceremony seemed a likelihood?

No matter that marriage held no appeal for him personally, Domingo sensed that the strong-willed Manuela needed an equally strong-willed husband, and he determined to do all that he could to see that she married Louis Saint-Denis. Though seldom disposed to choose the romantic outlook, he had sensed for some time that the two were made for each other.

"I've already assured Louis that Manuela and he will be allowed some private time before you two leave again tomorrow," Diego said when Louis seemed disinclined to comment about why Manuela and he were not together.

"Good," Domingo said. "How about after dinner? It's not too cold for an engaged couple to enjoy a walk outside."

Louis stuck a hand in his pocket and tried to appear at ease during the following light conversation. When the dinner bell sounded, he let out a breath of relief. The sooner the time came for Manuela and him to be alone and thrash out what rose up so adamantly between them, the better.

* * *

"Keep your voice down," Manuela warned, pulling her shawl closer about her shoulders. They were wandering aimlessly about the moonlit courtyard while the others sat over coffee in the living room. Openly eager to grant the young couple some private time, Doña Magdalena had insisted that the men come back inside and finish their cigars, remarking that the night air had a bite to it. "They'll hear you from inside."

"I don't think they're interested in listening for noises," Louis remarked. "Unless you were to scream for help." He puffed on his cigar, then poked it, red end down, into a container of soil as if angry at it. "They probably think we're locked in passionate embraces. Besides, I wasn't speaking loudly."

Manuela sneaked a look at him in the wintry moonlight, admiring the manly form in the blue suit in spite of her not wanting to. The smoke from his last puff on the cigar appeared suspended behind him, leading her to think for a heart-stopping moment that he might have just stepped from a separate world. All through the meal, she had sensed that he watched her covertly in between exchanges of talk and realized early on that she was guilty of like actions. If any of the others noticed that they seemed stiff with each other, not at all as a newly engaged couple might be expected to act, they pretended not to and carried on a lively conversation with the visiting priest from the far side of the province of Coahuila.

"You didn't call me a 'conniver' in a whisper," she countered.

"Connivers don't hear many whispers, except

from others of their kind."

"Our coming out here to talk was a mistake." Her voice sounded haughty, but she didn't care.

"It wasn't my idea to be alone with you."

"I could have figured that out by myself."

"You seem to figure everything out for yourself, don't you? I believe that's the crux of the matter."

"What was I supposed to do, Louis? Let Governor Anya kill you by neglect? From what Conchita and I learned, you weren't exactly being coddled in that filthy cell." She swept her skirts close so as not to touch him there on the narrow walkway and plopped down on the bench beneath the bare-limbed chinaberry tree. The murmur of the small fountain behind them did nothing to soothe her.

Louis watched Manuela settle herself on the bench and draw her shawl closer. All evening he had admired the way she looked in the yellow gown and the stunning jet jewelry. Like a tiny crown, the tall comb tucked into the braids atop her head gave her the elegant mien of royalty. Drawn to her as strongly as ever, in spite of his anger, he strode over to sit beside her, but not too close.

"What you were supposed to do was act like a well-bred young woman and let men handle their own affairs," he grated. "You can't take matters into your own hands, Manuela. That's not the way to act."

"Even if it saves the life of a ... someone special?" A thickness of voice showed that tears were struggling for life behind the huge, slanting eyes. When he would have put his hand on her arm, she shrugged out of reach and said in a harsh whisper, "Don't touch me!"

"We can't be man and wife and not touch," he reasoned.

"I don't know that we're going to be man and wife."

"We already are."

She swallowed hard. "Not actually."

"To me, it couldn't be more true than if we had already heard the words spoken over us." Didn't she feel that eternal thread linking them as much as he? he agonized. She seemed much farther away than an arm's length. "I can't believe you've forgotten what we said and . . ."

Manuela heard the resonant voice fade and wondered if some part of her hadn't faded since their tempestuous meeting in her bedroom. She felt no more than a shadow of her former self. "I'll tell Grandfather that we've changed our minds, that we don't care to go through with the ceremony." She gazed up at the sky, finding her usual wonder at its ethereal beauty replaced by awe of its brooding vastness. Their brightness diminished slightly by the half-moon, the stars twinkled secret messages; but all she heard was the sound of breathing, her own and that of the man sitting alongside her deluging her with washes of silvery gazes. Even the melody from the fountain lived outside the little sphere the two inhabited.

"You'll do no such thing!" Her slanted black eyes mirrored specks of starlight and made him think, against his will, how beautiful she was.

"What kind of life can we have together when you despise me for doing something I would likely do again if the circumstances were the same?" At his openmouthed gasp of disbelief, she added with a sidelong look, "I'm almost positive I would."

"Then you aren't even sorry that you meddled in men's matters and made me look as if I needed to hide behind a woman's petticoats?" All along he had thought he would need only to let her know of his displeasure and she would become overwrought with shame and overflowing with apology, even give promises never again to attempt such an unladylike feat. He could not believe her audacity.

"No, because that wasn't what I did."

Louis crossed his arms and concentrated on sitting straight and tall there on the bench beside her. Despite his willing it not to, the storm of anger overtaking him in her bedroom came sailing back from where it had obviously been hiding and gathering force. "I won the right to marry you, and I intend to do it. Domingo and I and a few of our men are leaving tomorrow to escort Father Hidalgo to the Mission of the Holy Saints. When I return, you're going to have your belongings ready, and we're going to marry out there in that church with the silver cross on top of it, just as we've planned."

"What a romantic proposal, Louis," Manuela taunted, letting irony override her own anger at the moment, but only for that brief space of time. Her chin lifted defiantly, she hissed, "So I'm no more than a prize you won, is that it? Strange how you manage to see all events only through your male viewpoint. I hope you'll have no trouble realizing why I'm refusing to accept — and don't you dare sneak into my bedroom again!"

"You've already accepted my proposal. As for

coming to your bedroom, don't worry. I won't have to 'sneak' the next time I'm in a bedroom with you, for we'll be man and wife before everyone by then." The beauty of the face lifted to his still charmed him, but its new air of disdain set his blood boiling. Her black eyes were crucifying him. "You need not try working any sly tricks to keep our marriage from taking place." He grasped her arms more firmly than he realized, but even when she tried to free herself, he did not loosen his hold. Unprepared for the debilitating pangs of anguish ripping his heart at her cruel denouncement, he could not endure the thought of losing her. He longed to shake her into submission. "You're already mine, and I intend to claim you before God and everyone." His words shot out like weapons, but he did not attempt to refashion them.

"You wan't me only because you won me, and your misguided sense of male pride won't allow you to admit you made a mistake in choosing me as a desirable prize," she snapped with fire as blatant as his. Where he held her arms, she felt branded, no longer belonging completely to herself—in the same way as when he had tried on the afternoon of the bird hunt to prevent her from plucking the flower down the bank of the mountain stream, she recalled with a jolt. Only this time, she was unable to jerk free. "I won't be here when you return."

"You had damned well better be, or I'll come find you wherever you are and drag you back."

Manuela heard a new note in his threat and shivered. She studied the harsh expression on his face, realizing that it resembled one she had seen there during the fight with Zaaro. She gulped, and her pulse leapt. "It won't do you any good, for I'm not going to marry you."

"Would you rather I told Diego about your little tricks? Would he like hearing that you forged his name on a message to the viceroy?" When she merely blinked in that heavy-lidded way, which intrigued him even in his anger, he went on. "Or that you took it on yourself to speak privately with Governor Anya about your betrothal? Since when have women claimed such actions as their own, or does the Spanish upper class have a separate set of rules?"

The pain splintering the fury in Manuela's eyes told him that he had hit upon a raw spot. If she did not love him enough to marry him and trust they could work out their differences, she at least seemed to care what her grandfather might think about her errant behavior, Louis reflected with a kind of perverse satisfaction at even a partial victory. "I'll expect you to be waiting for me to get back, with all in readiness for a grand ceremony and then our departure for Louisiana. Do we understand each other?"

Manuela listened to the nuances in his deep voice, unable to discern the varied emotions lurking therein. Beneath the uncharacteristic harshness and the orders, she suspected something far more compelling was attempting to surface, but the glitter of the silvery eyes there in the chilling moonlight caught her up in a kind of dizzying spell, and she found her thoughts centering on relief. She must have relief from the force emanating from him and threatening to surround her, suck her up. Weak all over, she answered, "Yes, I think we understand each other – and maybe for the first time."

Casting a look toward the lighted windows of the living room behind them, he commanded in a husky bass such as she had never heard before, "Then give your man a kiss for good luck on his journey."

Before the startled Manuela could mouth the protest forming, Louis seized her and pulled her against him there on the bench in the shadows. His lips captured hers with passionate force, stealing her breath and setting her heartbeat into a runaway gallop. Nothing had been settled except that he intended for the marriage to take place, she thought desperately. They yet had differences that needed to be resolved.

She recognized with trepidation that the fiery play of his lips on hers was branding her far more than the clutch of his hands on her arms had done. Crushed against his broad chest as she was, and with one of his hands cupping the back of her head, she felt overpowered. The lingering aroma of his earlier cigar blended with his usual manly fragrance and filled her nostrils. His masterful arms made her feel helpless against a strange, inestimable power threatening to possess her with a more telling certainty than she had ever exercised over herself.

For a crazy instant, Manuela was back in the stables that night when she had fallen atop him and he had kissed her until she was all weak and ripe for the unknown. Until his accusations in her bedroom before dawn, she had felt that Louis was no longer an unknown. Now that he seemed bent on devouring her very soul with his kisses, she suffered from serious doubts about the one she had envisioned as her cavalier. Cavalier? He seemed — and her mind trembled at the searing thought—every bit as savage as Mescatonaza had that eerie night when she had awakened to find him beside her in the tepee, bent on enticing her to surrender.

True, she had longed for relief from Louis's and her quarrel, but to have him wrecking her self-control was not what she had had in mind, Manuela realized with the last vestige of her ability to think of anything other than what his demanding caresses and plundering mouth were doing to her. She tried to draw away, tried to summon again the boiling anger sustaining her verbal attack on him. But a trickling of an essence raw and primitive was joining her racing blood, and she found herself responding to his devastating kisses against her will. Was it this heretofore unrecognized, hidden streak of constrained passion uncoiling deep inside to which the near-naked Mescatonaza had unknowingly signaled that frightening night?

There on the bench beneath the chinaberry tree, Louis tasted Manuela's lips with new delight for their spicy sweetness, felt her body try to wrench free, even as her lips spoke a different message against his. From the moment he grabbed her close, the remembered scent of roses had flirted outrageously with his nose. He could hear her little snatches of breath and the seductive song of silk playing against the fabric of his coat. He could feel her breasts spilling against his muscles, heating up his blood. For the first time, he gloried in being bigger and stronger, for, he confessed to the wounded part of himself, he wanted nothing more than to conquer her, prove to her that she belonged to him in all ways possible.

Feeling not at all ashamed over his mastery, he leaned away enough to send his hand to trace the shape of her breast, delighting to find that the nipple peaked and told him what he wanted to know. Yes, she wanted him, even more than her responsive mouth was admitting. Like a sword searching out that of an opponent, his tongue plunged beyond her lips. When her own accepted the fierce challenge, Louis recognized that the earlier fury from his temper had turned into one of raging desire. Not even that night in the prison cell when she had first offered herself had he felt so potently ablaze with need to claim her.

His breath was as ragged as hers, and he wondered if she might not feel the rapid drumming of his heartbeat against her own. Thoughts of not seeing her over the next several weeks heated his loins to new levels. Like an addict faced with the prospect of losing access to what he felt he could not live without, Louis found the prospect of even one day without the provocative Manuela frightening, not appealing from any aspect.

Defensively, for he had no wish to face up just then to how vital her love was to his well-being, he jerked her closer, a purring back in his throat only an echo of what tore at him inside. What was there about her that was driving him to want to possess her totally, possess her in ways he sensed went beyond the ordinary? She seemed different, somehow, and more desirable than ever. His hand found a silken ankle exposed and slid upward to caress the shapely legs, the curving thighs and hips, and then the springy little mound of hair barely disguised by a thin undergarment.

A discreet closing of a door behind them signaled that the courtyard now belonged to more than the couple close in frenzied embrace on the bench underneath the chinaberry tree in its concealing shadows. Breathing erratically, they pulled away as quickly as two drops of quicksilver from a sharp blow. With painful effort, Louis released Manuela and, as soon as he could, stood shakily, not sure that he could control his breathing for another few seconds yet. When he was able, he bowed mockingly, then offered Manuela his arm.

"May I escort you inside?" he asked, summoning from somewhere a voice loud enough for Doña Magdalena to detect from where she stood on the gallery peering in their direction. He felt a kind of lopsided gratitude for the *dueña's* lack of good eyesight and hearing.

"Please do," Manuela replied with even less breath control than he had managed in the brief time. Her pulse continued to assault her ears and create a light-headedness. Inside, she was a veritable mass of pulsating, moist heat.

Slipping her trembling arm to nestle in the crook of his, Manuela cut her eyes at the silvery-eyed young man looking down at her with an unfathomable gaze in the dazzling moonlight. How strange, she thought with a slight shiver, that she might well have met him tonight for the first time. Even stranger was her next thought: She was not at all sure what she felt for the new Louis Saint-Denis.

Chapter Twenty-six

"It's best that the men left at dawn," Doña Magdalena assured Manuela the next day, for she felt confident she knew what brought the wan look to the lovely face of her grandniece. Probably she had spent most of the night grieving that her beloved would be gone over the next several weeks. Only two years past forty, the silver-haired woman knew well what tormenting doubts love can create in a passionate heart. "Saying farewell again would have only proved more painful. Louis will be back before you know it."

Manuela made little attempt to dispel the uncharacteristic black mood claiming her and answered few of the older woman's remarks. She felt she might be drifting without known purpose in a kind of void, perhaps like the stars diminished by the brightness of the half-moon that she had gazed at last night while in the courtyard with Louis. Begging off joining those in the sewing room near the kitchen, she donned a riding costume and went to the stables after *siesta* time.

"You don't need to come with me," she told Eblo after he saddled Nightstar and led the

493

horse outside.

The old Indian grunted, saying in an offhand way as he turned back toward the stables, "I'll catch up with you if you don't wait."

Manuela mounted, truly not caring whether or not Eblo rode along with her, for she had no intention of talking at length with him, or anybody else, until she got things sorted out in her mind. Nightstar moved friskily toward the distant foothills, his white head sawing with eagerness to taste the chilly wind washing down across the sand dunes and flats. The sounds of his hooves pounding the sand and the silver trims jangling on his bridle rose up about his black-haired rider like one of the frequently sighted whorls of dust out on the landscape. A nearing drum of hoofbeats told her that Eblo was catching up.

When some of the tension inside let go, Manuela shepherded her thoughts from their grazing on distant, imperceptible fields of wasteland and acknowledged Eblo's presence. By then they were almost to the area of bird hunts in the past, and she reined Nightstar to a moderate canter.

"Missy trying to outride the wind spirits today?" Eblo asked. From beneath the floppy brim of a weathered hat, the old Indian's eyes seemed all-knowing.

"Maybe." An errant breeze slammed a spray of sand toward her face, and she dodged expertly while turning the spirited white horse back toward the *presidio*. The sun was sinking behind the mountains on the horizon, and, as she well knew, the night winds of December often brought with them the icy breath of snow falling high in the mountains. A mass of clouds towered

494

over the distant peaks, their outer edges turning into blazes of fiery pink and orange from the descending sun. Idly she wondered if one of the few seasonal rains to visit San Juan Batista might not be packing for a nighttime call. Breathing in deeply, she sniffed at a rare hint of moisture in the normally dry air.

"I hear wedding bells will ring when the lieutenant and your uncle return." Manuela had visited with him briefly one morning over a week ago, right after her return from the city. At that time, though the Frenchman had been the topic of most of her conversation, she had said nothing about getting married. How well he recalled his vast feeling of relief upon learning that Zaaro would no longer pose a threat.

While Manuela and he were being held in the Mescaleros' village, Eblo had overheard talk that the hot-tempered Zaaro, a renegade from another tribe to the north, would not be tolerated long, not after he had kicked up so much fuss with the young chief about his hatred of Manuela for her daring to bite him in front of his fellow warriors. It had seemed a bothersome certainty to Eblo that eventually the angered Mescalero would get lost in a mescal-induced fog and seek out Manuela to carry out his threatened revenge. Reflecting now on such things, he felt no grief that Zaaro was dead, only sadness for a wasted life.

Manuela waited a while before acknowledging that she had heard Eblo. "It's true that Lieutenant Saint-Denis and I are to be wed," she replied in a heavy voice, her eyes refusing to meet those wise ones studying her. She saw how the silver cross up ahead gleamed in the few remaining fingers of angling sunlight but marked mentally that as the sun was in its winter, the rays did not produce as much sparkle as during the rest of the year.

"Lieutenant Saint-Denis is a fortunate Frenchman."

Turning then to look at her companion riding alongside, she asked, "Eblo, do you think my sending the message to the viceroy was wrong for a woman to do?"

"I thought I sent it." Whatever made her ask that? he wondered. He realized he was still waiting for Diego to upbraid him for having done so without first checking with him. Could it be that the commandant knew nothing of it, even now?

"Yes, but I wrote it and asked you to send it without gaining Grandfather's permission."

Eblo saw the hurtful doubt deep in the black eyes and sighed inwardly at the seemingly needless pain young people inflicted upon each other, no matter what color their skins. So, he mused, the proud lieutenant had not approved of her interference, even though, from all he himself had learned, the unexpected arrival of the viceroy's detail to escort the prisoners to the city was the only thing that had kept Louis and his men from dying of neglect in their cells at Monclova.

Hoping to blot away some of the somberness marring her normally happy face, Eblo said, "It seems to me that all men like to make up images of themselves, images made perfect to hold up before other men. If the lieutenant was angered by your message when he learned of it, mayhap he won't be after he's had time to think upon it."

Drawing little recognizable comfort from Eblo's words, Manuela leaned forward then and gave Nightstar free rein to find the stables up ahead at his own speed. The wind, carrying a few grains of sand for spice, whipped wildly about the rider's face and dislodged the flat-brimmed hat, pushing it to flop upon her shoulders from the neck strap. Her unbound hair floated loose then, black ribbons of silk dancing behind her. The feel of her lithe body moving in rhythm with the surging animal beneath her erased everything except the pure pleasure of meeting head-on the exhilarating wind.

Like one deprived of what is craved, she lifted her face and sniffed the familiar scent of desert air, laced now with more than mere hints of the fragrant moisture rushing down from the foothills behind her. The walls of the *presidio* loomed ahead, but for the moment she luxuriated in the sense of complete freedom. Long before they reached the stables, Manuela was wearing a smile of partial contentment.

After midnight, the rain clouds broke over the *presidio* with fury. Manuela sat up at the first rumbling sounds signaling the rare event and rushed to open the shutters of her bedroom windows. Pulling on a robe against the rare chill of dampness, she went to the balcony, unmindful that wind snatched at her unbound hair and turned it into a tangled mass. For the first time, she drew out her troubled thoughts about Louis and examined them, thinking that it seemed right to do so during a time of turbulence. Overhead, lightning streaked the sky in the same way that thoughts illumined her mind – disjointed, with startling, short-lived brilliance.

She confessed to herself that upon returning to her room the previous night, after the impassioned scene with Louis in the courtyard, she had felt as if she had fallen off a mountain. All about her had lain broken dreams, and she had felt she might be as much a stranger as Louis had seemed while kissing her with such new fierceness.

Now, with the storm flinging fat raindrops against the curved-tile roofs in the *presidio*, she again sensed that she lay at the bottom of some despised dark pit, hurled there from a great height. If, as Louis had insinuated by his scorn of her willfulness, she had created the current misery, it seemed it would be up to her to resolve it. How could she climb once more into the world of light and love she had so foolishly thought she already inhabited?

If she could persuade Diego to allow Doña Magdalena and her to return to the city right away, would Louis really seek her out and insist on marrying her? Shivering a bit from the damp, chilly air hugging her there on the second-floor balcony, she recalled the threatening tone of his voice when he had assured her he would find her, no matter where she might go. The idea of escaping died aborning, fading as quickly as the last growl of thunder. In spite of her turning over countless ways to thwart the man she had once believed perfect for her, she found none made any sense. A flash of lightning seemed to jump down into the courtyard before her and bounce away with equal speed, and she sensed, with its same brief, eerie clarity, that her destiny lay intertwined with that of the French lieutenant. Were they truly meant to be man and wife?

She hardly knew Louis anymore, she agonized. She pulled her robe closer as drops of rain rode puffs of wind onto the balcony and sprayed her with cold mist. The man of her dreams, the Louis Saint-Denis she had known prior to his return, was the handsome cavalier plucking the rosebud in the Garden of Love. Her Lover. Against her will, her heartbeat sped up and her breasts warmed at the memories of their lovemaking, both in the prison at Monclova and at the inn at Saltillo.

The jagged memory of their frenzied kisses last night rose maddeningly then. That had been no genteel Lover seizing her and stirring to life those wanton feelings she had not known she possessed. His unspoken call to something savage deep inside her had been real, devastatingly real.

For the first time, she felt brave enough there in the roar of the storm to recall how deliciously frightening it had been. She closed her eyes and let memory wash over her, wondering if it might not drown her, then deciding she did not care as she relived those moments in Louis's arms in the moon-drenched courtyard. All of a sudden her heartbeat tore into a dizzying pace and her breasts did more than warm up; they tingled and hardened painfully in their thrusting points. The remembered mass of molten desire stirred once in warning down low, like an echo of the thunder disappearing toward the east.

Tears scalded paths down Manuela's tortured face. When the drops burned her lips, she licked at the saltiness and scolded herself for having fallen prey to what she viewed as a feminine weakness. To her way of thinking, crying offered no solution to all that troubled her.

Before she could come up with any answer, she realized with a start, she needed to define the problem rearing up between Louis and her. All along she had thought the only one they faced was the freedom to be together. Now that he had told her of his disappointment in her and that he wanted her as a wife only because he had won permission to claim her, she felt the burden of a problem far weightier than the first one. No longer was it one for others to make right, and she sought to frame it in her mind.

Wasn't the crux of the matter that she wanted Louis to love her and honor her as he had seemed to before learning about her acts of willfulness? As she stared through the falling rain in the direction of the bench beneath the chinaberry tree, parts of her chimed in that she had indeed stated the problem, and that all she had to do was apologize and promise never again to take matters into her own hands. A wayward part of her denied she could take such drastic steps, now that Louis had shown her he wanted to marry only because he had won her as a prize. Back when she had thought he loved her, she likely could have mustered whatever it might take to humble herself. But now ...

Like the violent storm overhead, Manuela's turmoil at last wore itself out, leaving in its wake a piercing calm. She no longer saw herself as a Rose in the Garden of Love awaiting her Lover with blind unawareness of the ways of love. That former dreamer had become a flesh-and-blood woman with a fiery, passionate love for the man determined to marry her. Shivering at the admission of her overpowering love and raw desire for

Louis, she felt she might be an airborne bird plummeting to earth from the loss of its wings.

When she turned to go back inside her bedroom, she heard her parrot making little throaty clucks and guessed the wind must have dislodged his covering and disturbing his sleep.

"Hot pepper! You'll be–" Zorro began to squawk as she cut off his favorite saying by throwing the cloth back over his cage.

Manuela smiled for no reason she could understand and returned to her bed. Right away, sleep spirited her off.

Christmas came and went, a holy day given over to ritual reverence at the *presidio*. Along with Diego and Doña Magdalena, Manuela visited the church early to admire the scene prepared each year by Father Dermoza and the youngsters at the *presidio*. Off to one side of the altar, she saw the same small thatched roof sheltering a stall with hand-crafted, half-sized figures placed inside and others standing about.

Manuela recalled how when Carlos and she had first come to live at the *presidio*, they had eagerly joined the other young people in rejuvenating the appearance of the varied parts of the display. Polished to a mirrorlike brightness, a silver star on the roof pointed toward the wise men approaching from the East, their splendid gifts held out before them. Inside the tiny stall lay the child made of wood, painted and gilded anew each year. During the mass attended by area ranchers and sheepherders, plus nearly all at the *presidio*– Indians, soldiers, and servants, sitting close on the straight-backed pews – Man-

501

uela's glances kept stealing back to the miniature Bethlehem, as if her eyes sensed on their own that this might be the last time she would spend the holy day at San Juan Batista.

"Hurry, Manuela," Conchita called from the door of her mistress's bedroom one mid-January morning. "Inez and Doña Magdalena have your wedding gown ready for a fitting."

Looking up from where she sat beside the window creating a new picture made of dried flower petals, Manuela asked, "So soon? They've been working on it only a few weeks." She placed a dried poppy leaf upon the stretched-fabric background lying on her small worktable and stood, smoothing at her rumpled pink shirt with suddenly trembling hands.

Ever since the night of the storm, she had puzzled over whether or not she could marry Louis if mutual love did not bind them. How could she bear to let the gown touch her? What if Louis came back and announced that he no longer wanted to claim his prize? Or what if he did not come back at all? She saw it as a bad omen to be trying on a wedding gown for a ceremony as unlikely to take place as the one being planned.

"Mama says that she woke up with a feeling that the men are on their way back now," Conchita confided as they walked downstairs and toward the sewing room off the kitchen. She had never determined what gnawed at Manuela with apparent persistence, but she was glad to see that over the past weeks she had at least managed to put on a happier face when others were

502

about. Several times, Conchita had crept upstairs late at night to stand outside Manuela's door and listen for tears, but she had never heard suspicious sounds. Despite the maid's voiced concern and frequent questioning, she could not learn what was going on behind that beautiful face. "Have I told you that Medar and I are going to have our own wedding the day after we get you two married?"

"Yes, and I'm delighted, Conchita." Manuela tried to visualize Louis riding Diablo toward the *presidio*, but, as ever since his departure, she could not call up vivid details of his countenance. His face always became a blur of handsome but vague features, and she wondered if that puzzling situation spelled some kind of misfortune. "I'm thinking you're going to be happy as the wife of the witty Medar Jalot."

"And handsome," Conchita reminded her with a girlish giggle and blush. "Don't forget to add handsome."

"What nonsense, Manuela," Doña Magdalena scolded when the sober-faced Manuela entered the sewing room but shied away from touching the gown, declaring she wasn't ready to put it on. "How can we make sure it fits you properly if you don't try it on? You're acting as if it's contaminated in some way."

"Maybe it's bad luck for me to try it on. Can't you go by measurements alone?" Unfamiliar moisture coated the palms of her hands. Her heart set up a fuss at the thought of trying on a wedding gown that might never be worn before any except those creating it. Should she go

503

ahead and confess that though her own love for Louis nigh consumed her, she could not marry a man who no longer loved her — even if he might insist on the ceremony due to his masculine pride? She felt she might smother if the white satin garment cloaked her face for more than an instant.

"Stop being so dramatic," her great-aunt said with a noticeable huff. When Manuela yet stood as if transfixed, Doña Magdalena's eyes softened, and she went to put her arms around the tensed shoulders. In a softer, caring voice, she went on, "You're just feeling the normal uneasiness of all brides. Every one I've ever known, including myself, suffers these moments of doubt. Come now, and oblige us, for we want to complete the gown and get to other items for your wardrobe."

Manuela called upon inner strengths she had not known she possessed to keep from screaming and fleeing the room. It was only fabric, she reasoned, only a garment much like any other. Her teeth holding her bottom lip still, she nodded to Conchita that she was ready.

Once she made herself look at the lovely gown and let Conchita and Inez help her into it, Manuela found breathing a little easier. She stood before the long mirror and saw the way she would look on her wedding day — if it ever came to pass. The shimmering white satin, she thought shakily, was pretty enough without the addition of the thousands of seed pearls embroidered on its thick surface, but with the ornate needlework, it fairly glowed.

"Lieutenant Saint-Denis will see that he has the most beautiful bride in the world," Conchita murmured, her voice showing her awe. She held up the lace *mantilla* to Manuela's head, where an ivory comb with inset, criss-crossed lines of diamonds decorating its tall crown-shaped top would fasten it to high-placed curls.

"Yes, Manuela will be a perfect vision of all that young brides should be," Doña Magdalena remarked, her eyes suspiciously bright. Her own talented hands had created some of the embroidery, and she felt pride in her work. "We lack little now before having it completed."

"It's a good thing, too," Inez spoke up. "I have yet to begin on the other gowns and riding costumes needed, though I do have most of the undergarments nearly finished. I plan to begin on the nightdresses and robes today."

Manuela heard the words and smiled her thanks for the loving compliments and assurances that everything would be in readiness by the time the men returned. Her mind whirled anew at the doubts that Louis would ever again find her more than one to fill his bed, more than the prize he had won for a job well done.

Suddenly weary of all that weighted her mind and heart, she turned away from the mirror and asked that the gown be removed. Time seemed to be marching both for her and against her, she agonized as she stepped back into the pink one and left the chattering women to their tasks. If Juanita's premonition turned out to be true and the men were actually on their way back, everyone might know soon that all was far from well between the pledged couple. She felt she had already done all the pretending she could endure.

That night after dinner, Doña Magdalena told

Diego that Manuela's gown was nearing completion. "You'll be proud to escort her down the aisle," she added when Manuela did little but give a weak smile from where she sat near the settee drinking coffee.

"Not unless she regains her blooming spirits when the dashing French lieutenant returns," Diego teased. "Sometimes I fear she might be coming down with some illness," he added when the nagging thought insisted on being voiced. Having watched his granddaughter droop like a neglected flower and become silent for long periods of time ever since the men had left over a month ago, he had stewed over what was troubling her.

Was she having doubts about her decision to marry Louis and go so far away to Louisiana? Since Diego had never understood what moved her, he assumed the drastic change in mood was perhaps no more than could be expected from one who faced such an upheaval in her life. No matter that she herself had chosen that path against his advice, he reminded himself. It was still more challenge than she had ever faced.

As Doña Magdalena and he had agreed several times in private, the air of calm about the *hacienda* was far easier to take than when the spirited Manuela was openly revolting against some imagined wrong. Sending the object of his thoughts a fond smile, Diego said, "When Louis and Domingo come back safe and sound, you'll wear your pretty smiles again, I hope. All any of us want is your happiness, my dove."

"I know that, Grandfather, but I don't know what you're talking about," Manuela denied, forcing herself to dazzle him with a semblance of a happy smile. Not understanding her new compassion, she disliked causing him unhappiness and often felt guilty for the hurts she had inflicted unknowingly in the past. "Just because I have much to think on – so much planning about what to take and what to leave for future trips down – I might seem to be more serious than usual, but I'm fine. Truly I am." She turned then to Doña Magdalena sitting on the other end of the settee beside Diego, remembering her kindness earlier when she had balked at trying on the wedding gown and hoping now for additional support. "I'm sure you must know how much comes to mind when one is getting ready to marry, Aunt."

The older woman surprised Manuela by turning quite pink and managing little more than an agreeable murmur. She became overly interested in the handle of her cup, her delicate fingers tracing its pattern idly.

"Have I said something untoward?" Manuela asked, seeing only then that Diego also appeared to be edgy and perhaps a bit flushed about the face. She laughed and set down her cup, asking, "Does anyone have an answer to help me solve this puzzle?"

"Well," Diego began hesitantly, sending little warm looks at his sister-in-law and obviously gaining courage, or permission, to continue in a strong voice, "Magdalena and I have discussed the possibility that we'll marry after you've gone to your new home in Louisiana."

Manuela jumped up from her chair and hugged Doña Magdalena, then rushed to embrace Diego. "This is wonderful news! I can't tell you how happy I am for both of you. More than once, I've thought about how you seem to belong here, Aunt, and not just as my *dueña*. Since you've come, we've enjoyed your way of bringing order and laughter, and I won't have to worry anymore about Grandfather being lonely after I'm gone." To see the shy smiles they exchanged lifted her heart and gave her a smidgen of hope that maybe the problems between Louis and her could be resolved. "Tell me about your plans. I'll feel so good knowing that you'll be here together. Why don't you marry when" — her voice failed her for a moment — "when Louis and I do?"

"No, no," Doña Magdalena replied, still looking softer and more pink about the face than usual. "That day should belong only to you two young people. We think it best to wait until later, mayhap around Easter."

"But I'll not be here for the ceremony then." Her eyes widening from a sudden thought, she asked, "Why don't you marry as soon as the men return? We've agreed that Louis and I will wait until the first Friday after he gets back, so as to give us time to get our packing done for the journey to Louisiana." She did not dare add what haunted her — that they might find, once they talked at length, that neither actually desired the marriage once dreamed of, now that mutual love no longer ordered it.

"Remember that your maid and Medar plan to wed the following day. You can see it will be a week of great activity without adding our ceremony," Doña Magdalena pointed out. Happy that now she could look at Diego without pretending he was no more than her respected brother-in-law, she eyed him with open affection as she went on. "We've made up our minds that

508

we prefer to wait until after all has calmed down here at the *presidio.*"

"That's true, my dove," Diego added, his black eyes twinkling first at Manuela and then at the silver-haired woman beside him. "Magdalena speaks our case well. We'll be sorry not to have Louis and you at our wedding, but we'll tell you all about it when you come for your first visit — accompanied by that Frenchman and his trade goods, of course."

Manuela hugged him again, knowing that his decision to allow even one trading expedition from Louisiana into Mexico had been most difficult.

One night scarcely a week later, Manuela visited the Garden of Love in her dreams for the first time in months. Again she found herself a restless rosebud imprisoned upon a stem, still awaiting the arrival of her Lover. The Keeper's same stern voice commanded one who approached with steady steps to hold himself at bay until he had suffered enough to pluck the blossom desired.

This time, to Manuela's surprise, the caller's deep voice overrode that other with certainty, and sure feet headed in her direction. The man's hand boldly snapped whatever held her and lifted her up in his arms, close to his face. She found she had not only a wildly hammering pulse but also a wondering voice that called out in joyful recognition, "Louis Saint-Denis!"

Black eyes popped open. Was that her own voice she had heard? Manuela wondered. She was still dreaming, she assured herself in the darkness. A rush of air against her face denied it though, and she sat up, half expecting to see the one she had called out to in her dreams.

Louis was not there, but Manuela had an eerie feeling that he was not far away. How was it, she agonized, that one could long for something to happen and yet dread it at the same time?

Conclusion

The Spanish rose in sunshine
Drinks in the force of life.
In bud, 'tis a lure to the wanderer;
Unfurl'd, a sweetheart become wife.

Chapter Twenty-seven

February, Manuela mused the next afternoon as she galloped Nightstar toward the irrigation stream while others observed *siesta* time, and she could already see the greening of the gracefully leaning willows and squatty underbrush up ahead. Even with the heat of the blazing sun, the water would be too cold for swimming, yet she felt it drawing her near.

Perhaps it was because she had first recognized her love for Louis here, she reflected after having tethered Nightstar near a patch of fresh grass. She stroked the white withers and spoke in a conversational way as she loosened the girth.

"Now you can eat all you can hold, you greedy boy," she told the horse. Putting her arms about the huge neck, she lay her head against the silky mane. "It doesn't matter that Carlos always teased me for talking to you. He's gone his way now, but you and I know that you've always understood, don't we?"

As if his mistress were right and it was time to tell her how much he appreciated the release of the tight band encircling his belly, Nightstar turned to look at her and swelled out his middle.

A prolonged, blubbery snort and a jingle of his silver-encrusted bridle must have disturbed a lingering bird, for a nearby whir of wings joined the sounds. Her hair blue-black against the whiteness of the horse, Manuela tilted her head and smiled upon hearing the cooing protest of a mourning dove as it flashed by in a gray blur on its way upstream.

Leisurely she drank in the idyllic scene, noting that lizards were beginning to poke out their heads nervously from hiding places now that the only sounds came from Nightstar's lipping at grass. The dream of last night had shaken her and had left her heart as vulnerable as the tender growth along the ground. She saw how each of her steps crushed something green pushing up from the soil.

Dropping her flat-brimmed hat to the ground atop the small embankment, Manuela sat beside it and stretched out her legs, her boots barely covered by the yellow riding outfit. With a sigh of contentment, she leaned back, setting her arms out behind her as support, and watched a large bird circling ever higher in the distance until she could no longer see it. Her hair, unbound because she had fled on sudden impulse and had not bothered even to gather it with a ribbon, grazed against the grass when she closed her eyes and lifted her face to the warming sun. Wafting to her nose, which aimed toward the bright blue sky, the clean smell of fresh water added its touch to the subtle fragrances of early spring sunshine, budding trees, and baby plants.

Her arms complained at serving as props, and she lowered her body with a whisper from the yellow silk, luxuriating in the nearly forgotten feel of lying full-length in the warm sunshine. Without ever realizing she was feeling drowsy, she drifted into sleep.

"What a delightful homecoming," came the voice Manuela had heard in her dream the night before. "All I need to make it perfect is a kiss."

Her eyelids lifted in their heavy manner, stopping short of opening all the way because of the glare from the afternoon sun. A kind of breathless excitement snaked over her. Her pulse awakened faster than the rest of her, and she struggled to make sense of what she saw.

Was that really Louis squatting close by in that relaxed, male fashion, wearing deerskin breeches and shirt and with his hair hanging over a broad shoulder in a long brown braid? With a start, she realized how much he resembled an Indian to her half-dazed mind, even without the red skin and dark eyes. About him there seemed that same aura of savagery she remembered from their last time together in the courtyard. How long had he been there lazily raking her body with those dark-fringed eyes made even paler and more mysterious by a deeper tan?

Sucking in a choppy breath and sitting up quickly, for he seemed about to rise and come closer, Manuela opened her eyes wide and replied in a voice sounding unlike her own, "Am I dreaming, or are you really here? Either way, Louis Saint-Denis, stay where you are. I don't feel at all like giving you a kiss." She was already groggy, and, an inner voice warned, she did not need him one step nearer before getting answers to some

515

of the questions that had haunted her over the past two months. Her hand rose in protest. Her eyes warned him to keep his distance.

Louis laughed, his teeth flashing in the bright sunlight. She was even more beautiful than he had remembered – and just as peppery, he added. How he had agonized over whether or not she would still be at the *presidio* upon his return! When he had left Domingo and the others and had reined in to rid himself of the trail dust, he had not believed his good fortune in finding her stretched out asleep, as if she had sensed his homecoming and had ridden out to greet him alone.

No doubt he had dreamed the part about her coming out to welcome him back, he reflected upon seeing the fire in Manuela's eyes. She seemed as put out with him as on their last night together in the courtyard. As he had promised himself at least once each day and night while away, he would take his time and woo her back into sweet humor. He smiled at her in silence, letting his thoughts run while he took his time in answering. She seemed as caught up in staring and ruminating as he.

Having left with their relationship on shaky ground had haunted Louis more with each separating mile. So what if she had stuck that pretty nose in men's business. She had managed to get him freed, hadn't she? The farther he traveled, the more he realized that she had shown far more bravery than many men he had known and fought alongside. Did it matter that Manuela moved to a rhythm all her own? Didn't he, as well?

Her unexpectedly wild response to his demanding kisses that final night had taunted him anew with his need to have her beside him for a lifetime. No woman had ever fascinated him as had the black-haired beauty fixing him now with such a belligerent stare. None had possessed so many intriguing facets, and he had pondered the delightful possibility that life with Manuela Ramon would never be static. Just loving her was adventure.

Deciding from a perceptible softening about her lips that she might be relaxing her guard, Louis assured, "Oh, I'm really here all right, and I can wait on the kiss as long as I have to. Anyway, I'd much rather have one as a gift than have to steal it." He glanced around, spotting Nightstar nibbling at grass not far away, then returning his attention to her.

The yellow of Manuela's riding costume set off her sultry beauty in a way that threatened to make Louis forget his promise to go slowly. He had the urge to grab her and kiss her into yielding softness. Her black hair was tousled most disarmingly, and he could see her breasts pushing too fast against the silk of her shirt. She might pretend his appearance didn't ruffle her, he thought with awesome tenderness, but he knew her too well. From his first sight of her sleeping there, he had wanted to scoop her up and carry her beneath the willows beside the stream.

"Should you be out here alone?" he asked. When she did not answer, merely shot him a haughty glare, he teased, his eyes crinkling, "I told Domingo I was stopping off to take a bath, but I could have been a highwayman or a sneaky Indian and—"

"But you aren't any of those things," she interrupted, her mind racing as she tried, for the millionth time, to figure out exactly who he was and what she meant to him. She seemed to have done little other than that during his absence, she reflected with ill humor at his visible high spirits. Her pulse had not stopped drumming faster at each beat, but her mind seemed not fully awake.

Glancing over her shoulder at the *presidio* in the near distance, she saw horses and riders almost at the gates. She must have been dead asleep to have missed hearing the noisy group pass not far away on the path, she realized. Or Louis come so close. All of a sudden, she was wide awake. "Is that your party over at the *presidio*? Is Uncle Domingo all right? Did you find Father Hidalgo's mission?"

Louis sank to the ground then, sitting crosslegged before her. "Yes, to all questions," he replied, watching her draw her silk-covered legs gracefully to one side there on the sparse patch of grass and sit up straight. "Domingo has never been in better health or spirits, saying he is going to petition the viceroy for permission to establish a *presidio* on the eastern boundary of New Spain, close to my own on the Red River."

Manuela was not ready to think about what place his fort might hold in her future. Instead, she recalled how she had heard her uncle state over the past couple of years that he would like more adventure, while at the same time serving the people of Mexico.

Half-smiling then, and combing back her hair with her fingers, she said, "That sounds like Uncle. But what about Father Hidalgo? Did he find his mission still standing, and did he stay behind?"

"Yes. He was disappointed, as we all were, to find the building had suffered mightily from neglect, but by the time we shored it up and got his things set up the way he wanted, it looked as solid as any mission on the frontier." At the gleam of interest in her eyes, he continued, "At first the few Indians riding by ignored his pleas to return to services, but we'd not been there over a week before some began showing up with gifts of game and their finest fur robes. He assured us that once we left, more would be coming to him for prayer and guidance. Those who hadn't known him personally had evidently heard of his good works, for they took him right in. We didn't leave until we made sure he was contented and reasonably safe."

Manuela watched Louis's handsome face while he talked on about how they had restored the mission near the lower Colorado River and what they had seen as they rode, spellbound by the way his resonant tones rose and fell naturally to lend drama to his accounts of all that had happened. The stray thought that she would never tire of hearing his voice recount his adventures nibbled at her hastily thrown-up defenses.

He paused to pluck a blade of grass and chew upon it idly, that simple action of an outdoorsman at ease blinding her to all but his sparkling white teeth and sensuous lips, until he withdrew it and flicked it aside. Without wanting to, she remembered the way those lips had covered hers and set her on fire. For a magical time, she forgot that they had quarreled and that he had told her he was marrying her only because he had won the right to do so. She became lost in the private world he created by his stimulating presence, his deep voice, and his admiring gazes.

"We need to be talking about us, Manuela," Louis said, leaning closer and speaking more softly.

Not ready to return to the real world, the one encompassing more within its boundaries than the two of them there on the little levee, she drew back in protest. "What is there to say about 'us'?" She fingered her tangled hair again, and tossed it back behind her shoulders, unable to meet those piercing gray eyes. "I haven't changed my mind about not wanting to marry a man who doesn't love me for what I am. You made it plain the night before you left that I wasn't what you thought I was when you first asked me to marry you." Black eyes no longer hid behind thick lashes as she talked, and by the time she finished, they were fencing boldly with his.

Louis snatched another blade of grass and stuck it in his mouth, sucking at its tart nectar before asking in carefully controlled tones, "Is that what I said?"

"You might as well have," she retorted, almost captivated again by the sight of his mouth attacking the tender grass. Remembered anger delivered her, though, and whisked away her former feeling of contentment at being with Louis. "You jerked me around and told me that I'd better be ready to marry you when you came back, for I was a prize you had won."

Having ridden hard since daybreak to get back to Manuela, then having to keep his hands off her once he had found her, Louis fought for control. Damn! He hadn't expected her to be so fired up after all these weeks. He managed to remember his vow to talk things out with her if they were allowed some privacy, and he said through clenched teeth, "I don't remember that you particularly despised the 'jerking around.'"

"Then you have a poor memory," she shot back, lifting her chin and flipping her hair. Her cheeks burned, and she wondered if the sun's rays had reddened them while she slept. Why didn't he take her in his arms and tell her he loved her as he once would have done? Once in a while she had dared hope that such would happen when he came back, but now she realized it was not going to.

"Have you been sitting here brooding all these weeks instead of getting ready for our wedding?" Hurt mingled with anger, lacing his words with a savagery akin to that detectable during their last time together in the courtyard. No need to let her know that he had thought of little but her and making her his wife since their uneasy parting. She obviously had given it little or no thought; or if she had, there had been no anticipation. Damn! Did she no longer care for him at all? Without his knowledge, his tongue flicked briefly as her lips pursed in a beguiling pink rosebud of a pout. "It's to be on the first Friday after my return, isn't it?"

She glared at him without answering, her mind already having marked that today was Wednesday. Ever since Conchita had told her that Juanita had the feeling the men were on their way back, Manuela, mocking herself for doing so, had made note upon awakening each morning of what day of the week it was ... and its relationship to Friday. But the maddening Frenchman was revealing that he didn't even know for certain what the plans were! He obviously looked upon their wedding as no more than a way to satisfy his male ego in having won Diego's permission to claim her. And, she fumed, to gain a woman for his bed.

"The day after tomorrow at sunset we'll become man and wife in church," Louis announced in a manner not at all as he had imagined he would say the words to her. Visions of the way he had dreamed their reunion would be punished his bruised heart. Where was the laughter bubbling from her pretty mouth? Where were the warm kisses of welcome? Messages of invitation weren't reaching out from those slanted black eyes. A heartrending question could no longer be denied. "Or have you told your grandfather there'll be no wedding?"

"I've told no one about our disagreement."

Encouraged at that admission, Louis asked, "Why not?"

"You told me I had no choice but to marry you when you returned, remember?" she retorted, her eyes lashing him as cruelly as her tongue. "I've no wish to have you parade before Grandfather my part in getting you freed and have him view me as immature or foolhardy, as you so obviously do. He has enough to worry over without adding disappointments over my rash actions. Besides, Eblo might get into trouble over sending the message without permission."

Each telling statement stabbed Louis deep in his heart. Guilt for his having given in to his wounded pride and making her feel like a culprit tore at him. Wondering at a vulnerable look about her full lips, he watched her incredible lashes block him from view. What was it she had told him at the start of their conversation about why she didn't choose to marry him? He realized he should have been listening more closely, instead of reeling inwardly from what the sight of her was doing to him.

"I'm surprised to hear you admit that what you did was rash," he said softly. Watching her eyelids lift in their slow way reminded him of the countless times he had observed the action, reminded him also that at each occurrence he became more under the spell of her beauty. His hands itched to touch her.

Boldly she declared, "I never said it wasn't. All I said was that I doubted I would have acted any differently, no matter if you liked it or not."

"Then I can expect more of the same after we're married—is that it?"

Manuela did not deign to reply. Her eyes again upbraiding him for his failure to understand what moved her, she prepared to rise.

The fearful thought that Manuela was going to leave before he could woo her into a receptive mood seized Louis, and he leaned to grab her before she managed to stand. The minute his hands touched her, unreasoning passion took control.

Caught off guard there on her knees, she struck out at him with a quick fist. "Get your hands off me!"

He ducked, losing his balance and pulling her to roll backward with him down the incline toward the water. In a blur of flying hair, arms, and legs, they tumbled until a flat place beneath a budding willow stopped them.

Very aware of the struggling, silk-clad body he still clutched, Louis raised his head and asked,

"Are you all right?"

From behind a lock of tangled black hair, Manuela glared up at him as she tried to free her hands from where they lay pinned beneath his heaving chest. "Do I look it?" she hissed with barely recovered breath. Her heart seemed about to jump from where it had lodged in her throat. All she could think of was the way her traitorous body was warming up from his nearness.

Louis laughed softly, his delighted gaze lingering over the debris-specked hair half-covering her indignant, flushing face.

"What are you laughing at? I could have been maimed for life from your attack!" She squirmed beneath his pinioning body, hating it when she acknowledged the heat in her cheeks must be coming from a blush. Even so, she strove for a haughty mien. "Damn you, Louis! Quit laughing at me."

Sobering a bit, he teased, "If I remember correctly, you had a hell of a good laugh when I fell down a bank once."

"It's hardly the same thing." Again she struggled to get out from underneath him, not wanting to recall that time she had laughed at the way he had looked sprawled in the water.

"Close enough." A pleased smile danced across his face and set his eyes to twinkling as he reached to push aside the hair lying across part of her face. Once his fingers touched the lovely skin, they stayed there, the knuckles bunching up and forming a brush as soft as thistledown to trace a loving path across the high cheekbone and wander down to her lower cheek. "Maybe we're even now."

"Nobody can be even with you. You're too busy

trying to make them into what you think they should be." The aromas of horse, saddle leather, and virile young man from a hard day's ride worked a devastating spell on her, despite her willing them to disappear. So close, his breath smelled of fragrant grass and sunshine. The touch of his hand caressing her face almost made her lose her breath all over again. Fearing she might suffocate, she wriggled again to free herself. If she didn't get away soon . . .

"Manuela," he growled softly while he continued without effort to force her struggling, unyielding body to lie upon the grass beneath his. All vestiges of his anger were gone now. He ignored her angry mutterings and attempts to free her hands from where his chest imprisoned them. "You belong to me. How can I bear to let you go?"

At the moment Louis had reached for her up on the levee, Manuela had seen again that fierce look upon his face that had held her captive that night in the courtyard. Panting from her renewed struggles for release, she barely heard his words, so caught up was she in baffflement at what was happening to her resolve to get their differences settled before making more plans to marry. She sensed with each passing moment that there was no other world and no problems other than what they created there beside the water.

His face was so close that she could see the individual lashes framing his eyes. He seemed to be drinking her into those silvery pools, and she felt strangely at home in their depths. His braid fell forward when he leaned the brief space to kiss her, and she shivered, feeling again that he was part savage. The fiery invectives she had felt pushing at her mouth only seconds ago died aborning as his covered it with a soul-shattering kiss.

The sound of his erratic breathing frightened her until she realized her own matched his and that it was the blending of the two causing the little uproar. At once, she became frightened of herself, that newly born part of her quivering in eagerness to answer the same aberrant streak she sensed controlled him now. She trembled, both inside and out, and a little animallike sound back in her throat lent credence to her thought that she herself might be less than tame. Her arms suddenly freed, she reached to pull him ever closer in deliciously wild embrace, and her silk-encased arms became entrapments of their own, as confining as the muscular ones holding her.

He had said she belonged to him, she agonized with a sudden, raw recognition that he was right. Only when she was with him did she feel fully alive, now that he had shown her the ways of love she had so willfully sought. Hadn't she lived in a half-state during his absence of the past two months, one even others had noticed as being less than what had once been normal for her? The brown-haired man kissing her with such thoroughness made her know why she had been put on earth.

Her hungry mouth invited his invading tongue, and her own made a fiery foray into that consuming mouth she would never tire of surrendering to. She loved it when his hands walked tenderly through her hair, then settled to nestle about her ears. For a moment, she wondered if he had not touched far more than those parts designed for hearing. Fires blazed within, heating up her womanhood and settling her heartbeat into matching, frenzied rhythm. Fraught with desire, she could no longer be still beneath that lean, leather-covered body covering her, only this time she was not seeking freedom. Her breasts throbbed as if he had already touched and kissed them. Her hips begged to find more intimate contact with the hardness pressing hotly against them.

"I love you," Louis whispered against her lips as he unbuttoned the yellow shirt and gave his hands license to rediscover the fullness of her breasts. His heart threatened to run away. "Nothing else matters. I love you so much that I know we can be happy together." His eyes begged her to agree.

A smile lighted Manuela's face and eyes as though an inner candle had ignited. "I love you, too. But why have you waited so long to tell me? I thought you hadn't loved me since you found out about—"

"Hush, sweetheart." He stopped her words with a kiss no less searing than the play of his hands on her neck and breasts. When he released her, he rose to his knees, pulling her to hers so as to remove her shirt and chemise.

"But you were so angry," she said, her mind and heart memorizing the endearment and her body tingling from the silvery washes of his eyes. The way he was looking at her bare torso set her on fire, and she reached to slip his leather shirt over his head, feeling daring and adventurous as she uncovered the brawny arms and broad, furred chest. She leaned to press her throbbing breasts against the thickly muscled plane. Her arms hugging him closer, her nipples peaking almost painfully as they rubbed against his, she peeped up into the handsome face so close and asked, "What made you change your mind?"

Mesmerized by the black eyes half-hidden behind sooty lashes, he opened his heart for her to read there in the afternoon shadows. "I learned that my love for you goes beyond anger and pettiness, beyond the need for a me to exist all by itself. To share my life with you is all I need." By the time the last word formed there in the diminishing space between their glowing faces, it floated with the barest of husky bass notes.

Forever, echoed in both of their minds and hearts as their lips met in a tender exchange of silent but fervent promises. Love sped up their caresses, added extra sparkle to wondering eyes. As they hugged and murmured endearments, his hands made new paths along her slender, silken back and dropped to tug at the yellow riding breeches, even as hers worked circles of worship across his shoulders and dared dip inside the leather garment covering that part of him she hungered to explore. Sending smiles of adoration there beneath the budding limbs of the willow, they parted long enough to rid themselves of all remaining clothing, not turning back to face each other until both stood naked, trembling at the wonder of whatever ordered the miracle of reunion.

That distantly drumming bit of savagery, which Manuela had sensed was demanding recognition in both of them, increased in intensity when they stepped to embrace. Stripes of afternoon sunshine fingered through the arching willow branches and bathed their naked beauty in a kind of celestial light. Her hair a silken cloud of ebon falling over the arms pressing her close to his hard nakedness, Manuela welcomed the blatant invitation in his eyes and opened her mouth to his.

A spark of something feral leapt in his pale eyes when his swollen manhood at last throbbed against the softness of her tempting furred nest. An answering gleam of primitive need from within the beloved midnight depths surprised him, pleasured him beyond his wildest desires. With an uninhibited growl of gleeful mastery, he lifted her high in his arms, watching her face grow more beautiful from the rosy hue of passion. He cradled her so as to kiss the love-swollen mouth, then the saucy breasts bobbing from her rapid breathing.

During his loving ministrations, Manuela reclaimed her old territory of his hair and corded neck, tender hands pulling his Indian braid forward to brush its ends across the nipples of her breasts while he kissed her and sent his tongue to conquer any recesses neglected earlier. Just when she was floating into a sublime level of ecstasy, he deserted her lips and became enamored of her breasts. The touch of his devouring mouth and stroking tongue upon her nipples took her farther into that sensuous sphere she sought, and she arched back across his arm in undisguised ecstasy, not surprised that a begging sound escaped from her throat.

"You're mine," he whispered as he lay her on the grass. "Tell me I'm right." With one arm cradling her head, he faced her, then slowly traced the shape of her hairline with a wandering finger. She was trembling satin skin and the scent of roses and perfectly shaped curves, yet he knew her passion purred as wildly as his now that he had awakened it. He felt masterful and blessed, all at the same time. His manhood pulsated impatiently against her tantalizing softness, gathering intensity from what was uncoiling deep inside.

"I'm yours, Louis. Take me now." Her voice was also a whisper, one heavy with the inner torment he was reading in her eyes. She was not sure how much longer she could wait for him to quell that burning inside her core, and she inched closer to that compelling pulsation.

He whispered huskily, "Not yet, my love."

Not once but again and again, he traversed the silken hills, the valleys, and the crevices of her yielding body with his mouth and hands. Once she found she was unable to lure him to take her until he was ready to bring the delicious torment to culmination, she gave free rein to the moaning monster growing inside her and discovered all the delightful surprises awaiting. The feel of his lean, hard buttocks beneath her wandering hands satisfied all kinds of senses she had not known lived within her. She gasped with awe at the undreamed-of dimensions their lovemaking was reaching; it was as if it were all brand new.

Nothing could stop her quest then for new adventure, not when she burned with such love for the one leading her into a new world of ecstasy. Her fingers moved with tender daring to close upon the velvety hot shaft throbbing in readiness. Great waves of need almost stole her breath, and she sensed from his own indrawn breath at her caresses that he was as near exploding as she.

With a bass sound much like a growl purring in his throat, Louis moved above her then, his claiming her at last a reality. Womanly warmth took him in and closed around him with eager possessiveness. Stunned for a moment at the awesome rush of desire for the beautiful young woman in his arms, he kissed her tenderly before beginning the rhythm of love. When she refuted tenderness, chose fierceness instead, he unleashed all that had been driving him since he had learned of her willfulness and had not known how to deal with it. Her legs encircled his hips in unabashed surrender, the telling action erasing any earlier doubt he might have had about her being able to give her every facet to him. He wanted nothing more than to take her in closer to his heart, willfulness and all. He gloried in the taste of her fiery, nibbling mouth, the sound of her wanton cries, and the feel of her fingers digging into his back.

The world of splendor they sought at each movement lay beyond the sphere of reason, but they sailed right to it as one. Manuela felt she might never wish to return to the world of sanity, so airborne and exhilarated were her senses, so unfettered there in that ethereal zone with Louis. His arms yet clutched her; his body yet claimed her; but languor and stillness reigned now. The elusive energy kept speeding out of reach, deserting them. What was there to do, they agonized as one, but drift back on a sigh and a wish to recall forever that perfectly attuned moment of savagery blended with love?

Feeling a shyness at her uninhibited responses to his lovemaking, Manuela lifted her eyes in that heavy-lidded way to Louis. "I believe you know now how much I belong to you, and how much I love you." With fingers devoid of their formerly passionate searching, she outlined the heavy brown eyebrows with tenderness, then did the same for the handsome nose and love-swollen mouth. She wondered if she might not always remember him as he looked at that moment.

"Discovering you is the finest thing I ever did," Louis replied. "I told you once that you're the treasure here, and you still are." He rolled to lie beside her and fit her head to his shoulder. For one who had fallen in love with a spirited, budding young beauty, he mused happily, he was even more in love with the peppery, blossoming creature she had become. He felt he might be the one who could claim he had truly found the pot of gold at the end of the rainbow. "I'll love you forever."

"You'd better," she murmured in a sultry threat. "You made me what I am, for I was nothing but . . ." Her voice faded when she thought of how she had almost confided about her girlish dreams and the rosebud on the bush in the Garden of Love.

"But what? Don't stop now." One hand lifted her face so he could look into it. How could one who had displayed such charming abandon only moments ago appear to be blushing now? "What were you before I came and fell in love with you?"

Manuela smiled mysteriously, her eyes veiling just enough to entrance him. "A foolish girl with a head full of dreams."

"Will I be able to make them come true?" He sensed she was withholding the complete truth, but he did not mind. In time he would learn all there was to know about her, and he sensed it would take a lifetime. He kissed her bruised lips, savoring their fiery sweetness as well as the brush of her fragrant hair against his skin. The thought of always smelling the sweet scent of roses fed his soul.

"I've no doubt you will, for you've already begun," she replied when he released her to snuggle again on his shoulder.

Only then did they notice that the shafts of sunlight had paled and were angling sharply there beneath the limbs of the willow. The air touching their nakedness was no longer warm. With reluctance, they rose and dressed.

"One question I've been meaning to ask," Manuela said before allowing him to help her mount Nightstar. "How did you get the scar on your cheek?" Her forefinger traced the little vee on his left cheekbone.

Grinning down at her, Louis replied, "Would you believe it resulted from a foolish boy's attempt to jump his horse over a fence back at his father's farm in Canada?" His eyes twinkled with mischief, but whether from the memory of the described incident or from the knowledge of a white lie he might be telling, Manuela could not say.

"No, I don't believe that. It sounds too tame for a cavalier."

He hooted then. "Who says I'm a cavalier? From what you told me, a cavalier leaves the ladies behind and keeps riding on in search of adventure." He leaned down to savor one more quick kiss. "You're all the adventure I'll ever need, Manuela Ramon, soon to be Mrs. Louis

Saint-Denis."

Her eyes flirting, she tossed her unbound hair and replied, "I'll make sure of that."

Louis helped her onto Nightstar then and mounted Diablo. Riding close and holding hands, they headed with eager hearts toward the *presidio*, where wedding plans were already being hurried into motion.